**"Maybe you should sleep elsewhere tonight?"
I suggested what I hoped sounded more
like a requirement.**

He grinned, and his fingers slid to the back of my head. His hand left my hair, both hands went under my armpits, and he hauled me up his chest then rolled into me so he was on top. Then he gave me the good-night kiss to beat all good-night kisses. It was long, hard, deep, wet and utterly delicious.

When he was done, I was breathing heavily, my lips were tingling, my nipples were tingling and there were other places that had started to tingle. Then he rolled to his back, reached an arm out to turn off the light on my nightstand and tucked me into his side.

My cheek was to his shoulder, my hand on his abs, and I was trying to control my breath. Once I got my breath under control, I said quietly into the darkness, "I guess this means you aren't going to go home."

His arm around my waist got tight before it relaxed, and he replied with humor in his tone, "Yeah, Red, that's what it means."

Then I realized I had no choice but to sleep with a naked Tack in my bed.

Praise for
KRISTEN ASHLEY

"I felt all of the rushes, the adrenaline surges, the anger spikes...my heart pumping in fury. My eyes tearing up when my heart (I mean...*her* heart) would break."
—Maryse's Book Blog (Maryse.net) on
MOTORCYCLE MAN

"[*Law Man* is an] excellent addition to a phenomenal series!"
—ReadingBetweentheWinesBookClub.blogspot.com

"[*Law Man*] made me laugh out loud. Kristen Ashley is an amazing writer!"   —TotallyBookedBlog.com

"Run, don't walk...to get [the Dream Man] series. I love [Kristen Ashley's] rough, tough, hard-loving men. And I love the cosmo-girl club!"   —NocturneReads.com

"I adore Kristen Ashley's books. She writes engaging, romantic stories with intriguing, colorful and larger-than-life characters. Her stories grab you by the throat from page one and don't let go until well after the last page. They continue to dwell in your mind days after you finish the story, and you'll find yourself anxiously awaiting the next. Ashley is an addicting read no matter which of her stories you find yourself picking up."
—Maya Banks, *New York Times* bestselling author

"There is something about them [Ashley's books] that I find crackalicious."   —Kati Brown, DearAuthor.com

MOTORCYCLE MAN

Also by Kristen Ashley

The Colorado Mountain Series

The Dream Man Series

The Chaos Series

MOTORCYCLE MAN

KRISTEN ASHLEY

FOREVER

NEW YORK   BOSTON

Copyright © 2012 by Kristen Ashley
Excerpt from *Mystery Man* copyright © 2011 by Kristen Ashley
All rights reserved. In accordance with the U.S. Copyright Act of 1976, the scanning, uploading, and electronic sharing of any part of this book without the permission of the publisher is unlawful piracy and theft of the author's intellectual property. If you would like to use material from the book (other than for review purposes), prior written permission must be obtained by contacting the publisher at permissions@hbgusa.com. Thank you for your support of the author's rights.

Forever
Hachette Book Group
237 Park Avenue
New York, NY 10017

www.HachetteBookGroup.com

Printed in the United States of America

Originally published as an ebook

First mass-market edition: January 2014
10 9 8 7 6 5 4 3 2 1

OPM

Forever is an imprint of Grand Central Publishing.
The Forever name and logo are trademarks of Hachette Book Group, Inc.

The Hachette Speakers Bureau provides a wide range of authors for speaking events. To find out more, go to www.hachettespeakersbureau.com or call (866) 376-6591.

The publisher is not responsible for websites (or their content) that are not owned by the publisher.

To Barbara Hunter Mahan
My aunt, my role model and my most avid reader.
She's an aunt who's interested in everything you do,
supports every decision you make,
wants nothing but your happiness
and gives love without conditions.
She's a woman who calls 'em as she sees 'em,
does what she likes and likes what she does,
says what's on her mind
and if you can't hack the honesty that's your problem.
She's the first woman I'd choose to shop with
and she's the only woman I'd want to get kidnapped with.
Love you, Aunt Barb.

Acknowledgments

To Chas, for again having my back.

PROLOGUE

Motorcycle Man

"BABE, YOU AWAKE?" he called, his warm hand moving down my spine, taking the sheet with it, making my skin tingle and coming to rest just above my bottom.

I smiled.

I had done it. I finally had done it. I found him. He was right there in bed with me and it wasn't the tequila talking. I had way too much but not too much that I didn't know he was it.

He was the one. This motorcycle man in bed with me was the man of my dreams.

I never would have guessed it would be a man like him but I knew it was. I knew it the minute I saw him across the forecourt, through the sea of people, all of them laughing, drinking, shouting, dancing, eating, necking or fighting. It wasn't my scene but Eloise had invited me, told me I needed to become a member of the family, so I went. This was going to be my new life, I'd made that decision and I had to embrace it. So I did.

He saw me too and it was my motorcycle man who sought me out. Then he plied me with tequila but he didn't need to. I was his the minute he sauntered through the crush to get to me, his eyes never leaving mine, his lips surrounded by that kickass goatee curved into a sexy grin. When he'd made it to me, he'd said, "Hey," in a deep, gravelly voice, and that was it.

Then we shot tequila, talked a bit and laughed a lot.

An hour later, he took my hand and guided me to a room in the motorcycle club's Compound, and now, several hours later, I was naked in bed with him having been given so many orgasms I lost count and I knew he was it. He was the shadowy-faced man I'd been daydreaming about since I could remember. And it wasn't the orgasms, it was him making me laugh a lot, drink a lot and feel so unbelievably, fantastically *alive* while the party raged around us.

This man called Tack loved life and knew how to live it to its fullest. And I knew, as crazy as it sounded, that I was going to live my life to its fullest by his side.

I was on my belly in bed, my arms crossed on the pillow, my cheek resting on them, my head turned away from him. I turned my head his way and looked up at him.

Dark, longish, somewhat unruly, definitely sexy hair with a hint of gray interspersed in it. Blue eyes with pale lines radiating from the sides that I knew, I just knew, came from laughing. A dark goatee around his mouth, the bit at his chin overlong in a biker way that was too cool for words. Fantastic tattoos slithering up his defined arms, broad shoulders and muscled neck along with one on his ripped chest and a big one on his back. The rest of his body hard and strong, I knew because with great relish I'd acquainted myself with every centimeter.

Beautiful. Perfect. Not my type and I never would have thought a man like him, a biker guy, a motorcycle man, rough and ready for anything, would be my type. But now that I found the man of my dreams, I knew he was perfect.

"I'm awake," I whispered, and a whisper was all I could manage. My throat was clogged with joy and excitement. I'd been waiting for him forever and here he was.

I knew when I'd jumped off the roller coaster that had been my life, I was doing the right thing and *here he was.* Living, breathing, gorgeous, tattooed, gravelly voiced, great with his hands, mouth and other parts of his anatomy proof that I was absolutely right.

His hand left my skin to smack my ass lightly before he said, "Time to get to your own bed, darlin'."

I blinked but the rest of my body froze.

He moved.

He exited the bed, grabbed his jeans and yanked them on. Then he sauntered to a door off the room, not even so much as glancing back as he said, "Leave your number and close the door on your way out, would you, Red?"

Then he disappeared behind the door and shut it behind him.

CHAPTER ONE

I'll Make You Coffee

IT WAS TEN to eight when I held my breath and turned off Broadway into the wide, cement-covered drive that took me around the big warehouse auto supply store that was part of Ride's operation. I made it to the forecourt of the three-bay garage that was the other part of Ride's operation.

I studied the mammoth garage as I approached.

Ride Custom Cars and Bikes, my new place of employment, was world famous. Movie stars and Saudi Arabian sheiks bought cars and bikes from them. Their cars and bikes had been in magazines and they were commissioned for movies. Everyone in Denver knew about them. Hell, everyone in Colorado knew about them, and I was pretty sure most everyone in the United States too. I was pretty sure of this because I knew not that first thing about custom cars and bikes. In fact, I knew nothing about non-custom cars and bikes, but I still knew about Ride.

I also knew the Chaos Motorcycle Club owned the garage and four auto supply stores, this one in Denver, one in Boulder, another in Colorado Springs and the last one that just opened in Fort Collins. I knew the Chaos Motorcycle Club too. They were famous because of Ride and because many of their rough-and-ready-looking members had been photographed with their custom bikes and cars.

I also knew them because I'd partied with them.

And that day I was starting as the new office manager of the garage.

And that day was only one, single day after I'd been laid by Tack, the president of Chaos Motorcycle Club and, essentially, my boss.

And lastly, that day was only one single day and one single night after Tack had slam, bam, thank you ma'am'ed me.

"God," I whispered to my windshield as I parked in front and just beside the steps that led up to the door next to the triple bays of the garage, a door with a sign over it that said "Office," "I'm *such* a stupid, stupid, *idiot*."

But I wasn't an idiot. No, I was a slut.

I didn't know how to cope with being a slut. I'd never been one before. I did not jump into bed with men I barely knew. I did not have flights of fancy where I thought they were beautiful, perfect, motorcycle man daydreams come to life and therefore did tequila shots with them and then had hours of wild, crazy, delicious, *fantastic* sex with them.

That was not me at all.

I was not the kind of person who lived life like Tack did. I was thirty-five and I had lived a careful, quiet, risk-free life. I weighed decisions. I measured pros versus cons. I wrote lists. I made plans. I organized. I thought ahead. I never took one step where I wasn't absolutely certain where my foot would land. And if I found myself in a situation that was unsure, I exited said situation, pronto.

Until two months ago, when I looked at my life and the toxic people in it and I knew I had to get out.

So I got out. I didn't plan it. I didn't measure the pros and cons. I didn't organize my exit strategy. I didn't think ahead. When I'd had the epiphany and realized where I was, how dangerous it was, how unhealthy it was, I had no idea where I'd land when I jumped off the ride that was my life. I just straightened from my desk chair at work, grabbed my personal belongings, shoved them in a box and walked out. I didn't even tell my boss I was going. I just went.

And I didn't go back.

For the next two months I bought the paper every Wednesday and opened it to the want ads section. On each page of the want ads, I closed my eyes and pointed. If I was qualified for the job my finger touched, I applied for it.

That was the extent of my plan.

My best friend, Lanie, thought I was nuts. I couldn't say she was wrong. I had no idea what I was doing, why I was doing it, where I was going and what would happen once I got there.

All I knew was that I had to do it.

So I was.

Now I was here and here was where I decided I needed to be. I'd spent all day the day before trying to figure out if I should show for my new job or not. I'd screwed everything up, literally, and I hadn't even started the job yet. I didn't want to see Tack. I never wanted to see him again. The very thought was so humiliating, I felt my skin burning and I had that very thought nearly constantly since I slid out of his bed, dressed and, mortified, slithered out of his room.

But I had been out of work for two months. I had a nest egg but I also had a mortgage. I had to find employment. I had to start my life again. Whatever I was supposed to be doing, I had to do it. Whatever I needed to find, I had to find it.

There was no going back now. I'd jumped out of the roller coaster at the top of the crest, just before it took the plunge and I was falling.

I had to land sometime and it was here that I was going to land.

So I'd been a slut. There were lots of sluts out there, hundreds of thousands of them. Maybe millions. They went to work every day and some of them surely went to a workplace where there were people with whom they'd had sex. They probably didn't blink. Their skin probably didn't burn with mortification. They probably didn't care. They probably just found a new workmate or random guy that made their heart beat faster and their skin tingle with excitement and then they slept with him. They probably liked it. No, they probably loved it.

That was part of life, wasn't it? That was part of living, right? You did stupid stuff because it felt good and if you screwed up, you moved on. Everyone did that. Everyone.

Now, even me.

And damn it, I'd been on a scary, freaky roller coaster for a long freaking time. That whole time, I had my eyes closed and ignored the scary, freaky stuff that was happening around me. I was too scared to open my eyes and take a risk on life.

No more of that.

So I slept with my boss. Who cared?

I sucked in a deep breath, hitched my purse on my shoulder, threw the door to my car open and got out. Then I looked around the space. It was early and clearly bikers didn't do early. There was no one there. There was a line of bikes, five of them parked in front of the Compound, which was a long, rectangular building to the side of the forecourt separating the garage from the auto supply store. There was a beat-up pickup truck parked behind the auto supply store. Nothing else. No movement. No sound.

Eloise was supposed to meet me at eight to show me the ropes. I figured I was early but I walked up the steps and tried the door anyway. It was locked. I turned to face the forecourt and looked at my watch. Seven minutes to eight.

I'd wait.

I took my purse off my shoulder, dug my cell out, slid my purse straps back over my shoulder and texted Lanie.

I'm here.

Approximately five seconds later, Lanie texted back.

OMG! Why? Are you nuts?

I'd told my best friend about the motorcycle club party I'd attended and I'd told her about my new boss's slam, bam, thank you ma'am. I did this in an attempt to stop my skin from burning when I thought of it because every girl knew, a problem shared with her best friend was a problem lost. Though I'd learned a new life lesson, and this was that those problems mostly were discussions of what to wear on first dates or whether or not you should invest in that fabulous wrought iron wine rack from Pottery Barn and not the fact that you'd had a one-night stand with your new boss. I learned this because even after sharing with Lanie, it didn't help.

Lanie was of a mind that I shouldn't show at my new job and what I should do was my want-ad finger-pointing thing for another two months, or twelve, just as long as I never entered Tack's breathing space again. Then again, Lanie had a really good job as an advertising executive and was living with her fiancé, Elliott. She didn't have to worry about her nest egg depleting not only because she was talented, in great demand and therefore made a more than decent salary but also because Elliott was a genius computer programmer and made big bucks. Huge. She was spending ten thousand dollars on flowers alone for her wedding. Their catering budget sent my heart into spasm. And her dress cost more than my car.

My thumb went across the number pad and I texted back, *Not nuts. I need a paycheck.*

Five seconds later, Lanie texted, *What if you see him?*

I was prepared for that and I'd spent a lot of time preparing for seeing Tack again. Indeed, I'd spent all night doing it considering I had all of two hours of sleep.

If I see him, I see him, I texted back. *I'm embracing my inner slut.*

To this, I received, *You don't have an inner slut!!! You're Tyra Masters. Tyra Masters is NOT a slut!!!*

She is now, I replied, adding, *or she was Saturday night.*

No more flying solo, Lanie texted in return, then right on its heels came, *Any and all future social events you attend, I'm your wingman.*

I smiled at my phone, heard a door slam and my head came up. Then my lungs seized.

Shit! There was Tack standing outside the door to the Club's Compound. He was wearing faded jeans, motorcycle boots and a skin-tight white t-shirt. Even from a distance I could see his hair was a sexy, messy bed head. And I knew why since he was currently making out with a tall, thin, dark-haired woman, and when I say making out, I mean *making out.* They were going at it, her hands at his fantastic ass, his hands at hers.

God, I'd been in his bed Saturday night and he had a new woman in his bed last night, Sunday. And he hadn't walked me to the door and made out with me to say good-bye. Hell, he hadn't even said good-bye.

Damn.

I closed my eyes tight and swallowed and when I did, it hurt...a lot.

Okay, maybe I couldn't do this.

I opened my eyes and pinned them to the phone, my thumb flying over the number pad.

He just walked out of the Compound, I told Lanie.

Two seconds later, I received, *OMG!!!!*

He's making out with a brunette, I informed her.

OMG!! OMG!!! OMG!!!! Get out of there! Lanie texted back.

I heard an engine cough to life and lifted my head to see the brunette in the beat-up pickup. My eyes slid to Tack to see his on me. My gaze shot back to the truck to see the brunette was waving at Tack but he was done with her. I knew this because she was waving at him but when I looked back to him he was not paying a bit of attention to her and was walking my way.

I looked back down at my phone and typed in, *She's taking off. He's coming to me.*

I sent my message and stared at the phone, not lifting my head and trying hard not to bite my lip or, say, have an embarrassment-induced seizure.

"Red," I heard when my phone beeped in my hand, and luckily I didn't have to lift my head immediately because I was reading Lanie's latest message.

Escape, Tyra, go, go, go!!!!

"Red," I heard from closer, and I finally lifted my head to see that Tack was three of the eight steps up and climbing toward me.

He looked good. Everything about him looked good. The way his clothes fit. The way his hair looked like he'd just got out of bed and run his fingers through it. The way those lines radiated out the sides of his eyes. The way his body moved.

Nope, I couldn't be a slut. I should have listened to Lanie.

"Hey," I forced out.

My skin started burning and I was pretty sure it was pink top to toe as his eyes slid the length of me. When he made it to the top of the steps, he looked down at me and he didn't look happy.

"What're you doin' here?" he asked.

I stared at him, surprised. I mean, I'd told him on Saturday night I was his new office manager.

Didn't I?

So I said, "I work here."

"You what?"

"I work here."

His eyes did a top-to-toe again then he repeated after me, "You work here."

"Yes, Eloise hired me. I'm taking over for her. I'm your new office manager."

He stared down at me and he didn't look any less unhappy. In fact, he looked unhappier.

Then he stated, "You're shittin' me."

I fought against biting my lip again, succeeded and shook my head.

Apparently, Tack wasn't a big fan of working alongside women he'd loved and left. Or, in my case, loved and then kicked out of his bed.

I found this interesting, not in a good way, but it was interesting nonetheless.

Then Tack announced, "You don't work here anymore."

I blinked up at him as my hand automatically reached out and grasped the railing beside me.

"What?" I whispered.

"Babe, not good," he growled. "What the fuck were you thinkin'?"

"About what?" I asked.

He leaned in and it hit my fogged, stunned, fired-before-I-even-started brain that he was even unhappier than before, and I had to admit, it was a little scary.

"I do not work with bitches who've had my dick in their mouth," he declared, and that was when my skin stopped burning and felt like it was combusting.

"But," I started when I could speak again, "I thought I told you I was your new office manager."

"You did not," he returned.

"I'm pretty sure I did," I told him.

"You didn't," he replied.

"No, I think I did."

He leaned even closer to me and growled, "Red. You. Did. *Not*."

"Okay," I whispered because he was now definitely scaring me but also because I actually wasn't pretty sure I did, I was just kind of sure I did.

"I do not fuck anyone who's got my signature on their paycheck," he again made his opinion perfectly clear, and my mind raced to find a solution to this new dilemma at the same time it struggled with fighting back the urge to run as fast as I could to my car and peel right the heck out of Ride Custom Cars and Bikes forecourt and get as far away from this freaking scary guy as I could.

I mean, what was I thinking? I thought he was beautiful. Perfect. My motorcycle dream man.

Boy, was I wrong. Very, very wrong. He wasn't. He was a rough-and-ready motorcycle man, the president of a motorcycle club, and he was downright frightening.

With effort, I pulled myself together.

Then I told him, "Okay, that works for me. Minor blip. We forget it happened and since it's never going to happen again, we move on from this and you don't have to break your no-sleeping-with-employees rule in order to, um... employ me."

"We forget it happened?" he asked, looking even angrier.

"Uh... yeah," I answered.

"The rule's broken, babe, no unbreaking it," he returned.

"It's not broken," I told him.

"Red, it's broken."

"It isn't."

"It is."

"It isn't," I stated, and he opened his mouth to speak again, his face hard, his eyes flashing and I quickly went on to explain my reasoning. "See, you said you don't sleep with anyone who's got your signature on their paycheck. Eloise hired me but I hadn't actually *started*. So, I didn't have your signature on my paycheck because I'd only had the job offer. I wasn't actually doing the job. I walk in that door," I pointed to the office door, "that's when I'm your employee and since we're not, erm . . . you know . . . and won't again, then, technically, you didn't break your rule and, um . . . won't."

"I know what you taste like," he informed me of something I already knew.

This was an odd and slightly rude thing to share so I had no response.

"And what you sound like when you come," he continued being rude.

This was not getting better and I clenched my teeth to stop myself biting my lip.

"And how fuckin' greedy you are," he went on. "Babe, you think you're around I'm not gonna want seconds, you're fuckin' crazy."

I blinked.

Then I asked quietly, "What?"

"Darlin', you're the greediest piece of ass I've had in my bed in a long fuckin' time. I got a taste for greedy, you think I'm not gonna take it?"

Now he was definitely being rude.

"I'm not greedy," I whispered.

He leaned back. "Jesus, you fuckin' are. So fuckin'

hungry, you nearly wore me out. And, darlin', that's sayin' something."

This was already not fun and it was getting less fun by the second.

"Can we not talk about this?" I requested.

"Yeah, absolutely, we can not talk about this. That works for me. It also works for me you showed since you didn't leave your number before you took off on Saturday. So give me your number, get your ass in your car and I'll call you when I got a taste for you."

Oh my God. Did he just say that?

I felt the blood stop rushing through my veins as my entire body solidified.

"Did you just say that?" I asked when I got my lips moving again.

"Red, give me your number, get your ass in your car and I'll call you when it's time for us to play again."

He did. He did just say that because he'd also just mostly repeated it.

I clenched my teeth again but this time for a different reason.

Then I asked, "Do you know my name?"

"What?" he asked back.

"My name," I stated. "I told you my name Saturday night and I know I did so don't tell me I didn't." And I did. I absolutely, *totally* told him my name. In fact, I'd done it at least three times when he kept calling me "Red."

"You're shittin' me," he said again.

"Stop saying I'm shitting you. I'm not. What's my name?" I demanded to know.

"Babe, who cares? We don't need names" was his unbelievable answer.

"Ohmigod," I whispered. "You're a jerk."

"Red—"

"Totally a jerk." I kept whispering and he crossed his arms on his chest.

"Two choices, Red, give me your number, get your ass in your car, get outta here and wait for my call or just get your ass in your car and get outta here. You got five seconds."

"I'm not getting in my car," I told him. "I'm waiting for Eloise to come and show me the ropes then I'm going to work."

"You are not gonna work here," he returned.

"I am," I shot back.

"No, you aren't."

"I am."

"Babe, not gonna say it again, you aren't."

That was when I lost it and I didn't know why. I wasn't the type to lose it. You didn't lose it when you planned every second of your life. Caution and losing it did not go together.

But I lost it.

I planted my hands on my hips, took a step toward him and lifted up on my toes to get in his face.

"Now, you listen to me, scary biker dude," I snapped. "I need this job. I haven't worked in two months and I *need* this job. I can't wait two more months or longer to find another job. I need to work *now*." His blue eyes burned into mine in a way that felt physical but I kept right on talking. "So you're good-looking, have great tats and a cool goatee. So you caught my eye and I caught yours. We had sex. Lots of sex. It was good. So what? That was then, this is now. We're not going to play, not again. We're done playing. I'm going to come in at eight, leave at five, do my job, and you're going to be my scary biker dude boss, sign my paychecks, do my performance evaluations and maybe, if you're nice, I'll make you coffee. Other than that, you don't exist for me and I don't exist for you. What we had, we had. It's over. I'm moving on and how I'm moving on is, I'm...working...this...*job*."

I stopped talking and realized I was breathing heavy. I also realized his eyes were still burning into mine. I knew he was still angry but there was something else there, something I didn't get because I didn't know him and I couldn't read him. But whatever it was, it was scarier than just him being angry, which, frankly, was scary enough.

When he spoke, he did it softly. "You think, Red, right now, I put my hands and mouth on you in about two minutes you wouldn't be pantin' to be flat on your back, legs wide open in my bed?"

At his words, I forgot how scary he was and hissed, "You're unbelievable."

"I'm right," he fired back.

"Touch me, you bought yourself a lawsuit," I retorted acidly.

"You are so full of shit," he returned.

"Try me," I invited hostilely, though I didn't want him to. Not that I thought he was right, but because he was a jerk. A *huge* jerk. And I'd just decided I'd rather be touched by any man currently residing on death row before I wanted Tack to touch me again.

"Is everything okay?" we both heard, and our heads turned to look down the steps to see Eloise at the bottom looking up at us with wide eyes.

I opened my mouth to say something to Eloise, what, I had no idea, but before I could speak, Tack did.

"You tell her she wears that fancy-ass shit to work again, her ass is canned," Tack growled, and I watched Eloise's body jerk in surprise.

She was in jeans, a tight t-shirt and high-heeled sandals and I was in a pencil skirt, blouse and high-heeled pumps;

therefore I had to admit I definitely made a mistake on the dress code but it wasn't worth termination.

I looked to him to see his eyes cut to me. "And you," he said, "I taste you again, *any* way I can taste you, and I will, Red, trust me, you're gone. Outta here. Get me?"

"You won't," I declared, and he glared at me then his eyes moved over my face. They did this for a while and while they did this, they changed. I could swear I watched the anger leak clean out of them and something else, something curious, something warm and therefore something far more frightening filled them.

His warm blue eyes locked on mine and he muttered, "We'll see."

Then he stepped away, jogged down the steps, sauntered to a bike, threw a leg over it, started it, backed it out and roared away.

"What was that?" Eloise asked. I jumped and turned to see she was standing at my side.

"I don't think I made a good first impression on my new boss," I answered. Eloise was staring after Tack but at my words she looked at me, eyes still wide, so I pulled my I-can-do-this mask over my face, smiled at her and cried, "Oh well, never mind! He'll come around. Now, let's get crackin'."

And I turned to the office door.

CHAPTER TWO

Bring It On

IT WAS DAY three at Ride. Eloise was gone, I was on my own and I had no idea what I was doing.

It would seem it was important to know a little bit about cars and bikes in order to be the office manager of a garage that made custom ones. Eloise did the best she could in the two days she had to show me around, but she had a job in Vegas to get to. She was a blackjack dealer as well as a garage office manager. Her man had already left to start his new job there and she had to get her ass out there (her words) because her man was getting impatient. Seemed there weren't many women who were equipped to run the office of a garage, or at least not ones that would meet Chaos MC (short for Motorcycle Club, one of the few things Eloise taught me that sank in) standards, and therefore her hiring efforts took longer than she expected.

She did not share what Chaos MC standards were but apparently they didn't include knowing that first thing about cars and bikes.

The good thing about these two days was that after Tack roared off on his bike after our incident, I only saw him twice. The first, he was roaring in when I was leaving the first day. The second, he was standing, hands planted on hips outside the back door of the auto supply store talking to two other rough-and-ready motorcycle dudes. His back was to me and the conversation looked unhappy. I had a list in my purse and was on my way to get lunch for Eloise, the mechanics and me so I didn't pay much attention. When I returned, Tack and the two rough-and-ready dudes were nowhere to be seen and didn't return before I left.

Now I was back, my third day, my first without Eloise, and Tack was there. I knew this because, as I drove up at ten to eight, one of the big bay doors was open and he was bent over the engine of a bright, cherry red car. His head turned to watch me drive in but that was all I saw because after I caught the initial glimpse, I studiously avoided looking at him as I parked. I equally studiously put him out of my mind as I grabbed the box of donuts I brought for the mechanics, got out of my car, unlocked the office, turned on the lights and computer then started coffee.

Forty-five minutes later, some of the boys were in. I could hear them and a few had been in for coffee and a donut. I was sitting behind the desk, sipping coffee, staring at an order for parts I was clicking into the computer, no part I knew what the hell it was and the notes I was using that were scribbled on a scrap of paper looked like Sanskrit, when the door that led into the garages opened.

My eyes slid to it as my mouth started to form a smile for who I thought would be one of the mechanics when Tack walked in.

My smile froze. Then my eyes went back to the computer screen.

I tried to pretend he wasn't there but I failed at pretending. I knew exactly when his body stopped at the other side of my desk even though I was studiously avoiding looking at it.

"Thought I told you 'bout those clothes, Red," he growled.

I didn't pry my eyes away from the computer screen, took a sip from my coffee and kept clicking the mouse.

"You don't have an Employee Handbook," I informed the computer screen.

"Say again?" he demanded.

My eyes slid to the side and up.

Damn, he was gorgeous. Another white t-shirt, skin tight across the wall of his chest, broad shoulders and lean abs, this tee stained with grease. His hands were also stained with grease even though he was carrying a grease-stained cloth. He'd obviously wiped them and, from the look of it, so had every other mechanic, all of them about ten thousand times.

I made a note to self to look into laundering the guys' grease rags as I repeated, "You don't have an Employee Handbook."

"So?" Tack asked, his hands going to his faded jeans-clad hips, the cloth dangling from one.

"So, you don't have an official dress code. Therefore, I can wear whatever I want. And I take this job seriously so I'm wearing serious clothes."

And I was. Another pencil skirt, this one bone-colored. A cute little pale pink blouse with barely there sleeves and darts up my midriff. And spike-heeled, pale pink slingbacks that I thought were awesome. So awesome, I bought the blouse, another skirt and a pair of slacks to go with them, I loved those shoes so much.

"Babe, this is a garage. You don't wear uppity, high-class shit at a garage. You wear jeans at a garage."

I straightened away from the computer and swiveled my chair to him, my head tipping back as I did so.

"Would you like me to draft an Employee Handbook that includes a dress code?" I asked.

"Yeah, Red, you do that," Tack replied.

"Certainly." I nodded. "Do you have a deadline?"

"End of business today."

I blinked. Then I said, "That's impossible. With everything else I need to do, that'll take a week. Maybe two."

"You got until the end of business. And I need those parts ordered and I wanna go over the order before you send it."

Oh boy. Now I was beginning to panic. I was working on the order and I didn't want to mess it up. Since I had a very loose hold on all that I was doing, I was certain I'd mess it up.

"It'll be ready in an hour," I told him, probably stupidly as it was highly doubtful I could learn Sanskrit in an hour and I knew for certain I couldn't learn anything about cars and bikes in an hour.

"You don't got an hour. I'm leavin' in thirty minutes. You got thirty minutes," he replied.

Damn!

"Fine," I bit off.

He scowled at me then he turned away but stopped dead.

"Shit," he muttered and twisted his torso to look back at me. "You bring in those donuts?"

"Yes," I answered.

"Why?"

"Why not?"

"'Why not' is not an answer to 'why,' Red," Tack returned, his whole body moving now to face me again.

"The guys like donuts," I told him.

"So?"

"So, I bought donuts for my coworkers. If you're a nice person, it's something you do. And I'm a nice person."

"It's something you do when you wanna crawl up their asses and make them like you. And it's not something *you* are gonna do again, got me?"

Jeez. What was with this guy?

"I was just doing something nice," I stated the obvious and kind of repeated myself.

"So you did it. Don't do it again," he returned.

"It's donuts, Tack."

"Don't do it again, Red."

I glared at him. Then I asked, "Are you this big of a jerk to just me or are you this big of a jerk to everybody?"

He shoved the rag in his back pocket and crossed his arms on his chest as he said, "Listen, darlin', I told you I didn't want you workin' here. You cannot be surprised I'm gonna be an asshole to you because I haven't changed my mind. I don't want you workin' here."

I stared up at him. Then I thought of the order for car and bike stuff I had no idea how to make. I knew my attempt would probably piss him off and maybe give him reason to fire me. Then I thought of the fact that I'd slept with him, I thought it was something special, something beautiful, and it was most definitely not. Then I thought of the fact that he didn't want me there so why was I so fired up to be there? I didn't like him, not at all. He was a jerk. The fact that I slept with him mortified me. The idea of dealing with him day in and day out wasn't something that filled me with delight. Sure, I liked some of the guys in the garage and when they came in, they gabbed like women, but I hadn't bonded with any of them.

So what on earth was I doing?

"Fine," I stated and looked back at the computer screen.

"What?" Tack asked.

"Fine," I repeated to the computer screen then went on

to explain to the monitor, "Eloise didn't have enough time to teach me the ropes. I don't know what I'm doing. You're going to figure that out in thirty minutes. You don't like me. I *really* don't like you," just my eyes slid to him, "so, fine. I'll finish out the day and then you won't see me again."

Tack's brows went up. "You slap me with attitude twice for this job and then you give in, easy as that?"

"I'm not going to work in a place where I can't eat donuts," I informed him, looked back at the computer screen and started tapping away. "You crossed the line with that one. So, yeah, easy as that."

Then I took another sip of coffee.

"I thought you needed this job," Tack said.

"I'll find another job where I can wear my fabulous pink slingbacks without putting up with annoying, unnecessary, scary biker dude hassle."

"So, you're sayin', you get in my face about keeping this job and then you give in 'cause you can't wear sex kitten shoes and eat donuts?"

My eyes moved back to him. "Yeah, handsome, that's what I'm saying."

He stared at me. I stared back at him. Then his face relaxed and his lips, surrounded by that kickass goatee, curled up into a sexy-as-all-hell grin.

"Jesus, Red, tell me, when you're such a pain in the ass, why do I seriously wanna fuck you right now?"

It felt like a strong, heavy hand pressed hard on my chest, pushing all the air out of my lungs.

"Don't be coarse," I snapped.

His eyebrows went up again. "Coarse?"

"Coarse, vulgar, uncouth... *rude*," I explained.

His sexy grin turned into an even sexier smile. "Only way I can be, darlin', 'cause all that's me."

"Well, good. Another reason for me to quit."

"You're not quittin'," he declared, and it was my turn for my eyebrows to go up.

"Pardon?"

"You're not quittin'," he repeated.

That hand at my chest pressed deeper. "I thought you didn't want me working here."

He jerked his chin up. "Changed my mind, babe."

"You changed your mind?" I asked.

"Yeah, and I changed my mind about your clothes and the donuts too. Bring whatever you want for the boys. Wear whatever you want. *Especially* those tight skirts that remind me how great your ass feels and those sex kitten shoes that make me want to feel their heels digging in my back."

Ohmigod! Could he *be* more of a *jerk*?

"You can't talk to me like that," I informed him bitingly.

"I can't?" he asked.

"No. It's sexual harassment."

He smiled again. "Darlin', don't think I have to remind you that you took a job, you knew I was your boss, you came to what amounts to a company party and then you fucked my brains out. I didn't harass you. You walked with me straight to my bed and you participated fully in everything we did in that bed. You could try but you'd have a hard fuckin' time convincin' anyone I'm harassin' you."

This was, unfortunately, true.

"I'm quitting," I announced firmly.

"So quit," he returned. "I can't chain you to that chair. It isn't me who's gotta look in the mirror in the mornin' and know I'm a coward."

My body jolted straight in my chair.

"What?" I snapped.

"Babe, you took this job knowin' it'd be a challenge and

you fought for it knowin' how that challenge changed. Now, two days in, your first head-to-head with me, you're givin' up. That's bullshit and it's weak. That's the way a coward would act. You give in, you gotta look in the mirror and know that shit. I don't. So you wanna quit, quit. That shit ain't on me, it's on you. You can live with that…" He trailed off and shrugged.

"So you wanted me to go, and I'm going, now you're trying to goad me into staying?" I asked with easy-to-read disbelief.

"I'm tellin' you the way it is. You're sittin' on your sweet ass in that sweet skirt knowin' you're gonna give in eventually and warm my bed. This isn't about donuts, Red, it's about you bein' weak. So don't try to bullshit me because I know your play and I'm callin' you on it."

"I am *not* going to warm your bed!" I fired back.

"Oh yeah you are," Tack returned.

"You don't even know my *name*," I retorted.

"Nope, and I didn't before when you sucked my cock, I ate you, you fucked me hard and I fucked you harder. Didn't bother you then."

"I thought you knew my name!" My voice was rising.

He bent at the waist, put a fist to my desk and said quietly, "If that what it takes for you, baby, then tell me, we'll go to the Compound and I guarantee you'll enjoy an extended break."

"Go to hell, Tack," I hissed.

"Or we can just lock the doors, close the blinds and I'll do you on your desk."

Total. Freaking. *Jerk!*

"Go to hell," I repeated.

"Or, if you're into that shit, we don't have to lock the doors and close the blinds."

I glared at him. He held my glare and did it with his lips twitching.

After we had our staring contest for a while, he whispered what sounded like a dare: "Gonna quit?"

"No," I snapped, his lips stopped twitching because he grinned and then I finished, "Not until I find another job. You're right. I need this job. I'll start looking immediately and I promise to give you notice."

"Right," he muttered, still grinning.

"And in the meantime, I will warn you that I have no clue what I'm doing."

"I'm patient, baby," he said softly, and I knew he wasn't talking about me getting car and bike part orders right.

"Well, that's good because you're going to have to be," I returned then added, "*Very* patient."

"You'll get it in the end," he muttered, his meaning clear.

"You're unbelievable," I whispered irately.

"Yeah, I think you whispered that in my ear Saturday night," he whispered back, not, I noted, in the least irately.

It was safe to say I was done.

"I have a lot of work to screw up, Tack. Do you want to stop annoying me so I can do it?"

"Sure," he agreed. I glared at him. Then, without warning and so fast I couldn't avoid it, his hand was curled around the back of my head. He pulled me to him, leaned into me and I had to execute evasive maneuvers not to have a desk covered in coffee.

I forgot all about the coffee when I noted his eyes were so close they were all I could see.

"To be fair, baby, I'm givin' you a warning," he said quietly.

"Let me go," I demanded just as quietly, mostly because I was freaking out.

"I want somethin', I get it."

"Let me go," I repeated.

"Only once I didn't. That shit ain't happenin' to me again."

"Tack—"

"You've been warned, Red," he whispered, and I watched his eyes drop to my mouth.

I held my breath and put pressure on his hand at my head. I was concentrating on both of these things so hard, I lost track of his other hand until I felt his fingers against my cheek. His thumb was sliding along my lower lip before I could do anything to stop it.

Then he released me, turned and, without another word or look, he sauntered out the door.

When the door closed behind him, I sucked in breath, closed my eyes tight and kept breathing deep until I felt my heart slow and my lower lip stopped tingling.

I opened my eyes and stared at the door.

Then I whispered, "I'm not coward and I'm not going to be your plaything. I don't know where I'm going or what I'm doing but I do know I'm Tyra Sidney Masters and Tyra Sidney Masters is not a coward and she's not a plaything. That's what I know. So, Tack Whoever-You-Are, bring it on."

Then I turned to the computer and royally screwed up the order.

CHAPTER THREE

Only I Call You Red

"HEY, LENNY," I called loudly to the mechanic (or body guy or whatever he was) closest to the door leading to my office. The big man in blue coveralls straightened, shoved back his welding mask and turned to me.

"Yo!" he replied.

"Do you know where Tack is?" I asked.

It was precisely thirty-seven minutes since my last encounter with Tack (I had timed it). I had the what I was sure was screwed-up printed parts order in my hand along with the Sanskrit notes and a pen. I was hoping Tack had already taken off and when he returned, he'd promptly come in and fire me due to the lateness of the order being completed as well as the fact it clearly stated I had no clue what I was doing.

These hopes were dashed when Lenny's eyes slid to the door of the bay and he jerked his head toward them.

"Out there, Tyra. Compound," he yelled over the garage noise. I looked toward the door but couldn't see anything so I walked down the steps and through the garage toward the doors.

Then I saw him. He was standing, back to me, at thc linc

of bikes in front of the Compound. He was with two other bikers. There were more bikes there today. Eight, I counted as I walked across the forecourt, my heels clicking against the cement, my eyes squinting against the powerful, bright July sun of a Denver day.

I was ten feet away when the attention of the two bikers with Tack shifted to me and I was seven feet away when Tack's body turned and his eyes hit me.

I will not blush, act like an idiot or a shrew. I will be professional. This is a job. Only a job. He's my boss. He's a handsome one but a jerky one and I slept with him, but he's just my boss. I embrace my inner slut. Sluts wouldn't blush, act like idiots or shrews. They would just go about their business. Therefore, I am a slut and I am proud, I said to myself as I approached.

I stopped close to their huddle and looked at the two bikers. One was huge, tall, blond, his long hair pulled back in a ponytail at the base of his neck. He had blue eyes, lighter and grayer than Tack's (which were a blue so pure it was nearly sapphire, no joke), and he was really cute in a rough-and-ready way. The other was also tall with a full beard that needed a trim and it needed that trim about two years ago. He had long russet brown hair that he'd bunched up at the back of his head in a man-bun. He also, unlike Tack and the blond guy, had a hint of a beer gut.

"Hey," I said, my eyes pinned to the two other men when I stopped at them. "Sorry to interrupt. Do you mind? I need Tack but this won't take a minute."

"Not at all, darlin'," the brown-haired guy said.

I smiled at him. "Thanks," I muttered then looked at Tack and wiped the smile clean off my face, something he saw which made him press his lips together at the same exact time his eyes lit with what could not be mistaken as anything other than humor. "The order," I announced curtly, holding out the papers and pen. "You can look over it. The notes Eloise gave me are on top. And there's a pen so you can make any changes."

I knew there would be changes so when he reached out with his left hand to take the papers and pen from me, I took a quick step away and went on, "You can bring it back to the office and I'll make any changes before submitting it." I looked at the boys and finished, "Sorry, gents, and thanks. You can go back to talking now."

I started to turn away and found my progress halted when a strong arm wrapped around my waist and I found myself three feet from where I was half a second before. I also found my front plastered against Tack's side, his arm an iron band around my waist.

"Brick and Dog won't mind I look at this here, Red," Tack told me when I tipped my head up to stare at him.

I heard his words but had no response since I was pretty certain my lips were parted in shock and surprise that he was suddenly holding me plastered to his side. I was also pretty certain my eyes were wide for the same reasons. And lastly, I was definitely certain I forgot just how hard and lean his body was because feeling my soft one pressed to his rock-solid one acutely reminded me of this fact.

Before I could recover, a rough voice came at me and I dazedly turned my head to look at the dark-haired guy. "You the new office girl?"

"Uh...yeah," I answered as I put pressure on the arm around my waist, something which made the iron turn to steel.

"Brick," he stated.

I nodded, still putting pressure on the arm. "Hey, Brick."

"Dog," the blond man said. My eyes went to his face to

see his gaze on Tack's arm around my waist and a grin playing at his lips.

I'd seen them both at the party but I hadn't met either of them. I also had a feeling they'd seen me at the party with Tack and very likely had seen me walk to the Compound and disappear inside it for hours, also with Tack. And therefore, standing in the Colorado sun, in the forecourt of Ride Custom Cars and Bikes, pressed to Tack's side with his arm tight around me, I had the feeling they were getting the wrong impression.

I fought the blush that was creeping along my skin and said, "Hey, Dog."

Then I said no more.

Therefore, Brick asked, "You got a name?"

My body tensed and my eyes went to Brick. "You can call me Red."

The steel arm tightened around my waist and my neck twisted, my head tipping back as Tack growled, "Only I call you Red, Red."

"Why do you only call me Red?" I asked.

"Because only I do," Tack answered.

I tipped my head to the side. "Is that really your answer?"

"Only one you're gonna get," he replied.

I stared up at him and he stared down at me. Then I gave up.

"Whatever," I muttered, looking away, pulling again at his arm and not getting anywhere.

"So, again, babe, you got a name?" Brick asked, and I looked up at him to see he was smiling.

"Is the name on your birth certificate Brick?" I asked a question I was pretty sure I knew the answer to.

"No." He gave me the answer I was pretty sure I knew.

I looked at Dog. "Is your name really Dog?"

"Nope," Dog responded, also smiling.

I looked up at Tack and pulled again at his arm and again it was ineffectual. "And you? Did your parents name you Tack?"

"No," he answered.

"Okay then," I turned to the boys, "since it's nicknames all around, I'll answer to whatever you christen me."

"Whatever we christen you?" Dog repeated.

"Sure," I told him on a shrug. "I invite you to be creative." Dog and Brick looked to each other and grinned, but I looked to Tack and demanded on a request, "Can you let me go? I have an Employee Handbook to write."

"No," he answered, and I felt my eyes narrow. He ignored the narrowing of my eyes and went on, "Darlin', this order is totally fucked up." And he shook the paper in his hand.

"I know that," I informed him. "I told you I didn't know what I was doing and I was going to screw it up. That's why I brought the pen, so you could make amendments."

He grinned. "Not enough room on this paper to write all the amendments, Red. How could you fuck this up so much when I wrote down everything I needed?" Then he shook the papers again, my eyes went to them and I realized the Sanskrit notes were his.

"Those are your notes?" I asked.

"Yeah," he answered.

"I can't read Sanskrit, Tack."

"It ain't written in Sanskrit, Red."

"You have worse penmanship than a doctor," I informed him.

"I can read it," he informed me.

"Of course *you* can, you know what it says. To me, it's a bunch of scratches and squiggles and since I don't know anything about car and bike parts, I couldn't guess very accurately. So you need to take some time and write out the changes…" I paused and concluded with emphasis,"…*legibly*."

"Eloise hired an office girl who don't know shit about cars and bikes?" Dog asked Tack, and I looked at him.

But it was Brick who answered for Tack. "Eloise hired an office girl who wears fuck-me shoes and skirts. Who cares if she don't know shit about cars and bikes?" Then Brick looked at me. "You just take your time, sweetheart, you'll get it."

"Thanks." I smiled at him, deciding to ignore his comment about my skirt and shoes being of the fuck-me variety. I thought they were cute and girly but I was a woman, they were men. Men, I knew, thought way different from women, and most of these thoughts, I knew, centered around sex so obviously cute to a woman would be something else to a man.

"You need any help, I know all about car and bike parts," Brick offered.

I kept smiling. "Thanks, that's sweet."

"That's me, I'm sweet." Brick smiled back, and it was then I felt Tack's body get tight. My head turned to look at him again and I saw that his neck was twisted and he was looking beyond Dog. My gaze followed his to two men walking from the door of the Compound toward our huddle. They were the two men Tack had been talking to the day before. And they were two men who didn't look laid-back and welcoming like Brick and Dog. In fact, they looked so *not* laid-back and welcoming that they were more than a little scary.

When my eyes swung through Tack, Dog and Brick I saw that they, too, no longer looked laid-back and welcoming and they, too, looked more than a little scary.

Yikes!

It was then Tack's arm gave me a squeeze and I looked up at him to see his head tipped down to me.

"Back to the office, Red. I'll be in in a minute to go over this with you."

I saw his face was serious and although this was an order, it was voiced quietly, even gently, and thus it felt weirdly sweet.

Therefore, I said quietly back, "All right, Tack." I looked at the boys. "Later, guys."

"Later, babe," Dog murmured to me but his neck was twisted to the two men who were now close.

"Later, girl," Brick muttered. He also was watching the two men.

Tack let me go. I smiled politely at the two men who were now stopping at the biker huddle then I turned and skedaddled across the cement of the forecourt, my heels clicking loudly as I went, all the while wondering what in the hell that was all about.

CHAPTER FOUR

Do You Want a Donut?

I WAS PLAGIARIZING an Employee Handbook I'd downloaded from the Internet when the outside door to my office opened and sunlight shone through around the dark outline of Tack's body.

Great, I thought.

"Hey," I said.

"Red," he replied and walked toward me, demanding, "call up the order."

"Okeydoke," I muttered, professional efficiency personified. I turned back to the computer screen and started clicking the mouse to call up the order. The screen with the order on it was loading when I felt movement close to me and heard papers rustling. I twisted my torso and looked up to see Tack plant his ass smack on the top of my desk, pinning me in my chair turned toward the computer with his muscled thigh.

"Um...could you not sit on my desk?" I requested.

"No," he replied.

"I asked nicc," I told him.

"Answer's still no," he told me.

I stared up at him. He stared down at me. He didn't look

serious like he looked outside before I left him, Dog and Brick. He didn't look laid-back and amused either. I didn't know what he looked like but I sensed everything was not okay.

"Is everything okay?" I asked.

"No," he answered with surprising honesty.

Oh boy.

Perhaps there was dissent in the ranks of the Chaos MC. This was probably not good. And it was probably even more not good if you were the president of the Chaos MC.

And because of this, for some insane reason, likely because I found the consumption of donuts soothed a variety of things that were not so good, I found myself asking, "Do you want a donut?"

He stared at me a beat and he did this with a strange intensity, something I did not get working behind his eyes.

Then, before I got it, he answered, "No."

"Have you had breakfast?"

"It's after ten o'clock, Red."

"Have you had breakfast?" I repeated.

"No."

"Then you need a donut."

"I don't need a donut."

"Okay," I gave in. "Do you want coffee?"

"No, babe, I don't want coffee. I don't want a donut. I want to sort out this order, get it sent and then I got shit to do."

I now knew what he looked like because he sounded like it too, and that was impatient.

"Okeydoke," I whispered and turned to the screen.

This was a mistake because one second later, I felt Tack's heat against my back. I felt this because he'd leaned in close. Then his hand covered mine on the mouse, his finger settling on mine, pressing in to click as he moved out of the order screen and back to the menu. Then, without a word or any instruction, he continued clicking through the screens, ordering the parts he needed, upping the numbers when necessary by clicking on arrows, then he went to our on-line basket and removed practically everything I'd added that morning. He did this quickly, with practiced ease, and the only time it took was waiting for the different screens to load.

"Uh…" I mumbled when I fought back the haze created by the rapidly flashing screens filling my eyes. "I'm not learning anything."

"You learn somethin', you don't need to come to me to help you."

I blinked at the screen. Then I twisted my neck to see his profile right there. And it was a very attractive profile. Not to mention he smelled good, a mixture of motor oil, musk and man.

Damn.

"I'd rather know what I'm doing," I told his profile.

He kept clicking, his eyes on the screen when he replied, "And I'd rather watch you strut your ass to wherever I am when you need to sort somethin' out."

"Tack—"

His head turned, I got a full frontal of his face up close, and stopped speaking.

"Red," he said softly. "You entered the game, it's my game, babe, you play it my way."

"I don't want to play games," I told him.

"Oh yeah, you do," he told me, and I shook my head.

"I want to do my job," I stated.

"You get to do that too," he returned.

"Not very well, if I don't know what I'm doing," I said.

"It'll be annoying to have to find you every time I run up against something I don't understand."

"You'll get used to it."

I stared at him, feeling my blood pressure rising, then I pulled my face back an inch and his hand on mine on the mouse tightened.

"Listen, seriously," I started. "This is ridiculous. Can't we just move on?"

"No."

Argh!

"All right, fine." I set my face and turned it to the computer screen, announcing, "You're not the only person here who knows cars and bikes. Brick said he'd help. I know Lenny knows what he's doing considering he's a mechanic or a body guy or something but whatever he is, he is what he is around cars so he has to know what he's doing. They might even be able to decipher your handwriting. I'll be perfectly fine."

"You ask anyone for help, Red, not only you but they'll answer to me," Tack warned. I tore my eyes from the screen to look at him to see he was gazing at the monitor then his finger pressed mine and the mouse clicked.

I looked back at the screen to see it said our order was submitted.

"Tack! You submitted the order and I didn't even get a chance to scrutinize it!" I snapped.

"Babe, have you not been listening?"

I turned to glare up at him, yanking my hand from under his on the mouse then instantly finding it caught, his fingers curling around mine tight, and then my hand was resting on his rock-hard thigh.

Crap.

"Tack," I clipped, still glaring at him and now pulling in vain on my hand.

He ignored me and said outrageously, "I gotta go. Tip your face back further for me, baby, I wanna give you a kiss before I do."

My stomach plummeted in a way that wasn't altogether unpleasant even as I felt my eyebrows rise as did my voice. "Are you nuts?"

"No," he replied calmly, his eyes moving over my face and settling on my mouth before he muttered, "Remember your mouth. It was near as sweet as other parts of you."

Ohmigod!

I felt my eyes narrow mainly because he was too much and none of the too much he was was good.

I yanked at my hand. His fingers curled tighter and his other hand came up to wrap around the side of my neck as his upper body started coming toward me. Therefore, I pulled at my neck at the same time I yanked at my hand. This not only didn't work, it made him slide his fingers around to the back of my neck, pulling up as he bent closer and lifted my hand from his thigh to press it against his chest.

I was watching his face get closer, specifically his amazing lips surrounded by his kickass goatee. My mind took that unfortunate moment to remind me that I'd never had a man with facial hair prior to Tack and I'd liked the feeling of those lips with that goatee on various parts of me. In fact, every part they'd touched. And it was then we heard the door open.

Both our necks twisted to see a woman was standing in the door. She was pretty, with wild red hair that had liberal streaks of very fake blonde, which I couldn't decide in that instant if I thought looked good or kind of skanky. She also had clear, light blue eyes. She was wearing biker-babe apparel of jeans, high-heeled boots and tight scoop-necked t-shirt with four buttons at the neckline, all of them undone exposing cleavage.

"Fuck," Tack muttered right before the redhead exploded.

"You are *fucking shitting me*!" she, for some reason, shrieked, walking in quickly after slamming the door loudly, her eyes going squinty, her face setting hard, and I saw what I didn't see seconds before. Her face was already hard prior to her setting it harder. There were lines around her mouth probably from smoking too much. There were also lines around her eyes that didn't look like laugh lines, instead they looked like she got squinty-eyed pissed-off frequently. And her skin looked like someone should have introduced her to sun block about three decades ago.

I pulled at Tack's hands and one let me go, the one at my neck. The other one dropped our hands to his thigh as his torso straightened and twisted to face her.

"Naomi, what the fuck?" he asked, and her squinty eyes cut to him.

"Are you doin' your new office manager?" she asked.

"For fuck's sake," Tack growled.

"Are you doin' your new office manager?" she repeated, her voice, unfortunately, getting louder.

"Don't know that's any of your business," Tack answered, and my hand jerked spasmodically in his hold, which tightened in return.

"You don't know that's any of my business?" she shouted. I winced at the volume of her voice at the same time I hoped that the noise in the garage was drowning her out.

"Woman, I divorced your ass four years ago," Tack reminded her, and I felt my lips part as I stared at Tack's ex-wife. I could see it, considering she'd been pretty once. She wasn't exactly pretty now, mostly because she looked and acted like a serious bitch. Furthermore, on closer inspection, the fake blonde streaks were definitely skanky. She shouldn't have gone for champagne highlights. Instead her stylist should have recommended honey or, maybe, caramel.

"So?" she shot back.

"So?" Tack repeated with unconcealed disbelief.

"Yeah, so?" she returned.

"You're hitched to another fuckin' guy," Tack replied.

"So?"

"So, who I do ain't no business of yours and hasn't been for four fuckin' years," Tack returned.

"We got kids, asshole," she retorted.

Oh wow. Tack had kids.

"Who I do ain't their business either unless I decide to make it their business instead 'a you makin' it their business. Which you should not fuckin' do but I know you will because you are one seriously twisted, stupid bitch which is the reason I divorced your ass four years ago," Tack fired back.

Um, it seemed to me a domestic situation was brewing. It also seemed I was due a coffee break, which I decided to take immediately and take it somewhere that was not there.

I rose from my chair, muttering, "I'll just—"

Naomi's eyes sliced to me. "Yeah, get your ass outta here, bitch."

That was when Tack let me go and he did this before he stood, turning to face her so he was standing between her and me. I didn't know him very well and he'd been scary around me, very scary. But even though I had his back and I might not know him very well, no one could miss the vibes emanating from him, and those vibes were so beyond scary it was *not* funny. They were so beyond scary I found myself holding my breath.

"Do not," he said softly, in a voice that seemed to slither

through the room in a sinister way, "speak to Tyra like that. Do you fuckin' hear me?"

My body locked when he said my name but my eyeballs swiveled to Naomi who was, shockingly, completely immune to the scary vibes sparking menacingly in the room.

"I'll talk to your latest piece of ass however the fuck I want, dickhead."

At that, Tack moved and I could swear I was watching but he went so fast, I wasn't certain what I saw. One second they were facing off, the next the bright Denver sunshine came in through the door and the next that door was closed and both Tack and Naomi were on the other side of it.

Even so, I heard their continued conversation starting with Tack warning, "Do not test me."

"Fuck you" was Naomi's rejoinder.

"You came here to say somethin', say it and get the fuck gone."

"Kiss my ass!"

"Fuckin' hell. Clue in, bitch, I'm done with this shit. I was done with it years ago. You got two seconds to say what you gotta say then I'm walkin' away." There was silence for two seconds then Tack again, "I'm walkin' away."

That was when Naomi said quickly, "I want her job."

My eyes locked on the door.

Ohmigod, she wanted my job. Holy crap!

"Say again?" Tack demanded as I aimed my behind to the chair and sat in it.

"I got canned from my other job. Pipe's outta work. I need to get somethin' quick-like. I heard Eloise was leavin' and I want her job."

"Position's filled, Naomi, and even if it wasn't, no way your ass would be in Tyra's chair."

"I did that job for twelve years, Tack, no one knows it

better than me," she stated, giving me history that made me bite my lip.

"I'll repeat, position's filled," Tack returned.

"Then unfill it," she shot back. "You want your kids fed, you'll sort shit out."

"You got money problems, woman, Rush and Tabby got rooms at my house and I got food in the cupboards. They're more than welcome to move in with me."

"The kids aren't movin' in with you."

"They are, you can't feed 'em, Pipe don't get off his fat ass and you don't stop actin' like a bitch and gettin' your ass fired from job after job."

"It wasn't my fault!" she snapped.

"In your twisted head, it's never your fault but it always is."

"I came here askin' for help and this is what I get," she returned.

"You came here and started shoutin', like usual, actin' like a bitch, like usual, so yeah, this is what you get," Tack replied.

"You know I can do that job and you also know I won't suck your cock as part of my job description like *Tyra* in there will so you're bein' a dick even when it's your kids who'll suffer."

"Naomi, I asked you to suck my cock, you'd have your mouth wrapped around it so fast, you'd break the sound barrier."

"As usual, right up your own ass, Tack."

"Jesus, honest to God, seriously? You need a favor, you drive here and give me shit and think you're gonna get it? What's the matter with you?"

"It took a lot for me to come here, Tack. And I walk into *my* office and have a flashback seein' as you like to play around, you always liked to play around and you're still fuckin' playin' around!"

Oh boy.

"Christ, you are fucked up. Still singin' that song?" Tack asked.

"Still lyin' to me that you didn't fuck everything that moved when you had *my* gold band on your finger?" she retorted.

"Twisted, totally twisted," Tack muttered and finished with "We're done."

"We are so *not* done."

"We're *done*," Tack stated, and I knew he meant it because suddenly he was in the office, the door was closed behind him and he locked it. Then his long legs took him across the office to the door to the garage and he locked that one too, all the while Naomi pounded on the front door shouting, "Open this goddamn door, motherfucker! We're not done!"

Tack ignored this and walked to the window that faced the forecourt and with a rough, angry jerk he closed the blinds.

Then he turned to me.

That scene was so nasty, so intense and so unlike anything I'd ever seen or heard before I couldn't fight it back so I stared up at his angry face while biting my lip.

"You all right?" he, for some reason, asked me.

"Uh..." I answered, because I could say no more but the answer was, no. I was not all right. Tack's ex-wife was a bitch, she wanted my job, he had two kids and he may or may not have fucked around on his wife. None of this I wanted to know but all of it was bouncing around in my brain in a way that I knew, no matter how studiously I did it, I wasn't going to be able to avoid thinking about it.

"My ex is a bitch," he stated the obvious.

"Um..." I replied, still unable to utter more.

"Your job is safe," he informed me.

"Uh...okay," I whispered, uncertain if I was happy about this fact or not.

That was when Tack shared even more stuff I did not want to know.

"She's got this in her head, she'll probably be back and she'll probably do other shit to fuck with your head," he told me. I stared up at him as my heart started beating harder and he went on, "She does, you tell me immediately. I'm not here, you phone me. Got that?"

"Um...okay." I was still whispering.

"Give me your cell," he ordered and, not thinking, wondering how that crazy woman was going to "fuck with my head," I grabbed my cell from the desk and stretched my arm out toward him. He took two steps to me, slid my phone from my fingers, his thumb started moving over the number pad and I heard beeping.

"Uh...Tack?" I called.

"Yeah?" he asked, head bent to my phone, my phone still beeping.

"How will she...erm, fuck with me?"

He touched a button, tossed my phone on the desk and then he was bent to me, his hand wrapped around the back of my neck, bunching my hair and his face was an inch from mine.

"Don't matter. Whatever she does, I'll deal with it. You won't. Got that?"

"But—"

"She calls, you hang up. She shows, you walk the fuck outta here, take your phone, go to my room in the Compound, lock yourself in and call me. Yeah?"

None of that sounded good except for the part about me calling him and him dealing with it. Therefore, I whispered, "Yeah."

"Don't be scared, Red. She's a bitch but she's stupid and I got your back."

"Uh…okay," I said yet again, not liking him having to have my back and now seriously wondering if I wanted to continue with employment at Ride Custom Cars and Bikes but for different reasons. Then I stared into his eyes, decided to change the subject and whispered, "You know my name."

His face softened in a way I'd never seen before but I liked a lot. Too much. Way too much to be conducive to healthy, functional employer/employee relations, and he replied quietly, "Yeah, baby."

"How long have you known my name?"

"Since the first shot of tequila I handed to you when you gave it to me."

"Why did you pretend you didn't know my name?"

"Because, Red, I'm gonna fuck with your head too."

Oh boy.

"Tack—"

"But you'll like the way I do it."

I wasn't so sure about that.

"Tack—"

"Gotta go."

"Tack—"

He interrupted me when his mouth hit mine for a hard, swift kiss that included his tongue touching my lips briefly in a way that made them tingle before he lifted his head.

My heart was beating wildly and my fingers were clutching the arms of my chair when his hand slid from my neck to my jaw, taking my hair with it, and his thumb swept my cheek.

"Later, darlin'," he whispered. Then he was gone and I blinked at the door when I heard the lock turn even though I no longer heard Naomi.

I closed my eyes tight for the second time that day and waited until my heart stopped beating hard and my lips stopped tingling before I opened them.

Then I whispered to the door, "Damn."

CHAPTER FIVE

Fair Enough

IT WAS SATURDAY night, twenty after six, and I was wondering what to have for dinner at the same time I was clicking through want ads on my laptop.

I'd just returned from yoga class with Lanie. I was still in my black roll-top yoga pants and cornflower blue stretchy racerback yoga camisole with the deep gray racerback yoga bra under it. I was also in a mellow mood. Yoga did that to me. It made me feel energized but mellow and after the week I'd had, mellow was a good thing.

I'd only seen Tack once since his ex came to call, he kissed me and then disappeared. It was last night, Friday, when I heard the roar of bikes come into the forecourt of Ride. I was getting used to the roar of bikes but this wasn't the roar I was used to. This wasn't one or two bikes. This was a lot of them so I got out of my chair and looked out the window to see Tack leading six other bikes into Ride. Two of those bikes carried Dog and Brick, the two directly behind Tack. The rest of the guys I'd seen around but had not met. They parked beside the two bikes already outside the Compound, got off and entered the Compound. Ten minutes later, three more bikes roared in, two of these carrying the two men I'd seen Tack have the unhappy conversation with. They parked and into the Compound they went. None of them reappeared before I called it quits for the day and I was glad.

I didn't need more of Tack screwing up my workdays. And I didn't need thoughts of how cool Tack looked sitting on a Harley. So the minute the clock hit five, I closed up shop and got the hell out of there.

Now I was perusing want ads on-line. I needed a new job. What I did not need was my body (and heart, I had to admit) to jump every time the door opened and I worried Tack was walking into the office to fuck with my head in his own unique scary biker dude way. And I certainly didn't need to leap off the roller coaster that was my life to leap right back on a different one.

Lanie was all for this plan. Actually, Lanie was all for the plan where I walked into Ride on Monday whereupon I would instantly give notice. But I'd spent Wednesday night paying bills and examining my bank and investment accounts. I'd downsized my living operations when my pay-checks quit coming, but that didn't mean the money quit going. My calculator and I deduced I could live frugally for another six months. I could live seriously frugally for seven, maybe pushing it, for eight.

But that meant no yoga classes with Lanie and I liked my yoga classes with Lanie. That also meant no Sunday night self-facials where I used the expensive stuff that made my skin feel freaking great. That also meant no Thursday pig-outs on takeaway. I could live but I couldn't live like I liked to live and I'd worked hard to get to a life I liked to live and I didn't want to let it go.

I bought my house ten years ago when it was a buyer's market. My house was two blocks from Porter Hospital. It was small but had a big yard and sat among a bunch of other small houses with big yards or huge houses that had been built after the old house was scraped off or small houses that were now larger because their tops had been popped.

Because I bought my house ages ago, my mortgage was low. It was a one-story, two-bedroom adobe with a living room, dining area and huge-ass kitchen. I'd fixed it up exactly as I wanted it, even splurging on a fabulous kitchen including top-of-the-line appliances and kickass countertops. There was a two-car garage out back and a nice-sized shed. There was also a great deck. I had fantastic furniture in the house and on the deck, fabulous décor and a well-landscaped yard that looked good only because I spent a bunch of time in it.

This was the one downfall of my house and if I had to do it again, I would buy a house with zero yard. I wasn't a fan of mowing my yard and had quit my job before I'd purchased a riding lawnmower. Even though I had a kickass power mower, it still took me hours to mow my huge yard. This was not my favorite activity. Part of the reason my yard was well landscaped and I spent so much time in it was because I was incapable of not having my surroundings be the best they could be. It gave me a sense of peace and if I had to work at that peace, so be it.

Still, that didn't mean I liked it.

I was about to get up, make myself a cup of tea and peruse my cupboards for dinner ideas when the doorbell rang.

I felt my brows draw together as I stared at my front door. No one came calling without warning unless it was some religious person wanting to help me find God (just as long as it was their God) or someone wanting to sell something, which were both kind of the same thing.

Damn.

I took the laptop off my thighs, put it on the coffee table, pulled my ass out of my couch and wandered to the door. I opened the little wooden baby door that had a wrought iron cross outside that gave me a view to my stoop and I stared at Tack.

What the hell?

"Hey, babe," he greeted.

"What are you doing here?"

"Open the door."

"What are you doing here, Tack?"

"Open the door, Red."

"Not until you tell me what you're doing here," I returned.

"Darlin', you don't open the door, a minor injury might turn into a major one," he stated.

"What?" I asked.

"I'm hurtin' out here."

Ohmigod! He was injured!

I threw the wooden baby door closed, unlocked the front door and pulled it open to see Tack wearing his uniform of tight tee (this one black), faded jeans and motorcycle boots. He was also carrying an enormous pizza box and a six-pack of beer. What he wasn't was visibly injured.

I blinked.

Tack pushed in.

"What...?" I started, and trailed off as Tack sauntered into my living room like he'd done it a million times before, dumped the pizza box on my coffee table then rested the six-pack on the inside of his forearm.

"Fuck, they don't mess around at Famous. That pizza burned the shit outta my arm," he muttered.

I stared at him.

Then I asked, "Are you saying the minor injury you were mentioning was a pizza box burn?"

"Yep," he answered casually, rounded the coffee table, planted his ass on my couch, put the six-pack on my coffee table (my *wood* coffee table, which required *coasters* or some other protective accoutrement) and flipped open the pizza box. Then he ordered, "Come eat."

I stared at him again.

Then I repeated his words in a question, "Come eat?"

His eyes lifted to me still standing in the open door. "Yeah, come eat." Then he tugged one of the beers off the plastic and snapped it open.

I resumed staring and while doing this watched Tack take an enormous swig of beer.

As he was swallowing, I started, "Tack—"

He dropped his beer and interrupted me. "Red, close the door and come eat."

"I—"

"It'll get cold."

"But—"

His eyes traveled the length of me and as they were doing this, he cut me off again. "Jesus, what the fuck you got on?"

I looked down at my yoga clothes then back at him. "I just got back from yoga."

His eyes took their time sliding back up my body before they locked on mine. "You finish that Employee Handbook, you make *that*," he tipped his head to me, "the dress code."

"I'm not wearing yoga clothes to work, Tack."

He held my eyes, his lips turned up slightly then he looked down at the coffee table, put his beer on it and reached for a slice of pizza saying, "Probably a good call. Every guy who works there is takin' their break in the bathroom, jackin' off, thinkin' of you in your tight skirts and sex kitten shoes. You wear that to work, no one'd get any work done."

Um…gross!

"They do not," I snapped.

His eyes lifted to me as his hands lifted a slice of pizza and he said only, "Darlin'," before he guided the pizza to his mouth and bit off a huge chunk.

I decided I was done.

Therefore, I informed him, "You need to leave."

Tack swallowed then informed me, "I'm eatin', babe."

"No, you're leaving."

"You're eatin' too," he replied. "Get your ass over here and grab a slice."

I crossed my arms on my chest and asked, "Are you nuts?"

"Nope," he answered and took another bite of pizza.

Gah!

All right, new tactic.

"Why are you here?"

"I'm here to have dinner with you," he answered, grabbed his beer while balancing the slice in his other hand and took another swig.

"Did it occur to you to *ask* if I wanted to have dinner with you?"

He put his beer down, grinned his sexy grin then stated, "No, since I know you wanna have dinner with me."

"I don't."

"Babe, you do."

"I *don't*."

"Red, you don't get over here, there won't be any left," he returned then took another huge bite of pizza.

"I'd like you to leave."

"I ain't leavin'."

"Why?" My voice was rising as well as the pitch going higher.

"'Cause Naomi has decided not to fuck with your head, she's fuckin' with mine. She calls every fuckin' five minutes, my cell, my house, the Compound, the store. I go home, she's waitin' for my ass out on my deck. I don't answer her calls on my cell, she calls every one of the boys until she gets to one who's with me and gives them so much shit, they hand her over to me because they don't wanna put up with her shit. She's on a tear about your job and she's on a tear about *you*. Two days 'a that, I'm done, 'cause I had fourteen years 'a that and I was done before so I'm definitely done now. I know she's at my house so I ain't goin' to my house 'cause I see her face again, honest to God, I won't be responsible for what I do. So I'm here, having dinner with you."

That sounded like it sucked.

It also was not my problem.

"Don't you have anywhere else to go?" I asked.

"Not anywhere I wanna be."

That, unfortunately, sounded nice.

Damn.

I studied him. He was clearly in for the long haul and it was doubtful I could take him on, best him and get him out my door.

Damn again.

I slammed the door, stomped into the kitchen, grabbed a couple of placemats, some paper towels and a plate then stomped back out to the living room. I approached the coffee table opposite him and then rearranged the beer and food so they were on placemats, dropped the paper towels on the table then I jerked a plate toward Tack.

"Eat your pizza, drink your beer and then go," I demanded.

He took the plate, set it on the coffee table and continued to eat with his hands and no plate. He did this with his eyes on me. I stood across from him, put my hands to my hips and watched him watching me.

"Babe," he said quietly after he finished his first slice, "sit and eat."

I looked down at the pizza. It looked like sausage and olive. It also looked really good even though I wasn't a raving fan of sausage.

"I don't eat pizza after yoga. Pizza defeats the purpose of yoga. I'm going to have a cup of rejuvenating green tea and, probably, a salad."

Tack stared up at me. Then he asked, "Say again?"

"I'm going to have a cup of rejuvenating green tea and a salad and I'm going to do both when you're done with your pizza and beer and you're gone."

"Green tea?"

"*Rejuvenating* green tea," I corrected.

"Christ, that sounds shit."

It actually kind of was. I wasn't certain why I drank it because I didn't like it but I felt it was important to be healthy so, outside of Thursday takeaway night and a donut indulgence here and there (and a cake indulgence, and the pie ones I sometimes had, as well as the cookie ones that weren't unknown to occur), I was studiously healthy.

"I thought you liked your donuts," he noted.

"Donuts are an indulgence," I explained. "You don't indulge every day. If you did, it wouldn't be an indulgence."

He studied me.

Then he ordered, "Red, sit down, grab a beer, eat a slice and fuckin' live a little."

"No, Tack, you drink your beer, eat your pizza and live a little and I'll make my salad when you leave."

At that, he suddenly stood and I found myself looking up at him rather than down, which was a change of circumstances I wasn't ready for. Tack sitting on my couch eating pizza and drinking beer seemed harmless. Tack standing, staring down at me and filling my living room with biker guy badassness seemed something else entirely.

"All right, Tyra, I'll give you a quick lesson seein' as you drink tea, eat salads, do yoga, live in a fancy-ass house with a fancy-ass yard, you probably don't get how this is gonna go 'cause I'm seein' you probably never fucked a man like me so I'll help you out and tell you how it's gonna go," he began.

Oh boy.

Before I could say word one, he went on, "How it's gonna go is you're gonna sit your ass down, eat pizza, drink beer and relax with me or I'll pick your ass up, plant it in the couch and *then* you're gonna eat pizza, drink beer and relax with me."

"You can't tell me where to sit or what to eat and drink, Tack, that's ridicu—"

I didn't finish because I found myself no longer standing opposite the coffee table. I found myself in the air then I found myself in his lap because he leaned forward, picked me up at my hips, hauled me over the coffee table, sat down and deposited me in his lap. Before I could move, he leaned forward again, yanked a beer off the plastic, leaned back and held it to me.

"Now relax," he ordered.

I stared into his eyes.

Then I stammered, "I can't...you didn't just..." I paused then finished, *"Relax?"*

"Yeah, relax."

"I can't relax in your lap!" I shouted.

"Then relax on the couch but you get off the couch, babe, just sayin'...two seconds you'll be back in my lap."

"You're unbelievable," I hissed.

"I see why you think that now, drinkin' fuckin' tea, Jesus," he said like no one but me on the entire earth drank tea and the very idea was repugnant.

"Fine," I snapped. "You win. I'll eat pizza and drink beer. Just let me off your lap."

He shook the can of beer at me, I took it, then his arm around my waist loosened and I slid off his lap.

"God, this is ridiculous," I muttered, popping open the beer.

"You didn't seem this uptight last Saturday night," Tack muttered back, reaching for more pizza.

"I was drinking tequila last Saturday night."

His head turned, his eyes captured mine and his voice was soft and low when he said, "Babe, do not bullshit me. Last Saturday night had fuck all to do with tequila."

He was right and that sucked. He also sounded strangely like that was important to him and that freaked me out. Therefore I glared at him, didn't respond and took a sip of my beer.

It tasted awesome.

I set the beer down, grabbed the plate and then grabbed a slice. Then I flicked as much sausage off the slice as I could and lifted the pizza to my mouth. As I did this, my eyes hit Tack to see he was watching me.

"Not a big fan of sausage?" he remarked.

"Sausage in the form of brats, affirmative. Sausage in the form of smoky links, again, affirmative. Sausage in the form of a breakfast patty next to pancakes, repeat affirmative. Italian sausage on pizza? Um, not so much." Then I shoved the pizza in my mouth and took a big bite.

Famous Pizza. The…freaking…best.

I leaned back against the cushions with my plate and chewed.

Tack sat back too, asking, "Pepperoni?"

I nodded. "And olive," I added then finished, "And mushroom."

"So noted," he muttered, lifted his legs and rested his booted feet next to the pizza box.

I tamped down a rant at him putting his boots on my table and took another bite of my pizza, holding it over my plate at my chest. Then I made a note to self that Famous Pizza worked wonders in helping you tamp down a rant.

Then, because I was an idiot, I asked, "Naomi's on a tear about me?"

"Yep," Tack answered, mouth full.

"Why?"

"She don't need a reason why, Red. She'll get on a tear because the sun rose, then she'll get on another one when it sets. She's just a bitch."

"Why did you marry her?" I asked before taking another bite, his head turned and his eyes came to mine.

"You been married?"

I shook my head and his brows went up.

"No shit?"

I chewed, swallowed and affirmed, "No shit."

"Why not?"

I shrugged and took another bite.

"Babe, seriously, why not?"

My eyes met his and my voice changed, it got soft when I said, "That's really none of your business."

He held my eyes and he did this a long time.

Then he replied quietly, "Fair enough."

I was surprised he gave in. So surprised, I was shocked. I was also somehow touched. It was a nice thing to do, letting it alone because I wanted him to, and I didn't know Tack had that in him.

"So, why did you marry her? She doesn't seem your type," I brought the subject back in hand.

"What's my type?" he asked.

"Not a woman who shouts at you and essentially stalks you," I answered.

He threw his head against the back of my couch and burst out laughing. He had a great laugh. It was as deep and gravelly as his voice. He also *looked* great laughing. I'd noted both of these things last Saturday night. I liked them then but I liked them a whole lot better in my living room.

Oh boy.

"So?" I prompted through his laughter.

Tack's laughter died down to a chuckle and he took a big bite of pizza, chewed, swallowed and looked back at me.

"She married a soldier then found herself tied to a general," he finally answered.

"Pardon?"

"There are soldier's wives and there are general's wives. Naomi ain't no general's wife. She liked the flow, she doesn't like headache. A general needs a wife who can handle headache, do her bit to make 'em better, not make 'em worse."

I wasn't certain I got this but I thought I did and I leaned forward to grab my beer, bowing my head to hide my face with my hair so he couldn't see me when I asked, "So it wasn't that you were cheating on her?"

"According to Naomi it was."

I looked over my shoulder at him. He saw me do it, lifted his boots off my table and leaned forward too. Putting his elbows on his knees, his head turned to facing me and, surprisingly, he shared.

"I filed for divorce, Red. She fought it. She didn't want to be quit of me. I don't know why. She was miserable, she made me miserable and she was makin' my kids miserable.

Life's too short for that shit. After she figured out that she was in a fight she wasn't gonna win, she started bitchin' about me steppin' out on her, spreadin' that shit far and wide and workin' so hard at it, she convinced herself. Honestly?"

He stopped speaking and I realized he wanted me to answer the unspoken question of if I wanted the truth.

I held his gaze, held my breath and nodded.

He leaned slightly into me, his leg shifting so his knee touched mine and went on, "She turned into a bitch and I was pissed at her. What we had starting out was good. So good I thought it would be that good for a lifetime. Not long after we made it legal, she started changing, it started goin' bad and that's all on her. She knew who I was and she knew what I wanted outta my life, it wasn't me who changed. And it pissed me off that she made it turn bad. And it pissed me off more she made it turn as bad as it got which, darlin', was seriously fuckin' bad. What you saw was the tip of the iceberg with Naomi. She gets on a tear, she's hell on wheels. So, I gotta tell you, I thought about it. I found myself not wantin' to go home to that and wantin' someone in my bed who wasn't bustin' my balls. So, I can't say I didn't look but before I found anything, I cut her loose. She was once a good woman but good woman or bad, no woman deserves that shit."

Oh hell, that was a really good answer.

I let out my breath, nodded, grabbed my beer, took a sip then snatched another slice and sat back, lifting my legs to sit cross-legged on the couch.

I felt him lean back as I was flicking more sausage off my pizza, my eyes slid to him and I felt something should be said. He was a scary biker dude but he laid it out for me, honest and straight.

So I said softly, "That sucks, Tack. I'm sorry that happened and I'm sorry she's still messing with your life."

"Better mine than yours," he muttered, and that was a good response too.

"It still sucks," I stated and his eyes caught mine.

"Yeah," he said quietly. "What sucks worse is in her mission to make me miserable she drags my kids into it. No hesitation. Now *that* sucks."

I tipped my head to the side to communicate my agreement then I looked down at my plate and took a bite of pizza.

Then I heard him order, "Fire up the TV, Red," and my eyes swiftly moved back to his.

"Pardon?"

"Turn on the TV," he semi-repeated.

I stared at him then turned my head to look at my TV then I looked back at him.

"I don't have TV."

His brows knitted, his eyes went to the TV then came back to me.

Then he asked, "So what's in the corner? A piece of modern art?"

I smiled at him because he was being kind of funny and answered, "No, I mean, I don't have cable and I only get one channel, PBS, and it comes in fuzzy."

He studied me then slowly asked, "You don't have cable?"

"I don't watch TV," I told him.

"You don't watch TV," he repeated.

"No. I only use the TV to watch movies."

"You don't watch TV," he said again.

"No, I don't watch TV."

"You drink tea, do yoga and don't watch TV," he stated.

"Yep," I answered.

"Jesus," he muttered, shaking his head, a small smile playing at his mouth then he ordered, "Then fire up a movie."

"Pardon?"

"You got movies?"

"Yes."

"Fire one up."

This was not good and the reason it was not good was because this *was* good. I didn't want to admit it but I was enjoying this. The beer tasted good, the pizza tasted great and Tack being funny, honest and forthcoming was even better.

I was in trouble.

"Tack—" I started.

"Fire up a movie, Red."

"I—"

He leaned into me and I leaned back but his torso was longer so his face got in mine. "Fire up a movie."

I looked into his eyes. They were really, really blue.

Oh hell.

Without my permission my mouth formed the words, "What do you want to watch?"

Tack leaned slightly back. "Your choice. Put in your favorite movie."

I stared into his eyes. Then I informed him, "I don't think you'll like my favorite movie."

"Do they speak English in it?"

I couldn't help it, I smiled again. Then I answered, "Yes."

"Then fire it up."

I sighed, made my stupid, stupid, *stupid* decision and murmured, "Oh, all right," then uncrossed my legs, put my plate down on the table and went to my TV. I opened the cabinet under it and sorted through my DVDs, found what I was looking for and "fired it up."

I unearthed my remote that I hid in a drawer in an end table, resumed my seat next to Tack, grabbed my plate and sat back, eyes pinned to the TV, and started the movie.

Fifteen minutes later, Tack muttered, "Jesus, Red, what is this?"

"*The Color Purple*," I answered, not looking at him.

He said no more and I didn't either. I finished my pizza, finished my beer and started another one and, as usual, got lost in one of the most devastating, most beautiful movies of all time. That was, I got lost in the movie until I started crying. When I started crying, I became acutely aware of Tack's presence. I didn't want Tack to see or hear me crying so I pressed my lips together and tried to breathe steady in an effort to control my tears as I kept my eyes glued to the screen.

This didn't work and I knew it didn't when I suddenly felt his fingers at my chin and he forced my face in his direction. I tried not to catch his eyes but this was difficult because I liked the way they roamed my face with that warm look in them. Then as suddenly as his fingers took hold of my chin, they let it go, his arm went around my shoulders, he pulled me into his side and again lifted his feet to put on the coffee table. He slouched, taking me into his slouch so I had no choice but to slouch with him. I did actually have a choice but I told myself I didn't and lifted my legs to rest my heels against the armrest as my side and back settled into his side and my head settled on his shoulder.

I knew I shouldn't lie like that. I knew it but I liked it. His body was warm and hard, his arm strong and the movie inspired a variety of deep emotions. It was good to have a warm, hard, strong body close when watching it. I'd never done it but I liked it so I did it.

When the credits rolled, I wiped the new tears from my face, twisted in his arm, placed my hand lightly on his chest and tipped my head back to look at him to see he was already looking down at me.

"What did you think?" I whispered.

"She shoulda cut his throat with the razor," Tack replied and I grinned.

Definitely scary biker dude.

Then I said, "She didn't have that in her."

"Right," he muttered.

"And if she did, he wouldn't have had the opportunity to learn how to be a better person and find absolution."

Tack stared at me intently for a few beats. Then he repeated quietly, "Right."

"So did you like it?" I pressed.

"Not really a movie you like, Red," he answered.

"I think it's beautiful," I whispered.

"Not sure you understand the concept of beauty, darlin'."

"Truth, honesty, perseverance, strength, love of all kinds and forgiveness are all beautiful, Tack. The most beautiful stories ever told are the most difficult to take."

For a few more beats he again stared at me intently then he said, this time on a whisper, "Right," and his eyes didn't release mine.

I liked him looking at me like that. I liked him being like this. I liked pizza, beer and sad movies with an easy-to-be-with Tack. This was what I thought I'd found a week ago and here it was, in my living room.

God, what did I do now?

"You got any movies that don't make you cry?" Tack asked and I blinked up at him.

"Yeah," I answered.

He shifted me off him, lifted his legs off the coffee table, got up and went to my TV. He ejected the DVD, crouched in front of the cabinet and dug through it, pulling out DVDs at random and totally ruining the alphabetical organization of my films. Then he opened a case, slid in another DVD and came back to the couch. He grabbed the remote from the end table and he settled in again.

And when he settled, he did not slouch. He did not put his feet up on the table. No, he lay down flat on his back, ankles crossed, head on a toss pillow on the armrest. While he did this, he arranged me tucked into his side with my back to the back of the couch and my front plastered down his side.

Oh boy. Maybe it was time for me to start being smart.

I lifted up with a hand in his chest and looked down at him.

His eyes were on the TV and his arm with the remote in his hand was stretched out and aimed at the TV.

"Tack—"

He didn't even look at me when he muttered, "Relax, Red."

I started to push up from his chest and his arm around my waist got tight as his head turned my way.

Then he whispered, "Relax."

I stared down at him. He turned his head back to the TV, hit some buttons and tossed the remote on the coffee table. His arm curled me deeper into his body as his other hand went behind his head.

Speed started on the TV.

"Tack—"

"Relax."

"Um—"

Another squeeze and his head turned to me.

"Baby," he said softly in his gravelly voice, I felt that one word in my belly and it felt nice. *"Relax."*

His eyes were warm, his arm was tight and his body against me was hard.

I bit my lip.

Then I made another decision and relaxed.

An hour later, I fell asleep with my cheek to Tack's chest, my arm curved around his gut and my legs tangled in his.

*   *   *

I woke up confused.

It was dark and I was trapped in some kind of comfy cocoon. I sluggishly surveyed my situation and it hit me that I was sleeping on the couch with Tack. My head was cushioned on his bicep, my cheek pressed to his chest, his forearm was wrapped around my shoulders, his other arm resting on my waist. My arm was draped around his, my leg was hitched over his hip and his leg was cocked and resting between mine.

Okay, damn, this felt nice. Beautiful. Special. Perfect.

Maybe I wasn't wrong a week ago because this felt right. Really right.

Dreamy.

I snuggled closer. Tack's arm around my waist tightened unconsciously before it went loose again and a second later, I fell back to sleep.

*   *   *

I was being lifted and I opened my eyes to see weak light in the room.

It was dawn.

My arm automatically slid around Tack's neck and I whispered, "Tack."

"Sh, baby," he whispered back, walking and carrying me.

I pressed my forehead into his neck and sighed.

Then I felt myself going down and I was in my bed, head on my pillow. I turned to my side and my eyes slid to him to see Tack standing beside the bed pulling the covers over me.

"Are you leaving?" I asked quietly.

"Got things to do," he answered just as quietly.

"Okay," I whispered, my eyes drifting closed and, as they did this, I felt the sweet sweep of his thumb across the apple of my cheek.

Then I felt his presence leaving me, my eyes drifted open and I saw he'd almost made it to my bedroom door.

"Tack?" I called.

He stopped and turned.

"Yeah, baby."

"Thanks for dinner."

He grinned and it was no less sexy when I was half asleep.

"You're welcome, darlin'," he replied, and I grinned back as my eyes drifted closed again. Then I heard a muttered, "Pepperoni next time," before I fell back to sleep.

CHAPTER SIX

We Play This My Way

I WAS IN my office at Ride. It was the Thursday after the second Saturday night I'd spent with Tack. The second Saturday night I'd mistaken him for my motorcycle dream man. The second Saturday night where I made the way wrong decisions and acted so stupid I'd humiliated myself.

Four and a half days of nothing from Tack. Not one thing.

This did not mean I didn't see him. I saw him. I saw him roaring in on his bike. I saw him standing outside the Compound talking to his biker brethren. I saw him working in the garage.

I did not see him anywhere around me. He didn't come into the office and he didn't pay another surprise visit to my house. But he was at Ride and he was either doing a bang-up job of avoiding me or he forgot I existed.

Now I was a slut *and* an idiot, and I decided that being a slut was more fun. A lot more fun. Being an idiot, melting toward Tack, letting him in over beer, pizza, sad movies and snuggling on my couch only to have him shut me out was not fun *at all*.

He'd used me. He needed a place to crash that Naomi couldn't find so he showed at my door with pizza and turned on the biker charm to get what he needed to keep clear of his crazy, bitchy, stalker ex-wife.

And I'd let him. I'd even thanked him for a dinner I didn't want to eat in the first damned place.

Yep. Totally an idiot.

My cell chirped on my desk, I picked it up, saw a text from Lanie, and read it even though I knew what it was going to say.

Did you give notice yet?

This was the same text she sent six times a day, every day, since Tuesday when I realized that I'd been an idiot with Tack (again) and I'd shared this knowledge with her. She went from thinking he was a jerk to actively hating him. This was not surprising. This was what best friends did. Before Elliott, I'd done the same thing with numerous boyfriends of Lanie's.

No, I texted back.

Five seconds later, I received, *I'll pay for your yoga classes until you get a new job.*

Yesterday, she started an incentive strategy. We were up to once-a-month facials at her favorite salon, weekly invitations to Takeaway Thursday at her and Elliott's place and now yoga classes.

I've applied three places. Give it time. I sent back.

Is he there today? She returned.

He was. He was currently in the garage working on that kickass red car I noticed no one touched but him. He was also currently avoiding me or forgetting I existed. It was nearly two in the afternoon. I'd heard him roar in at nine forty-five (I'd heard it and like the idiot I was, whenever I heard any bike roar in for the past four and a half days, I'd looked), he'd sauntered into the garage and I hadn't seen him since.

Yes, he's here. I told Lanie.

I'm e-mailing you your letter of resignation now. You just have to print it, sign it and give it to him. Easy. Lanie replied.

She'd written my letter of resignation. Totally Lanie. I smiled at the phone. Then the door to the garage opened, I looked up and Tack stood there.

Damn.

I felt my smile fade and my throat clog at the same time my palm itched to find something to throw at him.

He walked right to my desk, eyes on me, hand to his back pocket and he said, "Do me a favor, babe. I'm starved. Go out and get me a sandwich."

I stared up at him as he pulled out his wallet, opened it, yanked out some bills and tossed them on the desk in front of me. He was shoving the wallet in his back pocket when my throat unclogged but that itch in my palm intensified.

He hadn't said word one to me after barging into my place and pretending to be a decent guy. Four and a half days later, he strolls in and tells me to get him a sandwich?

"Pardon?" I whispered.

"A sandwich. Roast beef and Swiss. Get me a bag 'a chips and a pop while you're at it. Don't care where you go."

"Pardon?" I repeated and his eyes narrowed.

"A sandwich, Red. Roast beef and Swiss, chips and a pop." When I simply continued to stare at him and said not a word, he added, "Jesus, you want me to write it down?"

My stare turned into a glare and I snapped, "No, handsome, you wrote it down, I wouldn't be able to read it, and I'm not getting you a sandwich. I have things to do. If you're hungry, jump on your bike and go get your own damned sandwich."

Then I turned to the computer and opened up my e-mail

in order to find Lanie's resignation letter because I was done with Ride Custom Cars and Bikes but mostly because I was done with Tack, the big, fat *jerk*.

"Say again?" I heard Tack growl.

"You heard me," I bit out and clicked on Lanie's e-mail.

"Babe, look at me."

"Kiss my ass," I replied, double clicking on Lanie's attachment and ignoring the sparking, scary biker dude vibe that was suddenly saturating the room.

"Red, look...at...me."

I looked at him, or, more accurately, glared at him.

"You got a problem?" he growled.

Did I have a problem? What a jerk!

"Yes," I told him. "I have a problem."

"What's your problem?"

What was my problem? Ohmigod!

I didn't know what to do. I was so angry, I couldn't think. Anything I could say would expose too much. For some bizarre reason, I fell in love with him over tequila and really great sex. Then I fell out of love with him because he used me and he was a jerk about it. Then I started to fall back in love with him while he was using me again, being the jerk he was. In the meantime, I knew he slept with at least one other woman. And all I got out of all that was a lot of hassle, two beers, two slices of pizza and a number of really great orgasms.

Without any way to explain it and not put myself out there, I stated, "My problem is none of your business."

"You made it my business by telling me to kiss your ass."

"If you have an issue with the way I communicate, Tack, fire me," I retorted.

"Jesus." He crossed his arms on his chest then asked rudely, "You on the rag?"

I felt pressure build in my head and fired back on a near

shout, "No! And if I was, *that* wouldn't be your business either." The pressure kept building and it forced me out of my chair, it forced my torso to lean across the desk toward him and it forced out of my mouth, "In fact, *nothing* about me is any of your business. I'm in a shitty mood and it's none of your business why. So, if you're hungry, go get your own stupid sandwich. I'm busy."

Then I sat back down, turned to the computer and, without reading the letter, I moved the mouse so the cursor on the screen was at the print button and I clicked. As I did this, through the pressure in my head and the thundering of my pulse beating in my wrists and neck, I heard Tack moving through the room. It wasn't until the room darkened that what he was doing penetrated. But I had no opportunity to react before my chair was swiveled around forcefully making my body sway with the movement. Before I knew it, my head was tipped way back because Tack, hands on the arms of my chair, was leaned deep into my space.

"Explain the attitude, Red," he ordered, his voice a low, angry rumble that I felt pulsating against my flesh.

"Are you *insane*?" I cried.

"Explain the *fuckin'* attitude, Tyra."

"Move away!" I demanded then I gasped because he didn't move away.

No, he pulled me out of the chair to my feet. Then, I kid you *not*, his fingers curled into my skirt at the sides. He yanked it up so roughly my body jolted and my breath caught, then I felt his hands at my ass where he lifted me up, twisted and planted me on the desk. Reflexively, to stop from toppling back, my fingers curled into his tee as his hands left my ass. They went to the insides of my knees and forced them open. I gasped and then my back was flat on the desk. His hips were between my legs. His torso was pressed deep into mine. One of his hands was forcing my leg to curve around his hip and the fingers of his other hand slid into my hair, fisted at the back and his face was so close, it was all I could see.

"Ohmigod," I whispered. "What are you doing?"

"I'm teachin' you a lesson," he growled. "You do not test a man like me, Tyra. You've never had a man like me so you gotta learn. You do not test a man like me."

My arms were crushed between our bodies and I uncurled my fingers from his tee and pressed them flat against his chest as I whispered, "Please, get off me."

"You want this," he informed me.

I pushed harder against his chest. "Please, Tack, get off me."

It was like I didn't even speak when he went on, "I want this."

"Please," it was barely audible, "you're scaring me."

That penetrated, and it did it in a way that made him even angrier. I knew it because I saw it on his face, in his eyes and I felt it in the air around us.

"Do not be scared of me, Tyra. Don't you ever fuckin' be scared of me."

"Tack, you just manhandled me onto my desk," I pointed out carefully.

"Did I hurt you?"

"No," I answered, and it wasn't a lie but that also wasn't the point.

"Right," he growled. "Now tell me what your fuckin' problem is."

"Um…"

His chest pressed deeper into mine. "Tyra," he rumbled his warning.

"Can we continue this conversation maybe, erm… standing up?"

"I tried that, didn't work. Now I'm tryin' something else so talk to me."

I sucked in breath as I stared into his eyes.

Then I whispered, "No."

His eyes blazed into mine when he warned on a scary whisper, "I told you not to test me."

"And I told you my problem was none of your business."

"If it isn't my business then keep a hold on that attitude, babe, and don't make it my business."

"Okay," I thought it prudent to agree.

"I'm thinkin' you don't get this but when you turn off Broadway into Ride, you drive into my world. My world is different than the world you live in. Unless I allow the parts of it I like, you don't get to live like you live in your world when you're in mine. And when I'm in yours but you're with me, you live like you're in mine. Do you get me?"

I didn't, actually, not at all. I still nodded.

He examined my face then with a suddenness that I again lost my breath, his body was gone. He yanked me to my feet, tugged my skirt back down then turned away.

I sucked in another breath then nearly choked on it when his eyes hit the computer monitor and they narrowed. Then his head turned toward the printer, his arm reached out to nab the paper on top, he turned it over and in about two seconds, I watched his jaw turn to stone.

Uh-oh.

"Tack—" I started on an exhale and then he was on me again, this time he rounded me then moved in. I retreated fast, bumping into my chair which rolled away and then bumping into the wall where he pinned me with his body.

"I don't accept," he growled into my face.

I stared up into his and stammered, "Wha...what?"

"Your resignation, Red."

Oh boy.

"Tack—"

His hand came up, his palm warm against my jaw, his fingers curving around my ear and neck and his face got even closer.

"You gotta learn," he told me.

"Learn what?" I whispered.

"We play this my way."

"Honestly," I was still whispering, "please hear me, honestly, Tack, I don't want to play."

"I got two Saturdays, Red, two Saturdays that prove that a lie."

I clenched my teeth and stared into his eyes.

His fingers tensed and lifted up, pulling me closer.

"Gave you four days to play it your way. Don't like the way you play so we play this my way," he rumbled.

Uh . . . *what?*

I didn't ask. I bit my lip. I couldn't help it and at that point, didn't have it in me to try.

"You got me?" he asked.

"I got you," I answered softly.

His eyes moved over my face before they locked on mine. "Do not be scared of me," he ordered, his voice still firm but also weirdly gentle.

"Okay," my voice was trembling even on that one two-syllable word.

His eyes held mine captive then he let me go, stepped away, ripped my resignation letter in half and dropped the pieces on my desk.

I stayed pressed against the wall and watched him, knowing I had just lied. I knew he was a scary biker dude and now I knew he was *seriously* a scary biker dude.

"Get your purse," he demanded as he walked to the door

that led to the garage and unlocked it then went on to say unbelievably, "we'll get a sandwich together."

I swallowed and my mind raced for excuses why I couldn't get a sandwich with him because I needed him to go out and get his own sandwich so I could get in my car and drive to Vancouver.

"Uh..." I mumbled, he turned, his eyes slicing to me, and then the sound of someone trying the handle of the door to outside could be heard.

Tack's eyes went to it and my eyes went to it.

Then we both heard a girl's voice from outside. "Dad! Are you in there?" The handle turned again, its sound desperate. "Dad! Open up! God! Open up! Mom's bein' a *bitch*!"

I stared at the door.

Tack moved to it. Then he unlocked it and opened it.

Then two teenagers were in my office. Two teenagers who were most assuredly of Tack's loins. Two teenagers who were visibly in the throes of a serious drama.

Oh hell.

CHAPTER SEVEN

Tabby and Rush

"MOM'S BEIN' A *total bitch*!" Tack's daughter cried again, approximately a second after she cleared the door.

I stared at her. She had Tack's hair except long, its glorious waves cascading down her back well past her bra strap. She also had his sapphire blue eyes, hers were flashing because she was pissed way the hell off. She was petite and slim but rounded, wearing jean shorts, a sweet Harley-Davidson tee and flip-flops. Her blemishless skin, every inch of it, was tanned a beautiful brown. She was a teenage knockout. And she was pacing with extreme, teenage girl agitation.

"She is, Dad, totally," Tack's son stated, and I moved my stare to him.

He was near to the spitting image of his father. The same height though Tack's son didn't have the muscled bulk of his father, but that didn't mean he didn't have a lean, sculpted body. Like his sister, he had his dad's hair and olive skin tone. He was wearing his dad's uniform of faded, fitting-too-well-for-peace-of-mind jeans, motorcycle boots and t-shirt, his announcing he was a fan of Black Stone Cherry. He didn't have the goatee and he had his mother's light blue eyes but other than that, Tack was written all over him. Unlike his sister, he wasn't pacing. He was standing, his hands on his hips, but he looked angry, if not as angry as his sister.

"This isn't somethin' you both don't know," Tack's voice rumbled into the room.

The girl whirled to face her dad and leaning in, she declared, "All right, then she's bein' *more* than the *total bitch* she *normally* is!"

"No joke," the boy put in. "She's all over Tab like a rash."

"Why?" Tack asked.

"Because she's a bitch?" the girl asked back.

"I need more than that, Tabby," Tack told her.

"She took the keys to Tab's car and grounded her and swear, Dad, totally swear, there's no reason," the boy informed Tack, and Tack's gaze went from his son to his daughter.

"Is there no reason, Tabby?" he asked.

Hmm. The way Tack asked that it seemed maybe Tabby was a bit of a wild one.

"You know I'll tell you like it is, Dad, but Rush is right. She's off on one and...*again*...because she's a total, freaking nutcase...she's takin' it out on me," Tabby said.

My eyes slid to Tack to see his jaw was clenched.

Tabby kept talking. "I can't live with this shit anymore. I kid you not, no more. I never know when she's gonna blow or freak out about something or get in my face or...or... *whatever*. And that douche bag of a husband of hers, he gets in on the act—"

"How?" Tack barked. He said that one word so forcefully, so abruptly and so angrily, it startled me so much I jumped. Both Tack's kids went still and their demeanor instantly turned cautious.

"He's just a dick, Dad, you know that," the boy said quietly and carefully.

"How's he a dick, Rush?" Tack asked curtly, only a slim edge of patience in his tone.

Rush and Tabby looked at each other then back to Tack.

"He's the one who took my keys," Tabby stated softly. "Says I don't pull it together, he's gonna sell my car." I held my breath when Tack's scary biker dude vibe filled the air again but Tabby went on, "The problem with that is, I don't know what I gotta pull together because I didn't do anything wrong!"

"He just wants to sell her car because he's a lazy fuck," Rush muttered under his breath, eyeing his father who was at that very moment yanking his phone out of his back pocket.

"Dad—" Tabby started.

"Quiet," Tack ordered, beeping buttons on his phone.

"I wanna live with you," she ignored him in order to continue. "And, just to say, I'll lose my freakin' mind that douche sells my car."

Tack put his phone to his ear and scowled at his daughter. What he didn't do was reply to her. Instead, he spoke into his phone.

"Shut your fuckin' mouth," he growled into the phone. I held my breath again at his vicious tone and he went on, "That shithead thinks to sell my girl's car because he's a lazy-ass motherfucker and can't pull his finger out to get himself a fuckin' job, he buys himself trouble. And I'm warnin' you, Naomi, it's trouble he don't wanna have. I gave Tabby that car, that car belongs to her. It don't belong to you and it sure as fuck don't belong to him. You get his shit sorted and you get *your* shit sorted and you do not use my kids to sort it. Are we clear?"

He listened for approximately two point five seconds then went on.

"Bullshit," he bit out. "I hear you, or him, talk that way

about Tab again, swear to Christ, Naomi, both your asses are in front of the judge. Do not use my daughter to work out your shit. Your life ain't what you wanted it to be, that ain't Tabby's problem, it ain't Rush's problem and it ain't my problem. I'm sick of your games and I'm done playin' 'em. You stop this shit, Naomi, or honest to God, I'll make you wish you never started it and I'll be creative in how I do that. Now, are we clear?"

He listened this time for approximately point five seconds before he carried on.

"I don't wanna hear your shit. I asked you a question. Are we clear? There are two answers to that, woman, but only one smart one." There was a pause then, scarily, "That wasn't the smart one. Kiss your kids good-bye."

Then he disconnected, shoved his phone in his back pocket and his eyes sliced through his children.

Then he asked, "You guys have lunch?"

"No," Rush answered.

"Right, then you're goin' for a sandwich with me and Tyra," Tack announced.

My lungs seized and I felt my eyes get wide.

"Tyra?" Tabby whispered then both kids turned their heads and looked at me for the first time.

Oh boy.

"Uh . . . hey," I greeted.

Tabby looked me up and down. So did Rush. Their looks couldn't have been any more different. Then Tabby grinned. So did Rush. Their grins also couldn't have been any more different.

"Sweet shoes," Tabby told me.

"Erm . . . thanks," I replied.

"Shoes?" Rush muttered. "Didn't get that far. The skirt's burned on my brain."

My eyes moved to Tack to see now he was grinning.

Tabby looked at her father. "This your new woman that Mom's in a tizzy about?"

Tack didn't answer, Rush did, "Duh, Tab, you saw her skirt."

Tabby looked back at me and grinned, murmuring, "Right." Then she informed me, "Tyra's a cool name."

"Um...thanks," I said. "Is, uh...your name Tabitha?"

"Totally," she replied.

"That's a pretty name too," I told her.

"I hate my name. Mom gave me my name and I hate my mom 'cause she's a total bitch," she replied.

I couldn't argue with that and I couldn't agree with it. I also couldn't make myself vanish in a puff of smoke and reappear in Siberia even though I was using every fiber of my being to try.

Since my body wouldn't disappear in a puff of smoke and a response was required, I said, "Well, once a gift is given, no matter how you feel about the person giving it, it's yours. And even though you're angry at your mom now, she still gave you a pretty name. So you shouldn't think about her giving it to you. You should just think of owning it and you do so um...own it."

"Dig it" was Tabby's response made through a widening smile.

"I'm Rush," Rush stated. "My name's Cole but no one calls me that. They call me Rush."

"Hey, Rush," I said to him.

"He's always in a rush," Tabby explained. "Dad says even when he was a baby, the minute he could crawl, he was rushin' everywhere. And it's the *God's honest* truth, let me tell you, and he's got the speeding tickets now to prove it."

"You should probably, maybe, uh...check that impulse

when you're behind the wheel of a car," I advised Rush. "Speeding tickets are expensive."

"No shit," Rush grinned at me.

"You guys gonna shoot the shit with Tyra for the next four hours or are we gonna get a sandwich?" Tack cut in to ask.

Tabby jumped up and down twice, turning toward her father, shouting, "Sandwich!"

"I want enchiladas," Rush declared.

"I'll make fajitas tonight for dinner," Tack told his son, and I stared at him. The idea of rough-and-ready biker guy Tack in a kitchen cooking was something my mind violently wanted to expunge but it couldn't because he'd said it.

"Rock on!" Tabby exclaimed, throwing both her arms in the air, fingers extended in devil's horns. Then she whirled to me and dropped her arms. "You had Dad's fajitas, Tyra?"

"Um...no," I answered.

"Get ready to have your world rocked," Rush stated. "Dad's fajitas are *the shit*."

"I, actually...uh, can't make dinner," I started, all eyes, including Tack's, locked on me, and Tack's, I noticed, looked annoyed for reasons unknown since he hadn't actually asked me to dinner. "I have a ritual that I never miss on Thursdays."

"What's that?" Tabby inquired, her head tilting to the side.

"Thursday Takeaway," I told her.

"Thursday Takeaway?" Rush asked.

"Um...yeah," I answered. "Tonight I'm doing Imperial Chinese. I've been looking forward to it since last Thursday."

"Babe, you so *totally* don't want to miss Dad's fajitas. Imperial is sweet but Dad's fajitas *rock*!" Tabby declared.

"Seriously," Rush added.

"Red, get your purse," Tack ordered.

"Actually, um...I already had lunch so you just go on without me." I jerked my head to the door and smiled at Tabby and Rush. "But it was cool meeting you."

"Babe, get your purse," Tack repeated with a slight modification.

My eyes moved to him and I said quietly, "Tack, I have work to get done."

"Get your purse."

"But—"

"Purse."

"I—"

"Purse."

"I don't—"

He bent a bit at the waist in my direction. *"Purse."*

I finally snapped, "Tack!"

"Jesus," he muttered then moved while speaking and where he moved was toward me. "You're not payin' anyway so you don't need your fuckin' purse."

I had moved several inches away from the wall but I pinned myself against it again, now willing my body to dissolve through the wall but this also failed. I was in this position for approximately one point five seconds before Tack's strong hand curled around mine. He yanked me from the wall then he dragged me across the room. Then he dragged me through his children. He then dragged me out of the office and down the steps where he stopped me on the passenger side of a very cool, shiny black car.

"Keys," he called, lifted his hand, tagged a set of keys Rush sent sailing through the air then he ordered, "You two in back. Tyra's shotgun. I'm drivin'."

He unlocked the door and used my hand in a forceful, not-to-be-denied way where I had no choice but to plant my ass in the passenger seat. The minute my feet hit the floor, he threw the door to and rounded the hood. He opened his door, both his kids scrunched into the back and Tack folded behind the wheel.

I stared at the door to the office thinking, *Guess I'm getting sandwiches with Tack and his kids.*

Um. *Yikes!*

Tack turned the ignition, the car's engine growled in a totally kickass way and with no other choice, I twisted and grabbed the seat belt.

CHAPTER EIGHT

Open

I SAT TUCKED in the corner of my couch, my knees up, heels to the seat, plate wedged between my thighs and torso, and I ate Tack's fajitas which, just as Tabby said, *rocked*.

This was after I sat sipping a diet while Tack and his kids had sandwiches, chips and pops with Rush eating two huge chocolate chip cookies on top of that. Through this, Rush sometimes spoke, Tack sometimes interjected, I said a few words here and there but mostly Tabby chattered away, completely over her drama. She was talkative, animated, smart, charming and funny. This was the way she was but it was also the way she was around her father and brother, both of whom clearly adored her so she could safely blossom under their adoration, and she did.

This was also something I didn't need. Rush, the eldest at seventeen, nearly eighteen (Tabby just turned sixteen, upon which Tack gave her a car, the same as he did for Rush, this I learned while Tabby chattered away), I could see as he was her big brother. Tack, since he was her father and she was his only daughter, I could also see but that didn't mean I *wanted* to see it.

Badass biker Tack smiling at, teasing and openly adoring

his daughter was something I definitely didn't want to see. One could say the messages Tack had been giving me since I met him were most assuredly mixed. One could also say the personalities Tack had been displaying since I met him were most assuredly multiple. I wanted to focus on the bad messages and scary or annoying personality traits. Tack being a loving father, close to both of his kids, openly respecting his son and definitely being Daddy to his little girl were neither of those.

Fajitas on my couch were also after Tack took his kids and me back to Ride where Tabby hung out in the office with me and Rush worked on the red car in the garage with Tack. Tabby was just as talkative, animated, smart, charming and funny with me alone as she was with her brother and father there. This meant I got zero work done and also was unable to return any of Lanie's texts, all of them getting increasingly demanding that I inform her immediately that I gave notice. I did manage to send off an *I'm busy, got someone in my office* text, which finally quieted her down but only after she ordered me to text her the minute I gave Tack my resignation letter.

Tabby in my office also made it impossible for me to avoid fajitas. It was impossible because at five to five, Tack stuck his head through the door that led to the garage, his eyes hit me and he stated, "Tab's with you, babe, Rush and I'll follow. I'm on my bike. Rush and I'll go to the store to pick up the shit, you take Tab to rent a movie and we'll meet at your house."

The ten thousand words all rushing up my throat got jumbled and clogged on their way to my lips so I only got the chance to open my mouth before he disappeared behind the closed door and Tabby cried, "Awe...*some*! Let's rent *Saw*! That movie kicks *ass*!"

I didn't have the heart to tell her I had no interest in renting *Saw* nor did I have the heart to tell her I wasn't all fired up to have her dad make fajitas at my house for his kids and, apparently, me. What I did have was the desire to find her father and then find a way to explain to him that he was a big jerk, I wasn't playing his games and no matter how he told me to feel, he scared the freaking hell out of me and I wanted no part of it.

Since I couldn't do the last, I closed down the office, loaded Tabby in my car, we rented *Saw*, I took her to my house where I immediately opened a chilled bottle of white wine and got her a diet. She wandered my house, declaring it was "the shit," and I changed out of my skirt, blouse and heels into a pair of cutoff jean shorts and a camisole. We were out the back door off the kitchen and on the back deck when Tabby heard the growl of her brother's car and the roar of Tack's Harley. She popped out of her seat, raced into the house and I heard her greeting her family with loud exuberance at the door, shouting, "Rush! Wait 'til you see Tyra's pad. It's the *shit*! Her back deck is fah-*reeking awesome*!"

I closed my eyes and lamented for the fifty-fifth time since I buckled my seat belt in Rush's car the decision to show at work after Tack's slam, bam, thank you ma'am. Then Rush and Tack showed on the back deck and greetings were exchanged. Rush's was a "Hey, Tyra." Tack's included his fingers sifting into the back of my hair, a gentle tug that brought my head way back to see he was bent in and then he gave me a lip touch that was sweet and supremely annoying at the same time. The latter because he was a jerk and he had no business kissing me and further because I couldn't demonstrate this *or* inform him of this fact with his kids in attendance. Something he very well knew.

Tack went to work in *my* kitchen like he cooked in my kitchen frequently even though his motorcycle-booted feet never stepped into the damned room in his whole badass life, while the kids alternated between him in the kitchen and me on the back deck. Rush, being a gentleman (where he got this, I did *not* know as it wasn't from his father), filled my glass twice, even once topping me up when I didn't need it.

Therefore I was essentially on glass three of white wine when Tack declared dinner was done, the kids raced into the kitchen and I followed much more slowly. We all received piled plates and headed into the living room. Rush stretched out on the floor, Tabby collapsed in the middle of the couch, I took the end and Tack took an armchair.

And there I sat, eating Tack's fabulous (really, they were amazing, he was a scary biker but it couldn't be denied the man could cook) fajitas and watching a movie that scared the absolute crap out of me while sipping wine and wondering how in *the hell* I was sitting in my very own living room with Tack and his kids eating his fajitas, sipping wine and watching a movie that scared the absolute crap out of me.

I finished my fajitas, put my plate on the end table, grabbed my wine and drained the glass, deciding that was a good excuse to escape to the kitchen. I could tell them I needed a refill then wander to the back deck, sit there, drink wine and plan my escape. They probably wouldn't even know I was gone or, at the very least, I could manage a head start.

At this point, Tabby was on her back, knees bent, the soles of her feet in the couch, head on the armrest, eyes on the screen so I had a direct shot in front of the couch to the kitchen.

So I took my shot.

"Need a refill," I muttered, standing. "Anyone need anything?"

"I'm good," Rush mumbled from the floor.

"I'm okay, Tyra, thanks," Tabby said distractedly.

Excellent. They both were into the movie. A good start.

I walked across the front of the couch and was passing Tack's armchair when I was stopped and what stopped me was Tack catching my wrist in a firm grip. I looked to him to see him standing.

Then I heard him announcing, "Tyra and I are off-limits for a while."

"Cool," Rush mumbled from the floor.

"'Kay," Tabby said distractedly.

My head jerked back to look at Tack but his hand slid from my wrist to curl around mine. I found the wineglass not in my hand but on the end table by Tabby's head. Then I found myself being pulled down my hall to my bedroom. Then I found myself in my bedroom. Last I found the door to my bedroom closed.

I jerked my head back again to look at Tack, my mouth opening, my mind deciding I didn't care if his kids were just down the hall because when I finally made noise, it was going to be loud. But I found my mouth clamping shut because my body found itself in the air. Automatically I grabbed onto Tack's shoulders, his hands at the backs of my knees swung my legs around his hips and then he took three long strides and I was flat on my back in my bed, Tack on top of me.

I blinked up into his handsome, goateed face.

Not this again.

"Tack—" I started, his name vibrating because I was so...*freaking*...pissed.

"Now that I'm not pissed, baby, we need to take some time to talk shit out," he said gently.

Oh no, we did *not*.

I unwrapped my legs from his hips, shoved my feet into the bed and bucked up at the same time I pushed against his shoulders, but Tack didn't budge.

When this didn't work, I hissed, "Get off me."

He had a forearm in the bed beside me and his other hand came up to cup my jaw, his thumb moving out to sweep my lower lip. I fought back the urge to bite him as he spoke.

"Just settle, Red, and be quiet. I got something to say and I need you to listen."

"You do not have anything to say that I want to hear," I whispered irately.

"You're gonna hear it anyway," he replied.

I stopped pushing against his shoulders and glared at him. "Of course I am," I stated sarcastically. "You want to say something, you say it. You want to do something, you do it. And who gives a shit what *I* want? Is that the gist of what you were about to say?"

His eyes held mine. "Not exactly."

"Right, well, carry on, Tack. You're going to anyway."

"I see you're pissed—"

"Mm hmm," I cut him off. "Good call on that, handsome."

"Babe," he murmured, and I could swear his mouth was moving like he was fighting a smile.

Oh. My. *God!*

"Do you find something funny?" I snapped.

"Well...yeah," he answered.

"Interesting," I replied. "See, I don't find anything funny. Because, this afternoon, I was innocently working and the next thing I knew, I was on my back on my desk. That is not *cool*, Tack. That scared the holy *hell* out of me." I ignored his face changing, his eyes changing and what the way they changed communicated to me and kept right on talking. "And just now, I was innocently intending to walk to my kitchen and refill my wine and I find myself flat on my back in my bed, something else that's not cool."

"I needed your attention then and I want it now," Tack returned.

"Well done, handsome, you found a definite winner. You got my undivided attention then and you have it now."

"You pissed me off earlier, Red, and you been pissin' me off for a while. It wasn't a good play to take your shit out on me this afternoon."

I stared up at him a beat then asked, "I've been pissing you off for a while?"

"Yeah."

My head tilted on the pillow "How?"

"Jesus, Red, don't act stupid and don't think I am."

Um…*what?*

"Pardon?" I asked.

"I don't know how it works in your world but I'm guessin' in your world you can lead a man around by his dick by actin' sweet then turnin' on the freeze and ignoring his ass for days. Then you think you can shovel shit at him and he'll eat it for a chance to get another taste of your sweet pussy, but, baby, I'm tellin' you now, that's not how it works in my world."

"Ig…Ig…" I stuttered, "ignoring your ass?"

"Ignoring my ass."

"I…I don't even know what to say. That's insane."

"Red, you got my numbers in your phone, all 'a them. And your car has been at my garage for days and I haven't once seen your face until I walked into our office today. I left you sweet and smiling in this goddamned bed and I don't see you or hear your voice for four days? Then I walk into your office and you give me attitude and tell me to kiss your ass because you're in a pissy mood about some shit you refuse to share? No. You gotta know, darlin', that shit don't play with me."

"Well, Tack, that goes both ways because you showed and were all about biker charm and warm looks and then *I* got nothing from *you* for four *and a half* days. Then you walk in my office and tell me to *buy you a sandwich*! No. You gotta know, handsome, that shit don't play with me."

He studied me a few beats, his eyes flashed then his thumb swept my lower lip again and he murmured, "Well, fuck me."

"I see the light's dawning but I don't care," I announced. "Too late. I don't understand the rules to your game but what I do understand, I don't like. You have got to listen to me, a game is supposed to be fun, and this is no fun for me. This isn't fun at all. When it isn't infuriating, it's frightening and I don't like either of those. I like your kids. They're good kids so what I'm going to say next reflects on you, not them. I want you to let your kids finish their movie and then I'd appreciate it if you'd get yourself gone and take them with you. And, by the way," I finished, "I don't care if you accept my resignation or not. I won't be in tomorrow and I'm not coming back. Now, please, get...off...*me*."

"Listen to me, baby," he said gently.

"No," I replied sharply.

"Tyra, listen to me."

"No!"

His thumb moved to press lightly against both of my lips as his head dipped down and to the side and I felt his teeth nip my earlobe. My body stilled under his at the shocking headiness of his nip, my breasts swelled, my fingers curled into his shoulders and my belly dropped all before he growled into my ear, "Listen to me."

When I made no response, his thumb slid from my lips

and his hand spanned the side of my head, he kept his mouth at my other ear and he held me captive as he spoke.

"Shit is not good in the Club. Shit is not good outside the Club. Shit is not good with Naomi. I got a lot goin' down, it needs my attention. I need to stay sharp. I do not need to be thinkin' about your sweet mouth wrapped around my cock or my dick buried in your tight, wet pussy, which is all I wanna think about. When I say I gotta stay sharp, baby, I mean, I don't, I get dead, and when I say *that*, I mean the not-breathin'-anymore variety. You don't fit into all the shit that's swirlin' in my life right now unless I can make you fit. That's all I got to give you and that's all you're gonna get. And you're gonna take what I have to give, Red. You're not gonna resign. You're not gonna disappear. You're gonna be where I want you to be, you're gonna do what I want you to do and you're gonna listen to what I have to say and if you don't do it, I'll find a way to make you do it. That scares you, you gotta learn to get over it, and you'll learn not to be scared because I'd rather cut off my own arm than ever hurt you. But you fucked up, baby. You showed me somethin' I want and I get what I want and I do what I gotta do to get it. So this needs to sink in right fuckin' now, Tyra. You... are... stuck. Find some way to deal with it and my advice would be, don't fight it. You fight it, I'll take you on. That's a guarantee. Do you understand me?"

"You're scaring me right now, Tack," I admitted breathily because I was lying on my back, but everything he said made my breath ragged and there was nothing I could do to stop it mainly because I wasn't lying. He was *scaring me right now*.

He lifted his head, his other hand came up so both were framing my face and he looked into my eyes when he whispered, "What scares you?"

What scared me? My God, he *was* insane.

"All of it," I told him.

"Break it down," he demanded.

"Shit isn't good in the Club?"

"No, shit is not good in the Club."

He didn't elaborate, just confirmed so I went on. "Outside the Club?"

"Same outside the Club."

Confirmation not elaboration, and clearly I would get none of the last.

So, I whispered, "You could get the not-breathing variety of dead?"

"Yep."

"Ohmigod." I was still whispering.

"Baby—"

"What's going on?"

"It's better you don't know."

I was willing to go with that.

"Okay, then, can I just say that I'm not all fired up to live in your world if that's one of the problems you face."

At that, for some insane reason, Tack grinned. Then he said, "See I got more explaining to do."

Oh boy.

Before I could stop him (not that I could stop him), he went on, "Now, baby, you coulda taken your job with Ride and kept your shit separate. You didn't. You came and partied with the Club. Then you took my hand and partied with me. That means I get to claim you, and I have. There's no out once you're in and, Tyra, darlin', you're in."

"That's ridiculous."

"That's the way of the world."

"No it isn't."

"All right, babe, I'll amend that. That's the way of *my* world."

"Okay, Tack, but that's ridiculous!" My voice was rising and I declared, "I want out."

"You don't want out."

"I do."

"You don't."

"Trust me, *I do*."

"No, you don't."

"I so totally do."

"You want me to prove you don't?"

Uh-oh.

"No," I answered quickly as his hands tilted my head one way, his head slanted the other, his eyes dropped to my mouth and his face got closer.

"Too late," he muttered against my lips. I pressed them together. He changed tactics at the last minute, his tongue slid along my lips and my eyes drifted closed as my hands pressed against his shoulders. "Open your mouth for me, baby," he whispered against my lips.

I shook my head.

"I wanna taste you, open for me, darlin'." He was still whispering.

I shook my head again.

His thumb moved across my cheek, sweeping across my lips again, his tongue following and all that felt way, way, *way* too nice.

"Open for me," he urged gently.

I shook my head again at the same time pressing it back into the pillows.

His hand left my head and moved down my neck, my chest, as I felt his hips grind into mine.

Mm, that felt way, way, *way* too nice too.

Damn.

"Open," he ordered.

I squeezed my eyes tight.

His hand kept moving down.

"Open, baby."

I pressed my lips tight.

His fingers found the hem of my camisole, dipped under then the warmth of his hand was moving up my skin.

I squirmed under him.

"Open."

I turned my face away from his and his hand cupped my breast.

"Open," he whispered against the sensitive skin of my neck.

"No," I whispered to the pillow.

His hand at my head moved to curve around my jaw. He pulled my face to his again just as his fingers curled into my bra and yanked the cup down, scraping the nipple, making it go hard. I sucked in breath as my body instinctively melted under his, the inside of my thighs pressing into the sides of his hips, then his thumb swept across my tightened nipple, my lips parted and I gasped.

"There it is," he muttered, then his lips crushed mine and his tongue slid into my mouth.

God, he tasted good. I forgot how good. So good, he tasted *great*.

My thighs tightened against his hips, his finger met his thumb at my nipple and rolled. I felt a rush of heat between my legs. The rush was so strong I moaned into his mouth and arched into his hand as my tongue tangled with his and my arms slid to lock around his shoulders.

"Dad! Tyra!" Tabby shouted. "Someone's at the door!"

Tack's fingers stopped rolling, his hand curled warm around my breast and his mouth broke from mine to growl, "No fuckin' way."

"Should I answer it?" Tabby called, sounding closer.

"Ye..." My voice broke, I cleared my throat and shouted, "Yeah, honey, go ahead. I'll be right out."

"Fuck," Tack clipped, and I opened my eyes to see his were drilling into mine. "We're not done," he announced.

"Um...I need to go see who's at the door."

His fingers tensed on my breast and he growled, "Yeah, but we're not done."

"Um..."

"You'll see who's at the door then we're finishing."

I bit my lip.

"With me?" he demanded to know.

I stopped biting my lip to mumble, "Uh..."

Suddenly his thumb swept my sensitized nipple, my lips parted and my eyes drifted halfway shut.

"You're with me," he murmured, I snapped my eyes all the way open just in time to catch his grin.

Then his fingers were righting my bra, his hand was out of my top, his body was off mine and I was out of my bed and on my feet.

I wobbled slightly since my knees were not ready to take on my weight and Tack's arm went around my belly. He pulled my back to the front of his body, partly to hold me steady and partly to march me to the door with his face in my neck, against which he ordered, "Be quick gettin' rid of 'em."

"Tack—"

His arm around my belly gave me a squeeze and his teeth lightly nipped the skin at my neck.

My legs wobbled again.

"Quick," he commanded on a low rumble.

"Okay," I whispered.

He held me close but reached beyond me and opened my bedroom door.

CHAPTER NINE

I Can't Keep Up

I WALKED CONNECTED to Tack with his arm around my middle all the way down the hall. I was freaking out and I didn't want to like it but there was something about feeling his hard body and the power that naturally emanated from it surrounding me as we moved. He was not someone I felt safe with, at least this was what my mind told me, but my body felt something different.

I'd rather cut off my own arm than ever hurt you.

His words came to me, words I missed when he said them, and they filled my head so full, when we made it out of the hall into the living room, I had to blink my eyes to clear my mind.

Then I stared at Lanie's fiancé, Elliott, standing in my living room with Rush and Tabby. The movie was on pause and there was no Lanie in sight.

Weird. Elliott never came over by himself.

"You know this guy?" Tack's voice rumbled in my ear both audibly and physically.

"Yeah," I replied. "Hey, Elliott," I called, smiling at him.

"Hey, uh … Tyra," Elliott replied, his eyes, for some

bizarre reason, darting back and forth repeatedly from Tack to me.

Well, maybe it wasn't bizarre. Tack was a badass biker who was holding me and Elliott knew me pretty well so he knew I wasn't seeing a badass biker. He also probably got the lowdown from Lanie about Tack because I was pretty sure she told him everything. So he was probably surprised I was standing there in Tack's arm with two teenagers in my living room that could not be mistaken as the fruit of anyone else's loins but Tack's.

Still, it was bizarre the way he was doing it because it didn't seem like surprise or shock.

It seemed like fear.

Elliott was not tall, he was five foot seven and Lanie was five foot nine. Elliott had thinning blond hair and a receding hairline. Lanie had thick, lustrous, long dark hair akin to Tabby's. Elliott had a paunch and a weak chin. Lanie was slim and svelte, a human hanger, no tits or ass, amazing bone structure, beautiful green eyes, and she was pure elegance from top to toe. Lanie was a human goddess. Elliott was nowhere near a human god.

But Elliott was brilliant, a genius and not one of those socially awkward or arrogant geniuses. He was easy to talk to. He was funny. He was sweet. He was thoughtful. He was generous and he was kind. He never missed Lanie's birthday and always bought her the perfect present, not always something expensive, but always something she wanted or something meaningful. Ditto with anniversaries. She said he made her laugh. She said he listened when she had a bad day. She said he held her when they slept. And she said she knew beyond any doubt she was the most important thing in the world to him. So Goddess Lanie saw beyond Elliott's looks and he became the most important thing in the world to her.

They were a love match. Surprising to some, I was sure, but real. And because he made my best friend happy, I adored him.

"What's up?" I asked, moving forward only to be tugged back, again bizarrely, into Tack's body. This was bizarre not because he was holding me, which, I was getting, he intended to do whenever the hell he felt like it. No, it was bizarre *how* he was doing it.

In the hall, his natural badassness made me feel casually safe.

Right now, his tight hold and the feel of his hard body, statue-still and weirdly alert at my back, made me feel he was intentionally keeping me safe.

What on earth?

"Uh...I was wondering—" Elliott started.

"Is Lanie here?" I asked because I didn't want Lanie there. I was a little panicked that she'd come storming in at any moment, see Tack, see his kids, see the evidence of fajitas and the movie and lose her mind.

Lanie might be pure elegance from top to toe but that didn't mean she couldn't be pure drama, and when Lanie let it rip, watch out.

"No," Elliott replied, his eyes went over my shoulder and up and he asked, "Can I uh...Kane...er, Mr. Allen, can I talk to you?"

I stared at Elliott wondering what he was on about and who he was talking to.

Elliott's eyes flitted to me then back to Tack when he finished, "Alone."

That was when my body went statue-still.

It stayed statue-still for approximately a nanosecond before I heard Tack say to Elliott, "Don't move," then he turned me around, let me go, grabbed my hand and I found myself tugged down the hall. Then I found myself in my room and the door was again closed.

I tipped my head back to stare up at Tack.

"How do you know that guy?" he asked.

"He's my best friend's fiancé," I answered.

Tack looked down to the floor and muttered, "Fuck."

Okay, now he was scaring me again but for a different reason.

"What?" I whispered.

His head came up and his eyes caught mine. "I'm gonna take him out to the back deck. When I do that, I need you to promise me you'll stay in the living room with my kids and you won't listen. Can you promise me that, Tyra?"

Ohmigod! What was going on?

"Why?" I breathed.

"Promise me."

I leaned in and put a hand to his chest. "Why?" I repeated.

His hand curled around the back of my neck and his face dipped close. "I'll explain why later if you promise me now, baby," he said gently.

I stared into his eyes as fear filled my heart. Then, for some crazy reason, I nodded.

"Words, baby, give me the words," he demanded.

"I promise," I whispered.

His head tilted, his mouth touched mine, he let my neck go and grabbed my hand again. Two seconds later we were in the living room.

"Back deck," Tack growled then he prowled to the kitchen and disappeared, Elliott following him and the whole time he did, he avoided my eyes.

I heard the door slam and my body jumped when I did.

"You okay, Tyra?" Rush asked quietly. My eyes slid to him and it was then I realized I was trembling.

"Yeah, honey, I'm fine," I lied and threw him a fake smile. "That movie just freaked me out a bit and your dad was um...helping me out with that." I kept lying.

"Yeah, bet he was," Tabby said on a giggle then collapsed in a full-body plop on my couch.

But Rush didn't move. He studied me like his father had a tendency to do, and I guessed he didn't buy the fake smile or the lies. I didn't have time to consider the fact that Rush was seventeen, nearly eighteen, and astute. Something bad was happening and I only had time to consider that. So I curled into the armchair Tack had vacated and after a moment's hesitation and further study of me, Rush stretched out on the floor again and started the movie. We watched perhaps five minutes of it before we heard the back door open.

I jumped out of the chair and Rush paused the movie like he'd been listening for the door too. I was on my feet and Rush was at my side by the time Elliott and Tack reentered the room.

Elliott came straight to me and grabbed my upper arms. I felt Rush close to my side but all I could see was Elliott's pale, plainly freaked-way-the-hell-out face and panicked eyes.

"Don't tell Lanie," he begged on a whisper.

"Get your hands off her," I heard Tack growl and felt Rush get closer and Tack closing in but I only had eyes for Elliott.

"Don't tell her what?" I whispered.

"Don't tell her," he pleaded.

"Man, what did I say?" Tack bit out, and Elliott's head jerked to the side and up.

"She can't tell her," he told Tack and his fingers tensed, digging into my arms so much they caused pain.

"She'll do what she's gotta do. Now, I'm not gonna say it

again. Take your fuckin' hands off her or I'll make you do it," Tack warned.

Elliott paled further, released me and took a quick step away.

His eyes found mine and I saw his were wet. "I had to," he whispered. Both his hands went to his hair and he repeated, "I had to."

Then he ran, actually *ran* to and out the front door.

When it slammed behind him, I jolted out of my freeze and ran after him, calling, "Elliott!"

"Movie on, you and your sister stay in here, get me, Rush?" Tack ordered in a low, serious voice. I was interrupted in throwing open the door when he caught my hand and I found myself dragged yet again to my bedroom.

I didn't fight it and the minute the door closed behind Tack, I got in close. So close, my breasts brushed his chest and both my hands went to his tee at his abs and curled in.

I tipped my head back and whispered, "What's going on?"

I was freaked out and near tears. I felt a chill on my skin. And my stomach hurt.

Tack's hands came up, palms to my jaw, fingers curled around my ears and neck.

"Tell me what you know about him," he demanded quietly.

"Um…he's a computer programmer. He's a nice guy. He's really smart. He's getting married to my best friend in the whole world. Their wedding date is just over six weeks away." I shook my head in short shakes, not breaking eye contact. "I don't know…um, I like him. He loves her and I like him."

Tack's hands left my face and one went to his back pocket. He pulled out his phone, hit a few buttons and put it to his ear.

"Tack—" I started, but stopped when one of his hands came to my jaw again but his thumb rested on my lips.

"Dog," he said into his phone, "Elliott Belova just left Tyra's house. Pick him up. I want him at the Compound in an hour. I'll meet you there."

I felt my eyes get wide as Tack shoved his phone into his back pocket. Then my fingers curled deeper into his shirt and I pushed closer.

His thumb slid from my lips to my cheek and I whispered, "Please, talk to me."

"Your friend just offered me half a million to whack the big man in the Russian mob."

I blinked and swayed at the same time and Tack's arms went around me fast and tight.

Then I breathed, "What?"

"I think you heard me, baby," he said softly.

"Whack?" I whispered.

"Murder, kill, assassinate," Tack explained.

"I know what it means." I shook my head. "Do you...do you *do that*?" I asked.

His arms tightened briefly before he said low, "Fuck no, except five minutes ago when I was moved to consider it when that fuckwad stood on your back deck and offered me five hundred large to end another guy, but it wasn't the guy he wanted me to end I was considering ending."

"Then why...what...why...?"

Tack's face got close and his arms got tighter.

"This guy, Red, this guy is not a good guy."

"But he's Elliott," I said stupidly.

"He is not a good guy."

"Why do you say that?"

"I say it because he offered me five hundred K to kill someone. I say that because I know he's not as smart as you think because he's dumb enough to get involved with some seriously fucked up shit. And I say that because I just found out he's got the love of a woman who's probably a good woman and she's gonna end up brokenhearted, hurt or worse."

I felt my breathing escalate.

"Why do you say that?"

"This shit, the kinda shit he's in, leaks and no one's safe."

I gave him my full weight as I heard my breath hitch and felt tears fill my eyes.

"Tack," I whispered.

"She's gotta cut him loose."

"Tack—"

"Yesterday, Red."

"Oh my God."

"You get me?"

"My God."

His hand came back to my jaw, the pads of his fingers digging into my neck. "Baby, do you get me?"

I pulled myself together and nodded.

"You go to her," he ordered.

"Okay," I whispered.

"But you wait. I want you on the back of one of my boy's bikes when you do."

I nodded.

"I'm bringin' him in and he and I are gonna have a chat."

I nodded again.

"She needs to be here, she's on the back of one of my boy's bikes. I'm done with him, I'm comin' here. If she needs you, you bring her here. You do not stay there. I'm puttin' your house on radar. You're in this bed tonight when I get to you. Yeah?"

I nodded again.

"Give me the words, Tyra."

"If she needs me, I bring her here, only on the back of one of your boy's bikes, and I'm in my bed when you come to me."

"That's it, baby."

I swallowed and felt a tear slide partway down my cheek, but it didn't get very far before Tack swept it away.

"That's the only tear he gets, darlin'. This is not a guy you cry over."

"I'm crying for Lanie," I told him as another tear spilled out of my other eye.

That one didn't get very far either because Tack's head dipped in and his lips kissed it away. That felt unbelievably sweet but my heart hurt so much, when he did that, I closed my eyes and tears spilled down each side.

I felt his forehead against mine, another swipe of his thumb to wipe the wetness away and I heard him whisper, "Baby, I can't keep up."

"She's my best friend," I whispered back.

"She's in good hands," he said. That made me open my eyes and look into his brilliant blue ones.

I did not know this man. He freaked me out. He scared me. He infuriated me. And he excited me. I fell in love with him once and started to do it again. All of this in less than two weeks.

And I had absolutely no idea if I could trust him.

"Promise?" I whispered, and he nodded. "Give me the words, Tack."

To that, he grinned, his mouth moved to mine and he murmured, "I promise, Red."

Then he pressed his lips lightly to mine, touched his tongue even lighter to my lips and then his face moved an inch away.

Then he said, "Need a set of keys, darlin'."

I nodded and it was me who took his hand before I led him to my kitchen where there was a kokopelli key holder on the wall by the back door.

I grabbed a spare set and gave Tack the keys to my house.

CHAPTER TEN

Metal Detector

"You okay?" I asked Lanie, who was tucked into the double bed in my guest bedroom, her eyes red and puffy, her nose red and swollen, and about a thousand used Kleenexes littering the nightstand and floor by the bed.

"No," she snuffled, reached out to the Kleenex box, snatched another one out, shoved her face into it and burst into loud tears.

"Honey," I whispered, stroking her hair back.

I was sitting on the bed beside her, although for the last hour I'd been lying in it with her. She was inconsolable until about two minutes ago when she'd pulled it together and I thought it was safe to leave her.

Apparently it wasn't.

Earlier, Tack had taken off after having a quiet word with Rush in the kitchen, giving his daughter a kiss on the cheek and one on the lips for me. Rush and Tabby had hung around until Brick roared up on his bike. Rush walked me out to Brick's bike and promised to lock up behind him and Tabby. I'd gone to Lanie, explained what had happened with Elliott and what Tack told me about him, not including the fact he was picking Elliott up to have a "chat." I didn't think Tack's "chats" were like any kinds of chats Lanie and I could comprehend, and I figured Lanie would know that.

Not surprisingly, Lanie had not believed this at first. There was a drama where she accused me of being insane and blinded by hormones when it came to Tack.

Brick, who had been quietly standing inside the front door of the house, came in and confirmed my words by saying, "Babe, what Cherry here says is true. Everyone on the grid knows Elliott Belova is a serious bad dude. I got no reason to shit you. This guy is *whacked*."

Lanie had stared up at big, bearded, man-bun-haired Brick then she burst into tears.

I wrapped my arms around Lanie but looked up at Brick and mouthed, "Cherry?"

To which Brick grinned and muttered, "Creative."

I rolled my eyes. Brick yanked out his phone and called some guy named Hopper. Then I helped Lanie pack a bag. Then I climbed on the back of Brick's bike, Lanie climbed on the back of Hopper's bike and we roared back to my house. They made sure we were in safe, Brick told me to lock up after them then the boys rolled off.

Commence wild-ass crying jag, not a small amount of ranting, a couple of tantrums (one that included Lanie throwing her two-and-a-half-carat diamond engagement ring into my backyard, and I made a note to self to rent a metal detector prior to mowing my lawn the next time), Lanie texting Elliott about seven hundred times calling him every name she could think of and I finally got her to bed with a box of Kleenex.

Which brought me to now.

"You think you know someone," she sobbed into her tissue.

"Oh, Lanie," I whispered, still stroking her hair.

"I had to learn from a *biker* that my *fiancé* is *whacked*," she wailed.

I bit my lip.

"I mean..." She pulled the tissue away, started to look up at me, her eyes caught on something across the room, they grew huge, she bolted upright in bed and screamed bloody murder.

I leaped from the bed and turned to the door where her eyes were glued and saw Tack leaning against the jamb.

"Hey, babe," Tack greeted me casually over Lanie's screaming, which, fortunately, made Lanie stop screaming.

"Tack," I said softly.

"You...*you're* Tack?" Lanie whispered, and I looked down at her to see she was staring at Tack.

"That's me," Tack said.

"Holy shit, Ty-Ty, you were not wrong. He...is...*hawt*."

I closed my eyes and dropped my head but closing my eyes didn't mean my ears closed and therefore I heard Tack's very deeply amused chuckle.

Fabulous.

Apparently, heartbreak and finding out your fiancé was a bad dude didn't interfere with appreciating a fine male specimen. Good to know.

Before I recovered from my latest mortification that involved Tack, I felt his arm slide around my shoulders. My head came up when he curled me into his side and I saw that he was looking down at Lanie.

"How you doin'?" he asked gently.

"Uh..." Lanie answered, her eyes zipping back and forth between Tack and me.

"You need anything?" Tack asked.

"Uh..." Lanie answered, still doing the zipping thing.

"Ice cream?" Tack went on. "Whiskey?" he continued

when Lanie shook her head. "Weed?" Luckily he stopped there.

"Uh..." Lanie repeated, her eyes settling on Tack.

"I think she's good," I finally answered for her.

"Yeah, uh... I think I'm good," Lanie confirmed.

Tack pulled me closer, asking, "You done with Tyra for tonight?"

"Uh... sure," Lanie said.

"Is that a sure, sure or is that a not-so-sure sure?" Tack asked.

I looked up at him thinking he was being both very cool and very sweet. I didn't know what to make of this coming from him.

"I think I'm cried out... for now," Lanie told Tack.

"Right," he said quietly. "Then I'm gonna steal her."

"Okay," Lanie agreed.

"You rest good," Tack told her.

"Uh... okay," Lanie said.

Tack didn't speak for a beat then he said softly, "You'll be all right."

She blinked up at him. I did too.

Then he turned us to the door.

"Uh...'night," she called to our backs.

I looked over my shoulder at her and replied, "'Night, honey. I'm right next door if you need me."

"'Night," Tack said, not looking back. He guided me out of the room, closed the door then he guided me to my room, closed that door and curled me to him full frontal. I looked up at him and he asked, "How'd that go?"

"On the Drama Breakup with Your Fiancé Six Weeks Before the Wedding Because You Just Found Out He's a Bad Dude Scale of one to ten, that was a twenty-seven."

Tack's lips twitched.

I went on, "There's a fourteen-thousand-dollar diamond engagement ring somewhere in my backyard."

Tack's lips stopped twitching because they curved upward.

"Do you know where I can rent a metal detector?" I queried.

The curve turned into his sexy grin before he stated, "I'll get one of my boys to find it."

"That would be good considering she can hock that ring and add a room onto her house, make it a shrine to all the reasons she hates Elliott Belova."

The sexy grin turned into a bigger, sexier smile that included the lines radiating from his eyes deepening and his face looking like he was fighting laughter.

It was a seriously good look and I got so lost in it, I didn't notice it start to fade until his gentle voice came at me.

"You seem better."

I pulled in breath through my nose. Then I told him, "I'm better because she's going to survive and my hard part is done. Now I just have to offer support and that's easy."

He studied me again, his eyes moving over my face before they caught mine.

"You need sleep or you wanna know about this guy?" he asked.

I needed sleep. It had to be well beyond midnight, and although my boss probably would understand if I called off and hung with my best friend the next day, seeing as he was intimately involved in this drama, now that I was getting the hang of it, my job was pretty busy. Not to mention, the mechanics and body shop guys would not be good on their own. They needed direction. They also needed a listening ear. They further needed coffee and donuts. I missed donuts one day and I thought there was going to be a revolt. I had to get into Ride.

But I still wanted to know about Elliott.

"I wanna know about Elliott," I told him.

He nodded and gave me a squeeze. "Get ready for bed, baby, I gotta make a call. I'll meet you there and we'll talk before we sleep."

I blinked at him as he let me go, turned and walked out the door, closing it behind him.

What did he mean, *Get ready for bed* and *I'll meet you there and we'll talk before we sleep*?

The getting-ready-for-bed part I could do. My getting ready for bed left me in nearly the same outfit I was in when Tack left the room. Except it was drawstring pajama shorts rather than jean shorts and there was no bra under my camisole. Therefore I did that part.

I was sitting cross-legged on my covers, rubbing hand cream in my hands when Tack returned, again closing the door behind him.

"Tack, maybe we should—"

I stopped speaking when his hands immediately went to the hem of his tee. Then it was up and gone and I had a full-on view of his wide chest, tight abs and array of tattoos.

Holy heck. I forgot what a great chest he had. How broad his shoulders were. How much I really liked the definition of his collarbone. How much more I liked the ridges of his six pack. And how stupefyingly fascinating his tats were.

He'd undone his belt and two buttons of his jeans by the time I pulled it together, but I lost it again when he turned and sat on the bed to pull off his boots and I caught sight of his back.

Tack's back was tattooed too, from shoulder blade to shoulder blade, spanning his ribs and down his spine. It was an insignia I saw a lot around Ride and included wings, flames, the profile of an eagle and the American flag with a waving banner that spanned his waist in which, in old-style, old West writing it said, simply, "Chaos."

It was an unbelievably cool tattoo.

I hadn't recovered from it by the time he had his boots off and stood. It was then I snapped to, opened my mouth to suggest we talk in the living room prior to his leaving for the night and then his jeans were gone.

My breath caught and my eyes glazed over and before I knew it, Tack swept the covers down, climbed into bed, grabbed my hand, pulled me forward so I went up on my knees then toppled down on him. Finally, he swept the covers over us both.

I lifted my head and chest and stared down at him.

"Uh..." I mumbled.

"Elliott Belova is in some serious bad shit and I say that knowin' he was in serious bad shit before. The shit he's actually in is *serious*," Tack started the conversation and I snapped my mouth shut.

Then I opened it to ask, "So, he chatted?"

"Man wouldn't shut up," Tack answered.

Suddenly all ears, I dropped my chest to his to get closer and whispered, "Tell me."

To that, for some reason he asked, "Your girl in there, this wedding, it big?"

"Um...yeah. She's spending ten thousand dollars on flowers alone."

"Jesus," Tack muttered.

"Her dress cost more than my car," I informed him.

"Fuckin' hell." Tack was still muttering.

"And you already know about the fourteen-thousand-dollar engagement ring. I won't get into the catering," I finished.

"Christ, that explains that," Tack said.

"What?" I asked.

"Babe, her man loves her. Blinded by that shit. Wants to hand her the world."

"And?" I prompted when he didn't go on.

"And, Red, he can't afford fourteen-thousand-dollar engagement rings and ten grand on flowers and whatever the fuck on catering. That guy is in so deep he drowned about six months ago. He's dead man walking."

I felt my eyes get wide. "Really?"

"Really," Tack affirmed.

"I thought he made good money, *she* made good money. I thought—"

"They might make good money, darlin', but I'm guessin', the way they live added to that fuckin' wedding..." He shook his head. "He couldn't swing it. He also couldn't say no. He had some money, made what he called a 'bad investment' but what he means is, he got ripped off. Promised two hundred percent return in two months turned into a loss of one hundred and fifty K in the blink of an eye. The guy he gave the money to disappeared. Belova scrambled. Tried to find a way out usin' family ties but found himself hooked to some serious men who wanted to use his super brain to do some super-serious illegal shit. They paid him and these guys pay you, they own you. Now they own him. He can't get out from under it. I just called a cop I know and it's worse. He's not only on the grid, he's on radar. These men won't cut him loose, and Lawson at DPD didn't say it flat out but I get the sense the cops know what he's doin'. Belova's done, he wants out and he wants out bad. Your friend talked to him about me, this guy's got an idea about bikers, he came over here to talk to you to get to me but he got me. He made another stupid play, thinkin' I do that shit. Now he's owned by the Russian mob, he's on cop radar and he's not my favorite person, making assumptions like that about me. One way or the other, this guy is fucked. Far as I can see, he's got two options, jail or dead. But even if the cops get to him before the mob, he goes inside, he's dead. He even thinks of talkin' to the cops, he's dead. So, my guess is, he's dead."

I stared down at him and felt my nose start to sting as I thought of sweet, generous, totally-in-love-with-my-best-friend Elliott.

Then I whispered, "Damn, I don't think I'm better anymore."

Then I dropped my head and did a face plant in Tack's chest.

I felt his hand glide into my hair and cup the back of my head as I heard and felt him mutter, "Baby."

I turned my head, pressed my cheek to his chest and Tack's hand slid to under my ear but his thumb moved to stroke my cheek as I deep-breathed to fight back my tears.

Then I said softly, "Don't be mad at him, Tack. It wasn't cool, him asking you to do that. It was messed up. But it sounds like he's desperate, and I always knew he'd do anything for Lanie. He's got enough to worry about. He doesn't need to worry about pissing off a scary biker dude."

"Babe, he's still at the Compound which, right now, is maybe the safest place in Denver he could be."

I lifted my head and slid my hand up his chest to rest my chin on it as my eyes went to his. "You're protecting him?"

"For now, until I decide what to do with him, but, Red, that don't mean I'm not still pissed at him. Comin' to *your* house, talkin' to me on *your* deck, with *you* and *my kids* in the house and asking me somethin' that fucked up?" He shook his head. "No."

I nodded because he was right. What Elliott did was a big *no*.

Therefore, to change the subject, I asked, "What did he do for the mob?"

"Better question, what *didn't* he do. Hacks. Creative accounting. Creative banking. Wire taps. Camera feeds. Drops. Pickups. Messenger. It's lucky this guy works from home and I'll lay cake down on the fact he got zero real work done in the last six months, he's been so visible doing shit for Lescheva."

"Lescheva?"

"Grigori Lescheva, top guy in the Russian mob and distant relative of your boy Elliott."

"Oh," I whispered, my eyes slid to the side and I murmured, "All so Lanie could have peonies in August."

Tack's fingers still in my hair tensed against my scalp and my eyes slid back to him. "No. That woman in there with her mountain of Kleenex would be happy without peonies in August, Red. This is about him growin' a pair, mannin' up and tellin' her he can't hand her the world. She didn't want the world. She wanted him. He didn't have enough confidence in himself to believe that a woman like her would want a man like him and in the end, he took away the only thing she really ever wanted."

Um...wow. I liked that Tack knew that and I also liked how he said it.

I didn't tell him that. Instead, I whispered, "This is true."

"I know it's true," he whispered back.

"If he's broke, how was he going to pay you half a million dollars to whack this Lescheva guy?" I asked.

"Provin' irrefutably he's a moron, he was gonna use his skills to steal it from the mob."

Yes, that proved irrefutably that Elliott was a moron. Big time.

I turned my head, pressed my cheek against my hand on his chest and sighed.

Tack's fingers tensed against my scalp again and he ordered, "Come here, baby, I want a kiss then I gotta get some shut-eye. I'm fuckin' wiped."

I blinked at my room.

Now was the time to tell him he wasn't sleeping in my bed and he needed to go to another one. The problem was, he was naked in my bed and I was resting on his chest.

Oh boy. How did I let that happen?

I decided to blame Eiliott and Tack's tats.

Then I pulled in breath, lifted my head and looked at Tack.

"Uh...maybe you should sleep elsewhere tonight?" I suggested what I hoped sounded more like a requirement.

He grinned, his fingers slid to the back of my head and he started pulling me to him, saying, "Quit fuckin' around, Red, I'm tired."

"I wasn't, erm...fucking around."

His hand stopped putting pressure on my head and his brows knit.

"Say again?"

"I think you should, um...probably, uh..." Damn! "With Lanie here, you know...you should..."

His hand left my hair, both hands went under my armpits and he hauled me up his chest then rolled into me so he was on top. Then he gave me the good-night kiss to beat all good-night kisses. It was long, hard, deep, wet and utterly delicious.

When he was done, I was breathing heavily, my lips were tingling, my nipples were tingling and there were other places that had started to tingle but he'd stopped. Then he rolled to his back, reached an arm out to turn off the light on my nightstand, the room was plunged into darkness and he tucked me into his side.

My cheek was to his shoulder, my hand on his abs and I was trying to control my breath.

Once I got my breath under control, I said quietly into the darkness, "I guess this means you aren't going to go home."

His arm around my waist got tight before it relaxed and he replied with humor in his tone, "Yeah, Red, that's what it means."

I wondered what he would have done if I hadn't slithered out of his room when he'd kicked me out of his bed and instead just stayed. It was on the tip of my tongue to ask him but I couldn't call up the courage.

Then I realized I had no choice but to sleep with a naked Tack in my bed. And even though he'd been very cool about Elliott, with Lanie and even with me, this annoyed me to an extreme.

He'd said, *You don't fit into all the shit that's swirlin' in my life right now unless I can make you fit. That's all I got to give you and that's all you're gonna get. And you're gonna take what I have to give, Red. You're not gonna resign. You're not gonna disappear. You're gonna be where I want you to be, you're gonna do what I want you to do and you're gonna listen to what I have to say and if you don't do it, I'll find a way to make you do it.*

And when he'd said that, clearly he wasn't lying.

I decided we needed to have a conversation and when we had our next one we needed to have it when I wasn't flat on my back with Tack on top of me.

I rolled away from him to my other side, tucking my hands under my cheek and staring into the darkness.

He rolled with me, his arm curving tight around my ribs and pulling me deep into his body as his knee came up, taking mine with it and he leaned in, partially pinning me to the bed.

I'd rather cut off my own arm than ever hurt you.

He'd said that too.

Mixed messages and multiple personalities.

I closed my eyes tight, pulled in a deep breath and then let it go. When I did, Tack's arm moved out and up, his hand found my wrist, pulled it down and his fingers laced in mine before he tucked both our hands tight to my chest.

Then he whispered in my ear, "Sleep, baby, it's all gonna be all right."

He thought I was worried about Elliott and Lanie and he was being sweet about it.

I closed my eyes tighter, took another deep breath and let it go.

Then I whispered back, "Okay, Tack."

" 'Night, Red."

" 'Night."

I felt his lips touch the back of my neck then I felt his weight settle into me again and a little while later I heard his steady breathing.

A little while after that, mine joined his.

CHAPTER ELEVEN

You Forget Somethin'?

I WOKE AND felt the morning, bright Colorado sunshine on my eyelids. I rolled to my back and opened my eyes. Then I rolled to my other side and smelled musk and man.

Tack.

I breathed deep.

Mm. Nice.

I blinked and saw my alarm clock said it was ten to nine and I stared.

Ten to nine!

Damn! I was supposed to be at work an hour ago!

I threw the covers back and scrambled out of bed. My feet hit the ground running but I tripped and went flying, righting myself just before I took a header. I looked back to see what I'd tripped on and it was Tack's boots.

Then I stared at Tack's boots beside my bed, liking the sight of them lying there just like I liked the smell of him on my sheets.

Holy hell.

I scurried to the door, threw it open and was going to head to the bathroom but I heard the murmur of voices coming from the kitchen and stopped. I looked to Lanie's door and saw it was open. Something weird seeped into me, I stopped rushing and walked slowly toward the living room, rounded the wall and moved just into the kitchen.

My kitchen was long and narrow, running the length of the house. At the front of it was the dining area, the bulk of the kitchen was beyond a short bar with two barstools in front of it. One of those barstools held Lanie's firm, slim ass, her body encased in a shimmery, short silk kimono-style robe complete with beautiful embroidery on the back, most of which you couldn't see because her gleaming, thick dark hair was flowing down her back. Across the bar from her was Tack, wearing his gray tee from the day before and his jeans. They both held coffee mugs. Lanie was in profile and she'd not twenty-four hours ago found out her beloved fiancé was the kind of guy who would track down a biker in a failed attempt to have someone whacked. Not to mention, she hated Tack and wanted me to quit my job so I'd never see him again. But I still saw they both were smiling so big it looked like they'd just stopped laughing.

Something in my heart spasmed at this sight. Lanie was my friend and she had been for fifteen years. I knew she was beautiful, I'd been walking at her side or sitting on a barstool next to her or at a table with her enough times to notice the appreciating glances, see the drinks sent her way, watch the men slide in beside her, but that was the way of the world. Beautiful women got attention. And she was my Lanie, I was happy for her that she did.

But two weeks ago I watched Tack making out with a gorgeous, slim brunette and now he was laughing in my kitchen with one. And even though she was my friend who I knew wouldn't go there, whether or not Elliott was in or just dumped on his ass out of the picture, I didn't like it.

And I didn't like that I didn't like it.

Holy hell, now *I* was getting multiple personalities.

Tack's eyes went from Lanie to me, his smile stayed in place and his chin tipped up. "Mornin', babe."

Lanie spun on her barstool toward me. "Hey, Ty-Ty."

"Hey," I muttered, walking in directly to Lanie. I got close and slid her hair off her shoulder. "You okay this morning?"

"No," she answered, her eyes slid to Tack, she smiled beautifully at him, her innate elegance radiating from every pore, even makeup-less, in a kimono and with slightly puffy eyes from the crying jag yesterday. Then she looked back to me and stated, "But Tack's pancakes go a long way to soothe the ravaged soul of a woman who just found out her fiancé is *whacked*."

Tack chuckled. I looked down at my bar to see a plate that once held something covered with maple syrup.

Tack had made Lanie pancakes.

I didn't like that either.

"You want pancakes, Red?" Tack asked, and I looked up at him thinking he looked good in my kitchen. Really good. And also thinking he looked like he belonged in it with Lanie.

Damn.

"Nope," I murmured, giving Lanie a bump with my body and heading around the bar to the coffeepot. "I need coffee and to jump in the shower. I'm late for work."

I stopped in front of the coffeemaker, grabbed a mug and was in the process of dropping my arm when I suddenly found myself pressed to the counter and what was pressing me was Tack's long, hard body.

His arms curved around my ribs then I felt his goatee rough against my neck as his chin shifted my hair aside then his face was in my neck.

"You forget somethin'?" his gravelly voice rumbled in a murmur against my skin.

"Yeah, to turn on my alarm," I answered, my body still as a statue but every inch of my skin was tingling.

"No you didn't. I turned it off."

"You did?" I asked the cupboard.

"You're off today, seein' to your friend. Boss's orders."

"Tack—"

His arms gave me a squeeze and his goatee tickled my ear when his lips lifted there. "You forgot something," he whispered.

I turned my head and his came up as I did. When I caught his eyes I asked, "I did?"

"Yeah."

I was confused, freaked out about my weird response to Tack and Lanie laughing and maybe still a little asleep so my brows drew together.

"What'd I forget?"

One of his arms left my middle and cupped the side of my head.

"This," he muttered then his mouth was on mine.

It wasn't a morning mouth touch. It was a kiss, a serious kiss. So serious, his body moved back, turned mine to face him then it moved in again, pressing me into the counter. His hand cupping the side of my head slid into my hair to cup the back and hold me to him as his other arm locked tight around my waist, plastering me to his body.

It was such a serious kiss, and such a *great* kiss, I totally forgot Lanie was there, my confusion, my weird response to Tack spending time with Lanie and the sleep that lingered and my arms moved to wrap around his shoulders. I went up on my toes and I went at it right along with Tack. Maybe more. I was off guard plus I loved how he tasted and I was hungry for it. So without the barest thought about anything but Tack, his tongue and his mouth, I drank deep.

Tack broke the kiss but he didn't take his mouth away when he whispered against my lips, "Jesus *fuck*, Red, you can use that sweet mouth," and his arm around me squeezed tight on the word "fuck."

I gazed up at him in a haze thinking he could use his mouth too, thinking a lot more than my skin was tingling and also thinking I wasn't quite done with his mouth when I heard Lanie clear her throat.

I blinked and the haze cleared.

"Ohmigod," I whispered against Tack's mouth and watched up close as the lines beside his eyes deepened in a smile.

This would have been fascinating but I was belatedly mortified and therefore I pulled quickly out of Tack's arms and stepped to the side, my gaze finding my best friend.

"God, Lanie, sorry, I—"

"Don't mind me," she said, her mouth smiling but there was pain in her eyes. "I remember what it was like in the first throes of meeting someone. I remember it because it was a lot like what I still had with Elliott just the night before last." She stopped talking, the smile faltered and her eyes got bright.

Oh no. I'd seen that look a lot last night. She was going to blow.

"Damn," I muttered, and Tack's arm circled my chest from behind pulling me to him, which was the wrong, wrong, *wrong* thing to do because Lanie's eyes dropped to his arm. Her lips quivered and then she burst out sobbing, twisting a bit so she wouldn't face plant in her maple syrup plate, she face planted in her arm on the counter but her hair went into her maple syrup plate.

"I think the pancakes wore off," Tack muttered in my ear.

I yanked free of Tack's arms, whirled and glared at him.

His eyes caught mine but my eyes caught his mouth twitch before he asked, "What?"

I slapped his arm, lifted up on my toes to get in his face and hissed, "You don't make out like that in front of newly broken up people! In fact, you don't make out like that in front of *anyone*."

His face moved to within an inch of mine and he whispered, "Wrong, baby, *I* do. I make out wherever the fuck I want, which means you do too."

I squinted my eyes at him, whirled back around and ran to Lanie.

I put my hand on her back and carefully extricated her hair from the maple syrup.

"Honey," I whispered, "you got your hair in the syrup."

She sat back abruptly and looked to the ceiling, crying out, "I don't care! Who cares! I can shampoo with maple syrup. There's no one to care!" Then she flopped back down on the counter and I had just enough time to grab the plate and get it out of range.

I lifted my eyes to Tack and skewered him with a look at the same time I held the plate up and jerked it at him. He sauntered to me and took the plate while I pulled Lanie off her chair.

"Let's get you into the shower," I murmured to her.

"No shower. No work. No nothing. I'm going to eat Tack's pancakes until I weigh nine hundred pounds and die and they'll have to cut around your door to get my carcass out of your house."

I so totally told you that when Lanie let a drama rip, watch out.

"You'll feel better after a shower," I told her, guiding her out of the kitchen.

"I'll never feel better, Ty-Ty," she told me and I sighed. Then I guided her to her bedroom. I dashed to the bathroom and did my business quickly. After I was done, I went back to her bedroom and guided her with her toiletries and clothes stuffed in her arms into the bathroom. As I was doing this last, I heard the knock on my front door. I focused on Lanie and got her situated and as I was exiting the bathroom to see who on earth was at the door, I saw Tack was there before me.

"Hey, Tyra!" Tabby called chirpily.

"Yo, Tyra," Rush called after her.

I stood in the hall outside my bathroom in my drawstring pajama shorts and camisole with my wild bed hair staring at Tack and his kids in my living room and heard the bathroom door click behind me.

"Uh...hey," I called, stunned.

"Dad texted, said it was an impromptu Allen Pancake Morning so we came right over," Tabby stated.

"Nothin' better, not even his fajitas," Rush put in.

"Babe, get your ass in the kitchen so I can feed you and my kids and get on the road," Tack ordered while sauntering toward my kitchen.

His kids followed.

I stood in the hall and stared. Then I blinked. Then I stared some more. Then my body came unstuck and I motored into the kitchen to find Tack at the stove, Rush on Lanie's barstool and Tabby's head in the fridge.

I went direct to Tack and got close to his side seeing he was pouring perfect, silver-dollar pancakes on my griddle.

"Can I talk to you?" I asked quietly.

His head turned and he looked down at me.

"Yeah," he answered but otherwise didn't move.

"Elsewhere," I defined my request.

"Then . . . no," he said through a grin.

I opened my mouth to make my request sound more like a demand when a loud banging came at my door. It was so loud, my body jerked in surprise and Tack's head whipped around.

"What the fu—?" he started to mutter when we heard, "Open this motherfucking door!"

Ohmigod! It was Naomi.

More loud banging, so loud and violent I was uncertain my door could withstand it and I wondered if some of it was kicking, then, "I know you're all in there! I *saw* you go in there! Open this goddamned motherfucking door!"

Through this, Tack crashed down my fabulous pink Williams Sonoma mixing bowl with the little pouring thing-a-ma-jig in the lip, shoved the griddle off the burner, turned and stalked out of my kitchen.

Oh boy.

I hurried after him and felt Rush and Tabby at my heels but we weren't fast enough. Tack had the door open and he was standing in it. My body stuttered to a stunned halt when I saw Tack's torso rock back because Naomi shoved a hand violently in his shoulder to push in. She slammed the door behind her, took three steps in, turned to me, Rush and Tabby and I fancied I saw her head split right down the middle and fire pour out, such was her fury.

"You stupid, skank, *whore*!" she shrieked then came right at me.

I braced and she made an "oof" noise and bent double at the middle when Tack caught her at the waist and pulled her back at the same time Rush's arm went around my waist (a fair bit more gently, I might add), and he pulled me behind him.

Tack positioned himself between Naomi and me and planted a hand in her chest.

"Have you lost your fuckin' *mind*?" he growled.

"Get out to your car!" she screeched at Tabby.

Tack was shoving her toward the door and she was fighting it but losing.

"Get the fuck outta here." He was still growling, his voice low, deep, the gravel had turned to ice shards, and it wasn't directed at me but I still felt my skin rise in goose bumps.

"You do not spend time in that fuckin' bitch's home!" Naomi screamed, again, for some reason, at Tabby.

"Oh God," Tabby whispered, and her words were not filled with ice. They were filled with embarrassment.

Naomi landed against the door, Tack's hand still pressed into her chest and his face got into hers.

"You follow them here?" he asked, his voice still scary.

"Fuck you!" she shouted in his face.

"You follow the kids here?" Tack barked in hers.

"They are not spendin' time with your latest piece of tail!" she yelled.

"You're tellin' me you slunk out to your fuckin' car and followed your kids to my woman's house," Tack stated.

His woman? When did I become Tack's woman?

"Tabby's already part slut, spendin' time around you and all your bitches. She don't need to learn the high-class, fancy-ass way to spread her legs," Naomi fired back.

I gasped, Rush made a noise like a growl and Tabby whimpered.

Automatically, my arm stretched back, searching blindly until I found it, and then I wrapped my hand around Tabby's, held it tight and moved back until the back of my side touched the front of hers. The minute it did, Tabby's hand closed around mine like a vice.

"Did I just hear you?" Tack said in a soft, dangerous voice.

"You heard me, asshole," Naomi snapped.

"You're tellin' me I just heard you," Tack gave her another opportunity to stand down.

"You heard me," she clipped.

Another knock came at the door at the exact same time Lanie made her appearance.

"What on earth is going on?" she asked from the mouth of the hall wearing her shimmery, fabulous, short kimono, a towel wrapped around her head, her beautiful face and perfect bone structure no less beautiful with my pale pink terry-cloth towel framing it.

Naomi looked around Tack at Lanie then back at Tack and she shrieked, "*Fuck me*, you buildin' a harem?"

Another knock at the door.

Tack's hand wrapped around Naomi's arm and he yanked her from the door. Stepping back, he threw it open.

I peered outside and stared in shock at my favorite aunt, Bette, and favorite uncle, Marshall, who didn't live in Denver. They lived outside DC.

Aunt Bette's eyes were round and she took in the inhabitants of my living room, her gaze finally resting on me, and I knew she'd heard Naomi but then again, how could she not?

"Uh…surprise?" she asked and Uncle Marshall pushed in, shoving his wife in with him as Tack took a couple of steps back, dragging Naomi.

Uncle Marsh's eyes also looked around my living room then found me.

Then, just like Uncle Marsh, he grinned his shit-eating grin.

There was only one person on this entire earth that could hear a foul-mouthed woman shrieking in his beloved niece's house and find it grin-worthy and that was my Uncle Marsh.

I pulled in breath through my nostrils, tipped my head back to look at the ceiling then I looked at Uncle Marsh and grinned back.

CHAPTER TWELVE

Family Reunion

"YOU MIGHT WANNA step aside," Tack growled at Aunt Bette and Uncle Marsh.

Aunt Bette stared up at him, but Uncle Marsh shuffled Aunt Bette to the side just as Tack manhandled a struggling, spitting Naomi out the door. He slammed it in her face and locked it. And then he turned to face the room.

Pounding came at the door and Naomi could be heard screaming, "You did *not* just do that!"

With all that was happening and without having had that first cup of coffee, I was at a loss but luckily my feet weren't. They took me to Aunt Bette while more pounding sounds came at the door and I knew, being closer to them, they came from fists *and* feet.

I ignored them and Aunt Bette, who was staring at the door, jumped when I got close.

"Hey, Aunt Bette," I murmured and wrapped my arms around her.

"Open this goddamned door and send my kids out here!" Naomi yelled.

"Uh...hi there, Tyra," Aunt Bette murmured back, giving me a squeeze.

I let her go and smiled at her.

Naomi screeched over continued pounding, *"Open the fucking door!"*

I kept ignoring it and turned to Uncle Marsh. "Hey, Uncle Marsh." Then I wrapped him in my arms.

Uncle Marsh's hug was different than his wife's. My mother's cool-as-hell brother loved me and he loved me a lot. Therefore, his hug was tight, it was warm and it spoke volumes, every word beautiful.

"Hey, honey," he whispered in my ear.

"I said open the *motherfucking* door," Naomi shrieked with more hammering.

I stepped back but Uncle Marsh kept me close with his hands on my upper arms.

My Aunt Bette was petite, had short, curly hair and big, blue eyes. Aunt Bette was the kind of aunt who was interested in everything you did, supported every decision you made, wanted nothing but your happiness and gave love without conditions. She was a call 'em as she saw 'em, did what she liked and liked what she did, said what was on her mind and if you couldn't hack the honesty that was your problem, kind of person. I adored her.

Uncle Marsh looked like a shorter, but way cooler, Kevin Costner. Uncle Marsh got his news from Aunt Bette; therefore communication with Uncle Marsh was sporadic unless you were sitting on his deck (where, the last fifteen years, we had spent the vast amount of our time together). That said, he supported every decision you made, wanted nothing but your happiness and gave love without conditions. He was also a call 'em as he saw 'em, did what he liked and liked what he did, said what was on his mind kind of guy, but his way was that when he called 'em, did what he liked and said what was on his mind, you listened and learned because he was wise and he wasn't a fan of bullshit. I worshipped him.

"I'm here for some meetings," Aunt Bette put in over the continued pummeling heard at the door. "Your uncle decided to come with me, surprise you and make it a long weekend with his favorite niece. We thought we'd pop by and take you for breakfast." There was more pounding at the door and Aunt Bette gamely ignored it. "My meetings don't start until this afternoon then we have the whole weekend."

Uncle Marsh let me go and the minute he did, Tack was there, warm, lean body to my back, tattooed arm curved around my chest. When he did this, I was surprised for a variety of reasons. First, this was a claiming gesture. Second, it was meant to communicate, clearly, it was a claiming gesture. Third, it was a claiming gesture that was meant also to communicate togetherness *and* intimacy. And last, although we had been intimate, that wasn't something I wanted my aunt and especially my uncle to know, as I wasn't aware we were "together" as such and I wasn't certain how I felt about being claimed.

Aunt Bette's and Uncle Marsh's eyes immediately dropped to his arm. Then they shot to my face and I knew that neither of them missed a single thing Tack was communicating.

Aunt Bette's eyes turned openly curious.

Uncle Marsh's face wiped blank.

Aunt Bette did not judge. She was who she was and you took her as she was. She returned the favor.

Uncle Marsh had been a fighter jock in the Air Force. Now he was a golf pro. He wore Ralph Lauren and TAG Heuer watches. He still had a military haircut. He also didn't judge. That was, I learned in that instant, until a big, badass, scary biker dude with an arm covered in tattoos, wearing faded jeans and a tight tee, needing a haircut and needing it four weeks ago and who Uncle Marsh just witnessed man-handling a raving woman who assaulted my front door and hurled obscenities at it curved his painted arm around his much-loved niece's chest. On those occasions, he judged.

Oh boy.

Tack's other arm moved in the direction of Aunt Bette. "Kane Allen," his gravelly voice declared. I blinked, twisted my neck and looked up at him.

Elliott had said that name and apparently that was Tack's real name. It was a cool name. Though I wished he'd given it to me directly.

"Hello, Kane." Aunt Bette took his hand and shook. "I'm Bette, Tyra's aunt."

"Bette, you can call me Tack," he told her.

Her eyes slid to me, her brows went up declaring we were going to have a conversation later, but I knew this conversation would be so she could get all the juicy gossip then spread it widely throughout my extended family, all the way down to the cousins. Unlike Uncle Marsh, Aunt Bette was a communicator. She thought family was the most important thing on earth and thus made it her mission to be the hub of family information. If you needed to know anything, you asked Aunt Bette and if she didn't know it, she sure as heck found out.

Tack released her and his hand went to Uncle Marsh.

Uncle Marsh studied it. And while Uncle Marsh studied it, he also, I reckoned, was wondering if he should call all his fighter jock buds in order to spirit me away Mach Three. Then he took Tack's hand and shook it.

"Marsh, Tyra's uncle," he introduced himself.

"Right," Tack replied and let his hand go, stepping us back and to the side. "These are my kids, Tab and Rush."

"Yo," Rush said, coming forward to shake hands.

"Hey," Tabby said, following her brother. "Cool to meet you. We love Tyra. She's the shit."

Aunt Bette smiled. Uncle Marsh studied Tabby then Tack. I tried not to feel the warmth sliding through my system at being "the shit" after meeting Tabby and Rush once. I also failed in not feeling that warmth.

"I'm waiting!" Naomi screamed from outside. The hammering at the door had stopped but apparently she hadn't gone.

"This is so cool!" Lanie entered the huddle, and she did this to hug Aunt Bette and Uncle Marsh while gushing. "Ty-Ty talks about you guys all the time. Says if she wasn't related to you, she would have launched an investigation at the hospital to see if she was switched at birth. It's awesome to finally meet you!"

Lanie stepped back and smiled brightly at them. Aunt Bette smiled back at her. Uncle Marsh directed another shit-eating grin at me.

Lanie wasn't lying. I loved my mom and dad, but all evidence, except the existence of Uncle Marsh, pointed to there being a mix-up at the hospital. My mom and dad were Republicans. My mom and dad were religious. My mom and dad were both born in Ohio. They vacationed in Ohio State Parks. They considered themselves seasoned travelers because they'd been to Cooperstown and the Indy 500. They cheered for the Buckeyes. Their TV room was decorated in red, gray and white. And, last, they intended to die in Ohio and I knew this because they told me so.

My mom had a successful career as a housewife. She baked fabulous pies and listened to show tunes and gospel. My dad had a successful career as a cabinetmaker. He ate Mom's fabulous pies and bragged about them to all and sundry and he watched football, cop shows and action movies, the more bad guys blown up or filled with holes, the better.

Even at my age, my mom still lectured me that women should wear skirts, heels, never leave the house without makeup and earrings and lamented, often, through every means available (including phone, letters, e-mails and during visits) the fact that I had yet to give her grandchildren. My dad lectured me that I spent too much time working and socializing, not the right kind (the right kind being at church mixers where I would find myself a good, religious boy who liked football and God and had a job where he worked with his hands), and that I should find that boy and make sure his handkerchiefs were always perfectly ironed. This, as well as keeping a clean house and my boy in meat and potatoes, being my only reasons to exist.

My mom and dad had somehow managed to get thrown back to the '50's, they liked it, stayed there and, as with the great state of Ohio, they were never, ever leaving.

My mom and dad were nothing like me.

Suffice it to say that if it was not Aunt Bette and Uncle Marsh in my living room at that very moment while Tack (still) had his tattooed arm around me, and it was my mom and dad, things would be going very differently. Aunt Bette and Uncle Marsh had the ability to hold their tongues and act with decorum. Mom would be tight-faced. Dad would be asking Tack to have a chat on my deck where he would explain I was a "good girl" and probably go into detail about how he felt about tattoos and the importance of regular grooming and the only grooming that was acceptable left your hair in a buzz cut and not a single whisker on your face. Then Tack would likely refuse Dad's demand that he never have anything to do with me ever again. And finally Dad would promptly go to the nearest gun shop and buy a shotgun because Dad might be religious but he had no aversion to firearms.

I forced my mind from these reflections and introduced Lanie to my aunt and uncle. "This is Lanie, my best friend."

"Nice to meet you," Aunt Bette said. "Tyra's told me about you too, all of it good."

Lanie beamed. Uncle Marsh transferred his shit-eating grin to Lanie.

"Family reunion! Awesome!" Tabby cried. "And you're here just in time. You don't have to go out to breakfast with Tyra. Dad's making his world-famous pancakes."

Both Aunt Bette and Uncle Marsh turned eyes to Tack and even Uncle Marsh couldn't hide that he was startled at the idea of a scary biker dude making pancakes.

"Reminds me I gotta get that done 'cause I got shit to do," Tack rumbled from behind me, still not having let me go. "Tabby, darlin', get these folks a cup 'a joe. Rush, plates, forks, set Red's table." His arm gave me a squeeze and his mouth came to my ear where he said quietly but I knew my aunt and uncle could hear, "She'll go away and I'll deal with her. She doesn't and you see her again, you call me. She is not your problem, baby, yeah?"

"Yeah," I said quietly back.

That got me another arm squeeze, he let me go and I felt his heat leave my back as he sauntered to the kitchen.

"I have to go finish my shower," Lanie announced. "All that ruckus, I jumped out and I still have conditioner in my hair. I'll be back." Then she whirled around and raced down the hall to the bathroom where she disappeared behind the closed door.

I turned to my aunt and uncle, finding myself alone in the living room with them.

"Seems you missed some things in your last e-mail," Aunt Bette remarked.

I bit my lip. Aunt Bette grinned. Uncle Marsh looked at his shoes.

"How do you guys take your coffee?" Tabby called from the kitchen.

"Milk, two sugars," Aunt Bette called back, moving toward the kitchen.

Uncle Marsh looked at me.

"Deck. Explanation. First chance you got," he ordered quietly.

"Okeydoke," I whispered.

His hazel eyes bored into mine.

Then he looked away and started toward the kitchen.

I sucked in breath.

Naomi shouted through the door, "Fuck you! Fuck *all* of you!"

Damn.

CHAPTER THIRTEEN

Um . . . No

"SPILL," AUNT BETTE demanded while slapping hangers on a rack in Nordstrom.

I had escaped the Uncle Marsh chat on my deck because my day had started as mayhem and descended into bedlam.

Tack made pancakes for five people and Rush was again right, they were fantastic. Definitely better than his fajitas, and his fajitas were spectacular so his pancakes being better made them silver-dollar miracles. Then he took Rush and Tabby out on my back deck and talked to them for five minutes with this culminating in Rush shouting, "Fuck yeah!" and Tabby squealing in delight, rushing inside, looking at me and yelling, "Guess what, Tyra? We're movin' in with Dad!" Then she threw her hands up in the air with fingers in devil's horns and screeched nonsensically.

I had some concerns about this announcement mostly due to a fact that a judge usually decided something like that in a courtroom with lawyers in attendance. Not Kane "Tack" Allen deciding it on my back deck with only his kids in attendance. But it wasn't my business so I just smiled at Tabby and returned her big hug when she gave me one.

Then Tack announced he had to go. He did a bunch of

chin lifts but approached me in my chair at my dining table, fisted a hand in my hair, tugged my head gently back and laid a long, wet one on me in front of my aunt and uncle, my best friend *and* his children.

I scowled in his face after he was done (and after I recovered) to which he muttered to me, "Wherever the fuck I want, Red," gave my hair a playful tug and then he was gone.

I luckily could avoid the variety of looks I was getting from my audience because Elliott took that moment to call Lanie and she took that opportunity to give him a piece of her mind. She did this loudly, for a long time and while alternately pacing and stomping through my living room, kitchen and up and down the hall. Therefore, conversation was difficult but Tabby found the opportunity to explain to my aunt and uncle (when she could be heard) that the raving redhead in my living room earlier was her mother. Tabby also found the opportunity to go into detail about how she felt about her mother and further how gleeful she was she was moving in with her father.

My aunt had to go to her meetings and my uncle had a tee time at the Wiltshire because I might be his favorite niece and we hadn't seen each other for a while but he didn't miss the opportunity to golf. We made plans to meet up later for shopping with Aunt Bette while Uncle Marsh recovered from golf by drinking in the clubhouse and then later, dinner.

Rush and Tabby left soon after Aunt Bette and Uncle Marsh. I got ready to face the day and while I did this Lanie decided she was moving in with me until she figured out what she was going to do. I didn't mind this but it took a while because while she was packing at her place she frequently stopped to take calls from or make calls to Elliott, where she yelled at him loudly or sobbed hysterically.

We finally got her packed and moved in with me

whereupon it was time to go pick up Aunt Bette and go to Cherry Creek Mall. Where Uncle Marsh rarely missed an opportunity to golf, Aunt Bette rarely missed an opportunity to shop.

Which brought me to now, in Nordstrom, with Lanie and Aunt Bette.

"Spill what?" I asked though I knew exactly what.

Aunt Bette's big blue eyes hit me. She knew I knew. Aunt Bette also wasn't a big fan of bullshit.

I bit my lip.

"Are you talking about Tack?" Lanie asked, and Aunt Bette nodded to her and looked back to me.

"Let's start with that. Who's called 'Tack' and why?"

I slapped some hangers on the rack and replied, "Tack's called Tack and I don't know why."

"His kids are in your kitchen and he sticks his tongue down your throat as a good-bye and you don't know why he's called Tack?" Aunt Bette asked, her eyebrows to her hairline.

"Uh…" I mumbled.

"He's her boss," Lanie shared at this juncture, Aunt Bette's eyes got huge as her brows stayed glued to her hairline and her gaze stayed glued to me.

"Uh…" I repeated and Aunt Bette tipped her head to the side in a go-on gesture. I knew I had her undivided attention because she was standing in front of a rack of clothes at Nordstrom and paying no attention to it, but I had nothing more to give.

She looked back at the rack and started slapping hangers but I knew she wasn't looking at the clothes.

"Your uncle and I understood your need to check out, Tyra. Sometimes in people's lives, they need to check out. But I gotta tell you, your uncle isn't fired up about how you're checking back in." She slapped a hanger across the rack. "The tattoos, he could handle." Hanger cracking. "The needing a haircut, he could handle." Another hanging cracking. "The grown kids, he could handle." Another hanger went. "The grown kids cursing freely without him saying a word, he could handle." There was another hanger crash. "The hot and heavy make-out session as a good-bye in front of your uncle and Tack's kids, he could handle." And yet another hanger. "Even his ex shouting the house down, he could handle." No hanger as her eyes cut to me. "All of that together?" She shook her head. "Um...no."

"Things are confusing right now, Aunt Bette," I said quietly, and Aunt Bette's gaze grew sharp.

"I see this," she replied, hesitated then finished, "Clearly."

"I like him," Lanie announced, pulling out a top and holding it down her front as I stared at her in shock. "I think he's lush."

"I thought you wanted me to give notice," I said to her.

She stopped looking down at the top and looked at me. "I did, until he made me pancakes. Now I think he's lush."

That feeling I had that morning swept through me as Aunt Bette muttered, "Gotta say, those pancakes are definitely in the plus category."

I started slapping hangers, declaring, "I can't talk about this."

"Why?" Aunt Bette asked.

I stopped slapping hangers and looked at her. "Because I don't know what to think about it. He's a complicated man. There's too much going on, with him and just with me, and all of it is happening fast. One day, I knew where my life was heading. The minute I woke up, I knew what I would be facing. Two and a half months ago I changed that, and now I don't know what I'm doing, where I'm heading. All I know is, wherever it is, I have to get there. And as for Tack, he can be…" I stopped then started again, "a lot of things. Some of them are good, really good. Some of them are bad, really bad."

"What's bad?" Aunt Bette asked.

I shrugged and started moving hangers. "He's unlike any man I've ever met. He takes bossy to an extreme. I've never experienced anything like it," I answered. "And he has multiple personalities. He can be extremely gentle, thoughtful, warm. Then he can get angry and it's scary. Then he can, I don't know, disappear. He's there, we work together for the most part, but he's not."

"Has he ever handled you the way he handled his ex?" Aunt Bette asked quietly, and I took in a soft breath.

Then I admitted, "If he wants your attention, he finds a way to get it." Aunt Bette's eyes flashed and I hurriedly went on, "But it isn't exactly the same. She's a crazy woman and she makes his life a living hell *and* their kids. You heard it but what you saw is constant for him and they've been divorced for four years. And he said he'd never hurt me and he never has, not that way. He promised that. He said he'd rather cut off his own arm than ever hurt me."

"He said that to you?" Lanie asked.

"Yeah," I answered.

"Wow," she whispered then she looked at Aunt Bette. "He strikes me as a man of his word."

Aunt Bette looked at Lanie then murmured, "Well, that's two in the plus category, not exactly batting a thousand."

Oh boy.

I heard chiming coming from Aunt Bette's purse, she opened it, pulled out her phone and hit some buttons.

Then she hit some more while saying, "That's Marsh. He's done communing with the golfing brotherhood and he's hungry. I need to feed my husband. He says he's at a place called Club and he already has a martini. If we don't get there soon, he's ordering." She hit one last button and I sighed a relieved sigh that this particular conversation was over (for now). She dropped the phone in her purse and looked up at me. "Is this Club place close?"

"Yes, just outside the mall," I answered.

"But we have to drive there seeing as I'm wearing heels, and they have really cool cocktail glasses so it's likely a taxi night anyway since you have one cocktail in a really cool glass, you have to have seven," Lanie explained.

This was totally true and this also obviously worked perfectly fine for Aunt Bette for she nodded once then said, "Let's roll," as a reply.

With no other choice, since when Uncle Marsh was hungry, everyone ate, even I knew that, we left our rack and headed to the parking garage.

We motored through it toward my car since Uncle Marsh had their rental. I headed to the driver's side. Lanie to the passenger side back because Aunt Bette's legs were shorter than mine. And Aunt Bette to the passenger front.

I'd bleeped the locks, doors were opening all around when suddenly and with no warning I saw nothing but black. My body went solid in shocked surprise and I heard a scuffle right before I opened my mouth to scream.

But not a sound came out because I stopped seeing black when *everything* went black.

CHAPTER FOURTEEN

McGyvering

As I LAY on my side on a floor in the dark with my hands bound behind my back, my ankles also bound together, instead of freaking out and visualizing all the possibilities that would bring about what might be my imminent torture, violation and death, I took this time to reflect on why I had never married and why I fell in love with Tack over tequila and sex.

I did this because I wanted to think about Tack who was big and he was strong and he made me feel safe (when he wasn't making me feel unsafe) but mostly he made me feel alive. If there was nothing else to be said about Kane "Tack" Allen, he made me feel alive. Every minute I spent with him from his initial "Hey," to when he kissed me hard and wet and long before he left me that morning, I felt tingling. I felt excitement. I felt fear. I felt pleasure. I felt warmth. And I felt anger. I laughed. I wanted to yell so badly it made me want to explode. I wanted to cry so badly it hurt not to do it.

And I'd been one hundred percent *alive* through all of it.

What I did not want to think about was where Lanie and Aunt Bette were because they were not with me. And also I did not want to think about where I was. And further I did not think of why I might be there. And lastly I did not think about what might become of me because I was worried that what might become of me was that I wouldn't be alive anymore.

Instead, I forced my mind to Tack, a man who was not perfect.

But he'd seemed that way when I met him. He was everything my mind had made up in my daydreams of the man I wanted to be mine since I was fourteen and started having them.

He was handsome. He was strong. He had a beautiful voice and an even more beautiful laugh. And he laughed a lot. He had a light touch and he had a sweet touch and he had a sexy touch. He drank tequila like it was water and ate roasted hog sandwiches like they tasted as good as the finest filet mignon. And when I had his attention, I had all of it. That night at the Chaos party, he made me feel like I was the only one there. He made me feel funny and interesting and beautiful. And when he took me to his bed, he made me feel a lot of other things that were even better.

It felt like, all my life, I'd been living in black and white and didn't realize it and suddenly, across a rowdy biker party, I saw this man and the world filled with vibrant color. It didn't leach in slowly. It slammed in with a *kapow!*

I didn't know that was what I was looking for. I just knew I wasn't going to settle for anything less, not anything less than perfect. I was going to find the man of my daydreams and nothing else would do. So I never got married because I never found him, no one ever brought that color into my life.

Until Tack.

And lying on my side in the dark, bound, I realized that color shot back through my life every time he was filling it. It muted and trickled away when he didn't, but it would burst out bright and beautiful the minute he came into my space.

After all these years, I finally was alive, and now I feared I was going to die.

Tears filled my eyes only moments before I heard the door open and then I heard a thud. I instinctively knew what that thud was. It was a body hitting the floor.

I tensed and the door slammed.

"Who's there?" I called into the darkness.

"Tyra?" Aunt Bette replied.

Thank you, God!

"Aunt Bette." I started squirming toward her voice. "Are you okay?"

"No, I'm not okay. We've been kidnapped and Marsh is drinking martinis and probably flirting with the waitress!" she snapped, and it sounded like she too was moving but not in my direction.

This was likely true. Uncle Marsh flirted. It was harmless but he was hot, hot guys did this even if they were taken. Aunt Bette knew there was no one for him but her and he never flirted where the flirtee would get any sense it was going anywhere. But he was a good-looking man. It was pure instinct to keep those skills sharp.

And anyway, Aunt Bette had been shopping. Uncle Marsh would probably have a three-course dinner and four martinis before he worried where we'd gotten to.

"What happened? Where were you?" I asked.

"I was in a room tied to a chair where they asked me questions about an Elliott Belova. They thought I was Lanie's mother, do not ask me why. A, I don't look a thing like Lanie and B, I'm not old enough to be Lanie's mother!" she stated, sounding more than slightly perturbed and I had to admit, since her A and B were very true, and she'd been tied to a chair, she had a right.

"Elliott is Lanie's fiancé, or was until last night," I informed her as I stopped moving and listened to her continuing to do it.

"I think I got that from her shouting it to him fifteen times on the phone this morning," Aunt Bette returned.

"Right," I muttered.

"What's he into?" she asked.

"Well, according to Tack, the better question is to ask what he *isn't* into," I answered.

"Is Tack involved in this?"

"Um, not until Elliott involved him by asking him to whack the top man in the Russian mob," I explained then hurriedly finished, "He refused, of course."

"Of course," Aunt Bette muttered, still moving around.

"What are you doing?" I asked.

"So we're dealing with the Russian mob here?" she asked back instead of answered.

"I don't know," I answered.

"They had Russian accents," she told me.

"Then yes," I replied, thinking that was a good guess.

"Not good," she whispered and kept moving around.

"Aunt Bette, what are you doing?"

"Trying to find something sharp to cut through these restraints."

I fell silent. I did this because Aunt Bette had also been in the Air Force. That was how Uncle Marsh met her. This was before she "retired," and she did this early then took a contract job working for the Air Force. She told me what she did but it always confused me. She talked in a lot of acronyms like "TDY" and "PCC" and "FIGMO." I didn't speak Air Force acronym so I never knew what she was on about.

It sounded like a desk job. She boiled it down to "human resources" but I always got the sense that she likely wasn't filing away performance evaluations because I'd visited her office before and after she retired and seen how people were around her. There was respect and there was the respect people gave Aunt Bette.

I also fell silent because Aunt Bette had been in an avalanche. No joke. She'd lucked out and had an air pocket once the snow stopped covering her. She also picked the right direction to dig. Further, she used Aunt Bette Secret Skills to find every other member of her skiing party and dug them out too. It took her hours but she didn't stop. She had everyone out and even splinted someone who broke their leg before the rescue people found them. She made the papers. It was big news.

And there was the fact that she was in the Air Force at all. The Air Force didn't attract wusses.

Therefore, I had a feeling Aunt Bette was thinking of taking on the Russian mob.

I finally ended my silence. "Why are you doing that?"

"To get us out."

Oh boy.

"Maybe we should wait until Uncle Marsh figures out we're not coming and raises an alarm," I suggested. "Or maybe someone saw us being abducted from the parking garage and called the police."

"Tyra, this is the Russian mob."

"Yes, I know which is why I think maybe we shouldn't cause a ruckus and make them angry."

"We won't make them angry," she assured me though I wasn't feeling assured.

"Well, I'm thinking, they went to all that trouble to kidnap us, we try to escape, that won't make them happy," I returned.

"Excellent!" she whispered excitedly. "I think I found an exposed nail."

Oh *boy*.

I heard her sawing away at the plastic restraints and tried to push up to sitting, saying, "What about Lanie?"

"We'll get her before we go."

I got to my bottom and stared in the direction of my aunt's voice. "You mean rescue *then* escape?"

"Of course," she replied like I was a dim bulb.

"Aunt Bette!" I hissed. "We don't know where we are. We have no weapons—"

"I'll figure out something."

Wonderful. Visions of Aunt Bette McGyvering an explosive with that exposed nail, some lint from her pocket and spit filled my head just as the door opened quickly and shut just as quickly.

I went still and I heard nothing but booted feet moving on the floor. Aunt Bette had wisely stopped sawing away at the plastic restraints.

"You're safe," a deep voice growled. "I'm Hawk. I'm getting you out of here. Be quiet, be smart and do what I say. Yeah?"

Oh thank God.

Since he told us to be quiet, and he sounded like he knew what he was doing as well as a little scary, I was debating whether or not to answer with a "yeah" when Aunt Bette said, "Plastic restraints, wrists and ankles."

I heard movement, more movement, some more, then I felt strong fingers close on my wrist then both were free, movement at my side and then my ankles were free.

Hallelujah.

I rubbed my wrists and heard Aunt Bette ask, "Do you have an extra weapon?"

"This is gonna go quiet. No heroes. 'Specially not ones who don't know what the fuck they're doin'."

Aunt Bette replied with, "I know you. JTF Able Promise. I'm Lieutenant Colonel Bette Mansfield, retired."

Silence for a beat then, "Right."

There was more movement then I heard the sounds I heard on TV when people were fiddling with a gun.

Oh boy. I had a feeling the dude called Hawk spoke Air Force acronym but I didn't know if this was good or bad.

"You good?" Hawk asked.

"Talk to me," Aunt Bette ordered, sounding curt, bossy and scarily like she knew exactly what she was doing.

Oh boy!

"Neutralized the boys outside. No guard on this door. Two boys on the first floor. Two with your girl who's on the second floor."

Oh God. What were they doing to Lanie?

"You have backup?" Aunt Bette asked.

"Called it, the boys we're dealing with, couldn't wait. Right now it's just me. Plan is, I get you out safe, I go back for the girl. My backup should be here by then."

"Works for me," Aunt Bette stated.

"It doesn't work for me," I butted in. "We need to get Lanie."

"Quiet," Hawk ordered.

"No, seriously, this is the Russian mob. They might be—"

My mouth was covered with a big hand and how he hit the target with such accuracy in the dark was beyond me.

"Quiet," he growled, took his hand away and ordered, "Everyone up. Let's go."

I pushed myself to my feet feeling achy and stiff from being tied up and lying on the floor for so long. But I didn't take the time to stretch. The door opened and I felt Aunt

Bette grab my hand. She pulled me out the door into a dark, unlit hall.

We walked about five feet then I heard Aunt Bette whisper, "Stairs," right before I tripped up the first couple of them.

I righted my footing and moved up the stairs. Hawk opened a door and late evening sun showed through. It also showed on Hawk, who was tall, built, dark-haired, wearing a skin-tight gray tee and black cargo pants, and if I hadn't seen all the gorgeousness that was Tack our rescuer would be far and away the most handsome man I'd laid eyes on in my life. One word: *hawt*.

As hot as he was, he was also carrying a gun, surveying the area outside the door, giving us a nod and moving forward agilely and alertly. Aunt Bette had a gun too and Lanie was somewhere with two of the bad guys so I had no time to appreciate how hot he was.

Aunt Bette gave me a head gesture that told me to precede her, I did, following Hawk. We made it through the room, out the door and across a lawn with no incident. We stopped under a long, very tall, solid fence.

He looked down at me. "I'll give you a lift up. You're gonna have to pull yourself over. Drop down to the other side. Soft knees when you land. Fall to your side immediately and roll outta the way."

He didn't say, "Yeah?" to ask if I got it, he just linked his hands and bent so I was guessing time was of the essence.

Therefore, I didn't hesitate. I put my hands to his shoulders and my foot in his hands. I had misgivings about this mostly because I had limited upper body strength so I had the feeling there was no way I was going to be able to pull myself over that tall fence.

I didn't have to worry. Hawk didn't give me a lift up. He

gave me a *lift up*. Well past his waist, straight to his shoulders, boosting me with such strength and speed, he nearly hurled me over the wall. I was on my belly on the wall before I knew it. I swung my legs around and dropped down, soft knees, fell to my side and rolled.

Wow. Easy.

Not two seconds later, Aunt Bette followed me doing the same thing except hers was practiced, thus cooler like it wasn't the first time she did it. Or the second.

I was thinking I now had proof Aunt Bette had secret ways when she grabbed my hand and pulled me aside as Hawk followed her. Then he moved and we moved with him. The fence ran along the side of a sleepy road, sleepy as in no traffic. There was a black SUV some ways away from where we jumped over the fence. Hawk bleeped the locks. I went to the passenger side back, Aunt Bette to the front passenger seat.

"Down, no one sees you," Hawk ordered.

"Copy that, but do you have a secure phone? I need to call my husband," Aunt Bette replied.

"Glove compartment," Hawk answered, turned and through the gathering darkness another commando showed, Hispanic, shorter and leaner than Hawk. He didn't speak. Hawk nodded to him, turned and nodded to Aunt Bette, his eyes sliced through me and then he and the other commando moved away.

I scrambled into the SUV. So did Aunt Bette. I got low. So did Aunt Bette. I heard her searching the glove box, I heard beeping noises then I heard her talking to Uncle Marsh.

But all I thought about was Lanie. I was safe now. I was breathing. I was unhurt. The same with Aunt Bette. I just hoped with all I had that when our rescuers returned with Lanie, they'd do it in one piece and she'd be in the same condition. Then I was going to hunt down Elliott my own damned self and wring his neck.

"Tyra?" Aunt Bette called when she beeped off the phone.

"Yeah," I whispered.

"It's gonna be okay," she whispered back.

I bit my lip.

Then I said, "I'm sorry, Aunt Bette."

"You didn't kidnap me and tie me to a chair."

This was true.

We fell silent. Several minutes later, the door opposite me opened and Hawk deposited Lanie in the seat. I twisted and looked up at her, automatically reaching out to grab her hand.

"You okay?" I asked.

"No." Her voice trembled.

Oh God.

"Did they hurt you?" I asked.

"No." Her voice trembled more.

"Honey—" I started, but Hawk was folding in the driver's seat and he interrupted me.

"Debrief later," he ordered, started up the car and we took off.

I wanted to ask who he was, how he knew we were there and why he'd rescued us, but he scared me a little bit seeing as he obviously wasn't the police and entered an uncertain situation somewhat heavily armed. Not to mention, he could scale a twelve-foot wall without anyone giving him a leg up.

Since I figured Aunt Bette knew what she was doing, and she also kept her silence, I followed suit and held Lanie's hand squeezing tight. She didn't squeeze tight back and I heard a hitch in her breath so I knew she was crying.

I bit my lip again.

That was when I heard it, the familiar roar of Harleys. I turned and looked out the back window as I heard Hawk mutter, "What the fuck?"

I was right, Harleys and a lot of them. I saw Tack up front and it took everything I had not to cry out with joy or burst into relieved tears.

He'd been coming for me. Maybe he *was* the perfect man.

"One of you belong to Chaos?" Hawk asked.

"Um...I think that would be me," I answered.

Aunt Bette twisted her neck and looked at me through the two front seats.

From her look, I was seeing that during our Nordstrom talk I probably should have told her Tack was the president of a motorcycle club. However, I didn't expect us all to be kidnapped and then have Tack, and what looked like the entire club, come to my rescue (after an unknown commando rescued us, that was).

I looked out the windows and saw the Harleys overtaking the SUV, three bikes closing in at the front, two positioning on each side of the SUV, more at the back. I saw brake lights on the Harleys that held Tack, Brick and Dog in front of us, all of them coming on simultaneously as if they had biker brainwave synchronicity.

"Fuck," Hawk muttered on an annoyed growl, then he slowed and moved to the narrow shoulder. He didn't try to evade them. He just stopped, commanded, "Don't move," into the cab and knifed out.

I watched as he met Tack in front of the SUV. There was a boot-to-boot, nose-to-nose conversation that didn't look happy. Then Tack's head jerked to the SUV, Hawk's head turned and he looked our way. Then he lifted his chin and Tack instantly moved away from him, prowling to my side.

I had my hand on the door handle but before I could open it, it was opened for me. Then I found myself yanked out to my feet, the door was slammed and I was shoved back against it.

I lifted my eyes to his face, about to throw my arms around his shoulders and maybe dissolve into tears or perhaps declare that I was falling in love with him again because he turned my world to color and he'd been coming for me when his hand weirdly lifted to wrap around the front of my throat like he was preparing to strangle me and all movement and declarations of love died at this aggressive gesture.

"They touch you?" he barked, his tone sharp with what I belatedly saw in his face.

Rage.

I shook my head fighting the urge to shrink back. "No, not really, they…they just…just, hooded me, made me go unconscious, bound me and put me in a room. They did something to Lanie though."

With a quickness that stunned me, he let me go, jerked his head at Dog who was standing beside him, and then I watched him round the back of the SUV. Dog had hold of me by my upper arm and was dragging me toward his bike but I had my head turned and I watched Tack open Lanie's door and yank her out.

Uh…what?

Dog tugged me to a stop by his bike and threw a leg over it.

"Climb on," he ordered.

I kept staring at Tack who was now dragging Lanie to his bike.

Why was he dragging Lanie to his bike? Brick or Dog could take care of Lanie. Tack was supposed to take care of me. Wasn't he? I mean, just that morning he'd declared me his woman. Didn't he?

"Cherry, climb on," Dog repeated, but I couldn't tear my eyes away from Tack who was already on his bike, and Lanie, who was climbing on behind him.

"Cherry…"

I looked back at the SUV in time to see Hawk driving away with Aunt Bette who was giving me a sharp look incongruously mixed with a finger wave.

"Hey," I whispered, feeling the need to say something like "thanks" to Hawk or "Where the hell are you taking my aunt?" but not able to get anything more out and not knowing what the hell was happening.

"Cherry, get your ass on my bike," Dog demanded. My head swung back just in time to see Tack, with Lanie on his bike, arms tight around his middle, cheek to his shoulder, take off on a roar.

Bile filled my throat.

"Cherry—"

My eyes sliced to Dog.

"Right," I murmured, then I climbed on the back of Dog's bike.

CHAPTER FIFTEEN

Three Hours

I WOKE WHEN I felt hands turning me and my first thought was panic. Not exactly panic, as such. *Extreme* panic.

Therefore, I pulled violently free from the hands and scooted swiftly across the bed. Too swiftly and too panicked. I landed on my ass on the floor, cracking my head against the nightstand.

I didn't react to either of these things. I heard movement on the bed so I twisted and scuttled backward on hands and feet like a crab except not sideways. I hit wall and pushed up as the dim light coming from streetlamps filled the room and I saw a big, shadowed man heading my way.

I raised my hand to ward him off, his chest hit it, hands spanning my hips and I heard, "Baby, you're safe. It's me."

Tack. It was Tack. Not a bad guy there to hood me and hurt me but Tack.

I relaxed and the panic slid out of me.

Earlier, Dog had taken me to the Chaos Compound, dragged me with a hand on my upper arm to Tack's room and he'd locked me in. Not a word of explanation. Not a, "Have you eaten?" Not a, "Don't worry about your beloved aunt and best friend, all is well." He just walked out, locked me in and I heard his booted feet walk away.

Now it was the dead of night and Tack was back from whatever he did with Lanie. Not me. Lanie.

Reminded of this, my hand stopped going slack at the knowledge that nothing else terrifying was happening to me, it strengthened and tried to push.

Tack wasn't in the mood to be pushed away. I knew this because he leaned into my hand and my elbow buckled at the pressure just as the pads of his fingers bit into my flesh.

"Tack—" I started to say, what, I did not know, but he cut me off.

"Three hours," he growled.

These words were so strange, said in a growl so low it was almost guttural, and his tone had changed so significantly from his previous quiet words, I stopped putting pressure on my hand and blinked at him in the shadows.

"Pardon?"

My arm got crushed between our bodies when he invaded my space and his hands slid up my hips, into my shirt, pulling it up, skin to skin.

"Three hours," he repeated, his voice still that fierce, guttural rumble that kind of scared me and I didn't know why. It was like the tone communicated that he was trying to control something, some emotion, and he was failing.

"Three hours?" I asked.

His shadowy face got close to mine. "Yeah, Red. Three. *Fuckin'*. Hours."

Then his hands flew up, taking my top with it with such force I had no choice but to lift my arms. It was gone for nary a second when his fingers gripped me at the waist, I was up, twisted and he was walking, taking me with him. Then as quickly as I was up, I was down on my back in Tack's bed and he was on top of me.

All this happened and I didn't even have a chance to take a breath.

My hands went to his shoulders. "Tack—"

"Three hours."

"Why are you saying—?"

I didn't finish my question, his mouth crushed down on mine and there was no gentle coaxing to open for his tongue. It spiked out, forcing itself between my lips and then it was in my mouth. His kisses could be hungry, they could be demanding, but he'd never kissed me like this. No one had ever kissed me like this. I didn't even know you *could* kiss like this. It drained me dry at the same time it filled me up. Filled me full of what, I wasn't sure except all of it was good.

Then his fingers were in my bra. Pulling the cup down, they curved around the bottom of my breast and lifted it. His mouth released mine and he twisted his torso down and sucked my nipple into his mouth, hard.

"Oh God," I moaned as the heady sensations tore through me, my hands lifted, fingers sifting into his hair to hold him to me.

His other hand went to my shorts. He unbuckled my belt, unbuttoned the top button and pulled the zip down maybe half an inch before his hand was in, sliding through the instant wetness his mouth at my nipple created. His middle finger slid through, I gasped and then stopped breathing when it filled me.

Then it started moving as Tack released my nipple and demanded, "Get your other tit ready for me."

I didn't hesitate. He sucked my nipple back into his mouth, more wetness surged between my legs and my hand left his head, my fingers went to the other cup of my bra and pulled it down. Then my hand curved around the underside and his head shifted, his finger between my legs still moving, he sucked my other nipple sharply into his mouth as his finger and thumb rolled the one his mouth left behind.

God. *God.* Amazing.

My hips bucked and my back arched. Then my hips moved with his hand, fast, hard, demanding.

His mouth left my nipple and came to mine.

"Greedy," he growled, fingers at my nipple and between my legs still working.

"Yes," I whispered.

"You want more?"

"Yes."

"Now?"

"Yes, now."

"What do you want, Tyra?"

My arms moved around his shoulders, my hips still moving with his hand. "Your cock, Tack, I want your cock," I breathed against his lips.

His hands left me instantly then the zipper on my shorts zipped down. Tack tore them off, taking my panties with them.

He got on his knees between my legs and I watched him tug off his tee and toss it aside as I lifted up, my hands moving directly to his jeans. I opened them and tugged them down his hips, my eyes glued through the shadows to the beauty of him.

"Lie back, spread wide for me, baby," he ordered, my head tipped back and my mouth went dry with want.

Then I did as I was told, lying back and spreading my legs wide, and at first Tack didn't move. He just kneeled between my legs and I felt his eyes on me. Then he leaned in, put a hand in the bed beside me, arm straight. He lifted the other hand and trailed his fingers from my throat, down my chest, between my breasts, down my ribs, belly, down, sliding between my legs.

"Tack," I whispered, my voice urgent, my hips lifting to deepen his touch.

His finger slid inside and a moan slid out of my throat.

"Greedy cunt," he muttered and his thumb hit me right where I needed it, my body jolted and my neck arched. "My girl's got a greedy cunt."

I didn't respond. His thumb was moving. It felt good, unbelievably good, *fantastic*. So good, I was close to climax.

"Look at me, Red."

I dipped my chin, tried to focus on him as his thumb went away but the tip of his cock slid inside.

"Yes," I breathed, grinding down and taking him inside.

The minute I did, his body covered mine and he started moving, fast, hard, rough and deep.

"Yes, baby," I breathed in his ear, "fuck me."

My hips moved with his thrusts, my knees lifting, thighs tucking tight to his sides, my hands slid down his back so my fingers could dig into his hard ass.

God, he felt good. So good. And he was good at it. Great. Unbelievable. No one better. No one.

I felt his teeth nip the skin of my neck and it arched as that and his driving cock took me, already primed, crashing over the edge.

One of my hands released his ass and lifted, grasping his hair as I cried out. I lifted my hips, wrapping my legs around his back. I held on as he rode me through my orgasm, harder, harder, my body jolting, my limbs tightening, the beautiful pressure released only to build again instantly.

"You're done and your pussy wants more," he growled in

my ear, his hands spanning my hips, yanking me up to meet his deepening thrusts.

"Yes..." I gasped through his grunts as I started coming again, the beauty of it rolling over me, *"yes."*

My neck arched and my heels dug in his back as I lifted my hips further and he drove harder.

I was coming down, holding him tight, Tack thrusting deep, grunting with the effort, my tongue at the skin of his neck when his rhythm changed, slowed, but all the power of him shifted to his hips as he pounded hard and his grunts turned to groans.

Then he stopped, buried deep inside me, and gave me his weight. I liked his weight, his warmth, his smell, his body connected to mine and I held on tighter.

In my life, I'd had five lovers, and I had chosen them all carefully. I thought all were close enough to perfect before I took them to my bed. And none of them gave me what Tack gave me. Not even close.

He shifted some of his weight to a forearm in the bed as his other hand drifted up the skin of my side and with his lips at my ear he whispered, "Three hours."

My limbs convulsed and I whispered back, "Why do you keep saying that?"

He lifted his head and I felt his eyes on my face through the darkness. "That's how long they had you."

I forgot how to breathe.

Tack did not. He spoke. "They're gonna bleed."

It was a vow.

My body went as still as my lungs.

He went on. "Rivers of blood."

That was a vow too.

Oh. My. God.

"Tack—" I forced out.

His body shifted slightly to the side and his hand curled around my throat like it did outside Hawk's SUV. His fingers flexed in but the touch was light.

His tone was not.

"They took you," he stated.

"Yes, but—"

He interrupted me. "They hooded you."

"I know, but listen—"

"They touched you."

"Well, only to—"

"They bound you."

"Uh..."

"They scared you."

"This is true, but—"

"No," he ground out, his fingers flexing deeper into my throat, no pressure, no pain, his word final, his touch communicating the same—no response necessary.

My hand went to his cheek and I whispered, "Handsome."

It was like I didn't even talk. Tack stayed on target. "Had Roscoe on you. They clocked him with the butt of a gun. Six stitches. Shoulda put Hopper on you. Brick. No one would get the jump on Hop or Brick."

"Roscoe?"

"Recruit. Not fresh, he's been around a while. Smart kid. Seen some action. Done his part. Thought he'd do good. Fucked up."

Oh boy, I was worried about the unknown Roscoe and his six stitches but I was worried more about Tack and his fury.

"Tack, you need to let me—"

"No," he cut me off yet again. "I'll explain, Red. You belong to Chaos. *No one* touches what belongs to Chaos. *No one*. They don't touch it. They don't hood it. They don't bind it. They don't even breathe in its space unless they have Chaos permission."

Um. I had to admit, I liked that he was protective. I even liked that he was overprotective.

But it must be said I wasn't feeling the love for being referred to as an "it."

I thought it wasn't the brightest move to inform him of that fact in his current mood so I kept on my current target in hopes of getting through. "Please let me—"

"You gotta get that, Red. And I swear to fuckin' *Christ*, they're gonna get it."

I stared into his shadowy face and whispered, "You're scaring me again, Tack."

His fingers flexed into my throat again before his hand slid up, palm cupping my jaw, fingers wrapped around my neck and ear and his face came closer, his lips touching mine before he moved back.

"*You* shouldn't be scared. The point I'm makin' is that *you* should never be scared. But I promise, 'cause of this shit, someone's gonna feel fear. It just ain't gonna be you. Not again. Not ever again. Not for three hours, Tyra, not for three fuckin' minutes."

"Tack—"

"I'm not inviting discussion, babe, I'm sayin' it like it is."

"Tack!" I snapped, coming to my end. I slapped his arm to get his attention and demanded, "Listen to me!"

"What?"

He waited and I didn't know what to say.

Then I inquired, "If I ask nice, can I talk you out of rivers of blood?"

"Fuck no."

Firm. Resolute.

Damn.

"Okay then, if I ask nice, will you explain the concept of 'rivers of blood' so perhaps I can plan how long I'll need to visit you in the penitentiary?"

This was met with silence. Then Tack buried his face in my neck and burst into laughter. He slid out of me, his arms wrapped around me and he rolled to his back so I was on top and I felt him buck his hips as he jerked up his jeans.

I didn't find anything funny.

And I decided to inform him of this fact by lifting my head to stare down at him and explaining, "See, I figure you're commencing Operation Rivers of Blood because I was scared but mostly you're commencing Operation Rivers of Blood because you're a badass, scary biker dude who feels the need to piss around his property. Therefore, when you're sent down for twenty-five to life, I feel I should probably express my appreciation by visiting you for a year, maybe two, before I find myself an accountant who only utters the words 'rivers of blood' while referring to, say, a movie or book of that title."

Without buttoning his fly, his arms came back around me and gave me a squeeze, his head lifted, his mouth touched my neck to give me a light kiss and then he dropped his head back on another arm squeeze and muttered an amused, "Babe."

I was still not amused. "It's likely said movie or book title will be the true life story of Chaos MC and its president wreaking vengeance on the Russian mob in Denver." I paused then finished, "Sorry to say, it doesn't have a happy ending."

He chuckled.

I glared.

Then I asked, "Is Lanie okay?"

"Shaken up and rethinking her vow never to get back

together with Belova again because the shit they told her they were gonna do to him shook her up more than you all gettin' kidnapped did. So now she says she wants to move with him to Sri Lanka or wherever the fuck. But other than that, they didn't have time to do more before Hawk ended their party."

Well, that was a relief.

"And Aunt Bette?"

"Hawk took her to your uncle. Reported in and apparently your aunt's made of steel. Even fuckin' Hawk Delgado was all about respect when he talked about her."

Definitely Aunt Bette had secret ways.

I kept up my interrogation. "And why am I here?"

"Because you're Chaos. They ain't Chaos, darlin'."

"Let's explore that," I suggested. "I'm Chaos?"

"Was my dick just in you?"

I fought an annoyed growl and said, "Uh . . . yeah."

"Then you're Chaos."

"Is that all it takes?"

"That and pizza and puttin' up with your attitude and watchin' movies with you that make you cry, yeah, that's all it takes."

That was certainly interesting but I had other things I needed to explore.

Therefore, I moved on.

"What was that with Lanie?" I asked.

"What was what with Lanie?" was his uninformative response.

"Well, I'm naked in bed with you, who's mostly naked. I work for you. I fight with you. I watched a movie with you, actually two, almost three. You brought me pizza—"

He cut in to demand, "Get to the point, darlin'."

"You made her pancakes," I stated on what sounded like an accusation because, well, it kind of was.

"So?"

"That's it."

"And?"

"Well, I think, should you happen upon our rescue vehicle after we've been kidnapped, considering all that, it should get to be me who rides away on the back of your bike with you, not Lanie."

I saw the white flash of teeth surrounded by his dark goatee indicating he was smiling and got another squeeze before he whispered, "Jealous?"

Um... *hell* no.

So hell no, I was so pissed, I managed to yank straight out of his arms and I rolled. I got to my feet beside the bed righting my bra as I went in search of my underwear and shorts.

"Babe, get back in bed."

"No, I'm going home."

"Unh-unh, you're gonna stop bein' stupid and get your ass back in my bed."

Uh... what did he just say? Stupid?

Hell no again!

I found my shorts and panties, separated them and started to tug my panties on. I did not succeed in this endeavor because Tack's fingers jerked them from mine and he tossed them across the room. I watched their lightness flit through the dark and settle. I straightened, turned to Tack and then his fingers closed around my wrist and he jerked again, *me* this time. I went sailing, landing on him. He rolled us to our sides, his hands went into my pits and he hauled me up the bed then he rolled on top of me.

"Get off me, Tack."

"Like I said, stop bein' stupid." He didn't have to repeat the get back into bed part since he planted me there.

"Get off me."

"Red—"

I lifted my head an inch off his pillow and hissed, "Do not play my best friend against me. That is *not* cool."

This was met with silence and even though I was angry and felt I had a right to be, his silence was angry and it was scary.

Then he spoke. "No, Tyra, what is not cool is you thinkin' for one fuckin' second I'd do that."

"You yourself just taunted me with 'jealous?'" I mimicked his low, gravelly voice on the last word and the scary angry vibe ratcheted up about twelve levels on the scary and angry scale.

"I was teasin' you. I didn't think you actually believed I'd do somethin' that fucked up."

"Okay then, what's the deal with you taking off with her?"

"The deal with me takin' off with her is the reason you and your aunt got taken was because of her. They didn't want you. But these guys are lethal, serious as shit. They do not mess around, they do not care about collateral damage and they'll take every advantage they can get and suck it dry. They didn't want you but they would have used you if they needed to. Not gonna fuckin' happen. I told you this shit leaks, and it leaked. So for your protection, and hers, she needed to be locked down. I locked her down."

I had a lot of questions, including what the heck "locked down" meant, but I prioritized them quickly and out of my mouth came, "Do you mind explaining to me why it was *you* who needed to lock her down?"

"Do you mind explainin' to me why you're questioning why it was me?"

This was a good question I wasn't prepared to answer.

And the reason I wasn't prepared to answer it was because it hit me just then that he was right even though he'd been teasing. I was jealous. I was jealous of my own best friend. And acting like a moron. Acting like a moron in a variety of ways including the fact that I'd just had sex with Tack again. I didn't even think about it, not that he gave me a chance, but even so, I didn't think about it. I just did it and I liked it... a lot.

What was going on with me?

Having been kidnapped and having used Tack and how I felt about him as the way to keep my head straight while said kidnapping was happening and having just had sex with him, I felt it was time, finally, to figure that out.

Therefore, I ventured cautiously, "Um...perhaps we should discuss our relationship."

"Yeah, we'll discuss it by me tellin' you you're pretty fuckin' lucky right now seein' as I just came and came hard 'cause 'a you and that greedy pussy of yours so I'm feelin' patient," he stated, not sounding patient, not in the slightest. "So, since I'm feelin' patient, I'll take the time to explain even more shit to you. And the shit I'm gonna explain is that you do not tie a man like me down. You do not do that, Tyra. You try that shit, you'll find yourself cut loose."

It seemed pretty clear when I ventured cautiously, I didn't venture cautiously enough.

Therefore, I ventured even more cautiously when I told him, "I'm, um...uncertain what you mean by tying you down."

"Givin' me that shit about playin' you and your friend, askin' me to explain myself. I do what I do and you gotta trust that I'll do right by you. You tie me tight to you so I can't breathe, I'll find a way to get loose."

"Am I..." I found the need to swallow, so I did and tried again. "Am I tied to you?"

"Not yet and I gotta tell you, with this bullshit, I'm rethinkin' the hold I got on those strings."

Uh...

Ouch.

That hurt. It hurt so much I felt my chest jerk back into the bed like he'd dealt a body blow. But even as my body responded to his verbal strike, my brain didn't recover.

Yes, that's how much it hurt.

I was venturing cautiously. Things were weird and wild and confusing and happening too fast and they needed to be sorted out.

Tack was definitely not venturing cautiously. Tack was being Tack, laying it out and being honest about it, brutally honest.

But he'd never been *intentionally* brutal to the point of being mean.

And no woman needed mean no matter if it came with honest.

Therefore, I whispered, "I want you to get off me, Tack."

"I'm not gettin' off you, Tyra. I'm pissed and you're... whatever the fuck you are and we're talkin' this shit out. You're not gonna hide away, lick your wounds and think up more shit, that, mind, is pure shit, to hold me back."

"I'm not sure you get this but I'm not certain I want to hold onto your strings either," I said quietly.

"Right, that you just came twice?"

"Pardon?"

"Babe, I asked, you didn't hesitate to spread wide for me. I told you that mornin' you started workin' for me, I touched you, you'd spread wide and you did. You give attitude, darlin', I enjoy it. It works. You got a way of dishin' it out that makes me go hard and part 'a the reason I go hard is I know, I get in there, it's gonna be worth puttin' up with your mouth.

But what I do *not* enjoy is this cat-and-mouse bullshit you got goin' on."

"Cat-and-mouse bullshit?"

"Hot for me one second, cold the next. Sweet then tart. You need more?"

"Has it occurred to you that this whole thing is a bit confusing for me?" I inquired.

"No shit?" he fired back. "Has it occurred to you I get that and that's why I'm always explainin' shit to you? Which, while we're talkin', I'm just sayin', is gettin' tired."

Another verbal blow, direct hit, and the hurt spread.

I stared at him through the dark. Then I turned my head away and closed my eyes tight.

"Look at me, Red," he demanded.

"Get off me, Tack," I replied quietly.

"I said, look at me."

I looked at him and felt his eyes on me. Then his hand curled around my jaw and his tone gentled when he spoke again.

"Baby—"

It was me who cut Tack off this time and I did it by whispering, "No," then I turned my face away again.

His fingers brought me right back and when he had my eyes, he whispered, "Darlin'—"

"I want to go home."

"You're not goin' home."

"Please take me home."

"Baby, it's after three in the morning. I'm not takin' you home."

"Then I'll get a taxi."

"Tyra—"

I lifted a hand, wrapped my fingers around his wrist tight and whispered, "I want to go home."

His hand moved so his palm was against my jaw again and he whispered back, "You're pissed."

"No, I just want to go home."

"Baby, this shit's ever gonna work, we gotta be able to talk."

"Tack, I've just decided I don't *want* this shit to work."

"Jesus, Tyra—"

"No!" I cried, shaking my head. "No one has ever talked to me that way. I don't like it. It's not nice."

"It's not nice, Red, but it's real."

"Well, real *hurts*," I returned, then felt tears fill my eyes and I couldn't see him very well and I didn't know if he could see me but I didn't want him to see me cry. So I let him go, pulled my face away and tried to slide out from under him but both his arms wrapped around me. He turned to his side, pulling me into him. I pressed my hands against his chest and exclaimed, "Stop it! If I want to go, I should be able to just go!"

Then my breath hitched and he had to have heard it. It was loud and I knew he knew I was crying.

Damn it!

I dipped my chin and shoved harder at his chest but his arms just got tighter and he threw a heavy thigh over my legs.

"Calm down, baby," he whispered.

"Let me go," I whispered back.

"Calm down a second."

I bucked hard against his arms and shouted through my tears, "Let me go!"

"You need to settle and get it out," he told me and I stilled then my tears stopped coming and my head snapped back to look into his face.

"I do?" I asked sarcastically. "Is that what I need to do,

Tack? You know? Do you know what I need to do? Have you been hooded? Kidnapped? Bound? Have you ever lain in a dark room with your aunt, who you love like crazy, somewhere you don't know where she is? Same with your best friend, who you love just as much? Have you lain there wondering what would become of you? Has that happened? Because if it has, then I'll know you've got experience so I should listen to you and know how to behave."

"Tyra—" he started, but I kept going.

"I don't know what to do with you. So if you think I'm hot and cold, that's because *you* can be really nice and really not so nice so I'm just going with *your* flow. I've never known a man like you and I don't know what to make of you. Because the nice seems worth it and then, like just now, you're really, *really* not nice and I don't know what to do."

His hand slid up, fingers sifting into my hair, and he muttered, "Baby—"

I kept right on talking. "So if I'm taxing your patience, Tack, my apologies. I know what could help out with that. You could let me get out of your bed, get dressed, go home and quit my job so you won't see me again. Right now, I have to say, that works for me because when you get angry and impatient, your words hurt, and you don't know me enough to know if I can withstand that so let me explain something *to you*. I can't and I don't want any part of it. And that is not me running cold on you and playing games, Tack. That's me being *real*."

After I finished speaking Tack was silent but, I will point out, he was silent while not letting me go.

Then he murmured a question to the room because he certainly wasn't asking me, "What'd I get into when I got into this with you?"

But it was me who answered, "It doesn't matter because, if you'd just *let me go*, we're both out of it."

His hand slid from the back of my head to my face, taking my hair with it and he whispered, "You think about our Saturdays, baby, and what we had just now and you tell me that me lettin' you go is what you need, and you mean it, I'll let you go."

"I need you to let me go," I stated instantly.

"Fuckin' hell," he was still whispering, "you didn't even think about it."

"You told me you'd rather cut off your own arm than hurt me, Tack, and you just hurt me. Hurt is more than physical pain. You dished it out not knowing if I could take it. And I can't. That's you and that's me. You have to be you and you can't be you around me without me getting chewed up in the process, so no. I don't need to think about it because I know it's going to happen again and I don't want that in my life."

"You're right, Red, I can only be me but I'll tell you this then I'll let you go and you can leave or you can stay in this bed with me. I don't know you and you don't know me. But I know now I gotta handle you with more care and what you gotta trust is that I can do that. I let you loose and you roll outta my bed, that's tellin' me you don't trust me. But I'll say it straight. You can trust me to handle you with care. Now, baby," his arms went loose and his voice dipped low, "you decide."

I rolled immediately to my back away from him then to my side. Pushing up to sitting, I threw my legs over the side of the bed. My feet hit the floor and I moved quickly to my panties. Snatching them up, I yanked them up my legs.

They were blue. Pale blue with delicate pale green lace. The color combination was striking. I thought that when I bought them. Now, even in the dark, their shades muted, I could still see the colors.

I settled them on my hips and stared at the wall opposite

me, my hands lifting, my fingers sliding into the sides of my hair, nails scratching my scalp.

Colors, vibrant colors sifted through my brain. Tack's sapphire blue eyes. Tabby's matching ones. The bright, cherry red of the car he was working on. The purple of the flowers in the field that Celie and Nettie played in in *The Color Purple*. The embroidery at the back of Lanie's robe.

Vibrant.

Tack had been in this room maybe half an hour, forty-five minutes tops, and I'd had two orgasms, I'd made him laugh, I'd been angry, I'd been scared and I'd felt protected. Alive through every minute of it. Vibrantly alive.

I dropped my hands and wrapped my arms around my middle.

Oh God. Could I go back to black and white?

Then his words came back to me, not just the hurtful ones he just spoke, others. He lived in a different world and I had to fit into that world, he told me so himself. And, frankly, his world was more than a little scary. He asked me to trust him but he was who he was. He wasn't seventeen and becoming a man. He was...I didn't know how old but he sure as hell was not seventeen.

He was the man he was going to be. There was no more growing, no more learning. He was there.

I hadn't known him long but I knew enough about him, about *men*, that I knew he would expect me to shift and change and be who he needed me to be. He'd expect it like all men expected it because women did that shit all the time. But he was who he was and I had to take him as he was, shift and change into his life, and I had to make the decision now. Take him as he came and live in color but do it in *his world*, giving up my own. Or go back to black and white and hope my real dream man would come and color my world again.

I made my heartbreaking decision, dropped my hands from my hair, bent and grabbed my shorts, muttering, "I'll call a taxi."

I was pulling up my shorts while hearing movement in the bed. And I was just about to search for my shirt when two arms slid around me from behind, one at my ribs, one at my chest, both pulling my back into Tack's hard, warm front.

I felt the tickle of Tack's goatee on the skin of my neck where he murmured, "Baby, you aren't makin' the right decision."

Feeling his arms around me, the tickle of his goatee, I had second thoughts.

But my mouth didn't.

"I need to go."

"Don't fuck up, Tyra," he warned and I pulled in breath.

Then I quietly told the shadowy wall, "You don't know this because you didn't ask but I jumped off a roller coaster, Tack, one that was out of control, and jumping off that took me to Ride. I don't need to get off one and jump right back onto another. I have to get off the roller coaster."

His arms gave me a squeeze and his lips still at my neck moved. "Tell me about your roller coaster, darlin'."

"Too late," I whispered. "Too late to ask now, Tack."

He was silent a moment then he whispered back, "Don't do this, baby."

"Let me go." I was still whispering. "I need to go."

He didn't let me go. Not for long, breathtaking moments.

Then he did.

He let me go.

I felt tears clog my throat but I rushed through the dark room to tag my tee.

As I was pulling it over my head, I heard his gravelly voice say, "I'll get one of the boys to take you home."

There it was. It was done.

Done.

Oh God.

I yanked the tee down and, with difficulty, swallowed the tears that were threatening to choke me. Then I asked softly, "Can Lanie call me tomorrow?"

Tack's voice was remote when he replied, "I'll get her that word."

"Thank you," I whispered, watching him moving toward the door.

"One 'a the boys will be in to get you," he told me, striding out the door.

"Thank you," I repeated quietly to the door.

But Tack was gone.

CHAPTER SIXTEEN

You Matter

IT WAS AFTERNOON the next day and I was sitting on my deck, Uncle Marsh at my side, and he was telling me stories of growing up with my mom in Ohio. Aunt Bette was sitting at the bar in my kitchen, her fingers flying over the keyboard of her super-slim laptop, taking care of business even though it was Saturday. Mostly, she was giving me and Uncle Marsh alone time. But from my experience, Aunt Bette shut down approximately thirty minutes before she conked out for the night. All other times she was on the go, working, scrapbooking, shopping, serial communicating with family and friends and generally making everyone around her tired just by watching her.

She was, not surprisingly, none the worse for wear after being kidnapped. What was surprising was that she and Uncle Marsh were happy to let the kidnapping rest in Hawk Delgado's hands with no police interference.

"Hawk knows what he's doing," Aunt Bette muttered then charged into my kitchen to set up her super-slim laptop.

Apparently, Aunt Bette had been briefed. Also apparently, she didn't intend to fill me in.

I was happy to let it lie. I had other things on my mind.

When she and Uncle Marsh had shown that morning, I'd curtailed discussion of Tack by telling them straight off that things were over. I didn't explain but they both knew me enough to take one look at my face and leave it alone. So they did.

As Tack promised, I got a call from Lanie who I found out was with Elliott. She was still freaked so I didn't push her to share about her experience. I just listened as she told me that Chaos was helping them lay low and they were talking, which meant working things out. This didn't fill me with happy thoughts. Elliott might love my BFF but he also did stupid shit that got her kidnapped by the Russian freaking mob. However, I decided to throw my hissy fit later when my heart didn't hurt so much and when Lanie wasn't recovering from the drama to end all dramas.

Mostly, all day, I focused on getting through the day because, as I mentioned, my heart hurt. How this was, I didn't know. I kept telling myself I barely knew Tack and most of what I knew scared me, some of it confused me and some of it I didn't like. Even with that, the parts I did like, too much, kept pushing through and as hard as I tried, I couldn't tamp them down.

I wanted to call him. I wanted to take back my decision. But every logical bone in my body (what there were of them, which, I had to admit, were not many) kept holding me back.

His life was a nightmare, his world was frightening and he hurt me. The first night he met me, he kicked me out of his bed without a glance back and took another woman to it the very next night. Then he immediately commenced playing games. I needed to see these red flags for what they were and steer well clear. I knew it.

I knew it.

But that didn't mean it didn't hurt.

I loved my Uncle Marsh, and one of the things I loved most about him was his stories.

But sitting beside him on my deck, the kind of time I would normally cherish, I wasn't listening.

"You got a head full of biker."

I blinked at my backyard then looked at my uncle.

"What?" I asked.

His eyes went from my yard to me. "Honey, you got a head full of biker. You know I know it. You're miles away. And you know I know it's not about you and your aunt being kidnapped by the Russian mob."

These were words I never expected my uncle to say. Or anyone, for that matter. Then again, I never expected to be kidnapped by the Russian mob.

I pulled in breath through my nose and looked back at my yard.

"It's over," I said softly, hoping that would end it.

I should have known better. This was Uncle Marsh. He had something to say, he said it.

So he said it.

"That might be but the day after you get kidnapped by the Russian mob, my guess, as it's never happened to me, you'd normally have a head full of getting kidnapped by the Russian mob. Not a head full of biker and a face that says you just got your heart broken," Uncle Marsh returned.

This was true.

I didn't reply.

"How long were you with him?" Uncle Marsh asked.

I counted it down.

Then I answered, "Not long."

"He seemed rooted here, Tyra," Uncle Marsh noted. My heart squeezed at his words and my eyes went back to him.

"Pardon?"

"Him, his kids, pancakes in your kitchen. None of what I saw yesterday said 'not long.'"

Damn.

He was right.

"Maybe so, Uncle Marsh, but—"

He shook his head. "Don't know the man. Do know he's not going to win father of the year. That said, doesn't mean he doesn't think the world of those kids. He does. One thing about that man is clear. He loves his kids. And you don't have family pancake mornings with your kids in the house of a woman you're going to be together with for 'not long.'"

I hadn't thought about that and, thinking about it, Uncle Marsh was right about that too.

Oh boy.

"We weren't actually even together-together," I shared. "We weren't actually anything."

"Maybe *you* weren't but he sure as hell was."

I blinked.

Then I repeated, "Pardon?"

Uncle Marsh leaned into me and said softly, "I'll be honest with you, honey. I'm not sure about that man. Circumstances weren't such that he made a good first impression. So, truth be told, you telling me this morning that you two were over, I felt relief. You moping all day…" He trailed off but his hazel eyes held mine. "I don't know what happened. I do know I'm surprised that the man I saw in this house yesterday morning is no longer with my niece. He was comfortable here. Rooted. Him *and* his kids. All of them comfortable… with you. Makes matters more surprising is you got kidnapped and that may be part of his world but it isn't part of yours and my guess, he knows it. So I don't understand why he'd let you go the night you had that happen to you."

"Because I asked him to," I whispered.

Uncle Marsh shook his head. "Man's any man at all, that kind of shit doesn't fly."

"That's exactly it, Uncle Marsh. He's that kind of man and that scares me. He didn't want to let me go. I made him."

"That kind of shit doesn't fly," Uncle Marsh repeated.

"He can't *make* me stay with him. He wanted to but I didn't let him."

Uncle Marsh leaned further into me. "That kind of shit does...not...*fly*."

I stared at my uncle.

He kept talking.

"Something matters to you, you do not let it go. Ever."

My heart clenched again.

Uncle Marsh kept talking.

"Man I saw here yesterday morning, the situation we walked into, not good. Way he was with his kids, way he looked at you, I could let it slide. You mattered to him yesterday. No man who's any man at all has something, especially some*one* matter to him one morning and that night, she doesn't. No matter what happened, what was said, who was hurt and how. Your aunt tried to walk away from me, told me to let her go, I wouldn't. I'd find a way to make her stay. Because she matters and it's worth whatever I have to do to make her stay. That's the way it is, Tyra. Simple."

God, I loved him but he was killing me.

"This isn't helping, Uncle Marsh," I whispered because, well, it wasn't. It was making it worse.

"It isn't now, honey, and I know that. But it will when it sinks in. I'm telling it like it is. I'm telling you what you should expect. You matter, Tyra, and that's what you should expect."

I felt tears sting my eyes and turned my head away.

"I take it I should come back."

This was Aunt Bette from behind us and I took in another huge breath, turned in my chair and aimed a big, fake, bright smile in her direction.

"No, it's all good," I lied then pushed up from my chair. "Take a load off. I'll go in and see what I can rustle up for dinner."

Aunt Bette stared at me then she looked at Uncle Marsh.

"Biker roadkill," she remarked.

So Aunt Bette, cutting right to the chase.

"No truer words were spoken," Uncle Marsh muttered.

"Guys, can we let this go?" I requested. "You leave tomorrow. We've had shrieking women attacking my door, mob kidnappings and a breakup of a nonrelationship that was more relationship than any relationship I've ever had. Not the happy-go-lucky surprise visit to sunny Denver you were expecting, I'm sure. Let's just enjoy the rest of the time we have. Sound like a plan?"

Uncle Marsh opened his mouth to speak.

Aunt Bette got there before him. "Marsh."

His eyes cut to his wife.

"Let it go," she ordered softly.

Uncle Marsh held his wife's eyes. Then his came to me.

"Last time you were at our place, you bragged about your cooking. Dazzle me."

I looked to Aunt Bette. She rolled her eyes. I rolled mine back.

Then I went into the kitchen and rustled up some dinner. I didn't know if it was dazzling. I just knew there were no leftovers.

*   *   *

Standing outside security at Denver International Airport the next day, Aunt Bette gave me a tight hug.

She also slipped a business card that had the name "Cabe Delgado" on it into my hand when she was done.

"You have any problems, you call Hawk," she told me.

I nodded.

That was when Uncle Marsh moved in for his hug. It was longer and it was tighter.

Right before he let me go, he whispered in my ear, "Tyra, never forget. You matter."

Then he walked to the security line.

Aunt Bette looked back and waved.

As was his way, Uncle Marsh did not.

As was my way, I watched until I couldn't see them anymore. Then I went home. Then I typed out my resignation later. The rest of the day, I waited for Lanie to call.

She didn't.

Tack didn't either.

And when I went to bed that night, my heart still hurt.

CHAPTER SEVENTEEN

Foregone Conclusion

IT WAS MY luck the next morning at eight o'clock when I drove into Ride to deliver my resignation letter that stated I'd be giving no notice, Tack was working on the red car. He was the only one there.

Seeing him and watching his head turn my way even as he stayed bent over the opened hood of the car, I should have been used to the pain my heart clenching caused. It had happened enough times the last two days. But I wasn't.

I looked away, parked, jumped out of my car and hustled up the steps to the office. I unlocked it with the key I'd already taken off my chain and hurried in.

Drop the key and the letter on the desk and get the hell out of there.

That was my plan.

This plan was thwarted seeing as I barely made it through the door when Tack came through the door that led to the garage.

Damn.

I ignored him and went straight to the desk. I dropped the key and envelope on it. I also ignored the sound of the lock turning on the door to the garage.

Damn!

I turned and, eyes directed at my feet, I started to hurry to the outer door, escape the only thing on my mind.

I caught movement in my peripheral vision and my head came up.

Tack was at the door to the outside and he was locking that too.

Damn!

I stopped moving.

"Tack," I whispered. "Don't."

His head turned and his burning, blue eyes pinned me to the spot. Then his body turned.

At this point, I understood my mistake. I should have mailed my letter with the key.

Definitely.

"Please," I kept whispering, "don't."

He held my eyes.

I held his.

This lasted a while, both of us staring at each other three feet away.

Finally, I could take it no longer.

"Please, Tack, move away from the door."

Tack moved. He just didn't do it away from the door.

He came at me.

My heart started hammering in my chest and my feet took me back. I bumped into the desk and scooted to the side, still retreating. Then my thigh bumped into the chair and it went flying, such was the hastiness of my retreat.

Tack kept coming at me and my retreat might have been hasty, but his advance was far more rapid. My thundering heart skidded to a halt when his arm shot out, hooking me at the waist right before I would have slammed into a file cabinet. He jerked me to the side but kept coming until I was

back against the wall. Then his arm around my waist tightened, yanking me against the hard wall of his frame.

My hand went to his chest to try to force him back but
he stood firm as his other hand came up, palm at my jaw,
fingers curled around my neck and ear.

"Please," I whispered, bracing as his head descended
toward mine, *"don't."*

Just when I thought his lips would hit mine, they veered
to the side opposite where his hand was at my jaw. His fingers dug in, his arm around me tightened even further, plastering me against his body and his lips went to my ear.

"You fucked up, Red," he whispered.

I closed my eyes tight and pushed against his chest, my
other hand going to his waist and fisting in his tee, pushing
there too.

"Made the wrong decision," he went on in a whisper.

I opened my eyes.

God, *I had to get out of there.*

"Please, let me go."

"You been asleep, baby."

My body went still at his words.

Tack kept talking.

"Green tea. Yoga. No TV. Placemats for your coffee
table. Thursday-night takeaway. You got a night for takeaway. Scheduled. A narrow, little world. Fuck me. Crazy.
Fuckin' whacked. I woke you up, opened your eyes to a bigger world and scared you shitless."

Oh God.

This was not good. He had me figured out.

"Let me go," I begged.

His arm tightened even further and his lips stayed at my ear.

"You give it good, darlin', that attitude. So good, I
thought that was you. That isn't you. Not all of you. I got on

my hands the girl at the party who looked at me like I was the only man on the planet even when she was in a sea of people, took my hand with all the trust in the world that I was gonna make things good for her and followed me to my bed. You fucked up making the wrong decision Friday night. But I fucked up forgetting about that girl."

I closed my eyes. I liked that. I liked that he saw that. And I liked that he admitted he fucked up. I didn't think he had it in him but I liked it that he did.

Oh hell.

"Please, let me go," I pleaded.

"So much to you, never had a woman who has so much that makes her. Every day more comes out, and all of it is a surprise."

Ohmigod!

If I wasn't wrong, that was a compliment. A good one.

I opened my eyes on the word, "Tack—"

"Day in, day out, you peel the layers back for me. Smart mouth, funny, sweet, wild in bed. Chattin' with bikers like they were insurance brokers. Holdin' my girl's hand, givin' her strength when her mom's bein' a bitch. Keepin' your chin up when your people show in the middle of a full-blown drama. But so fuckin' vulnerable, you're scared shitless of livin' life."

"You don't know me, Tack."

His head came up and his eyes pierced mine. "I know you, Tyra."

"You don't."

"Life's a roller coaster. Best damn ride in the park. You don't close your eyes, hold on and wait for it to be over, babe. You keep your eyes open, lift your hands straight up in the air and enjoy the ride for as long as it lasts."

Seriously?

When did he become a sage?

He was beginning to piss me off mostly because he was making sense.

"Some people aren't roller coaster people, Tack."

"And you're tellin' me you're one of them?" he asked.

"Damn straight," I answered.

"Bullshit," he replied.

I glared.

He grinned his sexy grin.

I pushed at him with my hands, but this only made both of us rock two inches then Tack pushed back and he was stronger so I ended up not only plastered to him, I was also plastered to the wall.

"Let me go!" I snapped.

"No." He shook his head, still grinning. "No fuckin' way. Did it once, not doin' it again."

"You did it twice," I reminded him and his brows shot up.

"Twice?"

"That first night. Though it wasn't letting me go. It was kicking me out of your bed."

He grinned again, the jerk!

"See that stung," he said softly.

See? Total. *Jerk!*

"Truthfully?" I asked then didn't wait for an answer. "Yes. I'll let you in, handsome, just a little bit. Jumping into bed with a man I don't know is not my style. Getting kicked out of a bed I'd jumped into was something that never happened to me. So yes, that stung. But you know what else has never happened to me?"

"Tell me," he ordered, still . . . freaking . . . *grinning.*

"Seeing him just a day later in a clinch with a brunette."

"You knew me, you'd know she didn't have staying power and you'd know you do."

"And how's that?" I snapped.

"She's dark, you're red. I'll fuck dark, I'll fuck sun, but only red has staying power. Considered sun once. Lost her. Now it's you."

He was still kind of grinning and I was still definitely glaring. "I suppose I'm supposed to take that as a compliment."

"Just laying it out, babe."

"I see this isn't sinking in, handsome, but I don't want you to lay it out. I don't want anything from you except for you to let me go."

"Right back at you, Red, seein' as it's not sinking in that I'm not gonna let you go. We're talkin' this shit out."

"There's nothing to talk out!" I cried. "We're done."

Suddenly his face dipped close, the room filled with his badass biker vibe and he was all I could see.

"Truthfully," he shot my word back at me, "you were funny, you were sweet, you're gorgeous, you have great fuckin' hair and a great fuckin' body and I had fun with you, darlin', in bed and out. But you didn't show me all that's you so all I knew was the parts of it I wanted and I know that shit stung and this is gonna sting too, there were only parts. And I'll warn you, babe, this is gonna sting as well but you were too easy. A man like me can get easy, *easily*. So that's not what a man like me wants."

He paused, I kept glaring though I suspected my glare was more heated then he went on.

"Until you squared off against me. That first night, I didn't have it all. And I still don't have it all but every piece you give me, baby, I like. So now I want it all and I'm gonna fuckin' get it, Tyra. You aren't gonna hold back, you aren't gonna retreat, you aren't gonna push me away and I sure as fuck am *not* gonna let go."

"You're unbelievable," I hissed.

"You said that before, babe, what you need to get is you like exactly that about me. You're just too fuckin' scared to admit it."

"Oh," I started sarcastically, "so now you're in my head and you know what I'm thinking?"

"Yeah, I do. You may not have lived your life suckin' it dry but *I have.* I've jumped into bed with more than my fair share of women and I've spent time outta bed with more than my fair share of women and I know that a woman does not go wild for me in bed and that woman is not wild in life. You want wild, babe, because you *are* wild. You're just too fuckin' scared of it to embrace it."

"Wrong. You just happen to be an excellent lover, Tack. The problem is, outside of bed, you're mostly a jerk."

"You like that too, all of it," he shot back.

"God!" I yelled. "Seriously?"

He was losing patience. I knew this when he growled, "Seriously."

"News flash, Kane Allen, women do not go gaga over men who brag about their exploits and replace them within *a day.*"

"Tyra, do not shit me or yourself. There was nothing to replace, not back then. You came to a party, got drunk and got laid. Same as me. The minute you gave me more of you, I took it, wanted even more and I didn't keep that a secret, babe, and you fuckin' know it. And you kept givin' it. You coulda walked away and you didn't. And along the way as we've been playin' our game, you got your hooks in me and I got mine in you and you know that too."

I definitely did if the heartache I'd experienced the last two days was anything to go by.

But I wasn't going to tell him that.

"Your hooks aren't in me."

"Then why'd you drop that shit at the office instead of droppin' it in a mailbox?" he asked, jerking his head back to indicate the desk.

Fuck.

He totally had me figured out. Even I didn't know until that moment that was my play.

Fuck!

I gritted my teeth and glared at him.

He grinned again and gave me a squeeze.

Total jerk!

"You wanted this," he said quietly.

"I want closure," I returned, at this point mostly lying in order to save face.

"You want me."

Whoosh.

There went my breath.

Tack waited but I didn't reply.

Then Tack stopped waiting. "You know how I got my name?"

"Does it matter that I don't want to know?"

There it was. Another lie. I totally wanted to know. I'd been curious since he gave it to me.

"No," he answered.

Figured.

I glared at him.

"Sharp as a tack," he stated.

I blinked.

Then I found my mouth asking, "Pardon?"

"That's what my dad said about me. Sharp as a tack. Said it so much, they started callin' me that. Tack."

"Fascinating," I muttered sarcastically though the sarcasm was all for show. It actually was fascinating. And it was also true, regrettably.

"Clue in, Red. What I'm tellin' you is that you are not pullin' shit over on me. I'm a biker but I'm not an idiot. You entered this game, you knew it was a game and you made the decision, conscious or unconscious, to play it with me. And you're playin' it with me. I won't allow you to throw in the towel, babe. We're seein' where this goes because we both want that. And we want that because what we got is hot and parts of it are sweet and parts of it are wild and parts of it are frustrating as all fuckin' hell but all of it is *alive*."

God, he was so annoying when he was right.

"You hurt me," I reminded him, and damn, his face got soft, his eyes flashed with remorse and both looked really good.

"Yeah," he whispered.

"I'd had a really bad day and you hurt me."

His hand at my jaw tensed and he kept whispering when he said, "I'll probably do it again, Red, because I'm a man and any man can be a dick. But I won't do it like that, not again. I know you got soft under that attitude and I'll have a mind to that."

"I don't trust that to be true."

"Then you'll have to wait it out while I prove it to you."

"I don't have to do anything, Tack."

The pads of his fingers pressed into my skin, his eyes changed and the way they changed, I could do nothing but stare.

Not remorse.

Not intensity.

Determination.

Steely determination.

Crap.

"Tyra, get me right now. You are *not* gonna slip in a movie about love and redemption and cry by my side because, even though you've seen it before, it still moves you and then rip that shit away from me. You are *not* gonna ride my fingers, whisper to me to fuck you and take my cock the way I wanna give it to you, panting for more and then rip that shit away from me too. You are *not* gonna clash with me, toss your attitude my way when most every other woman shies away when I'm me then rip that away. And you are *not* gonna expose that soft spot you got that I like and I wanna protect and take that away from me either. Babe, I told you, you didn't get it and you need to *get it*." His fingers pressed deeper into my skin. "You are Chaos now. I am Chaos. You think you got the option but you don't. There is no goin' back. I've *claimed* you."

He wanted to protect my soft spot.

And he'd claimed me.

Oh boy.

"You let me go," I whispered.

"Does it feel like I let you go?"

No, one could say it absolutely did not since he had me in his arms pinned to a wall.

Still.

"It doesn't work that way, Tack."

"Try me and see."

I was right.

Determination. Steely.

"I don't want to live in your world," I informed him.

"You took my hand and walked with me to my bed."

"A bed you kicked me out of."

"And a day later, you walked right back into my world and demanded to stay there. You knew the risks, babe. And you took them. And here we are, here *you* are and this is where you're stayin'."

"You're scaring me again," I said softly.

His palm slid to below my ear, fingers in my hair, thumb pressed to the side of my face and his face dipped closer. "No, baby, I'm not scaring you. You're just scared. You give me a little more, you'll see I'll protect it. More, I'll protect that too. More, I got that too. When you give it all to me, if it works with us in a way that lasts, you'll never be scared. You'll feel safe enough to have your eyes open, your arms up and you'll enjoy the fuck outta the ride. I'll see to that, Red, and that's a promise."

God. Seriously. Totally annoying when he was right. And, I decided just then, when he was being sweet. And reassuring. And protective.

Damn.

I kept at it.

"Your whole world scares me," I admitted. "In fact, your entire life scares me."

"Like I said, baby, you give a little, you take my hand again like you did that night, I'll guide you through the nightmare. We'll make it to the other side and I promise, along the way, you'll enjoy the ride."

Oh hell. He was getting to me.

"I need to think about this," I told him.

"That's exactly what you don't need to do. But still, I'll give that to you."

I felt my back straighten as the words came out of my mouth sharply. "Well, thanks. Big of you."

Tack grinned.

"You know," I started, "it's annoying when you grin all know-it-all."

"This isn't my know-it-all grin, Red. This is my I'm-gonna-get-me-some-later grin."

I felt a couple of quivers that were on the high end of the pleasant scale.

Still, I shared, "That's even *more* annoying."

"Don't know why since me gettin' some means you're gonna get some."

More quivers that were climbing the scale of pleasant, but that didn't mean I didn't roll my eyes. I rolled them back when I heard and felt Tack chuckle.

"I told you I needed to think about this," I reminded him then went on, "What I decide isn't a foregone conclusion."

"Uh, yeah it is."

I had a strong feeling he was right partly because he wanted to protect my soft spot, a spot he liked. Partly because he was hot. Partly because he looked good grinning and he felt better chuckling. And partly because, even as he was annoying, he was kind of amusing.

But mostly because he was treating me like I mattered and he was making it clear he was not going to let me go.

Uncle Marsh said I should expect that and there it was, holding me tightly in his arms.

I didn't let Tack in on this information. Instead, I declared, "That's annoying too."

He grinned again.

"Tack! Stop grinning!" I demanded.

He didn't stop grinning but said through it, "You got the day. I'm rippin' that shit on the desk in half too. Tonight, I'm at your place. Tomorrow, your ass is back at your desk but it's gettin' there on the back of my bike. Now you're gonna kiss me so I can get back to work, you can go home and come to a foregone conclusion."

Totally annoying but kind of amusing. Again.

I didn't share that.

"Actually, I was thinking more that my day would include a visit with my best friend to ascertain she's all right after being kidnapped and interrogated by the Russian mob."

His grin died a quick death and he returned, "Actually, you are not gettin' anywhere near your girl or her fuckup of a man. Phone communication only until I got that shit locked down in a way that makes me comfortable for you to pay a visit."

That didn't sound good and my heart clenched again but a different way this time.

"Lanie isn't safe?" I asked.

"Lanie's safe and so are you, you stay away from Lanie."

I studied him closely, noting, "So, reading between the lines, Lanie is only kind of safe."

"Lanie's as safe as I can make her seein' as she won't leave him and he's *not* safe. You're nowhere near either of them and you're gonna stay that way. You also don't know where either of them are and you're gonna stay that way too so you can stay completely safe."

"This is not making me feel warm and fuzzy, Tack," I said quietly, still studying him closely.

"You made your decision, sparrin' with me, takin' up the challenge and playin' the game. She made hers reclaiming her man. Friday she became intimately acquainted with the risks that involves. She still made that decision. She hooked herself a fuckup of a man. You did not. You hooked yourself to a man who will not, under any circumstances, allow you to be in harm's way. It sucks you don't feel warm and fuzzy but that's not on me, babe. That's your girl. Her choice. My choice is to keep you safe and I'm takin' it. You get me?"

Okay, well, *that*... that made me feel warm and fuzzy.

"Do I have a choice *not* to get you?" I asked and his lips twitched.

Then he answered, "No."

My eyes slid to the side and I muttered, "I didn't think so."

"She's learning," Tack muttered back and my eyes slid back to him.

"FYI, that's annoying too."

His lip twitch turned into a big, white smile surrounded by a sexy, dark goatee.

Shit.

"FYI, baby, havin' your attitude back is so far from annoying, it's not fuckin' funny."

And he proved his point by pressing his hard body deeper into me, sliding his hand back into my hair and dropping his eyes to my mouth.

"I think it's time for me to go home and come to a foregone conclusion," I whispered as my stomach started to melt when his eyes didn't leave my mouth.

"Wrong, it's time for that kiss you're gonna give me," he whispered, his face getting closer, his lips a breath away, his eyes lifting to mine and they were again determined but a different way this time.

More pleasant quivers and they were way, *way* up the scale.

"How about you get that kiss when I come to my conclusion?" I suggested as my heart started beating faster.

"How about, seein' as that conclusion is inevitable, you kiss me now."

"Tack—"

"Red, quit fuckin' around."

"I'm not fucking around. I have a lot on my mind. I'm not in the mood to make out with a man who may or may not end the day being kind of my boyfriend."

His head came up and his brows drew together. "Kind of your boyfriend?"

"The conclusion is only foregone to you, handsome," I lied.

"Babe, I'm not anyone's boyfriend."

I blinked again but this was so I wouldn't flinch.

"What?" I whispered.

"You have a boyfriend when you're sixteen. You fuck a man casually, you don't have anything except, if he's good, a supply of orgasms. You got what we're building, you got everything. But bottom line, I've claimed you. This means you're my woman, which in turn means I'm your man."

Whoosh.

There it went again, my breath.

"You're my man?" I forced out.

"And you're my woman," Tack confirmed.

"We haven't even been out on a date," I pointed out.

"Babe, I also don't date."

I blinked again but this was so I wouldn't scowl. "What?"

"I don't date."

"So I'm your woman and you're my man after only a couple weeks of arguing, confusion, misunderstandings, game playing and breaking bread a few times, most of them with other people in attendance?"

"Yep."

I felt my eyes narrow. "Is this another part of being in your world?"

"Nope," he returned. "This is another part of being with me."

"So, what you're saying is, you're not going to treat me to dinner or any attempts to woo me."

His lips curved and he asked, "Woo you?"

"Woo me!" I snapped.

His lips curved deeper into a full-on amused smile. "No, Red, I'm not gonna attempt to woo you."

"Not liking that," I clipped and his brows went up again.

"Are you shittin' me?"

"No!" I cried. "I deserve to be wooed!"

"Right, then I'll amend my statement. I'll woo you by gettin' you off as many times as I can with my mouth, fingers and cock, cookin' for you when I have time, not firin' your ass when you fuck shit up, which is often, and puttin' up with your bullshit. Bullshit like now when you're playin' even more games because you know I like it when you also know what you really wanna do is kiss me."

"Actually, handsome, I don't want to kiss you. I want to kick you."

His smile came back. "Bullshit games."

"No, seriously, Tack, if I could land one right now, I'd kick you. Unfortunately, you have me pressed to a wall so I don't have room to move."

His lips came back to a breath away but his eyes stayed locked to mine and he went on quietly, "While I cook for you, while we eat it and after I fuck you, I'll also listen to you when you tell me about that roller coaster you jumped off and why you haven't had a man before me that you tied yourself to. That's another way I'll woo you, baby, but that's all you'll get from me. That said, that'll be enough for you because you'll like it just like you like it right now."

"Correction, Tack, I don't like it right now. I'm pissed right now."

"Feel good?" he asked.

"No!" I snapped.

"You feel alive?"

I closed my eyes.

Seriously. I *hated* it when he was right.

I felt his lips brush mine and I opened my eyes to look right into his.

"You feel alive," he declared quietly.

"Annoying," I muttered.

I felt his lips smile against mine as I felt his hand shift down then slide up under my top so his fingers could curl around my side, skin against skin.

I held my breath.

Tack held my gaze then his lips slid from mine down my cheek to my ear as his fingers lightly stroked my skin at my side.

"Straight up, baby, no excuse, but that night, after they took you, hooded you, bound you and held you for three hours, I was not in a good state. I already had issues with these guys. But I was pissed. I was worried. I was feeling things bigger than I expected when it came to you but mostly you being in danger, and I took that out on you. I shouldn't have. I let you go because I fucked up and needed to give you time. You had your time. Now your time is up."

I was feeling things bigger than I expected when it came to you...

Oh God. That *seriously* got to me and the foregone conclusion was cemented in my brain. So much, my body relaxed and melted into his.

Tack kept talking as his fingers slid up, up, *up* until they were stroking me at the side of my breast and my quivers went into overdrive, setting a new level on the pleasant scale. "Now, we gonna explore what we're buildin'?"

"Yes," I whispered.

His head came up and his gaze captured mine.

"Good, Red," he whispered back, "now fuckin' kiss me."

"Okay," I said softly, my hand at his chest moving up to curl around his neck and sift into his hair. My hand at his waist becoming an arm around his lower back. And my feet rolling up on my toes.

I pressed my lips to his.

That was all I had to do. Tack pressed me back into the

wall, his hand in my hair moving so his arm could curve around my shoulders and hold me close as his tongue thrust into my mouth. I liked that, the feel of it, the taste of him, and I melted fully into his body.

Tack growled into my mouth and held on tighter, his tongue thrusting deeper, faster.

I liked the growl. I liked what his tongue was doing. So I returned the gesture of holding on tight.

It was going from good to *really* good when we both heard the doorknob rattle.

Tack tore his mouth from mine on another growl, this one annoyed, and his head snapped around to look over his shoulder at the door. I tipped my body to the side and looked around him, also at the door.

"Locked," we heard a woman say from the other side of the door.

"What? Why? Says right there, office hours, eight to five," another woman snapped.

"It may say that, Elvira, but that doesn't mean it isn't locked," a third woman pointed out.

"Fuck," Tack muttered, his arms giving me a squeeze just as an imperative knock came at the door.

"Hello!" the second woman's voice shouted. "Anyone in there? Open the door!"

"Fuck!" Tack clipped tersely, let me go but grabbed my chin between thumb and finger and tipped it up to him as he bent his neck. His mouth touched mine then he released my chin and stalked to the door.

I watched.

Seriously, he looked good in jeans.

And tees.

And motorcycle boots.

And moving.

He also looked good standing still.

And holding me close in his arms.

Hmm.

Yes, the conclusion was most definitely foregone.

I watched him open the door and then I watched in surprise as three women surged in, practically bowling over scary biker dude Kane "Tack" Allen in order to do so.

One was a gorgeous, curvy blonde. Another was a gorgeous, curvy brunette. And the last was a gorgeous, very curvy black woman.

The blonde smiled broadly at Tack and said, "Yo."

The brunette smiled more timidly at Tack then her eyes slid to me.

The black woman didn't even look at Tack. Her eyes came straight to me then shocking words came straight out of her mouth.

"Looks like Tack was in the middle of givin' the business." She finally looked at Tack. "Early Monday mornin' nookie during office hours. You biker boys know how to live."

I blinked again. The blonde's smile got broader. The brunette's giggled quietly.

Tack did not giggle, not that he could giggle. He also didn't chuckle. And further, he didn't smile.

What he did was level annoyed eyes on the black woman and demand to know, "What are you three doin' here?"

"Uh, Hawk rescued your girl," the black woman replied, jerking her head in my direction. "Then he told Gwen you'd claimed a woman. This is juicy and you ain't stupid. You had to know we'd be here to check her out, schedule the test then, if she passes, bring her into the fold."

Tack glared at the black woman then his eyes went to the ceiling.

Then they went to the blonde. "Peaches, never thought I'd regret that day you strutted your ass into Ride. But right now I'm regretting that day you strutted your ass into Ride."

Test?

Bringing me into the fold?

Peaches?

"Can't go back. Have to go forward," the blonde replied, still grinning huge.

"Fuck me," Tack muttered.

"Um...hi," the brunette said to me. "Don't be alarmed. We're harmless. Or at least Gwen and I are. I'm Mara." She pointed to herself. "This is Gwen, Hawk's woman." She pointed to the blonde and I could see this. Hawk was hot therefore it was not a surprise that Gwen was stunning. "And this is Elvira." She pointed to the black woman. "We're not really here to test you. We're more like a welcoming committee."

Uh. What?

"No, we aren't," Elvira contradicted, eyes narrowed on Mara. "She doesn't have sass, she's not in the club."

"I don't have sass," Mara returned.

"Girl, what you been smokin'? You totally have sass," Elvira shot back.

Gwen leaned toward Mara. "It's the quiet kind of sass. It's different but it's good."

"Fuck me," Tack muttered again.

"I wish," Elvira muttered back, eyes on Tack then she looked to me. "That's part of provin' you got sass, lettin' us know how he is when he's in action. But, I'm warning you now, I don't do too much information. Just enough to confirm he's not only hot on the outside but he's also got the moves. I can't function around a man if I know his ability to give pleasure."

I stared at her and I was pretty sure my mouth was open. Was this actually happening?

Finally, seeing as no one was speaking, I figured it was up to me to respond so I mumbled, "Um..."

"Elvira, you're scaring her," Mara warned.

"I scare her, she don't have sass," Elvira retorted.

"Then that proves I don't have sass because I know you and you're scaring *me*," Mara returned.

"Whatever," Elvira murmured and looked at me. "Cosmos. Tomorrow night. Club."

"That doesn't work for me," Tack put in, moving in my direction. "Tyra'll be at my place tomorrow night."

I would?

"We get that. It's new. Things are intense when it's new," Gwen allowed.

"Tyra," Mara said, smiling at me. "That's a pretty name."

I decided I liked Mara.

"Thanks," I replied, smiling back.

"Right. Cosmos. Wednesday night. Club," Elvira threw out an alternative.

Tack made it to me and pulled me partially away from the wall so he could slide an arm around my shoulders and tuck me into his side, a maneuver he conducted under the avid gazes of all three women and while speaking. "That doesn't work for me either."

"My man, you gotta let her up for air," Elvira advised.

"No I don't," Tack returned.

Oh boy.

Another quiver *way* high up on the pleasant scale.

Elvira grinned then she asked, "Okay, macho man, so when can we have her?"

I felt Tack's eyes and tipped my head back to look up to see them on me. "You wanna have a drink with these women?"

"Um…" I mumbled.

"Sho' she does," Elvira answered for me.

"Uh…" I mumbled again.

"Babe, Elvira's a nut but Gwen and Mara are good people. You wanna expand your girl base, they're good additions," Tack shared.

"I take no offense to that, by the way," I heard Elvira say then she went on in a mutter, "not that you care."

I didn't know these women or what this was about. What I did know was that Gwen's man rescued me. I also knew they knew Tack. And, lastly, he'd asked me to trust him.

I figured I should probably start that now.

"Okay then, yeah. I'd like to have a drink with them."

"Awesome," Gwen whispered.

Tack looked at the women. "You can have her Wednesday."

"Done," Elvira agreed. "Now, we'll be gettin' on so you can resume the festivities. Later."

And with that, she took off.

Gwen and Mara didn't.

"See you Wednesday. And don't worry, it'll be fun," Mara assured, and I smiled at her.

"Look forward to it," I replied.

"Little black dress. Or little-anything dress. And heels," Gwen advised, and I turned my smile to her, finally looking forward to this. I hadn't dressed up in a while and I loved to dress up so even though drinks with the girls was a crapshoot, at least that would be fun.

"I can do that," I told her.

She smiled, both waved, I returned the wave and then they followed Elvira.

The door hadn't closed on them when Tack turned me into his front and both of his arms closed around me.

"Is it me or was that weird?" I asked.

"It's not you. Like I said, Elvira's a nut. Gwen's a nut too but the cute kind. Mara I don't know very well but what I do know of her, she's solid."

"And what was that all about?" I went on.

Tack's eyes roamed my face and the way they did I wasn't certain I liked.

"Right," he said softly. "A while ago, Gwen had a thing. Like yours, it involved kidnapping. Unlike yours, it also involved drive-bys."

Holy crap!

Tack continued. "I got involved in her thing. I wanted to be more involved with her. That didn't work out which, at the time, sucked for me."

Peaches.

Gwen was blonde. Gwen was the "cute" kind of nuts. This meant Gwen was the "sun" he said had "staying power."

Now I got it, all of it, and I didn't like it.

Tack's arms gave me a squeeze.

"At the time, babe," he said quietly. "Now it doesn't suck for me at all."

I remained silent as I considered all this information.

Tack's arms squeezed me again and stayed tight.

"Baby," he started, still talking quietly, "her thing was intense. We got close during it. And we stayed close. But she's Hawk's and, a man like Hawk, she...is...*Hawk's.* They're not only married, they're tight. I got that a long time ago but that didn't mean somethin' didn't keep growin' for her and me. It did. We still got that and I hope we always do. And part of us havin' that is, she heard about you, and although Elvira looked like the ringleader of that sneak attack, Gwen was the brains behind the operation. Hawk told her I'd claimed you and she wants to be sure it's all good for me. It's sweet. It's friendly. And that's all it is."

Okay, to trust him I had to trust that. I still didn't like it but...whatever.

Moving on.

"And Mara?" I asked.

"Mara's a long story that I'll tell you while I'm makin' you chops tonight."

I didn't know if that was good. What I did know was that chops sounded great.

"Pork chops?" I queried.

"Are there other kinds of chops?" Tack queried back.

"I don't think so."

He grinned then confirmed, "Yeah. Pork chops."

"Do you make good chops?"

"Cooked for you twice, Red. What do you think?"

That answered that. He made good chops.

I hadn't had breakfast and my mouth started watering.

But I had to know.

"Did you get...*involved* with Mara too?"

"Fuck no. She's bangin' a cop."

Well, that was firm. It was also good to know.

"And last, Elvira?"

"Elvira works for Hawk. She's in Gwen's posse. She lassoed Mara into Gwen's posse. The shit that went down with Gwen meant four men were involved. One of them was Hawk. One of them was me. One of them was Mara's man, Lawson. And one of them was a man named Lucas who claimed himself a woman named Tess and it's likely she'll be wearin' a dress and heels at Club come Wednesday night. I don't do chick so I have no clue what's in store for you. All I know is, Gwen's got a big heart. Elvira's is arguably bigger. And Mara's is off-the-charts big. Gwen's drama started that posse and with each new drama, that posse grows. They wanna suck you in, worse things could happen."

"Right," I whispered, intrigued but I'd let it go until chops. "So, I'm at your house tomorrow night?"

"Yeah."

"Did you think of maybe asking if I'd like to be at your house tomorrow night?"

His lips twitched.

Then he said, "No."

"Annoying," I muttered.

"Yeah, you say that, baby. What you didn't say was that you aren't coming to my house tomorrow night."

Damn. I was totally figured out.

I sighed.

Tack chuckled.

Then he squeezed me with his arms and dipped his face close. "Give me that mouth again, babe, then get outta here."

"Is the word 'please' in your vocabulary?"

"No, but you throw more attitude at me before givin' me your mouth, tonight, that word is gonna be in your vocabulary and I'm gonna make you use it often."

Oh boy.

That didn't cause a quiver. That caused a quake and it shook me from top to toe.

"Babe," he growled, *"mouth."*

"Oh, all right," I muttered, saw humor light his eyes then I gave him my mouth.

He took it and the way he did, that caused a quake too.

He'd let me go, turned me, scooted me toward the door with a hand at my ass and I was wandering there, slightly dazed by his kiss, slightly dazed by the girl posse's visit but mostly dazed in a happy way I was hoping I was right about when I heard Tack call, "Red."

I turned to him and my hand shot up automatically as he sent the key to the office I'd dropped on the desk sailing in my direction. Dazed, it was a miracle I nabbed it in the air but I did.

Then I stood at the door watching him pick up the envelope that contained the resignation letter I'd laid on the desk. I watched him rip it in half. Then I watched him toss it in the trash.

Finally, I watched his eyes settle on me.

Heated but it was again there.

Steely determination.

Instead of clenching, my heart grew light.

That felt a whole lot better.

I smiled at him and waited for Tack to smile back.

He did and it was great.

Then I walked out the door.

CHAPTER EIGHTEEN

Really Glad He Did

"Can I say, I'm not sure about this?" I said into the "secure phone" Tack handed me when it rang.

My ass was on the counter in my kitchen close to where Tack was working. And my ass was there because Tack planted it there with a muttered, "Keep me company while I cook," which was kind of an invitation but him doing it after lifting me up and planting my ass on the counter was more a command.

It was the evening after our showdown in the office. As promised, Tack came over with grocery bags full of food to make our dinner that I discovered was going to be chops, potatoes and green beans. The minute he closed the door behind him, he grabbed my hand, dragged me to my kitchen and planted my ass on the counter with his kind of invitation to hang with him while he cooked. So I was hanging with him while he cooked.

This was after I spent the day cleaning my house, doing yoga and opening the door to a scary-looking, boy-man biker in training who introduced himself as Roscoe and was wielding a metal detector (it took him half an hour, but he found Lanie's ring).

I did all this while anticipating that night.

I didn't have to think about my decision since both of us knew it was already made.

I was kind of scared.

I was mostly excited.

And I was excited because maybe, just maybe, I wasn't wrong about Tack being my dream man.

But in the two weeks we'd been playing our game, things had been anything but normal. Your man coming over to make dinner with you knowing he was going to do it as well as understanding he was your man was normal.

I was scared of normal.

I was also excited about it.

And normal started out good. As I sat on the counter watching, Tack slid right into it like we'd known each other years rather than weeks and most of those years had been normal.

Though, he did it while unpacking food and preparing the potatoes, which looked like they were going to be awesome. Sliced super thin, arranged in a casserole dish, layered with salt, pepper, paprika, pats of butter and minced garlic then smothered in cream and milk before he slid them into the oven. He also did this while telling me about Detective Mitch Lawson and his woman, Mara Hanover-very-soon-to-be Lawson (as they were engaged).

And what he told me was scary.

It also confirmed Mara Hanover-very-soon-to-be Lawson had an off-the-charts big heart.

But, although I got the drift that cops were not Tack's favorite people, the way he told the story shared that Detective Mitch Lawson's heart was so off-the-charts big, it needed its own zip code. Cop or no, Detective Lawson had Tack's respect not for being a cop but for being a good man who took care of his woman and the two kids they'd taken under their wing.

When he was done, I was looking forward to getting to know Mara better. And I was hoping I'd meet Mitch.

That was when the phone Tack had placed on the counter rang. He grabbed it, picked it up and handed it to me.

"Yours. Burner. Secure. How you communicate with your girl. She's callin'."

Even though I didn't fully understand a couple of his words, I wanted to kiss him. He'd arranged for me to have access to Lanie and that was thoughtful. It was also sweet.

Unfortunately, I didn't get to kiss him because checking in with Lanie took precedence. So I answered the phone and was assured by Lanie that she was okay after her abduction and interrogation. Then I was very *not* assured when she told me she and Elliott were planning to make their problems go away by disappearing.

Disappearing!

I didn't even know what that meant. I just knew it didn't mean good things.

This brought me to now, telling Lanie I wasn't sure about this scheme (by the way, this was a *massive* understatement).

"Eli and I have talked about it, Ty-Ty, and it's our only option," Lanie replied.

I sucked in breath. Then my eyes slid to Tack who was at the stove making what appeared to be homemade stuffing that had sausage and mushrooms in it and, incidentally, also looked awesome. Unfortunately at that moment with the prospect of my best friend doing something bonkers, like disappearing, I suddenly wasn't hungry.

His hand was holding a wooden spoon that was moving stuffing around in a pot but his eyes were on me.

"There's another option," I ventured carefully, my eyes holding Tack's.

"What?" Lanie asked.

I looked to my knees and suggested quietly. "You could let him go. Let him face the consequences. I know that's harsh but—"

Lanie cut me off. "I can't desert him."

"Yes, honey, you can. We're talking *the Russian mob*. We're talking *you disappearing*. We're—"

"Tyra," she interrupted me again, "in just weeks, I was going to pledge my troth to this man. What would it say about me when, days ago, I was intent on spending my life with him, for better or for worse, that I fall at the first hurdle?"

"Lanie, honey, really, I don't want to be mean but this isn't a hurdle. This is a twenty-foot, steel-reinforced concrete wall. I know I don't have to tell you because you were there, and so was I, but we were *kidnapped* because of his shit."

Tack made a noise that sounded like an amused grunt and my eyes went to him to see he was grinning at the pot but Lanie spoke in my ear.

"I'm sorry, Ty-Ty. So sorry. And Elliott is too. He feels so bad. He won't stop talking about it. Not only that it happened to me but that it happened to you and your aunt. But *he* didn't kidnap us. He just messed up. And, sweetie, the thing is, I've had a long time of better. This is the worse part of for better and worse. And he got in this pickle for me."

My back went straight and I looked at the wall in front of me. "Oh no. I'm being cautious here because I know you love him and things are crazy but that's not going to happen, you taking any blame for his actions."

"Say it like it is, baby," Tack muttered and my gaze went back to his, my eyes widening in a mute communication of "no comments from the peanut gallery." This simply got me a bigger grin before Tack turned off the burner, picked up the pot and moved to the thick chops he'd laid in a tray.

Lanie was silent a moment then she whispered, "Ty-Ty, I love him, and love scales twenty-foot, steel-reinforced concrete walls. If it doesn't, it isn't love."

Damn, she had me there.

"What are you going to do for money? What about your job. His job? Your house? The wedding?" I asked, leaving out the selfish but (I thought) important *Me?*

"We'll figure it out."

Gah!

"Lanie—"

"Tyra, sweetie, that's also what love is. You figure it out."

She had me there too.

I sucked in breath, my head dropped and my shoulders drooped.

Then I said softly, "I'm worried about you."

I heard the door on the oven go up and half a second later a strong, warm hand curved around the back of my neck. I looked up and saw a now-unamused Tack holding my neck and my eyes, his serious and searching. Then, when he found what he was searching for, his eyes warmed and his hand gave me a squeeze.

That was thoughtful and sweet too.

"We'll be all right," Lanie assured.

"But—"

"And if we aren't all right then we'll be not all right together, which is a form of all right."

As nuts as it was, as insane as the situation, I was both glad for my friend that she had that conviction about the man she loved just as I was jealous and wanted that for me.

And thinking that, my eyes held by the deep warmth in

Tack's, my heart clenched yet again, but it was the good kind of clench.

Scared but excited.

And hopeful.

"Okay," I whispered.

"I'll keep you in the loop as much as Tack says is okay," Lanie told me.

There it was. More. Tack was protecting Lanie (and Elliott) as well as me.

"I'd appreciate it."

"I'll tell Elliott you said hi."

I wanted her to kick Elliott in the shin for me and, maybe, shove his shoulder and, possibly, lecture him for being an idiot in love and doing stupid shit the caliber of which ended in the mob snatching three women from an upscale mall parking lot, but I didn't share that.

Instead, noncommittally, I said, "Right."

Lanie giggled quietly because she knew what I didn't share.

"Roscoe found your ring. Did he get it to you?" I asked, changing the subject, and Tack's hand gave me another squeeze then he let me go and moved away.

"Got it. Thanks for that."

"Thank Roscoe, he was the one wielding the metal detector."

"Already did."

"Good," I muttered.

"I have to go, Ty-Ty. They just brought in our food."

"Okay, honey, stay safe and stay strong."

"Will do. And next time we talk, I want to know all about you."

Translation: She wanted an update on me and Tack.

"Will do," I repeated her words. "Later, honey."

"Later, Ty-Ty."

I slid the phone shut. When I did, Tack was right there sliding it out of my hand. He set it on the counter then he positioned in front of me, pulled my knees apart then he positioned *in me*. He did this by wrapping his arms around me and yanking me forward on the counter so his hips were between my legs and I was crotch to chest against him, tight.

His hand slid up and sifted into my hair while he muttered, "That sounded like it went okay."

"Then it sounded wrong since she's making the wrong decision, I'm scared as hell for her and I think the decisions Elliott has made has put in question his ability to make other important decisions in their future."

"You'd be right about that," Tack agreed.

Great.

"But, babe," he continued, "I know about their plan and I'm arranging safe passage, new identities and a jumping-off point where they're gonna go. The Club is also gonna deal with the Russians. But that won't matter for them. They'll be long gone, buried in their new lives and all will be good. At least with that. We deal with the Russians, they can come back. Now, him not fuckin' up again..." he trailed off.

But I was staring at him.

"You're arranging safe passage, new identities and a jumping-off point?"

"Yeah."

"You're arranging safe passage, new identities and a jumping-off point?" I repeated then went on, "For Lanie and Elliott?"

His brows drew together. "Uh, yeah, babe."

"Isn't that...doesn't that kind of thing cost a lot of money? New identities?"

"It does, you're in the position you have to pay in cash. It doesn't, you got someone who does good work who owes you a marker."

I didn't get into why Tack might know someone who did good work with fake identities and more, why whoever that person was owed him a marker. I had bigger fish to fry.

"You're pulling in a marker for Elliott and Lanie?"

Tack cocked his head to the side then asked, "That woman mean something to you?"

"Yes, Tack, she's my best friend."

"Then yeah, Red, I'm pulling in a marker for Lanie. Normal circumstances, Belova could go fuck himself, but unfortunately Lanie comes with him, she means something to you so that means I'm pullin' in a marker for him too."

"No you're not," I whispered, still staring at him and his brows drew together again.

"Say again?"

"You're pulling in that marker for me."

His hand twisted in my hair, his face got soft and so did his voice when he answered, "Yeah."

God. Oh God.

That was thoughtful and sweet too. And it was also evidence that Kane "Tack" Allen had a big heart.

My head fell forward and to the side until it collided with his shoulder as my arms slid around him and got tight.

I felt his head turn and in my ear he said quietly, "Fuck, baby, just with that, you made callin' that marker worth it."

God.

Oh God.

My head snapped back, my hands fisted in the back of his tee and I ordered, "Be a jerk."

His chin shifted back sharply and he asked, "What?"

"I can't deal with sweet, thoughtful Kane 'Tack' Allen.

You need to be a jerk. Immediately. I can deal with jerky Kane 'Tack' Allen."

Tack grinned but said, "Sorry, darlin', got you tucked to me, good food cookin' in the oven, we're alone and no one's bangin' on the door. Not in the mood to be an asshole."

"This is unfortunate," I muttered. Tack chuckled. I felt his humor from crotch to chest. It felt *way* nice and his arms got tighter as his face got closer which was way nicer.

"You'll get used to my sweet," he promised.

"I'm not sure about that," I warned.

His eyes changed.

Steely determination.

Oh boy.

Then he stated, "I am."

Yep. I was right.

Oh boy.

"Tack—"

His face moved back a couple of inches and he said, "Roller coaster."

"Pardon?"

"Food needs to cook a while. While it does, you're gonna tell me about your roller coaster."

I could do this.

"Can we get some wine and move to the couch where it's more comfortable?"

"You uncomfortable?"

I wasn't. Not in any way.

Though I'd be more comfortable with a glass of wine in my hand.

"You're on your feet," I pointed out.

"Red, you're pressed to me crotch to tits. This is not uncomfortable."

Right. Good to know.

Suddenly, I didn't need wine.

"Roller coaster," I said quietly, and Tack nodded but I didn't know what to say. Thinking about it after having been kidnapped, it seemed to pale in comparison.

"Tyra," Tack prompted and I focused on him.

"I . . . well, you have a stalker ex-wife and problems in the Club and out of it that put your life in jeopardy. And Aunt Bette, Lanie and I were kidnapped. In light of all that, the roller coaster I jumped off that led me to Ride doesn't seem much like a roller coaster anymore."

"Pain fades," Tack declared. "But tell me about it anyway."

I held his eyes. Then I admitted, "Actually, now, it seems kind of lame."

And it did. Total bullshit. Office politics. Stuck in a job I didn't like mostly because the people around me were toxic but feeling my feet encased in molasses or, maybe, it was simply that I was too scared to take a risk and get the hell out.

"Red, those chops and potatoes need to cook a while but not a millennium. Tell me."

"I was targeted," I blurted and he blinked.

"Say again?"

"Targeted. I had a desk job. I was a supervisor. I liked what I did. It was challenging. It wasn't a normal desk job where you do the same thing day in and day out. Every day was something different. I had a lot of work to do. I was never bored. I got paid well. I got to wear nice clothes. It wasn't a passion but I was content. Content enough that I'd been there for a while and had no plans to leave. But, unbeknownst to me, one of my coworkers hated me and she'd been campaigning behind my back for ages. Shit-stirring and the brew was toxic. She'd turned a bunch of people against me. I just went to work, did my job, liked it and went home. I had no idea this was happening. It blindsided me when her brew was done and she started her spell in motion. I had no idea. She was kind to my face. No, not even that, friendly, out and out. I liked her. I cared about her. I knew about her life, her family. It wasn't like we were best friends and she was over for dinner every night, but she was, or she acted like she was, the kind of person in my life that she'd stay in my life no matter which direction we went. We'd exchange birthday and Christmas cards and stupid e-mails we thought were funny even if she moved to Florida and I moved to New Zealand. We'd be friends on Facebook. But it was a total lie. And all the people she filled with her toxin were two-faced too. I'd never experienced such poison. Such hypocrisy. It didn't feel good to be lied to, that kind of thing never feels good. But smiling at me and sharing recipes while you're stabbing me in the back? I don't understand that kind of behavior."

"Jesus," Tack muttered.

"Yeah," I agreed. "And I was stupid. I was surprised, sure, but when it started going down I should have said, 'Fuck this,' and got out. Life's too short to deal with people like that, their small worlds, their small minds, their venom. I didn't and I got buried under it. I thought it would just pass. I was a supervisor and promoted to that position and I think, though I have no clue why anyone would do that to someone, she was pissed because I was promoted and she wasn't. She was there longer than me. Or it could be I was younger. I don't know. I don't care. My boss said I didn't have anything to worry about, ignore it, keep my chin up, but it just kept coming. It went on for months. Stuff happened, things were said, done, just mean, catty, awful. I let it get to me. I wasn't sleeping. I wasn't eating. I couldn't understand how someone would hate me so much even to begin a campaign like that much less go full throttle for months on top of trash talking me for years. And she had been, Tack, behind my back trash talking me *for years* while to my face she was sweet. I let it get in my head to the point I wasn't only not sleeping, I wasn't eating and I couldn't even brush my teeth because just brushing my teeth made me gag and I'd end up hurling."

"Red," Tack whispered.

I shook my head. "No, it's okay. I've decided just now to let it go because, looking back on it, it was stupid. I should never have let it get to me."

"It ain't stupid. That shit is whacked," he clipped.

This response surprised me but the vehemence with which it was uttered surprised me more.

"Really?" I asked.

"Fuck yeah," he bit out. "Christ, bitches. They're the worst. I'll take a pissed-off man, his fists and the best man wins any time. But bitches, no. They play their mind games, fuck with your head. Jesus, darlin', I hate that happened to you."

Wow, that was sweet too. Very sweet.

"Are you, um...speaking from experience?" I asked.

"Yeah, experiencing you tellin' me that shit," he answered. "But no. There's a reason I am who I am, where I am and do what I do. I got a minefield of politics I have to negotiate but I also got a brain in my head, I'm smart enough to be cautious, I got my own weapons and I'm not afraid to use them. What I don't got is bitches who play mind games because they're pissed off about somethin' in their lives. Or they're pissed off that they're small, not good enough and know it and instead of doin' better, workin' harder, they gotta tear down someone who doesn't carry their load of shit. Jealousy is an ugly emotion that makes people do some seriously whacked shit and when a woman is experiencing it, it's worse. No, I am who I am, where I am and do what I do to avoid that kind of bullshit hassle."

I had to admit, it felt nice not only that he didn't belittle that situation but also that he understood it. And more, that he was angry on my behalf because it happened to me.

Before I could find the words to share this with him, Tack spoke again.

"So what'd you do?"

"I quit."

His head tipped to the side. "That's it?"

"Well. Yeah. One day, I'd had enough and it hit me. I wasn't going to be incarcerated for quitting my job. I had enough money to get by for a while. I wasn't eating and I couldn't even brush my teeth. That poison was infecting me. She was winning. So I packed up my desk and walked out. I didn't even tell my boss I was going. I just left."

"You didn't fuck with her back?"

"No. I just left."

"Babe, someone fucks with you, you fuck back."

"Looking back, she didn't deserve the effort."

"Wrong."

It was me who blinked this time. "Pardon?"

"Wrong. Bitches should not get away with that."

"Tack, she has to live her small life knowing she's not good enough and swimming in her own poison. That's her penance."

"Wrong again, Red."

"But—" I started, his arms gave me a squeeze and I stopped talking.

"That shit starts, you key her car. It continues, you slash her tires. That shit keeps goin', you get creative."

His words surprised me so much my "What?" was high-pitched.

"Life is lessons and she needs to learn hers."

"By keying her car and slashing her tires?" That was high-pitched too.

"She's got shit in her life she's gotta deal with, she's got less time to focus on makin' your life miserable."

"That's a strange way of solving a problem, handsome," I told him. "Not to mention illegal."

"Maybe strange to you. Maybe illegal. But, no doubt about it, Red, it'd work. Luckily, your ass is in your office at my garage and you work with all men so you don't gotta deal with bitches anymore. For some asinine reason you take some other job and you got bitches targeting you, you tell me and I'll see to it they stop."

I blinked again.

Then I stated, "Well, first, I like my job and I'm fucking it up less every day so it's unlikely I'll be moving on."

"Babe, you resigned this morning," he reminded me then finished with, "Again."

"Yes, because I was fighting with you. Now we're not fighting so I'm sticking."

He grinned and muttered, "Good to know."

I kept on target. "But, second, if some great opportunity came my way and I took it and the same thing happened, you wouldn't stop it. I'd just know next time to quit before it gets to me."

"Uh . . . no. You'll tell your man and he'll deliver a lesson."

"Tack—"

"Tyra," he cut me off quietly, leaning into me, "baby, listen to me because right now I'm delivering a lesson *to you* and I'm doin' it gentle-like so you'll get it and not freak. This is your new world. People don't fuck with people like us. They do, payback. This bitch might have been jealous you got promoted over her. But, my guess, she's butt ugly, possibly overweight and you said she was older. It wasn't about the promotion. It was about you bein' funny and sweet and smart and beautiful and she couldn't find a way to work with what she has and find happiness in herself so she saw all you had goin' for you and she had to drag you down. That's bullshit. You don't get to walk all over people without retribution."

He said I was beautiful.

Nice.

Further, that was the second time he said something like that today.

Very nice.

And he had my work situation figured out too even with limited information. She hadn't been exactly attractive, though not overweight but definitely older.

Even so, I said softly, "I'm not sure we agree about this, handsome."

"That's all right, darlin'. If what we're building doesn't go south, we're good and the job you got, you're surrounded by men so that shit's not gonna happen. And if it does, any man at the garage who's stupid enough to fuck with you will answer to me."

I could do that seeing as he was my boss so that would be his job anyway.

Still.

"And, if what we're building doesn't go south, something happens, an opportunity I can't refuse, I move on job-wise and someone targets me, then what?" I asked. "I mean, if you're my man, I should be able to talk with you about stuff like this without you going scary biker dude and laying a trail of devastation to someone's life."

Tack's hand moved to my neck and his body and face got even closer. "You move outta the office and not outta my life and shit goes down, then, Red, you don't hesitate to tell me.

You talk, I'll listen. I'll talk, you'll listen. And unless it's extreme, we'll sort it out before I take action."

I could do that too, maybe.

"But," Tack went on, "bottom line, no one fucks with my woman. So, if we sort shit out and my advice is you move the fuck on, that's what you do. You sleep beside me, Red, no fears, feeling safe. You do not lose sleep over bitches. And I like your mouth but I won't like it if you can't brush your teeth and you're pukin' all the time. Further to that, I like your body. You can't eat and you're pukin' all the time, you lose weight, I won't like your body as much. That don't work for me. So, you don't move on from a bad situation when that's the advice I'm givin' you, I'll be forced to take action to take care of you. And I will. We agreed?"

"Boiling that down, I do what you want me to do or you do whatever you want to do. Is that what I'm agreeing?"

Tack's mouth twitched.

Then he muttered, "Yeah."

"I'm noticing a theme to Life with Kane Allen," I remarked.

"Yeah, and that theme is, I got your back. I take care of you. You sleep easy. You eat good. And you feel safe. Are you tellin' me you got a problem with that?"

Well, presenting it like that, I didn't.

That said, I still did.

Carefully, I replied, "Do you see how my concerns over your responses to the way people treat me in life would make me think twice about sharing important things with you?"

"Yeah, baby, but do you see that when you're stuck in a box someone slammed over you and can't see clear, I give you advice that's lookin' out for you, you don't take it 'cause you can't see clear and the result is you come to harm in any way, I'm gonna act but I'll be doin' it in your best interests?"

Okay, well, presenting it like that, I did see.

Damn.

"You don't keep shit from me," Tack continued. "I will admit, there are times when I'll react, do it fast and do it on gut. But I lived through some serious shit and I'm still doin' it. I learned you don't carry through with a knee-jerk response. You think about shit and you do it smart. Eliminate blowback. Get the shit job done in a way you can move ahead free and easy."

This took us to a new topic of conversation, one I wanted to talk about less but also one that I had been able to avoid when I wasn't officially pronounced Tack's woman.

One I couldn't avoid now.

"Speaking of that," I started, "the living-through-serious-shit part. Now that circumstances have changed, are you going to share?"

"Yeah, I am," Tack surprised me by replying. "But I'm not gonna do it now."

"Why not now?"

"'Cause I gotta get my woman a glass of wine. Then I got green beans to cook. Then I want you to enjoy what you're eatin' and not be thinkin' about that shit while you do it. And after that, we'll be in your bedroom and we won't be doin' much talkin'."

A number of things to look forward to.

Nevertheless.

"Although I don't want to know, I kind of want to know and maybe sooner is better than later."

Tack's hand slipped down me so his arm curved around my back and he dipped his head so he could touch his mouth to mine.

When he lifted it, he said quietly, "My chops are fuckin' superb. My stuffing, better. Those potatoes, babe, you let loose and enjoy your food, they'll rock your world. And I made the effort to cook it because I want you to enjoy it. And I like this easy with you and I don't wanna lose it. Not tonight, our first night of having it. What I will tell you so I can shift that worry outta your eyes is, I've lived through worse and I'm still standin'. This Russian mob shit is a pain in my ass and has been a good long while. That said, it's also turnin' out to be the means to bring cohesion back to the Club. You're new but you're also Chaos, new or not. No one fucks with Chaos because Chaos fucks back, as a unit. You fuck one, you fuck us all. So at least I got one less problem because the boys are at my back with that shit and not arguin' about other shit. The kids are right now at my house and they're happier there. That's a Band-Aid but it's workin'. Another problem down. And you and me have shifted to a place I like and, way you are right now, you like it too. Let's have this. Later, I'll fill you in. Now, let's keep this good."

I couldn't argue with that so I whispered, "Okay." Then I set out to confirm. "But you'll tell me later?"

"Said I would, I will."

I nodded then pressed, "About all of it?"

"All of it?" he asked.

"You've lived through worse and you're still standing," I clarified.

His arms gave me a squeeze. "You wanna know, Red. I'll tell you. Just not tonight."

He'd tell me.

I let him in, he was letting me in.

And cooking for me while doing it.

I was thinking I could ride this new roller coaster. I was even thinking I liked it.

I pressed closer as I said, "FYI, handsome, I can cook too."

"You're up tomorrow night."

I edged back half an inch. "But tomorrow night is at your house."

"Yeah, my house. And bein' a house, it's got a kitchen. So you're cookin' at my house."

"But I won't know where anything is."

"I don't have kitchen utensils from Mars, babe. I found my way around yours. You'll find your way around mine."

Of course.

"Right," I murmured then told him, "If you want to get on with the green beans, I can get myself a glass of wine. Do you want a beer?"

"Yeah, I want a beer and I also want you to keep your ass where it is. I'll get your wine."

"Tack, I can get my wine and your beer and come right back and hang with you while you finish dinner," I offered, thinking I was being nice.

Tack's eyes flashed with amusement as he said, "I bet you can, Red, but what's up for debate is if you cannot argue about every fuckin' thing."

My back went straight. "I was being nice!"

"I see you can't," he muttered, his lips tipped up at the edges.

"Whatever," I snapped. "Wait on me. See if I care. I'll just sit here and sniff chops."

"Honest to God," Tack kept muttering as he moved away from me and toward the fridge, "she's pissed I'm gettin' her a glass of wine while I'm cookin' for her."

"I'm not pissed, pissed. I'm *mildly* pissed but only because you won't let me help," I amended.

Tack stopped, fingers wrapped around the fridge door handle, and he twisted to me. "Tomorrow, you can take care of me. Deal?"

I stared at him. Then I agreed, "Deal."

If I wasn't mistaken, I saw his grin right before his head disappeared in the fridge.

Then it occurred to me that I could argue about every fucking thing, including Tack getting me a glass of wine.

Which even I had to admit was ridiculous.

But, if that grin was any indication, Tack liked it.

So I looked at my lap and grinned too.

Because I was, at that moment, really glad he did.

* * *

My head snapped back and I gasped, "Oh my *God*."

Then I came. Hard.

The instant I did, Tack whipped me to my back and kept pounding deep. So I wrapped all four limbs around him tight and kept coming. Harder.

"Fuck," Tack muttered against my mouth between grunts, "my girl's got a greedy fuckin' pussy."

He was right. I did. Because I was *still* coming.

When I stopped coming, Tack was still driving deep and it felt so freaking good, it started to build again.

I held him tight, lifting my hips to take him deeper, and slid one hand up his back, his neck and into his thick, longish hair as I whispered against his lips, his goatee tickling my skin, "Honey, you have to come or I'm gonna come again."

"This is a problem?" he grunted back.

I saw his point.

So I smiled against his mouth.

He slanted his head and kissed me.

About thirty seconds later, I came again.

About a minute after that, Tack did.

About thirty seconds after that, Tack's hand slid lightly down the skin of my side, causing tingles that hit midrange on the pleasant scale but high on the soothing scale and his lips at my neck whispered, "Like that."

I liked it too. All of it. Going down on him and Tack returning the favor. Then, because he was so good at it, getting greedy, pushing him to his back and him letting me. Then climbing on and riding him until I came. And last, finishing when he flipped me and rode me until I came again and he did too.

Yeah, I liked it. All of it.

"I like it too," I whispered then suggested, "maybe we shouldn't talk, just have sex. Obviously, that works for us."

His head came up and his dancing eyes caught mine. "Obviously. But that wasn't what I was talkin' about."

"What were you talking about?"

"You called me 'honey,'" he answered then muttered, "Sweeter, hearing you say that when I'm buried inside you."

His words hit me and that hit was well above the midrange of the pleasant scale.

"Though, wouldn't know," he went on, "since you haven't called me that except just now when I was buried inside you."

My head tilted on the mattress. "I haven't?"

"Nope. You've called my kids that. You've called your girl that. You haven't called me that."

Boy, he'd really been paying attention.

"Well, I didn't know I liked you until about eight fifteen this morning so that's not surprising."

He grinned. "You knew you liked me."

Arrogant. Annoying. But hot.

"I didn't," I retorted. "Except that first night but I thought that was a fluke because, since then, you were a jerk."

His grin got bigger.

"Sometimes a scary jerk," I went on.

His grin turned into a smile.

"And, I will admit, sometimes a sweet jerk."

He started chuckling and I liked *that* since he was still on me and inside me so I tightened my limbs around him and enjoyed the ride.

But, like all rides, it ended. Fortunately, it ended with Tack pulling out gently then rolling both of us so we were righted in the bed and I had one side in the covers and one side resting on him. I slid my arm along his belly, laid my cheek on his shoulder and relaxed into him.

"Now that you know I'm not a jerk, I gonna hear more of that?" he asked when we'd settled and I lifted my head to look at him to see his goateed chin dipped down to look at me.

"You want to hear it?" I asked back, my voice soft.

"Yeah."

"Why?"

"Why?"

"Yes, why?"

"'Cause, babe, you say it to people you like and people who mean somethin' to you and clue in, I wanna be both."

Oh God.

I closed my eyes and dropped my forehead to his shoulder.

Damn.

Yes. This definitely felt like I had my dream man.

"You really can't handle sweet," he noted on a mutter.

"No, I really can't," I replied to his shoulder, and his arm came around so his fingers could sift into my hair.

"Fair warning, Red, you're gonna have to suck it up."

A startled laugh fluttered out of my throat and I lifted my head to look at him. And when I did, I saw his handsome head resting on my pillow, I felt his hard, warm body under mine and I liked both so much it hurt. But in a good way.

Therefore, stupidly, I blurted, "I like you here."

His eyes warmed, his fingers curled around the back of my head and he murmured, "Red."

"Please take care of this with me," I whispered.

His head gave a slight jerk then his eyes focused intensely on mine.

"The reason you haven't been tied to a man," he muttered.

"What?"

"You've been fucked over," he guessed inaccurately.

But I couldn't tell him the reason I wanted him to help me take care of what we had. It was too new. Way too new. I didn't trust it yet. I couldn't trust him with the knowledge that he colored my world.

He knew, in essence, that I feared what he made me feel.

He just didn't get how big it was.

And I wasn't ready to share that with him.

"Men are men and they do stupid shit that hurts, handsome, but that's not it," I shared. "But I'll tell you what it is. Later. Tonight, let's just have this."

He was silent a moment, eyes holding mine, then he replied, "I'll give you that play."

I grinned at him and whispered, "Thanks."

He grinned back and used his hand at my head to pull my mouth to his.

Once he'd touched my lips lightly to his, he let me back a couple of inches and asked, "Your pussy get enough or does it need more attention?"

"I think it's good," I answered then finished, "for now."

His eyes danced again. "You'll tell me, I need to get down to business."

"I'll keep you in that loop."

I watched his eyes dance more before he asked softly, "You wanna clean up or sleep with me inside you?"

I felt my heart flutter at this question. I liked the intimacy of it. I liked the language he used. What I never liked was sleeping after sex without cleaning up. But the way he asked that made me want to keep him with me.

So I answered quietly, "You inside me."

"Good, baby, now shift under the covers," he ordered, but he was still talking softly.

I liked that too.

Moving with Tack, I shifted under the covers. He twisted to turn the light off on his side of the bed and I rolled to turn the light off on mine. Then he claimed me and settled us exactly as we were before, me tucked to his side, my cheek to his shoulder, arm around his gut and his arm under me, wrapped around, hand resting on my waist.

This, I'd never had. Five lovers, two longish term, none was a cuddler. And I knew Tack was one because he settled us this way, because he'd curled into me the only other time we slept in the same bed and he'd snuggled with me when we slept on my couch.

And I liked this too.

"Thank you for dinner. It was yummy," I murmured to his chest in the dark, and this was no lie. His chops and stuffing rivaled his fajitas. His potatoes were so good, they rivaled his pancakes. And he melted butter to pour on his green beans and sprinkled them with real, crispy bacon bits. The dinner was a triple pork threat. The calories and fat it contained had to be off the charts. It was also divine.

"Glad you liked it, darlin'."

"Is the office going to be a nightmare now that I've had two unexpected days off?" I asked.

"Don't know. Don't work in the office. But you'll find out tomorrow."

This was true.

I kept talking. "Do you cook like that all the time?"

"It's worth eatin', it's worth puttin' the time in to make it taste good."

This was true too.

"So is that a yes?"

"No, it isn't a yes. It's a, if I cook, I do it right. But a lot of the time I don't have the time so it's takeout."

"Even when you have your kids?"

"Even when I have the kids. Though sometimes Rush or Tabby'll get a wild hair and try something. Rush has inherited his old man's talent in the kitchen. Tabby gets workin' near a stove, it's a crapshoot."

"Oh," I mumbled, finding this both interesting and his telling of it sweet. Then I asked, "What's that red car you're working on?" and when I did, Tack burst out laughing.

I lifted my head and looked at him through the dark. "What's funny?"

"Babe, you goin' to sleep or we gonna have a conversation in the dark?"

"I thought we were getting to know each other."

"We are and we did, in a lot of ways, Red. You provin' you can ride me even harder and faster than that first night we had together bein' my favorite part. But now I'm wiped. You wanna talk, store that shit up and we'll do it at my place tomorrow night."

"You're wiped?"

I felt his hand land on my face, his palm at my jaw, fingers light on my cheek and he replied, "Two nights ago, I fucked up and hurt a woman I'd come to care about. I been waiting for this morning, hopin' you'd roll up to Ride and I wouldn't have to hunt you down. But if you were really pissed at me in a way I couldn't fix, this morning could have gone different.

Thinkin' on that and all the other shit swirling in my life, the last two nights I haven't slept all that great. But I ate good, I just came hard, I'm in your bed, you like me here and you called me honey so I'm thinkin' tonight's my night. That is, if you'd shut up and let me sleep."

"I'll shut up and let you sleep," I offered immediately because I liked all of that and I liked it most of all.

And what I liked best of that most of all was knowing that he was worried I wouldn't forgive him and if I hadn't come to Ride, he was going to find me.

He wasn't going to let me go.

I *did* matter.

"So, you gonna settle in and let me sleep or you gonna stare at me in the dark while I do that?" he asked when I didn't move and kept staring at him in the dark.

"I'll settle," I whispered then did what I told him I'd do.

I was looking at the shadowed planes of his chest, feeling warm and fuzzy, and I'd been doing this for a while when Tack muttered, "Every day, somethin' new. Will I ever get to the heart of you?"

I pulled in a deep breath.

Damn, but I liked that too, and the part I liked was it sounded like he both wanted to and didn't but either way would be fine with him.

"I don't know. No one has ever tried," I answered quietly.

"Well, darlin', gratitude. 'Cause you just ensured I'll sleep good knowin' I'm the first man who gets that shot."

That made me turn my head, press my face in his skin and deep breathe to control happy tears.

"Fuck me, she really can't handle sweet," he muttered to the ceiling.

"So stop doing it," I suggested.

"Not a chance," he returned.

God, I hoped not.

I really, really did.

*   *   *

My eyes opened to the early dawn light weakly shining through the curtains and dimly lighting the room.

And what I saw was Tack's chest and his tats.

We were in the same position we'd fallen asleep in, me tucked tight to his side, cheek cushioned by his shoulder, his arm wrapped around me, mine wrapped around his gut.

We hadn't moved, either of us, all night.

I liked that. So much my hand slid up his side, over his chest and to his neck where my fingers curled around but my thumb moved out to glide along the stubble next to the edge of his goatee. As I did this, I turned my head to kiss his shoulder. Then, with the tip of my tongue, I trailed a path to his nipple where I let my tongue swirl.

He tasted great.

His arm around my waist tightened and I lifted my head just enough to see his sleepy, sexy, already heated blue eyes on me.

"You need to get down to business," I whispered, and his eyes went from heated to *hot.*

Then his other arm locked around me. He rolled me to my back and he did what he needed to do, proving Elvira right.

Biker boys knew how to live.

CHAPTER NINETEEN

Except Better

"OH LORDY, STOP talking."

This demand came from Elvira and when it did, the table full of women at Club burst out laughing. This was because I'd just explained precisely Tack's ability to give pleasure. And I did this because I was highly inebriated.

It was Wednesday night and we were at Club.

The last two days I'd spent in the office at Ride's garage dealing with work and man drama. As far as the work was concerned, it wasn't like I was gone two days. It was like I was gone two weeks.

And, kid you not, men were crazier than women. Each mechanic and body guy's life was like a soap opera, and they did not leave it at home. Over donuts and coffee, they were in my office telling me about it. Breaking up with women, making up with them, juggling two at a time (or three and, in one case, four), exes entering the picture, hysterical pregnancies, real pregnancies, STD scares, women who didn't "get them," skanky 'hos they fell for and who stole from them, financial troubles, car troubles (yes, mechanics had car troubles!), family troubles.

It wore me out just listening to it. Then again, I'd been

listening to it for two weeks, they'd broken me in early, so I figured one day, I'd get used to it.

And going to Tack's house after work the night before was no less exhausting.

The good thing was, riding on the back of Tack's bike with Tack was phenomenal. I'd ridden on the back of a bike before but I'd never done it with a man who I could press close to and hold tight.

It. Was. *Awesome*.

The other good thing was that Tack had a fantastic house. He lived on a quiet, secluded lot up in the foothills, his house built into the mountains, and nearly the whole front was a deck that had spectacular views. You walked into an open entryway that fed to the left into a big comfortable living room that jutted out past the deck. Straight off the entryway was a big kitchen with views to the deck and beyond. The house was long, three bedrooms (one Tabby's, one an office and one Tack's master that had its own bath) and bathroom all off one side down a hall. The other side had more windows with Tack's spectacular views.

What surprised me was that it didn't scream *Biker!* Not that I would know what that was, just that it didn't look rough and tumble and lived in and mostly filthy like the Chaos Compound. Just lived in. It wasn't tidy but it was relatively clean and the kitchen was clearly used but immaculate. The furniture in the living room had been chosen for comfort only, wide seats, slouchy cushions, lots of throws and toss pillows, all inviting you to take a load off.

Although it didn't scream *Biker!* it was decorated in "the Biker Experience." A framed black-and-white picture of what Tabby told me was Sturgis, South Dakota, circa some other time when there were oxen and horses in the dirt streets. A framed, greasy motorcycle sprocket that Tabby told me was from Tack's first bike. Jumbled frames holding pictures of Tack's kids as well as men I knew or had seen (in other words, members of Chaos) and others I didn't know. All of them wearing tees or leather jackets or leather vests with their arms slung around each other's shoulders. All of them wearing shit-eating grins. All of them hairy, rough poster boys for the biker lifestyle. Some of pictures had Tack in them at varying ages from teenager to who he was today. And rounding out the décor was a number of motorcycle rally posters.

Tack carried my bag to his bedroom with Tabby and me following (Tabby talking). I found it had a big bed, two nightstands but only one that had a lamp, no alarm clock. A dresser across the room from the bed, tall, six drawers. There were two big windows covered in beige curtains. Tacked to the wall above the bed was a huge, slightly tattered American flag. And there were more picture frames filled with snap-shots but not on the walls, on the dresser. Rounding out the look of Tack's room were jeans, t-shirts, socks, belts, boxer briefs and boots in a tangle on the floor.

The night at Tack's was exhausting because Tabby and Rush were there. I found teenagers had a lot of energy. And they were noisy.

I discovered the last part of this when we showed and there was music coming up from the basement where Rush had his room. It was metal and it was loud.

Clearly in her element and entirely comfortable, Tabby assumed the woman-of-the-house role and claimed me immediately. She showed me around, gave me the lay of the land in the kitchen, got me a drink and gabbed animatedly to me the whole time. It was like she'd been deserted on an island, hadn't seen another human being in ten years and was beside herself with joy that she finally had more than a coconut to talk to.

That day, Tack had called and sent Rush out with a grocery list I prepared so all the fixin's were available to make dinner for Tack and his kids. This I did to the stylings of Led Zeppelin. No, strike that. This I did with a continual loop of their song "Rock and Roll." It was a kickass song but the twelfth time, I had to admit, I was over it.

Fortunately, Tack was too and I knew this when he stalked to the open door to the basement and shouted down the stairs, "Either you move to the next track or your fuckin' stereo is sailing over the deck!"

"Black Dog" immediately came on.

This was such a relief that I smiled at Tabby. She burst out laughing.

And I thought that was nice. Not Tack shouting threats of stereo mutilation but the whole thing. Cooking with Tabby jabbering to me. The comfortable, lived-in house with spectacular views and a fantastic kitchen. The way they had about them that firmly said a family lived there.

Yes. I decided I was liking this roller coaster.

I made spaghetti with my homemade meatballs, garlic bread and Caesar salad with homemade dressing. I followed this with pistachio/chocolate parfaits made in some of Tack's tumblers with pistachio and chocolate pudding (instant, I didn't have the time to make homemade and, further, I didn't know how to make homemade pudding) and Cool Whip sprinkled with pistachio nuts. The meal wasn't as good as Tack's food but Tack and his kids hoovered through it. It also packed close to the same calorie and fat wallop so I figured I did all right.

We ate all of this in front of Tack's huge, flat-screen TV in the living room where I was treated to a marathon of *Storage Wars*. Seeing as I didn't watch TV, I'd never heard of this program. But by the second episode I was hooked. I declared that I thought Brandi and Jarrod were "adorable" together, which for some reason he didn't explain made Rush laugh so hard I thought he would bust a gut. Rush might find that funny but I decided I was going to start dressing like Brandi. She always looked the shit. I also shared that Dave was my favorite "character" to which Tabby told me with grave seriousness, "But, Tyra, he's the bad guy."

I thought he was the guy who knew what he was doing and I liked his grin, but what did I know?

Since the kids stayed up late, Tack and I went to bed before them. This I found uncomfortable and what made it more uncomfortable was Tack doing it like he often took women to bed with his kids around. Not to mention his kids acting like this was nothing out of the ordinary. Further, I found myself in the unusual mood of not being in the mood with Tack.

Kids, I discovered, were a wet blanket.

But when we hit his room, Tack made no moves on me.

He just said, "You get the bathroom first, babe. I gotta tell Rush something."

He took off and I rooted through my bag. I was wearing a sky blue shelf-bra cami and a pair of mocha drawstring pajama short shorts with sky blue and grass green swirls on them, sitting cross-legged on his unmade bed when he returned.

It was then I found Tack's nighttime routine included taking off his clothes and dropping them on the floor. Considering the thick layer of clothes on the floor, this wasn't a surprise.

It was also then I found, when he climbed into bed with me, turned out the one lamp then tucked me in his side, Tack wasn't in the mood either.

And last, I found that in his bed, we had different sides.

Not that we had sides, as such, since, in our limited experience, we slept cuddled together. But in my bed I was on the right. In his, he positioned me on his left.

I lay cozied up to him in the dark for a while before he spoke.

"Dinner was good, Red."

"Thanks," I whispered.

"And I get you. Dave from *Storage Wars* is the man."

I smiled into the dark. Tack must have felt my cheek move on his shoulder because his arm gave me a squeeze.

We fell silent.

Then I started, "Um…"

Then I stopped.

"Yeah?"

"Nothing," I whispered.

"Um…what?"

"Nothing."

"What?"

"Nothing, Tack."

"Start it, say it," he ordered.

I sighed. Then I said it.

"The, uh…kids didn't seem surprised you and I headed off to bed together."

"They wouldn't, seein' as I called them and told them you were comin' up to make dinner and you were spendin' the night. Rush even went to get the food, darlin'."

This was true.

"Is this a, uh, normal occurrence?"

"It ain't normal. It also ain't out of the ordinary."

Damn.

Honesty was usually good except at times like these.

"Though, none of them made my kids dinner," Tack continued then concluded, "or sat around and watched TV with them."

This was something, but it didn't make me feel a whole lot better.

Tack's arm tightened and he pulled me on him and up so we were chest to chest and face to face in the dark.

"I ain't no choirboy," he said quietly.

"I know that," I said quietly back.

I knew it but still, I didn't like this aspect of it.

"Kids were younger, no way. Women up here only when they were at their mom's. They got older, way of the world."

Hmm. I might disagree with that if they were my flesh and blood.

Tack continued, "That said, babe, none of those bitches got here on the back of my bike either."

"Is this a significant distinction?" I inquired.

"Yep."

"Do they understand that?"

"Yep."

"Are you going to explain it to me seeing as I don't?" I asked.

Tack's chuckle rumbled all around me and *through* me, which sounded and felt nice.

When he stopped chuckling, he explained.

"Some bikers have a code about who they put on the backs of their bikes and when. Rally, party, road trip, could be whoever you pick up. Your wheels are takin' you home, for me, for Chaos, only the old lady. A woman comes up here, she has her own ride. That way, I'm done, she can go. *You* gotta wait for me to take you where you need to be. This means, unless I take you, you aren't goin' anywhere."

I'm done, she can go.

There was a lot there to get angry about so I decided to avoid it.

All of it.

"I'm thinking, handsome, it might be good to end the biker lesson now seeing as this particular one might piss me off."

"Not surprised, babe, but we had a good run."

"Pardon?"

"Took you to work, brought you to my house, you cooked, we ate, we watched TV, all good. No fights. No backtalk. All day. But all good things come to an end."

It was at this point I was *glaring* at him through the dark.

"I'm thinking now, handsome, it might be good for you to stop talking *altogether* seeing as everything you're saying might piss me off."

"Sound of it, babe, no 'might' about you getting pissed. You just are."

At that, my glare became a stare because not only did he sound like he was amused, I could see the white flash of his smile in the dark.

But to confirm, I asked, "Are you amused?"

"Fuck yeah."

I sought further confirmation. "You're amused that I'm pissed."

His other arm stole around me and he gave me a squeeze on his repeated, "Fuck yeah."

It was then, light dawned.

"You like it," I said softly.

"Definitely."

"You like me pissed off?"

"No. I like not knowin' what to expect. I like that even though you say I scare you, you are not scared of me. The way you face off against me, you're not scared. Not one fuckin' bit. I like that you don't hesitate to speak your mind. I like that you don't hide your emotions. I like that when you get pissed, you just do and let it all hang out. You don't store up that shit and let it explode all over the fuckin' place when I least expect it. So, yeah. I like it. Definitely."

How did he do that? Answer questions that had no good answers with a good answer.

"You're still pissed," Tack observed, clearly feeling my vibe.

"Well, yeah."

"Why?"

"Because you have good answers to questions that have no good answers and that's annoying."

"Why is that annoying?"

"Because I'm a woman. We get annoyed at all sorts of things that make no sense."

"Now who has a good answer to a question that doesn't have a good answer?"

Argh!

Sharp as a freaking tack!

"Now you're annoying because you're too clever for *my* own good," I informed him then I found myself on my back with Tack on top of me, his face so close to mine I could feel his goatee tickling my chin.

"She's gettin' it," he muttered.

"Getting what?"

"Why we work."

I felt my breath start to get heavy so I had to force out my, "And why's that?"

"Because I ain't stupid and you aren't stupid either. Because I'm wild and, you let loose from that green tea, salad and no TV shit, so are you. Because people are scared of me but you aren't. We're on equal footing, Red. No one has the upper hand." His lips moved so they were touching mine when he finished, " 'Cept you're a damn sight prettier than me."

Oh God, he was making me melt at the same time he was turning me on.

"You're hot," I told him, my hands sliding up the sleek skin and hard muscle of his back.

"Pleased you think so," he replied, his hand sliding up the skin of my side.

"No, everyone would think so. Even a nun. She'd pray for your immortal soul but, if pressed, she would have to admit you're good-looking because it's a sin to lie."

His hand stopped at my side and his thumb swept out, grazing the curve of my breast causing a delectable shiver to glide over my skin when he ordered, "Stop bein' cute, baby. You're makin' me hard and I can't fuck you when the kids are awake."

My hands slid back down his back, down, *down* until my fingers curved in his hard ass as I breathed, "You can't?"

"Fuck no. You're a moaner."

"I am?"

"Yeah. Loud."

Oh God.

"Really?"

"It's good. Really fuckin' good when my mouth is on you or my dick's inside you. When it ain't good is when Tabby and Rush are down the hall."

"I can see this," I whispered, sliding my hands back up, fingers and palms flat, taking in all I could get, my touch light.

"And it'd be good, you stop touchin' me."

"I like touching you," I said softly.

"I like it too, baby, but it ain't helpin' my fight to stop gettin' hard."

My hands stopped and I advised, "Then you might want to stop whispering against my lips, Tack, because that's turning me on."

"Yeah?"

"Mm hmm."

"Doesn't take much for you, does it, darlin'?"

With the others, it did.

But not with him.

I didn't share that.

Instead I said, "It's the goatee."

"Bullshit, it's me."

He totally had me figured out.

"Well, it is *your* goatee."

That was when I felt his lips smile against my mouth.

Then, alas, he lifted his lips from mine and stated, "Right, been a good night, Red. I learned somethin' gets up your ass, you don't delay and with only a little coaxing, you ask me about it. I learned you think I'm hot. I learned you can be cute when you're turned on. And it's a definite that I'm never shavin' off this goatee." I grinned at him through the dark but he concluded with, "Not that I was goin' to anyway."

"Well, I'm glad you've declared that as a definite," I told him with humor vibrating in my voice. "Brings me relief."

"Babe, you're still bein' cute."

"Oh. Right. I'll stop doing that right away."

"Christ, still fuckin' cute," he muttered, and his thumb did another sweep and grazed the curve of my breast, causing another shiver at the same time my nipples got hard.

Time for a subject change.

"When something gets up my ass, I don't delay in asking you about it?"

"Nope."

"What was up my ass?"

"You cottoned on to the fact the kids didn't blink I had a woman in my house. That crawled up your ass. You sat on it for about fifteen minutes. Only a little pressure from me, you put it out there."

"Oh."

"Before you ask and so you don't have to think about it, I like that too. Definitely."

"Good," I whispered, giving him a squeeze with my arms.

"Fuck me, now she's bein' sweet."

I laughed softly and offered, "You want me to get pissed and maybe throw a rant?"

"No, 'cause that makes me hard too."

"What doesn't make you hard?"

"Comes to you, not much."

Oh boy.

That was nice.

"Honey," I whispered.

"Fuck, baby," he growled, pressing his hips into me, "seriously, stop being sweet."

"Maybe we should go to sleep. I can't be anything unconscious."

"Yeah you can. You go back to cute."

I blinked up at him and asked, "Pardon?"

"You go back to cute. You got these times when you press close and you make noises."

"I make . . ." I paused, *"noises?"*

"Yeah."

"Are you saying I snore?"

"No. I'm sayin' you make noises."

"What kind of noises?"

Tack didn't respond for a moment then he asked, "You don't know you make 'em?"

"No."

"No other man told you about them?"

"No."

"Fuck, how many men have you had?"

"Tack," I steered him back to target, "noises?"

"In your throat. Like little moans. They're cute."

Oh God.

"They're also hot."

Well, that wasn't so bad.

Tack went on. "They sound like you sound when I'm buildin' it."

"Building what?"

"Buildin' you up to coming."

"Great," I muttered. "I don't know whether to be mortified or turned on."

"How about just bein' you. It isn't mortifying 'cause it's cute, it's sweet and it's hot. But it don't matter since there's nothing you can do about it anyway."

This was good advice so I decided to take it.

"Though," he continued, "when you do it pressin' up against me, it wakes me up, I hear it, you're close, I don't know whether to lie there and enjoy it or wake you up and fuck you."

At that moment, I would have advised him to choose the latter.

Instead, I suggested, "Go with your gut."

"Gut tells me to fuck you."

"Like I said."

Tack threw his head back and burst out laughing and I grinned through the dark at him while he did it. My arms around him, holding his big, shaking body close and really liking the sound and feel of his humor all around me.

When he was mostly done, but still chuckling, he dropped his head and took my mouth in a hot, sweet, wet, long kiss that left me slightly breathless and holding him even closer.

"All right, Red, time for some shut-eye," he muttered when he released my mouth.

"Okay, honey."

"Three."

"Pardon?"

"Three honeys."

He was counting.

"Now *you're* being sweet," I whispered.

"You gonna fall apart on me?"

"I'll try not to."

"Good," he said softly then dipped his head again and touched his mouth to mine before he rolled, taking me with him and settling us with me tucked into his side. "Now sleep."

"Your wish is my command."

"Attitude," he muttered.

"What do you expect? You just ordered me to go to sleep."

"You wanna watch TV with the kids?"

"No."

"So what's with the sass?"

"It's me."

"It is," he sighed. "Fuck me."

"You said you like it," I reminded him.

"Gotta shut up to sleep, Tyra," he noted.

"Apparently I don't since I make noises while sleeping."

"Fuck," he murmured.

"All right, all right. I'll shut up and sleep."

"'Preciate it, baby."

I snuggled closer. Tack's arm around my waist tightened while I did so and only relaxed after I did.

Then I studied the planes of his chest in the dark, the darker marks of his tats until my eyelids drooped and I fell asleep.

Tack woke me in the dead of night, hand between my legs, lips to mine and I could feel I was already wet. I knew this because I was totally turned on.

The second my eyes opened, he whispered, "Goin' with my gut, baby."

I smiled against his mouth.

Tack kissed the smile from my lips.

Then he fucked me.

Then he let me go back to sleep tucked to his side.

He fucked me again in his shower the next morning. Apparently, the shower drowned out my moans. It didn't matter anyway, the kids weren't up.

Then we got ready, he put me on the back of his bike and took me to work.

More soap opera from the boys at work before it was quitting time and I could go home and gussy up.

This brought me to now. Sitting in Club in a little halter-top dress that was clingy, had a short skirt, serious cleavage and was the color of aquamarines. I wore it with spike-heeled, strappy silver sandals. I also wore it with lots of chunky, kickass silver jewelry, three times as much makeup than I normally wore on my face and my hair out to *there*.

And I was sitting with Gwen, Mara, Tess Lucas (Mitch's partner's wife) and Elvira. Our posse also included Gwen's friends Camille and Tracy and Mara's friend LaTanya. And last there was a woman with loads of strawberry blonde curls who looked like a fairy princess. Her name was Sadie Chavez. I drunkenly didn't remember how she factored into the group but I did know she was semi-famous in Denver though I didn't remember how.

I watched the women laugh, fuzzily noticed that Elvira wasn't laughing but scowling and that Gwen was the first person to quit laughing and she did it with her eyes on me.

"So, Tack has kids?" she asked when the laughter died down.

"Yeah, two. Rush is seventeen, nearly eighteen. Tabby just turned sixteen," I answered.

"I didn't know Tack had kids," she muttered, and I lifted my cosmo to take a sip in order to hide my drunken elation that Gwen didn't know Tack had kids. And I felt this elation as any woman would, sitting and drinking with a woman her man had feelings for with those feelings once including the fact he thought she had staying power.

Being hooked up with Hawk, Gwen wasn't competition, this was true. What she was was a stunning, tall, curvy blonde wearing a fabulous little black dress, even more fabulous shoes and having a great sense of humor. Until I knew her better, she was going to be the stunning, tall, curvy blonde with excellent fashion sense for whom my man had feelings. Me not only knowing Tack had kids but meeting them and spending time with them meant I had one up on her.

"Seventeen and sixteen," LaTanya said, surprised, then looked at me. "How old is he?"

"Forty-one," Gwen answered, and I instantly took a shot to the heart.

First, because she knew how old Tack was and I didn't. That took away my one up.

Second, because Tack was forty-one.

Forty-one.

Ohmigod!

"Forty-one!" I shrieked, calculating it, the time it would take to make sure all was good, the length of an appropriate engagement, the time we'd want to have just him and me and coming up with a very bad figure while all eyes turned to me.

"Yeah, forty-one," Gwen stated then asked, "How old are you?"

"Thirty-five," I replied and I was. Thirty-five. Tack was forty-one, had two grown kids and my calculations put him at at least forty-three, maybe forty-four depending on when his birthday was when, if all worked out, we could start a family.

Oh…my…*God!*

"Oh my God. Oh my God. *Oh my God!*" I cried, slamming my drink down and covering my face with my hands.

This was a disaster!

"Thinkin' this is when the night turns bad," I heard Elvira mutter but I wasn't really listening. I was freaking out, despairing and shaking my head behind my hands.

"Tyra, are you all right?" I heard Sadie ask, and I brought my hands down sharply, slammed them on the table and exclaimed, "No!"

"Why?" Camille asked, watching me closely.

"Because this screws with my dream. I didn't think he was forty-one. He doesn't *look* forty-one. He looks thirty-six, *tops!*" I was close to yelling, and I noticed now Gwen was looking at me closely too and it wasn't hard to read, even inebriated, she didn't like what she saw. "How can he be forty-one and look thirty-six? He drinks beer. He shoots tequila. He eats more pork in one meal than most people have in a week. He rides motorcycles in the sun without a helmet. And he lives wild. That isn't possible!"

"Uh, forty-one isn't exactly old. And he's hot," Gwen remarked.

"I *know* he's hot. I'm intimately acquainted with all the ways he's *hot*," I returned.

"No, no, no," Elvira chanted, hand up, palm toward me, "don't go back there, girl. We already had the pleasure discussion and I might look recovered but, the shit you shared, I'm not."

"So, I don't get it, what's the problem?" Tracy asked the second Elvira quit talking, and I rocked my ass in my tall stool, making it wobble but getting closer to the table, settling in and I started to count it down.

"It's supposed to happen like this." I lifted a hand and grabbed my other index finger. "I find my dream man. No one else would do. I promised myself that. Dream man or nothing. No settling. So I didn't. I would have preferred to meet him ten years ago. I didn't. I met him at a party at Ride two and a half weeks ago. I didn't know this because he was fantastic in bed and gave me so many orgasms, I lost count—"

"What'd I say about pleasure discussion?" Elvira asked sharply, interrupting me, eyes narrowed. But I was on a mission, ignored her and kept right on talking.

"I knew it because he was funny. I knew it because he made me laugh. He made me feel beautiful. He made me forget about all the worries and shit in life and just have fun. Be alive. Then he was a jerk and I mean...*bad*. Then we fought, like, *a lot*. Then we had a drama that involved kidnapping and neither of us responded to that well but even though it sucked and hurt something awful, it was good in the end because I exposed my soft spot and Tack promised he'd handle me with more care. Now he's hot, great in bed, gentle and unbelievably sweet, all this proving he's the one. He's my dream man."

Distractedly I noticed Gwen wasn't looking at me like she didn't like what she was seeing anymore but was smiling at me.

"So, again, I don't get it. What's the problem?" Tracy somewhat repeated, and my eyes went to her.

"The problem is," my voice was rising and I let go of my finger, "the dream is, after I found my dream man, he'd woo me, which Tack doesn't do but I'm okay with that since he's a great cook, he thinks I'm cute, sweet and likes it when I get pissed which happens with him a lot and he's awesome in bed."

"Is no one listening to me?" Elvira asked, but I talked over her.

"Then he'd win me, marry me in a big-ass wedding that rivals anything the Windsors could dream up and then..." I leaned toward Tracy, "we'd have..." I leaned closer, nearly teetering off my chair, "lots of babies!" I slammed back in my stool and threw up my hands. "But he's forty-one! He's got two grown kids! He's not going to want to start again *now*! And he might be enough for me, being all that is Tack. That's a consideration. And he has two kids, good kids that I like. But they're older, almost grown up so it isn't like I can ride the wave of helping to raise another woman's kids to get my kid fix so I'd have to give up that part of the dream. And I promised I wouldn't give up any part of my dream. And *I want kids*!" Now I was mostly shouting and ended my shout with *"Gah!"*

Then I slapped my hands to my face again, covering it.

"I'm seeing her point," Tess whispered.

"Me too," Mara whispered back.

I dropped my hands and nabbed my clutch that was resting on the high round table we were sitting at, declaring, "I'm calling him. We're going to talk about this right now."

"No!" Elvira said loudly. "Girl, don't do that."

"I'm doing it," I mumbled, digging through my clutch.

"Don't do it, really, don't do it," Elvira advised.

"Why?" Tess asked.

"Because, she's been seein' this guy for a couple of

weeks. It's been drama most of that time, it's been good for only a few days, she's drunk and no way she should be talkin' to some biker about her dream wedding that rivals the shindigs of the Royals and lotsa babies after a few days of good," Elvira explained. "I don't know, I haven't read the handbook, but my guess is, bikers don't do royal weddings. More like rowdy weddings that end in someone gettin' stuck with a knife."

It was then I decided it was imperative I talked with Tack about his thoughts on weddings too. Though, maybe later.

"I'm with Elvira on this one." Camille put in her two cents. "Especially the drunk part seein' as Tyra's not drunk, she's hammered. I do not see good things with this talk. Men like drunk women who get horny. They do not like drunk women who get hysterical about future babies..." I looked at her and she finished, "or not, as the case may be."

Oh God.

I was totally calling him.

I dropped my head and started digging through my clutch again.

"But this is important, she shouldn't waste time if they don't see eye to eye on their future. She should talk to him." Sadie cast her vote.

"I agree," Tess agreed with Sadie.

"I'm on the fence," Tracy put in. "I see all your points."

"Why am I not surprised about that?" Elvira muttered, and I yanked out my phone and held it straight up in the air.

"Found it!" I cried.

"Oh shit," Elvira muttered again.

"Jesus," Camille murmured.

"Oh man," Gwen whispered.

I dropped my hand, dropped my head and started stabbing the phone with my finger.

"I'm guessing this means we're calling it a night," Tess declared. "I'm calling Brock. Anyone need a ride home?"

"Hawk's coming. He already texted me that he's on his way. We have room. I can give rides too," Gwen offered as I messed up and accidentally called my friend Susie in Tennessee so I had to disconnect and start over.

"Mitch is on his way too so we can take a few people," Mara stated and, at her words, I got distracted and looked at her because I suddenly forgot what I was doing seeing as I wanted to meet Big-Hearted Detective Mitch Lawson.

"I took a taxi here and Tack told me this would go long so he decided he's at his place tonight. I'll take a ride with you and Mitch," I told her.

"Cool," she said softly and smiled at me.

I went back to my phone and successfully hit Tack's contact so I put it to my ear and listened to it ring.

It rang once then his gravelly voice came at me with, "Everything good?"

Damn, I liked his voice. Even on the phone.

"We need to talk," I declared.

Silence then, "Say again?"

"Where are you?" I asked.

"The Compound havin' drinks with the boys," he answered.

"We need to talk. Now or close to now. My place when, of course, I get there and, uh, you do too. Mitch and Mara are taking me home."

"We need to talk?"

"Yep."

"About what?"

I brought the mouthpiece of my phone closer to my lips and whispered with heavy meaning, *"Everything."*

"Oh shit," Elvira muttered.

"Jesus," Camille murmured.

"Oh man," Gwen whispered.

"Everything?" Tack asked.

"Absolutely everything."

"That's gonna take a long time, Red," Tack observed.

"No. The everything we need to talk about requires yes-or-no answers from you."

"It's nearly two in the morning," Tack noted.

"Are you too busy to talk about everything, which means everything important...*in life*?" I asked with grave, but drunken, seriousness, and the drunken part was communicated by me slurring my words more than a little bit.

Silence then, "Are you smashed?"

"Completely and totally."

"What are you wearing?"

"Who cares?"

"I do."

"Why?"

"'Cause you're smashed, you been with your girls, you somehow got riled up about somethin' and once I settle you down about whatever's aggravating you, I'm gonna rile you up a different way."

My toes curled. Promptly after that, I got annoyed.

"Stop turning me on when I have the weight of my future happiness on my mind!" I snapped.

"Oh lordy," Elvira muttered.

"Right on," Gwen whispered.

"Why do I suddenly want a scary biker dude?" LaTanya asked.

From Tack with a smile in his voice, I heard, "I'll be there in ten."

"No, I'm getting a ride with Big-Hearted Mitch."

"Big-Hearted Mitch?" Tack asked.

"Big-Hearted Detective Mitch Lawson," I clarified.

"Seems she knows your story," LaTanya muttered to who I guessed was Mara though I wouldn't know since I was staring at the table.

"I like that title for Mitch," Mara muttered back, confirming my guess. "It fits."

"I'll be there in ten, Red," Tack repeated.

"No, really, I want to ride with Mitch and Mara. I'll meet you at my place."

"Baby," his voice gentled, "this is me seein' to that soft spot when I say quiet-like that I...will...be...there...*in ten*. And what I mean is, when I get there in ten, your ass better be there."

Oh boy.

"Are you coming on your bike?"

"Yeah."

"I'm in a tight, short little aquamarine dress with high heels. I can't get on a bike."

"You're in a tight, short dress and high heels?" Tack asked.

"Yes."

"I'll be there in five."

"Tack!" I exclaimed but he'd disconnected.

I did too and looked at Mara. "Tack's ruining my ride home experience with Big-Hearted Mitch. He's going to be here in five."

Mara smiled and offered, "We'll have you over for dinner. That way you can meet Bud and Billie."

Bud and Billie were Mara's second cousins. Bud and Billie were also the kids Mitch and Mara were raising because their dad was a criminal asshole.

"Awesome," I breathed, grabbed my glass and sucked back the last of my cosmo.

"We shoulda confiscated that while she was distracted by her scary biker dude," LaTanya noted, eyeing the empty glass I put back on the table.

"Too late now," Elvira replied.

Sadie whispered, "Excuse me," slipped off her stool and disappeared.

I stared after her thinking she totally looked like a real-life fairy princess. And I kept thinking this, my gaze growing hazy and unfocused, until she slipped back on her stool two minutes later. This woke me up, my body gave a slight jerk and my head filled with the possibility that Tack wouldn't want to have more kids when I did, badly, which would mean bad things for us. I was doing this, my heart beginning to hurt, as my head did a distracted scan of the still-heaving restaurant/bar but my eyes caught on something. Then my head snapped back and I felt my eyes grow round. When the fullness of all that was meeting my vision penetrated, my hand shot out to curve around the edge of the table and my breath left me.

"Holy crap," I whispered as I stared at the men sauntering to our table.

One was Hawk.

Suffice it to say, considering I'd been in the throes of a kidnap rescue, I hadn't taken him in fully when I first met him. He was not wearing a tee and cargo pants. He was wearing a dark gray, slim-fit shirt and jeans. They looked good on him. Way good. Otherworldly good. And he wasn't hot. He was *smoking hot.*

With him were three other men. Two were tall, dark and gorgeous and both gorgeous in a way that was also otherworldly. One was older and had unusual but unbelievably beautiful silver eyes, these soft and aimed at Tess. One was younger and had soulful, dark brown eyes, these gentle and they were on Mara.

And last, there was a Hispanic man who was rough around the edges and needed a haircut about three weeks ago but he worked it almost as good as Tack. His eyes were black, they were intense but sweet and they were on Sadie.

"We've hit the hot guy mother lode," I whispered reverently when they were about five feet from our table.

"Welcome to my nightmare," Elvira muttered. "Though you got yourself a biker who fills his Levi's so well he should be in Harley-Davidson ads and has an off-the-charts ability to give pleasure so you can't really understand my pain."

I again ignored Elvira because the Hot Guy Crew hit our table and I was busy leaning forward and breathing in their general direction. "Hello, boys."

Two pairs of black eyes, one pair of brown and one pair of silver shifted to me. All the men grinned but only Hawk had dimples. Two of them.

They were *hot*.

My heart fluttered.

Hawk looked down at Gwen, claiming her by sliding an arm around her shoulders, and I decided instantly they looked freaking *great* together. "See you had a good night," he muttered.

"Tyra, this is Mitch," Mara said, and I tore my eyes off Hawk to see Mitch had done the claiming shoulder thing with his woman on her stool.

"Big-Hearted Mitch," I whispered.

"Sorry?" he asked.

"That's your new title," Mara answered, her head tipped back to look up at him and he dropped his chin to look down at her. "Big-Hearted Mitch."

I watched his full, beautiful lips twitch and I felt a different kind of flutter.

"And this is Brock," Tess put in, and my eyes went to him.

"Do I have a title?" Brock asked.

"Silver Hottie," I answered and I heard girl giggles all around.

"What?" Brock asked, smiling, his deep voice amused.

"I just christened you that. Your eyes," I answered and then *his* lips twitched which caused another flutter.

"Hector's already known as Hispanic Hottie or Double H," Sadie put in, and I tore my eyes from Brock's mouth and looked at Hector who was staring at me, his dark eyes dancing. "Meet my husband," Sadie went on, "Hector Chavez."

"If anyone tells you you need a haircut," I advised, "tell them to jump in a lake."

"Will do," he muttered on his own lip twitch while sliding his arm around Sadie's shoulders.

"I see Tack found it," I heard Hawk say softly. I looked his and Gwen's way to see they were looking at each other, Hawk bent slightly toward her so they were close.

"You don't know the half of it," Gwen said softly back, smiling, and I was about to ask what they were talking about but I didn't get the chance when Hawk straightened and spoke.

"I'll get the check."

"Oh no!" I cried, opening my clutch. "Let me—"

"I'll get it," Brock interrupted me.

"We'll split it," Mitch put in.

"I got it," Hawk replied.

"Four ways," Hector's deep voice rumbled.

"You got it last time," Brock remarked.

"And I'll get it again this time," Hawk returned.

"Fuck, we'll split it," Mitch repeated but with an extra word.

"Oo lordy," Elvira whispered. "Normal men fight over the check and it can get nasty. Badasses fighting over the check, I don't see good things."

"I already got it," Sadie threw in at this juncture, and four sets of male eyes turned to her and although she looked like a fairy princess and was married to a serious hot guy, I didn't want to be her at that moment.

"Fuck me," Hector sighed then asked weirdly, "Did you also buy the restaurant while you were at it?"

"No!" Sadie snapped.

"That's a first," Hector muttered.

"I've never bought a restaurant, Hector," Sadie retorted.

"Way you spread your money around, *mi amor*, we won't be able to put our kids through college," Hector returned.

"I could buy three restaurants and still we'd be able to put our kids through college," she shot back, and I was surprised. First, because, obviously she was loaded. Second, because she'd seemed sweet and funny but not sassy. Clearly, she was sassy. It was way cute.

"Red," I heard a gravelly voice say and my head whipped around to see Tack standing at the other end of the table. "Bike."

Even though his presence ratcheted the hotness quotient surrounding our table up about seventeen notches, not to mention he was mine, I started glaring.

"Well, hello to you too, handsome."

"Bike," he repeated.

"Would you like to say hi to everyone?" I suggested.

He cast his eyes around the table and grunted, "Yo." Then he locked his eyes on me and reiterated, "Bike."

Picking a girl at random, I chose Tess. "He's not scary biker dude. He's *bossy* biker dude."

"Red," Tack cut in, and I looked back at him. *"Bike."*

I kept glaring at him.

"Now I see the other half of it," Hawk muttered at this point.

"Tyra," Tack stated in a warning, growly voice.

"Oh, all right," I snapped and hopped off my stool, catching Sadie's eyes. "Sadie, thanks for the drinks. That was sweet. My turn next time."

"Okay," she replied.

"Like that's gonna happen," Hector muttered.

Sadie rolled her eyes.

I smiled at her and looked at Hawk.

"I didn't get a chance to thank you for rescuing me."

"Don't mention it," he replied.

"I already did," I pointed out and got the dimples.

Wow.

"Then, you're welcome," he said.

I smiled at him then gave my good-byes and nice to meet yous and made my way to Tack. The instant I got close, his hand closed around mine and he dragged me toward the door.

I turned back and waved at the crew.

The girls waved back.

The men watched with lips tipped up.

I memorized the view because, seriously, they were like out of a movie about cool, badass macho men and funny, sassy women that dressed kickass who all bantered and got kidnapped frequently.

Except better.

CHAPTER TWENTY

Bright Orange

"WHAT'S THE HURRY?" I asked, running through the parking lot to keep up.

"The hurry is, you told me about the dress and shoes, babe. But you did not let me in on the face and hair. So, now that I got a look at it all, *especially* that hair, I wanna get this talk about everything outta the way so I can fuck you 'til you stop breathing."

At his reply, I stopped breathing.

Approximately a nanosecond later, he stopped us at his bike.

I forgot about Tack fucking me until I stopped breathing and stared at his bike as I drunkenly swayed.

"I'm not going to be able to get on that thing," I informed him as he swung a leg around.

"Climb on," he ordered when he settled in and was tinkering with starting the bike and my eyes went from his kickass Harley Dyna Glide to him.

"How?"

His eyes came to me. "How you always do it."

"Tack!" I snapped then concentrated on enunciating, "I'm in a short skirt."

"So?"

"So?" I asked back. "It'll be indecent."

"Not to me."

"Tack—"

"Climb on."

"Tack!"

He leaned toward me. "Babe, normally, you know practically anything you do makes me hard. Now you're drunk, you're wearing that dress, those shoes and you got that hair and just lookin' at you is doin' a number on me. We need to get home. Fast. Climb…the fuck…*on*."

I stared at him thinking, *nice*.

So I climbed on.

Although I was more than tipsy therefore it was wobbly and not the most graceful mount, it wasn't as hard as I thought it would be. Luckily no one was around so if there was a crotch shot to be had, there wasn't anyone to witness it.

The instant my hands slid around Tack's belly, the bike roared then we roared out of the parking lot. I held on tight and enjoyed the warm night air, the refreshing breeze, the feel of my soft body pressed close to Tack's hard one, and it seemed like we were at my house in seconds. This was unfortunate since during the ride I was thinking I could ride in the warm night air, pressed to Tack for years.

We got off, Tack grabbed my hand and walked up the walk. Since I was attached to him, I followed, carefully putting one foot in front of the other. At my front door Tack commandeered my keys and let me in. Once in, I immediately tossed my clutch across the room to the couch and turned to him. He was locking the door and the second he turned to me, I grabbed onto his tee and started walking backward, pulling him with me.

"Are we talkin'?" he asked and my hands in his tee yanked up fast and hard so he was forced to lift his arms so I could tug his shirt free. This I did.

I threw his tee to the side and latched onto his belt loops with my fingers, pulling him with me as I resumed walking backward.

This was when, stupidly, against Elvira's good advice, I commenced our important talk and I did it not only drunk but recklessly.

"We're multitasking because even if the results of our discussion means we're over or I have to take you and only you and give up part of my life's dream, we're still enjoying the rest of the night and I'm not in the mood to waste time."

Tack stopped dead and since he did, I was forced to do it too.

"Tack, we're nowhere near the bedroom," I pointed out.

"The results of our discussion could mean we're over?" he asked.

I went still at the sound of his voice. Low, more gravelly than normal and somewhat sinister.

"I told you it was important."

"The results of our discussion could mean we're over?" he repeated.

Suddenly, what I said in my drunken state penetrated and I whispered, "Yes," then said, "Maybe."

"Fuck, how did drinks with the girls bring us back here?" he growled.

"You're forty-one," I told him.

"Yeah, I am."

"Gwen told me," I shared.

"And?"

"And..." I hesitated then carried on, "I want kids."

"And?"

I blinked.

"And, well, you're forty-one."

"We covered that, Red."

"Plus, you have two kids," I reminded him.

"I know that," he told me.

"And they're almost grown."

"This is also something I know."

"So, I'm thirty-five."

"Got your job application, babe, read it. I know that too."

"So I have no time to waste," I said softly.

"Say again?"

"My biological clock is ticking," I explained.

His hands came up and curled around either side of my head as his head came down and his face got in mine. "We're skippin' this back-and-forth shit, babe. Spit it the fuck out."

"I calculated it," I told him and stopped speaking.

"Think I already told you we're skippin' the back-and-forth shit, Tyra," Tack warned, and I hastily went on to explain.

"I calculated it. If this works with wooing time, as it were, engagement, wedding, time alone together, by the time we could get down to making babies, you'll be forty-three, forty-four. And you've got two kids already grown. You won't want to start over."

His hands slid down to the sides of my neck and he asked, "Who says?"

I blinked again and my heart jumped.

Then I whispered, "You want more kids?"

"Sure. I like kids."

My heart leaped and my voice was pitched high when I asked, "Really?"

"Yeah."

"With, uh...me?"

"Seein' as I've made it clear we're buildin' somethin' here, then the answer to that is, yeah. Not gonna go out and find another bitch and make babies with her when you're in my bed."

I lifted my hands to his chest and slid them down to his flat abs while I leaned into him and whispered, "Seriously?"

"Seriously, babe. What the fuck?"

"I really want kids, Tack. I always have and I was worried you wouldn't want to do it all over again."

His hands slid down and around so he was holding me while he stated, "Wasn't hard the first time."

I pressed closer to him, my hands sliding around his waist to wrap around his back as I said, "You'd know more than me but still. You're a guy who lives wild and free. Your kids are almost grown so, when they finish growing and move on, you can be wilder and freer."

"Baby," he whispered, giving me a squeeze, "kids are not a ball and chain. There is no greater joy than creating a life, watching it grow and, while it does, helping it thrive. Didn't feel stuck when God gave me Tabby and Rush. Kids are a big part of the ride of life. Not to mention one of the best parts of that ride. With the right woman, I'd be all over doin' it again."

Oh.

My.

God!

That was *so* beautiful.

"Tack," I said softly.

"How many you want?"

"Two, maybe three."

"Figure I could do that," he muttered.

My arms grew tighter around him, I pressed close and whispered, "Honey."

His arms grew tighter around me and he asked, "We done with this talk about everything?"

"Yes," I answered.

"You good?" he asked.

Oh yes. I was good.

I nodded but added another soft, "Yes."

His hands slid down over my ass and he ordered, "Then hop up, baby. Time to fuck."

My skin erupted in goose bumps and I hopped up as his fingers dug into my ass and helped by pulling me up. I wrapped my legs around his hips, my arms around his shoulders and I dropped my head, my mouth aiming for his. I hit the target, one of his hands slid up my bare back to my neck and up into my hair, holding my head to his as his tongue spiked into my mouth and he started walking.

Before I knew it, my back hit bed and the heavy warmth of Tack's body hit mine.

I instantly planted my spike-heel-shod foot in the bed and rolled him to his back, me on top, where I adjusted so I was straddling him.

"Baby," he whispered.

"I get to play."

He was silent a moment before he muttered, "Won't argue with that."

This was good since I'd already started and I didn't start slow. Hands, lips, tongue, I explored his chest, spent some time at his nipples, discovered every inch of his neck, I took my time doing it and I ended at his mouth.

As I kissed him, his hands that as I'd been playing wandered my back and my ass, yanked up my skirt. They slid over the small of my back and down into my panties where his fingers clenched into my ass. Our kiss was so hot, I started grinding my very female parts against his very hard male parts and one of Tack's hands slid from my ass, around and in. Then his fingers slid inside the gusset of my panties. At this, I was forced to break the kiss when he hit the spot, my head jerked back and I gasped.

"Oh God," I whispered after I gasped and his finger slid inside as his thumb hit the spot and I gasped again then repeated a breathy, *"Oh God."*

"Ride that, baby," Tack growled and my hips acquiesced to his demand.

He did this a while, it felt good and I tried to kiss him while he did it and succeeded, at first. But I ended up giving up because I was so turned on I was panting against his lips.

I'd moved onto moaning, my hips were bucking and it was seriously building when Tack grunted, "Jesus. Fuckin' hell. Greedy."

He was *so* right. I *so* was.

Then his hand between my legs was gone, his hand at my ass was gone, both were at my waist and I was flying through the air while being twisted.

I landed on my back deeper in the bed and my panties were torn down my legs. Then my legs were yanked apart. Then Tack's mouth was there.

Yes.

I slid my fingers in his hair, Tack tossed my legs over his shoulders, I dug my heels in, lifting my hips to get more of his mouth and I whispered, "Honey."

Tack growled between my legs and it felt so good my hips jerked. He cupped my ass in both hands, pulling me up, taking me harder with his mouth and my hips jerked again.

It was building, about to burst and I needed him inside.

"I want your cock," I begged, my fingers fisting in his hair, my heels digging deeper into his back.

Tack didn't reply. He kept eating.

God, his mouth felt good.

"Honey, *God,*" I breathed. "Please."

His head turned and he kissed my inner thigh then muttered, "You'll get it, baby, come in my mouth."

Then he went back to eating.

God!

My hips jerked again then they bucked then it built and I cried out when I gave him what he wanted and came in his mouth.

Brilliant.

I hazily felt him kiss my belly while he slid a finger through the wetness between my legs making my hips jerk again before he was gone. I didn't have my wits about me but I vaguely heard boots and a belt buckle hit floor and then he was back, rolling me to my belly. With hands spanning my hips, he pulled me up so I was on my knees. I felt him move in the bed as his hand glided along the skin of my ass but he was shifting to my front.

I lifted my head from the mattress in time to feel his hand curl around the underside of my jaw, using it to pull me gently up to my hands. His hand slid from my jaw into my hair at the back where he clenched his fingers and pulled back lightly so my head went back.

"Take my cock in your mouth, darlin'. Gonna fuck your face. Stay on your hands and knees," he ordered softly. "Wanna watch while your mouth takes me."

Oh yes. Hell yes. God *yes.*

He guided the tip of his cock to my lips. I opened them and he slid inside.

Oh yes. *Hell* yes. *God yes.*

He started moving and I sucked and stroked him with my tongue. I liked it so much, it was building again and I started moaning against his quickening thrusts.

"Mouth is greedy too," he grunted then ordered a rough, "Touch yourself."

My hand moved between my legs, I moaned deep and my hips jerked yet again as my knees slid a bit out to the sides. I was so turned on, my own touch sent shockwaves throughout my body.

"Fuck, beautiful," Tack whispered, his strokes deepening, going faster. "So fuckin' beautiful, baby."

I took him in my mouth, touched myself between my legs, moaned and let it build until suddenly Tack pulled out.

I gave a small cry of protest but before I could complete it, I felt the short zipper at the back of my dress going down. When it was down, my torso was yanked up because Tack was yanking off my dress. Then he had a strong arm around my waist and I was moving swiftly toward him and up. His other hand was between his legs and my legs automatically wrapped around his hips just as he jerked me down, guiding himself inside at the same time and I was full of him.

"Finally," I breathed, and Tack moved.

Connected to me, he shifted on his knees until I was back against the headboard.

Then he fucked me.

"Told you you'd get my cock," he muttered against my mouth.

Well, he gave me what he promised in more ways than one.

"Shut up and concentrate," I ordered, and his hips thrust harder.

Oh yeah.

"Now who's bossy?" he grunted.

"You're not concentrating."

He pulled out and then slammed back in. "Oh yeah, baby, I fuckin' am."

He sure was.

"Tip your hips, Red, I wanna go deep," he grunted, and I did. He went deep and I moaned. "You like that."

"I do," I gasped. "I like everything about you, honey. Everything. Lived in black and white seems like all my life. Never noticed. Not until you colored my world."

Tack went completely still.

I tightened my arms and legs around him, demanding, "Tack, don't stop!"

He started again. His hand at my ass tipping my hips further, he went faster, harder and a whole lot deeper and it took about two seconds before it built so high, it exploded and, clutching him close, I came again.

I was recovering, he was still thrusting and I felt his eyes on my face in the dark. Then I felt the tickle of his goatee and the movement of his lips against mine as he groaned, "Beautiful," buried himself inside, took my mouth and came, growling down my throat.

I knew his orgasm left him when his kiss gentled. He kept me tight to him and the headboard as he kept kissing me, soft, sweet but still wet and deep.

After he did this a while, and I enjoyed it that while, his lips slid down my cheek to the skin behind my ear and he whispered, "Love that greedy pussy of yours, Red."

I turned my head and with my lips at the hair curling around his neck I whispered back, "Good."

"And your hair," he went on, and I smiled against his neck.

"Good."

"This ass," his hand at my ass gave me a squeeze, "your long-ass legs, those heels."

"I like your cock," I shared.

"I got that."

"And your tats."

"Good to know."

"And, um, lots of other things."

He was silent for long moments before he said quietly, "Yeah."

Then he unfortunately pulled out but held me to him as he yanked the covers from under his knees. He set me in the bed on my back but he didn't move into me. Straddling me, he bent and kissed my breastbone. Then he moved down and kissed between my breasts. Down and another kiss at my belly. Down and then, one by one, he took off my shoes but when he did, he kissed the arch of each foot before setting my leg back in the bed.

And as he did this, I watched and deep breathed because something was happening. I was too sated from sex and too drunk to know what it was. I just knew it was something.

Something big.

Mammoth.

Colossal.

"Honey?" I called, and he moved back up, straddling me, now at my hips but he stopped there and reached out an arm, his hand curling around my throat like he'd done those two times after I was kidnapped.

He didn't speak but his eyes were on me. I saw them through the dark and I *felt* them.

"Kane?" I whispered when he didn't move for a long time.

His hand slid from my throat gliding down my chest, between my breasts to my belly but he did this not saying a word. Then he moved, shifting to my side and settling there.

He reached out to yank up the covers before he tucked me tight to his side, his arm not around my waist but up, his fingers cupping the back of my head and forcing my cheek to his shoulder.

"Is everything all right?" I asked his chest.

"Oh yeah."

"You sure?"

"Abso-fuckin'-lutely."

Well, that was firm.

I stared at his chest.

Then I whispered a hesitant, "Okay."

"How drunk are you, babe?" he asked.

"Drunk."

"So drunk you're gonna forget tonight?"

"No. I've never been that drunk."

"We'll see about changin' that," he muttered.

"Why?" I asked.

"Because you're gonna live life, Red. I'm gonna teach you to suck it dry."

I took in a deep breath thinking he already was.

Then I whispered again, "Okay."

"Sleep."

"Okay."

"And you forget tonight, I'll be pissed."

"I won't forget, Tack."

"Be sure about that."

"I won't forget."

"Good," he murmured.

"Are you going to shut up and let me pass out?"

His hand left my head, his arm sliding down and he wrapped it around my waist, pulling me closer.

Then he whispered, "Yeah."

I snuggled even closer.

Something had happened. I didn't know what and I stared at his chest while I tried to figure it out.

I did this for about two seconds before I passed out.

*   *   *

I opened my eyes and smelled musk and man. Correction, *my* man. I liked it but I also felt something else that wasn't nearly as awesome and instantly I groaned.

Hangover.

Damn.

Tack rolled into me and I groaned again.

He settled, chest partly on mine, and his slumberous eyes caught mine.

"Queasy?" he guessed accurately, which made me wonder what I looked like because I knew I had wild hair. I also knew I had leftover makeup, which was never attractive, but I was deducing I also was green at the gills, which was even less attractive.

"Yes," I answered.

"Day off," Tack stated.

"Pardon?" I asked.

"You feel shit, day off."

"But . . . I'm hung over."

"Yeah. So you're gonna take the day off."

"Tack," I started to inform him, "you're my boss. You should frown on an employee taking the day off because she tied one on the night before."

"Tyra, I'm your boss, I'm your man and I'm a biker. As your boss, you feel shit, you're not gonna be on your game so you might fuck shit up, which means it's better you're not in and work doesn't get done instead of you bein' in and work gettin' fucked up."

I had to admit, this made sense.

He continued, "As your man, you feel shit, I want you to rest and get better."

And I had to admit to this, it was sweet.

He kept going, "And as a biker, I live wild, I want you to too and I don't give a fuck if that has the consequences of a day off work to get over a hangover. In fact, I like it. You can make up the time. You can blow it off. The work'll get done. Work isn't important. Livin' a good life wild and free is."

Maybe it was the hangover but I couldn't figure out how he could be making sense; I agreed with him at the same time I thought he was sweet when just two and a half weeks ago all he said I would have thought was wrong.

"I'm not up to conversation," I shared.

"You up to bacon and eggs?"

I fought back a gag and groaned, "No."

Tack grinned then advised, "Babe, food is good for a hangover."

I fought back another gag and ordered, "Stop talking about food."

"Okay," he agreed. "You want coffee?"

"I could do coffee. And aspirin."

"Then I'll get you coffee and aspirin," he muttered.

"Thanks, honey," I muttered back, and his eyes locked on mine.

"I color your world."

I blinked and my heart stopped.

How did he . . . ?

Oh crap! I told him!

Drunk, in the middle of great sex, I told him!

Ohmigod!

"I—"

"I was right. You were asleep but you were dreamin'. You

dream in black and white, babe. I gave you color. Now you're awake."

"Tack—"

"You admitted it."

"Tack, please—"

"You were drunk, wet, hot and way the fuck turned on but you still admitted it."

I did and the way he was looking at me, his blue eyes drilling into mine, I couldn't deny it.

And also, it was true.

Damn.

"I'm in no state so can we not talk about this?" I requested.

"Yeah, we can not talk about this. Just want it confirmed you get that you gave that to me."

"I get that I gave that to you," I whispered, powerless to do anything but.

"Okay, baby, then now I'll confirm that you get what it means to me."

I stayed silent and stared.

Tack didn't stay silent.

"Seen a lot, done a lot, met a lot of people. Most of 'em, I like. Some of 'em, I don't. Some of 'em, I hate. But did so much and knew so many, the unexpected is rare. I color your world, you give me the unexpected. We're now totally balanced, Red. You didn't know it but you had the upper hand. Now I know what I give you, it means as much as what you give me, we're on the same level. And I like it like that."

He was kind of freaking me out.

And, contradictorily, he was kind of not.

Either way, I couldn't deal with this hung over.

"Stop talking, Tack."

"I will when you assure me you took in what I said."

"I took in what you said," I replied quietly.

"Are you processing it?"

"I'm hung over, Tack."

"You got the day to process it. You also got the day to get over that hangover. Tabby says she's cookin' tonight, which means you're on the back of my bike tonight and spendin' the night at my place."

My heart was pumping fast and my stomach was roiling.

"You're talking about food again, Tack."

"Pack a bag."

"Okay."

"No, I mean *pack a bag*."

I blinked.

Then I asked, "Pardon?"

"You're gonna be spendin' lots of nights in my bed in the mountains, babe. Come equipped to do that. I'll load the saddlebags on the bike."

My mind was whirling.

"Tyra, did you hear me?"

"Saddlebags. Come equipped. Tabby making dinner. I heard."

"Good."

"Coffee, Tack."

"Right."

"And aspirin."

"You got it, baby."

He touched his mouth to mine and I concentrated on not hurling as he rolled and angled out of bed, making it shift and sway in a way that was supremely nauseating. When he was out, I rolled to my side, shoving my hands under my cheek, and concentrated on his fantastic body as he yanked on his jeans finding this helped you forget you were hung over, if only for seconds. Still, it worked.

What worked better was, once he had his jeans on, him turning to the bed, bending over, putting a hand into it, arm straight, other arm stretched to me so his hand could come to my jaw and his thumb could sweep the apple of my cheek.

Yes, during that maneuver, I totally forgot I was hung over.

Then he moved away and was at the door when he stopped and his eyes came to me.

At the look in them, I braced.

"You have no clue," he whispered.

"No clue about what?" I whispered back.

"What you handed me last night."

I took in a deep breath and asked softly, "What did I hand you, honey?"

"What's lyin' in that bed."

That was when I stopped breathing.

"I claimed it," he went on. "But last night you gave it to me. Gift's given, no takin' it back. You get that, Tyra?"

"I think so," I whispered.

"Get that, baby, it's important."

I didn't have it in me to do anything but nod.

He took in my nod. Then his eyes shifted down my body in the bed.

When they came back to my face, he said gently, "Coffee and aspirin," and he disappeared.

I rolled to my back, ignored my queasy stomach and fuzzy head and stared at the ceiling, replaying last night.

It was awesome, from start to finish. I was losing Lanie, which sucked and I hoped she came back soon. But last night, I gained an entire posse and that felt good.

And knowing Tack didn't mind having more kids, actually wanted them was way better.

Then I replayed that morning.

It was awesome too. Most definitely.

"Roller coasters aren't so bad," I whispered to the ceiling. Then I smiled.

*   *   *

Five hours later, I was at Ulta buying stuff to take up to Tack's when my phone rang in my purse. I yanked it out, looked at the display, grinned, took the call and put the phone to my ear.

"Hey, honey," I said softly, grabbing a bottle of my shampoo.

"Like that," Tack's gravelly voice came at me. Then he asked, "How you doin'?"

"Not great but better. I'm at Ulta getting supplies for your bathroom."

"Good, baby," he said softly in a way that communicated he liked that too then he carried on, "Be by around five."

"Right."

"Later, babe."

"Tack?" I called quickly to catch him before he disconnected.

"Yeah?"

I looked at my shampoo bottle.

Then I said, "My shampoo bottle is bright orange."

"Say again?"

"My shampoo bottle is bright orange."

"Right. And you're tellin' me this because...?" He trailed off.

"Because I've been using this brand of shampoo for years and I never really noticed what color the bottle was. Not once." I drew in breath. "Until you."

Silence then a soft, very sweet, "Darlin'."

"See you at five, honey."

Again sweet, "Five, babe."

"Later."

"Later."

We disconnected.

I reached and grabbed a bottle of conditioner.

Same style bottle as the shampoo but it was beige.

It was the lettering that was bright orange.

CHAPTER TWENTY-ONE

Cool Whip

"Bye!" I shouted, standing outside Tack's front door, Tack behind me, his arm tight around my chest and I was waving away Dog and Sheila, the last of Chaos to leave our impromptu Friday night party at Tack's place.

Sheila, who I *loved* and who was on the back of Dog's bike, shifted to lift her arm to wave back.

"Later!" I yelled as they made their way down Tack's lane.

It was three weeks since I told Tack, drunk and turned on, that he colored my world and then confirmed it, hung over and with my wits about me, while standing in Ulta holding a shampoo bottle.

Three *great* weeks.

I didn't screw up at work (much).

No one had been kidnapped.

Naomi had been laying low.

Lanie and Elliott were somewhere Tack assured me was safe, and we still had our secure phones so I could talk to her.

After I sent my e-mail to Aunt Bette giving her the news that Tack and I worked it out, neither she nor Uncle Marsh lost their minds.

And Kane "Tack" Allen had proved he could handle me

with care, which further proved he was absolutely, without a doubt, my dream man.

Now it was now. I was at Tack's. Tab and Rush were out, Tabby at a party and then spending the night with a girl-friend. Rush was on a date, which was a double feature at the drive-in and he wouldn't be home until late.

Hop, Brick, Dog, Boz and Hound, all members of Chaos, and their women had come up. We drank beer. We shot tequila. We ate chips out of the bag (I didn't even put them in bowls!). We dipped those chips in jars of store-bought dip that I also didn't put in bowls. We laughed. We played music loud. Some of the boys and girls smoked pot though Tack didn't and they didn't press it on me. I thought that was cool since I was riding a happy vibe and didn't want to discover the consequences of saying no to a high biker. And the night ended when most of the couples started making out (yes, even Tack and me) so Tack gave the sign that the party was over (he did this by announcing, "The party's over") and the boys loaded the girls up on their bikes.

It was a blast!

Now it was late and Chaos was gone and I was standing outside Tack's wondering when I became the woman who would serve chips in a bag and then make out relatively hot and heavy with her man with a bunch of bikers and their babes in attendance.

Then I quit wondering because I was tipsy, happy, Chaos was gone and the *real* party could commence.

When Dog and Sheila disappeared, Tack released my chest but grabbed my hand and tugged me into the house. Then he shut the door and locked it.

This done, he turned me into his arms.

"You drunk?" he asked a question he knew the answer to, grinning his sexy grin down at me.

"Yep," I answered, rounding him with my arms, leaning into him and allowing his sexy grin to do a number on me.

"How drunk?" he asked, still grinning down at me, and I rolled up on my toes, pressing close and holding him tight.

"*Smashed.*"

"Good," he muttered, let me go but grabbed my hand again and dragged me to the refrigerator.

There, I watched him open the door and tag a tub of Cool Whip.

"What's that for?" I asked as he closed the door.

His eyes came to me.

Looking in his eyes, I knew what the Cool Whip was for.

Then I got a top-to-toe tingle that I fancied shimmered straight off my skin.

I grinned.

Tack didn't grin. He tugged on my arm and dragged me down the hall to his bedroom.

Dinner was chips and dip, beer and tequila and good company.

Dessert was Cool Whip and Tack.

In other words, dessert was *the bomb*!

*   *   *

I woke naked, draped over Tack, smelling the musk of him I loved, feeling sluggish, mildly hung over and definitely sated.

I didn't know the time since Tack didn't have an alarm clock.

"Babe, I get up when I get up. Don't need a machine tellin' me what to do." This was Tack's explanation for not having an alarm clock, and seeing as he was an early riser, it worked for me as when he rose, he saw to it I did too. Therefore, I couldn't find out the time.

I did know the sun was shining bright but since it was Colorado in August this could mean anything.

I also knew it was Saturday so whatever time it was, it didn't matter.

I lifted my head and saw my man was sleeping. As in *out*.

This wasn't surprising. He drank a lot of beer, shot a lot of tequila and ended the night energetically in a sex marathon that lasted a long, long time where he insisted on doing all the work.

But I was up in a way I knew I was *up*. Not to mention, I had to go to the bathroom.

So, carefully, so as not to wake him, I slid away and rolled off the bed. Rooting around on the floor which now included a tangle of my clothes, I found a camisole that I'd worn to bed a couple of nights before for approximately ten minutes before Tack took it off. Then I went to my bag in the corner, rooted through that and grabbed a new pair of undies before I picked my way through the clothes on the floor on my way to the bathroom.

I did my business, put on my undies and cami, washed my face, brushed my teeth and flossed. After I was done rinsing my toothbrush and was putting it in the holder with Tack's, my eyes caught my reflection in the big mirror that spanned the long vanity and I went still.

My belly had never been concave but it had been (mostly) flat. Now it was slightly rounded. My hips were never slim but they were now more rounded. My breasts were clearly fuller and straining the camisole.

I knew it by the way my clothes were fitting but I didn't really pay any mind to it.

Now I saw it. I was gaining weight.

Three weeks of eating whatever I wanted, that was bound to happen. But I didn't think of it, not once, until then.

I was deciding no more chips and dip and definitely no more beer when my mind moved over last night. Tack's mouth on me, his tongue, his hands, the way he rolled me, shifted me, hauled me, tossed me around the bed. His focus solely on me. The looks on his face, the heat in his eyes, the noises he made.

Not to mention the Cool Whip. We went through the whole tub.

My eyes went over my body in the mirror and I thought of Gwen, who was definitely curvy, and even Naomi, who was curvier.

Tack liked it like that.

I put my hands flat on my belly and slid them across to my hips, back to my belly, up my midriff to my breasts.

As I did, I was thinking I liked it like that too.

And I definitely liked Cool Whip.

My eyes caught their reflection in the mirror and I grinned.

Then I wandered back out of the bathroom and stopped at the side of the bed.

Tack had turned to his side, one arm thrown out, his other hand stuffed under the pillow under his head.

My eyes drifted over him.

He had the tattoo of a dragon taking up the whole of his upper right arm, its scaled, taloned feet slithering down the inside of his upper forearm. The tattoo curved around his bicep, over his shoulder and even up his neck. I'd asked why he got it and he'd explained it was because of Naomi. She told him when he got angry, he breathed fire. She was not wrong. Luckily, that tat was cool as all hell so even if it held nuances of his time with Naomi, that didn't shadow its coolness.

I could also mostly see the tattoo on his bicep on his

inner left arm. Swirling and spiking curlicues around the word "Cole." The curlicues were so intricate, you actually had to study it to find Rush's name in their midst (I knew this because I'd done it). He told me he got that because his bicep rested close to his heart. The same style curlicues around the mostly hidden word "Tabitha" was on his heart so no explanation necessary about that one.

Jutting up the wrist on his outer left forearm was another design, not in curlicues. It included wings, smoke, fire and parts of a motorcycle around four words randomly inked into the design, "Wind," "Fire," "Ride" and "Free." Those words, he told me, were essentially Chaos's motto. When a recruit was taken fully into the fold, they got the Chaos emblem emblazoned on their back and they also each had their own tattoo of their own design somewhere on their body that contained those words.

And last, all around the curve of his left shoulder was a kickass design that included a hooded skull and a set of scales. I had asked but he hadn't explained that one to me.

That tattoo, as with a number of other things, Tack wanted to share "later."

I didn't press. I was enjoying the now. And I knew, when he was ready, Tack would give me later.

Studying my man in bed, his tats on display, the sheet resting at his hip, his hard, defined muscles and the power of him at rest, his hair a mess, some of it falling over his forehead, he looked such that any woman, no matter her bent, would take a walk on the wild side if this was what she got to wake up to.

And she'd stay.

On that thought, I put a knee to the bed and Tack's sapphire eyes opened, his head turned on the pillow and those eyes locked sleepily on me.

"Come 'ere," he muttered, his voice deeper, rougher, even in a mutter rumbling over my skin.

I went there, moving on my knees into the bed as he pulled partially up, his hands coming out to me and grasping my hips. He rolled to his back and I swung a leg over to straddle him. His hands slid down then up so they were warm against the skin on the inside hem of my cami and his eyes moved over me.

My eyes moved over his tats and I was thinking that beyond anything on this earth, I wanted me to be inked somewhere permanent on his skin. And not like Naomi, an admittedly kickass dragon but one that laid testimony to the fact she pissed him off so bad he breathed fire.

One like Rush and Tabby's that was beautiful, its meaning hidden to anyone but Tack or someone he allowed close enough to study it long enough to find out.

"Baby," he whispered, and my eyes moved from Tabby's name to his.

"I'm gaining weight," I announced, and his fingers gave me a squeeze.

"Yeah," he agreed but said no more.

"I keep going, I'll need to buy more clothes."

"So buy more clothes."

There it was. Not, "Stop drinking beer," not, "Quit eating the Big Grab of chips with lunch and dipping into the boys' donut stash," but, "Buy more clothes."

He didn't care.

Good.

I bent over him and put my hand to his chest, my eyes dropping there and to watch my finger tracing the curlicue where Tabby's name was written. While I did this, his hands slid up my cami and moved soothingly over the skin of my sides and back.

"You hung over?" he asked.

My eyes went back to his, I shook my head but said, "A little bit. You?"

He shook his head.

My hand slid up his chest, his neck to his jaw and my thumb moved over his stubble on its path to glide along the edge of his goatee where my eyes had dropped to watch.

"You okay?" Tack asked, and I looked back at him.

"Yeah," I answered.

"You're quiet," he observed.

"I want to be inked on you," I blurted.

Yes, I blurted that. Right out.

His hands went completely still.

Damn.

We were having fun. It was easy. It was good. No, it was *great*. We were in that time when we were getting to know each other, enjoying it, seeing how we fit into each other's lives.

But it was too new, too soon for something that heavy.

Panicking, I blathered, "I mean...I don't know, not now—"

I stopped speaking when his fingers tensed into my skin so hard they dug into my flesh. Then I was flying through the air as he lifted and rolled so I landed on my back with Tack on top of me and between my legs.

"You want you inked on me?" he growled, and I stared up in his eyes, uncertain what I read there and for the first time in a long time I fought against biting my lip.

"No," I finally answered and his eyes narrowed scarily. "Yes," I amended hastily. "I mean, maybe. Eventually. Not now, of course, but—"

"I'm on you."

I blinked.

He was but I didn't think that was what he was talking about.

So I asked, "Pardon?"

He didn't exactly answer. He spoke and maybe he thought it was an answer but he didn't actually answer.

"I know what. I know where."

"Tack, honey—"

"A dragon, upper ass, spanning it, near to your waist, almost to your hips. I wanna see it when I'm takin' you from behind. I wanna see it when you're on your hands and knees and I'm fuckin' your face. And I wanna know it's under my hand when you're sleeping."

I got him then and what I got made my head jerk.

"A dragon?" I whispered.

"Yeah," he replied.

"But that's . . . that's . . ." I paused then said so softly it was barely a breath, "Naomi's."

"The dragon's me, babe. The tat I got is me, not her. She said it. I *am* it. She had that dragon, she lost it. Now it's yours."

Oh wow. I liked that.

Then it occurred to me he wanted me to get a tattoo. Not just a tattoo, a tramp stamp.

What he wanted, where he wanted it and why was hot.

But I wasn't sure.

"I don't think I'm a tattoo kind of person," I informed him carefully.

"You weren't a lotta things before you met me, babe," he pointed out.

This was true.

"I hear it hurts."

"Like fuck," he confirmed.

Not good.

"But it's worth it," he continued.

"If I got a tattoo, my dad would have a conniption," I shared, and this time, his head jerked. "My mom would also lose her mind," I added, he didn't say a word so I finished, "And Uncle Marsh would be none too happy, and he's a pretty laid-back guy."

"Any of them in this bed?" Tack asked.

"No."

"Then what do you care?"

Good point.

"Only two people who matter are in this bed right now," he told me, making my heart flutter. "This is your life, your body. Not theirs."

Well, I couldn't argue with that.

Tack kept talking, "I'll take you to my guy, have him sketch somethin' out. You like it, you get it. It isn't your gig, don't get it. I'm tellin' you what I want. That don't mean you gotta do it."

Well, that was nice.

"Okay," I said quietly.

"Now what do you want?"

I stared.

Then I started to ask, "Are you saying, I mean . . . are you going to get—?"

"Not tomorrow. Not next week. But this keeps on like it is, Red, it'll happen. Absolutely."

I felt my body melt underneath his.

That meant the world to me. The absolute *world* and I had no idea why.

It just did.

"So, I get your ink, what do you want?" he pressed.

My hands slid up his back, one going in to his chest and

up to wrap around the side of his neck and I answered softly, "I don't know."

"Link with Tabby's, under my pec, on my ribs," he decided.

Link with Tabby's. His daughter. His *beloved* daughter.

Close to his heart.

Tears instantly filled my eyes and I dipped my chin and turned my head to the side in a ridiculous and futile effort to hide my emotion.

And I knew the effort was futile when Tack's sweet whisper came at me.

"Baby, look at me."

"My turn to make breakfast," I said, but my voice was wobbly.

"Tyra, baby," he was still whispering and his hand wrapped around my jaw, forcing me to face him so the tears slid out the sides of my eyes, along my temples and into my hair.

"Inexplicable hangover crying jag," I lied stupidly and futilely. "It happens all the time."

"Bullshit, Red, you been hung over around me more than once and you have not cried."

"You're still getting to know me. I keep drinking like I am, you'll see it."

He ignored my idiocy and stated, "That meant somethin' to you."

I took a shaky breath in through my nostrils but didn't reply.

"It means somethin' to you," he mostly repeated.

I licked my lips and still didn't reply.

Tack's thumb moved out to glide along my lips and his face dipped close. "Admit it, baby, that means somethin' to you."

I pulled in breath through my nose again and whispered against his thumb, "No," and his eyes flashed but I kept going. "It means *everything*."

His thumb pressed into my lips as did all of his fingers along my jaw and his eyes shifted to heated and intense.

"Fuck, came three times last night, built seven in you and now I'm gonna fuck you again," he muttered, his thumb sweeping away and his lips getting closer.

"Tack, you don't—"

"Shut up, Red," he said against my lips, "I'm gonna kiss you. Then you're gonna sit on my face. Then I'm gonna fuck you on your knees and imagine my mark on you. Don't got time for your games."

My games?

"Tack!" I snapped. "I'm not playing any—"

I didn't finish. His head slanted and he kissed me. Then he deviated from his plan, yanked off my cami and spent some time at my breasts. Then he pulled me over him, tugged off my panties, yanked me down on his mouth and ate me. Then he fucked me from behind, his hands spanning the area just above my ass, under my waist, his thumbs meeting in the middle, his fingertips at my hips.

And during it I decided I was definitely a tattoo person. Absolutely.

CHAPTER TWENTY-TWO

Later

"Don't worry, Cherry, I'll get the pig."

This was Brick accepting the task of finding the pig Chaos was going to roast the next Saturday.

"He always gets the pig," Hound muttered, grinning at Dog, who was grinning back. This told me they were sharing an inside joke. I knew they'd explain if they intended to, they always did, or didn't as the case may be.

This time they didn't for no further words were spoken about getting the pig. And seeing as it was a whole pig and that whole pig was a dead pig that would be roasted, I really didn't want to know how Brick got his hands on it.

I was in my office at Ride's garage. It was Friday after the Saturday morning that Tack and I had our discussion about tattoos. My office was now filled with rough-and-tumble bikers. Brick, Dog, Hound and Boz to be exact.

Like the mechanics and body shop guys, members of Chaos hanging in my office was not unheard of. Shortly after Tack officially declared me his woman, this began to happen. It wasn't frequent. It wasn't rare. And the boys who came to hang included what I'd discovered was my man's inner sanctum, in other words, the guys who were closest to him, Dog and Brick (who Tack himself told me were his lieutenants), Hop, Hound and Boz. But I also got visits from all the members of Chaos including the three recruits, Roscoe, Tug and Shy.

Surprisingly, it further included the two bikers that Tack confirmed at my question were dissenters but who were back in the fold now that they had to band together against the common enemy of the Russian mob, Arlo and High.

Arlo and High hanging with me at the office wasn't only surprising because they were the two men I had more than once seen having what appeared to be unhappy conversations with Tack. It was surprising as well because they didn't seem the type to hang out with a woman and shoot the shit, seeing as they were scarier than the other guys. By that I meant scary in a dangerous, menacing way and not just a general, dangerous, rough-and-tumble biker way. And lastly, this was surprising because, although none of the boys was a gentleman, Arlo and High treated me in a casual, friendly biker way exactly like the others albeit they were more serious and less fun-loving. Nevertheless, the point was made. Whatever beef they had with Tack and/or the direction of the Club was not directed at me.

I'd talked with Tack about this and he *wasn't* surprised.

"Like it or not, babe," he'd started, going what he called gentle-like, and I knew he was having a mind to my soft spot with what he was gearing up to tell me. In other words, I wouldn't like it much. "Chaos, fuck, most MCs, women don't factor. Only men are members, only men make the decisions. A member takes a woman on, she's got the protection of the Club. She's a good woman, she can earn the respect of the men. But she won't have a say, ever."

I had nodded and made no response. He was right to go gentle since I didn't much like what he was saying. But although I didn't like the information he was sharing, it didn't surprise me.

Tack kept talking.

"But if a man claims a woman, she's in the fold and even if she hasn't yet earned it, they'll show her respect because doin' that shows their brother respect. All the men, including Arlo and High, are showin' me respect by gettin' to know you."

That made sense.

"They're also feelin' you out," Tack continued. "Says a lot about a man, the woman he chooses, for a lot of reasons. One 'a those is it's the way of the world that men talk to their women. Only men can be brothers but not a one of us is stupid enough to think if a woman has claim to a man's dick, she doesn't also got time to whisper shit in his ear. They take her shit in, it can sway how he behaves during sit-downs. So, with you havin' my dick and my ear, they're gettin' the lay of the land."

Again, that made sense.

Though his use of the word "shit" as pertains to a woman's point of view didn't make me feel melty and squishy.

Tack wasn't done.

"That said, she doesn't earn their respect, they'll make the show but, in reality, she won't get it. A brother, they'll respect always no matter his choice in women unless that woman guides him to doin' something seriously fucked up. They get you're my woman now, but the last one they didn't like all that much. Naomi wasn't popular. The brotherhood is all-important. She made me miserable and she made my kids miserable which made me more miserable. They didn't like that. And her shit reflected on me and *I* didn't like *that*. She also turned into a bitch and no one likes a bitch. And last, there was a sect of brothers who were on a certain path, a path she didn't agree with and made that clear. This made that path a fuckuva lot less easy and it was already serious as shit."

Oh boy.

"And what was that path?" I asked cautiously.

"You knowin' about that path is for later," he answered immediately.

I accepted that because I trusted him to give it to me later. I also accepted it because he explained what was happening gentle-like, telling me stuff many women would find hard to deal with or even abhorrent. But it was him and his world. To live in his world, I had to know it. He shared it and he did it honestly but carefully with a mind to my response. So I decided not to press.

Though, I had to admit, time was passing. We'd been "official" now for a month. In that time, although there were times when I went to bed without him, I never woke up without him. Most nights we had dinner together, usually at his house because that was where the kids were. Naomi was laying low. Lanie and Elliott had settled in wherever they were (and I didn't know where they were, I just knew they were both still alive and breathing). I was getting to know and like his kids more and more. And life was settling. It wasn't a pattern, Tack didn't do patterns. But that didn't mean it wasn't settled.

But I knew Tack hadn't forgotten those three hours the Russian mob had me.

Chaos was setting up for something. I just hadn't been let in on what. And I was beginning to get a little antsy because, even though the guys were planning a hog roast, the vibe was constantly alert. There were lots of close-huddle discussions all over the forecourt and garage. Tack and the boys had a number of sit-downs and, lately especially, I went to bed alone because Tack was "seeing to business." Business he didn't explain. Business I'd cautiously began to ask about. Business Tack brushed off giving me explanations with his "laters."

And since this business involved the mob, my man, his brothers (who I was also getting to know and like) and vows of rivers of blood, I was getting a bit impatient with "later."

Although this made me antsy, the boys hanging with me I liked. They didn't hang for hours. They were funny. They liked and respected Tack openly (except, of course, Arlo and High, but they hid it well, mostly). They didn't mind if I worked while we chatted. And, it must be said, it broke up the day.

They also made me feel weirdly like I was part of a family. An unusual, scary, badass biker family, but a family all the same.

This gave me a sense of why they pledged their lives and loyalty to the brotherhood. There was an honor to it, a beauty. It was nonconforming and some might think twisted, but it was there all the same.

And I liked that too.

"Roscoe's in charge of gettin' the hooch," Dog told me and I came back into the room.

"What can I be in charge of?" I asked, thinking party plates, napkins and red Solo cups for beer.

"Wearin' a short, tight skirt, showin' cleavage and strappin' on a pair of high heels," Boz answered, his lips surrounded by his full salt-and-pepper beard tipped up.

"And inviting your friends who'll wear short, tight skirts, show cleavage and strap on heels," Hound added.

I mentally drew a line through the item on my to-do list that said I needed to go to Costco.

"I'll see what I can do," I muttered, smiling at Hound,

thinking that Gwen, Elvira and the girls would like a hog roast. I thought this because, before my time, a few of them had already attended one or two. And I thought this because I'd spoken frequently on the phone and I'd twicc shared drinks with my new posse since our first night. I had found they were pretty much anything-goes types of gals. Though Mara was kind of shy and Tess was settled in home life with her and Brock's two boys, still, they'd be up for it.

I heard Dog's phone beep.

He pulled it out, looked at the display then his gaze cut through the group.

There it was. The alert vibe made its presence known and it did this when, with only that glance from Dog, the boys quit lounging around on my chairs and the beat-up couch under the window, their faces got serious and they all started to make a movc.

They'd been called to action.

"Business, Cherry," Dog told me what I already knew. "Later."

"Later," I replied, lifting my hand to flick it out when the phone on my desk rang and I could see the display said "Tack Calling."

I reached for it, calling out laters in response to laters as the men shifted out my door. They were still filing out when I put the phone to my ear.

"Hi, handsome," I greeted.

"Hey, babe. Just checkin' in to tell you you're at your place tonight. I'll meet you there but I'll be late. Probably way late. Called Tug, he's takin' you home. Go to bed without me."

"All right. So you're saying I'll wake up with you?"

"Do you ever not?"

"No," I whispered, liking that.

"Then no."

"Okay." I heard the boys' Harleys rolling out of the fore-court when I reminded him, "Tabby and I are shopping tomorrow."

We were and I was looking forward to it.

Rush and I were forming a bond.

Tabby, on the other hand, was melding herself to me.

I didn't question it and I didn't mind it. Her relationship with her mother was strained (to say the least), something it wasn't hard to notice at first because it was so out there, it was in your face. But since then I'd discovered it was more. From what I could tell, Naomi loved Rush and showed it. Her daughter, not so much. Why, I didn't know. But it was happening.

Therefore, Tabby had latched onto me as the woman in her life. I liked it because I liked kids so I just liked it but also because Tabby was sweet, charming and funny. I enjoyed her company immensely and we had a good time together. It helped that I was giving her that. It felt good. A good woman in a teenage girl's life was important and it was cool as all heck she chose me.

Tabby was shopping for school clothes. I was still on my mission to dress like Brandi from *Storage Wars*, a show that Rush now taped for me so I didn't miss it and caught up on episodes when I was at Tack's. So I needed Brandi clothes. They were probably going to be one size bigger than what I normally wore but...whatever.

"Gotcha," Tack replied.

"I'll call her and tell her to come down the mountain and meet me at my place at ten."

"Make it noon."

"Malls open at ten, Tack."

"And my woman'll hit them after I have plenty of time to hit her."

Oh.

Well then.

"Right," I said into the phone through a smile. "Noon then."

"Right. Noon," he confirmed, and I could hear his smile. "And do me a favor. Top drawer, back, in the dresser in my room in the Compound is an envelope. Go in, grab it and bring it home. I'll need it tomorrow."

A mysterious envelope.

Hmm.

"Got it," I replied. "Top drawer, back."

"Right, darlin'. You leavin' soon?"

I looked at the bottom right corner of my computer screen to see it was ten after five. Part of being Tack's woman, him being my boss and living the biker life with a biker, my eight-to-five workdays became nebulous. Weeks ago, Tack told me my responsibility was to get the work done; how I saw about doing that was up to me. It didn't matter what the office hours said on the door, I went in when I went in, I left when I left and as long as the work got done, he didn't care. If I didn't happen to be there to take a call, customers would have to deal, and I found they did. They knew they were dealing with bikers.

Bikers didn't do office hours.

This I liked a lot. I didn't take this freedom and fuck over Tack, Ride and thus Chaos. I got the job done and these days that meant actually getting it done without fucking up, finding or calling Tack to ask how I'd fucked up and then redoing it properly. Sometimes Tack rolled in with me on the back of his bike at seven, seven thirty in the morning and I'd get started then. Other times or, say, after energetic mornings it was closer to nine (or even ten). Sometimes we swung out of the forecourt close to six at night. I worked until I didn't need to anymore, and if Tack wasn't ready to go or he wasn't around and I didn't have my car, one of the boys took me home or I hung in the store, in the office, in the Compound common area or outside it with the boys.

Life was, except for the upcoming rivers of Russian mob blood, entirely stress free.

And thus life was, except for the Russian mob, entirely good.

"Yeah," I answered Tack. "Closing up shop now."

"I'll call Tug, find out where he is and either he or I'll call you back and give you his ETA."

"Thanks, honey."

"Later, babe."

"Later, Tack."

He disconnected. I shut down the office, grabbed my phone and my purse, headed out, locked up and clicked to the Compound on my high heels.

As I moved over the tarmac of the forecourt, I noticed there was only one bike outside the Compound. This I found surprising. It didn't take a master strategist to figure out that Dog's text and Tack's call stating he would be late meant Tack had given them the order to be on some mission. Their missions didn't always require every member in attendance, this was true. But if it didn't, there were always at least two or more bikes outside the Compound.

I'd never seen only one.

Well, whatever. It wasn't as if I had the comings and goings of the members of the Chaos MC down pat.

I walked into the deserted common area of the Compound, an area that looked a lot like a seedy bar except seedier. Tatty or chipped mismatched furniture including chairs, tables, couches and armchairs. A pool table. A long, curved bar that started almost at the front door and curved around toward the side wall. A door at the back wall beyond which held the boys' rooms. There were neon beer signs on the walls but not many of them. Most of the adornment were pictures of boys in the Club, past and present, all candid. There were not a few but several framed Chaos emblems. One of them was a large white flag tacked to the back wall that had the Chaos emblem in the middle with the words "Fire" and "Wind" on one side and "Ride and "Free" on the other. This same flag, incidentally, was flying from a flagpole on the top of Ride underneath an American flag. And last, there were a number of Harley-Davidson insignias here and there, framed, tacked and some were stickers randomly stuck to the wood-paneled walls.

It wasn't clean. It was, as I mentioned, seedy. Still, for some reason, I thought it was cool.

I headed across the room, my heels clicking on the wood floors, and made it into the back hall. I turned right and moved down it toward the end where Tack's room was.

My timing was bad for many reasons. Me just being there was one. Me hitting the hall opposite an open door when the noise came out was another. And what the noise meant had happened at that exact moment was the last.

The noise made me stop in shock, my head turned, and in the open door, for anyone walking by to see, was the brunette I saw Tack kissing that morning I started my first day at Ride. She was naked astride a naked man who I saw beyond her, his shoulders and most of his back up on the headboard, his muscled, tattooed arms spread wide and holding on, was Hopper. And the noise I heard was Hop groaning through an orgasm.

For some reason, instead of riding Hop facing him, she was riding Hop facing his feet.

And the door.

And, when her eyes hit mine while she was still bouncing on top of Hop, *me*.

Three things hit me, they hit me hard and they hit me all at once.

First, I didn't like seeing her again and the reasons why didn't need to be explained.

Second, I didn't like seeing what I was seeing *at all* and it wouldn't matter who the participants were. But it was exponentially worse that she was one of them.

And last, I didn't like seeing her riding Hop because Hop had an old lady who I knew had been in his bed for years. Her name was Mitzi. She wasn't exactly the warmest, fuzziest woman on the planet, but our paths had crossed more than once at the store or the Compound. We'd partied together the Friday before. And although she was a little hard and definitely tough, she was also kind of nice, could be funny and it was clear she loved Hop.

I was frozen to the spot even though I really, really wanted my feet to move or, preferably, my whole body to go up in a puff of smoke and rematerialize in the forecourt, back in time one minute before where I would have remembered I needed to go back to the office for something, anything. Instead I stood there, staring into her eyes.

And when I did, slowly, she smiled. It was catty. It was knowing. It communicated something I did not get but I did get that I didn't like it one bit.

Luckily, it also made me come unstuck and I hurried down the hall to Tack's room. The door was closed, I opened it, entered then I closed it. Once in his room, I stood still. But inside I was shaken.

I tried to remember if anyone had told me how long Mitzi and Hop had been together and I couldn't. Though I did know it was a long time. I also knew they weren't married but they lived together and had two kids together. This I knew because Mitzi told me herself. And although Mitzi was a tough broad, it wasn't only clear she loved Hop, it was super clear she loved their kids. So however long they'd been together, it had been long enough to have two children.

And, door open for anyone walking by to see, he was screwing another woman.

"Okay, this isn't good," I whispered to the empty room, and jumped when my phone rang in my hand.

I looked at the display, sucked in a calming breath, and put it to my ear.

"Hey, honey," I greeted with false brightness to cover my freak-out.

"What's the matter?" Tack asked immediately.

Damn. I could never pull one over on him, not even on the phone.

"Nothing," I lied then quickly moved on. "What's Tug's ETA?"

"I'll tell you when you tell me what's up."

"Nothing's up. I'm in your room about to grab the envelope. Is Tug going to be here soon?"

Silence then, softly, "What's the matter, Red?"

"Nothing, Tack," I lied again. "I talked with you maybe ten minutes ago. How could something be the matter in ten minutes?"

"The how is that you're you. Something could be the matter in ten seconds."

He wasn't wrong about that. Our run was going well, it was fun, it was stress-free, we had easy but that didn't mean I wasn't me and Tack wasn't Tack so the banter had not died.

But this wasn't about him being a bossy biker, me being sassy and us trading slightly heated words that were mostly lighthearted.

This was something else. I just didn't know what and I wasn't going to explain what until I knew why I was feeling the edgy I was feeling.

So I hid behind a veil of sass and snapped, "Well, something isn't the matter now but it will be if you don't quit asking me what's the matter."

This brought more silence that Tack didn't break.

"Kane," I called then prompted, "Tug?"

To which he said quietly, "Hop."

Oh hell.

I supposed, being the president of a motorcycle club, having your finger on the pulse of absolutely everything and being able to read people and figure them out was a good thing.

Being that man's woman and him having all that sometimes was not. And one of those times was now.

"Yes, Hop," I confirmed because if I didn't, he wouldn't let it go, which was something else I decided in that moment I wasn't all fired up about. "Or, more precisely Hop, who has an old lady and two kids. Added to that is Hopper's old lady, Mitzi, who isn't my bestest bud but she *is* in the sisterhood, considering she has a vagina. So, clearly, seeing Hop doing what Hop was just doing, something I'm guessing you knew he was in the middle of doing and that's why he's not on his way to you, didn't make me want to do cartwheels since we sisters need to band together no matter if we're not best buds. And, incidentally, seeing what I saw *at all* wasn't much fun. Hop has his own brand of hot but I don't want to see a brunette riding it. And last and mostly what's the matter is, that brunette was *your* brunette."

"She's not mine, baby," Tack replied quickly and gently.

"No, apparently she belongs to Chaos. What? Do you pass her around?" I clipped back.

"We don't but she does."

Ohmigod!

I might need to learn the ways of the biker world but that, *that* was something I didn't need to know. At least not now, alone, in the Compound, two doors down from a skank and a cheater and nowhere near a bottle of wine or, better yet, one of tequila.

Tack might know all, see all and figure it all out, but he also had to learn when to shut up and let it go.

"Okay, handsome, before I didn't want to talk about this. Now I *really* don't want to talk about this," I warned.

"This is another way of our world, Red, and if you keep control on that attitude long enough, when I have time, I'll explain it to you," Tack replied.

I'd heard that before.

Way, way, *way* too often.

And just then, with that brunette's catty, knowing smile burned on my brain, I'd had enough.

"Would that time be later?" I asked sarcastically.

"Uh...yeah."

"Seems you're going to explain a lot of things later and it seems you avoiding doing that, that means those things are like that brunette. Shit you aren't explaining because you don't actually want me to know."

"Tyra—"

"Ignorance is not bliss, Tack."

"Red—"

"Sometimes it's lies in the form of keeping something from someone with bullshit promises of 'later,'" I kept ranting.

"Darlin'—"

"And in the end, any lie is a hurt that burns and sometimes that burn can kill."

Tack was silent.

I was not.

"Call Tug. Tell him I'm getting a taxi. And as for you, you need to send someone else to get that envelope. I'm thinking I need a little time so I'd prefer to wake up alone tomorrow. When I'm ready to talk, I'll call you. But you need to know, whenever I'm ready, it'll be *later*."

"Goddamn it, Tyra—" I heard him grind out, but I disconnected.

This time we would talk *my* later.

I yanked open the door and stomped down the hall. I didn't look into Hop's room and I avoided it so studiously, I didn't even know if the door was open.

I would discover Hop was done when I walked out of the Compound, my phone up in my hand in preparation to make a call to the taxi company, and I saw him on his bike.

When he saw me, he lifted his chin and called, "Cherry! Yo!"

I didn't know if, when I saw him in his room, he was so in the throes of what was happening he didn't see me. Or if he didn't care. Or if he expected me to get the way of their world and not care because he didn't look embarrassed or, indeed, anything except Hop.

I gave him a chin lift as his bike roared then he roared off with another flick of the wrist to me.

I glared after his bike, spared some time thinking about poor, cheated-on Mitzi while I called a cab then I stood outside the Compound knowing exactly what that edgy meant.

Chaos, fuck, most MCs, women don't factor.

What? Do you pass her around?

We don't but she does.

Crap.

Truth be told, it hurt when I fell in love with Tack over

tequila and he kicked me out of bed. But until that moment, I didn't realize the hurt that burned deeper was seeing him with the brunette only a day later. He'd explained it. I hadn't made an impression on him, and clearly that had changed since.

But every girl, or at least the ones I knew, hoped like everything that when they met *the one*, they'd make an impression. And thus they wouldn't *ever* be replaced and certainly not the very next night.

And as ridiculous as it was, as inflated an expectation, as admittedly unrealistic and even stupid, that didn't mean it wasn't downright true.

I didn't know how Mitzi felt about Hopper. Maybe she understood this. Seeing the hard in her face, the tough in her manner, I suspected she did.

But I didn't.

And I might not watch TV and I might have lived in black and white but I wasn't literally unconscious all my life. I might not be savvy to the ways of the world like Tack but I wasn't an idiot.

Bikers chose their lifestyles for a reason. And men became members of motorcycle clubs for deeper reasons. And it wasn't a secret sect of society that lived quiet and kept clandestine.

Fire and Wind. Riding free. That was their motto.

Free.

Free.

Tack was avoiding all the "laters" because rivers of blood and the Russian mob freaked me out. But also because he knew this wasn't my world and he wanted me mired in it before he lowered the boom.

Unfortunately, shit happened and he couldn't control when the boom lowered.

And, damn it all to hell, that boom fucking *hurt*.

And unfortunately, that boom wasn't near done with me.

"You got your place with the Club, I got mine."

I jumped, twisted at the waist, tearing my eyes from their angry contemplation of the forecourt to see the brunette standing two feet outside the door to the Compound. She was dressed, fortunately, though she didn't wear a lot of clothes. Unfortunately, seeing her and processing all that was her, not only was she gorgeous in her skanky, slutty way, she also had a great body. Making matters worse, she was standing one hand on her hitched hip, which every woman knew meant she was prepared for our upcoming verbal smackdown. And last, she was also wearing her catty, knowing smile.

I didn't reply and turned back to the forecourt. Weirdly, my mind conjured up the image of us, two exact opposites standing in front of an MC's compound, me in my tight skirt, cute but smart blouse and sex kitten heels and her in her cutoff, ragged-edged, very short jean skirt, barely there, skin-tight top and platform slut sandals.

And it wasn't lost on me which one of us didn't fit.

I heard her heels clicking to me and I kept my eyes glued to the tarmac but I felt and heard her stop close.

"Had 'em all, 'cept the recruits. Don't fuck recruits. They get their cut, that's when I break 'em in."

Something for Roscoe, Tug and Shy to look forward to.

I pulled in breath and kept my eyes on the forecourt.

"Tack's my favorite," she whispered, and that was when I turned to her.

"He's also mine."

Her catty, knowing smile got bigger, cattier and more knowing. "As you can tell, girl, I don't mind sharing."

My hand itched to slap her. No, actually, my hand itched

to slap someone else. Her, I wanted to know why she did what she did to the sisterhood but worse, what she did to herself. But instead of asking, I again turned my gaze to the tarmac, willing the cab to show the fuck up already.

"You're up for it, we can share together. Tack likes it like that. Won't be the first time I gave it to him like that so I know."

I took that blow and while I did it took everything else not to react visibly to it.

But inside it burned deep.

He wasn't a choirboy. He was a biker. But I didn't need some skanky brunette reminding me of that.

What I needed was a man who knew I didn't need it and shielding me from it. Not setting me up by sending me into a Compound that contained it to get a mysterious envelope.

My eyes went back to her just in time for her to keep talking.

"You're his old lady so I'll let you have his dick. I'll sit on his face," she offered her take on our plan of attack to pleasure my man together.

"Maybe it would be a good idea for you to quit talking," I suggested quietly.

"Right, he's good with his mouth. I get you want that. I'll take his dick."

I held her eyes. She kept smiling at me.

This went on a long time.

Finally, her eyes slid to the side and she murmured, "Cab's here."

"FYI," I started, "that party you invited me to. I'll take a pass."

She shrugged then delivered her next blow. "That's okay. He wants it like that, he knows where to find it."

I had no retort. None at all. It wasn't my place to tell her to get gone. It wasn't my place to tell her I better not see her again. She belonged to Chaos in her way and I did in mine. We accepted our places and the boys called the shots.

Damn.

I had that box Tack talked about over me, closing me in, I couldn't see clear, and Tack was the one who put it there.

No, it was me.

I put it there.

God.

I tore my eyes free of hers and walked to the cab.

Then I got in and gave him my address.

The driver had pulled out on Broadway when my phone rang and I saw it was Tack.

Over it, *way, way* over it, when I put the phone to my ear, I asked as greeting, "Do you not understand the concept of me needing some time?"

To this, my heart stopped beating when he replied on a growl, "You call Mitzi and share, you answer to me. And if you answer to me, when you do, I won't go gentle."

Then I heard the disconnect.

Unseeing, unfeeling, not hearing a thing, not thinking a thing, I let the hand with my phone fall to my lap.

I didn't cry until I closed my front door and I was home.

CHAPTER TWENTY-THREE

Dish Out Retribution

MY CELL PHONE sitting on the nightstand ringing surprised me and it surprised me because it woke me up. After what had happened at the Compound I never thought I'd get to sleep. Apparently, I was wrong.

My eyes slid to my alarm clock to see it was just after one in the morning.

I knew the caller had to be Tack calling to argue with me, patch things up with me or tell me he was in an emergency room because Operation Rivers of Blood didn't go too good.

I was not ready for any of those options and even though I was still hurt, still pissed and had no intention of answering, this didn't mean I wasn't a woman. And women were like cats.

Curious.

Recklessly so.

So I picked up the phone in order to stay my course as a woman, in other words, torture myself and I saw the display said "Tabby Calling."

I felt my brows draw together and I sat up in bed, took the call and put my phone to my ear.

"It's late, honey. Everything okay?"

I heard a loud, agonized, hitched breath and nothing more, and I shot up straight in the bed.

"Tabby?" I called. "Honey, talk to me. What's going on?"

"My . . ." another hitched breath that hurt to hear, "my . . . Ty . . ." another sob, "Tyra, my boyfriend hit me."

Her boyfriend?

Tabby had a boyfriend?

Since when?

And he *hit her*?

I threw the covers back and swung my legs out of the bed.

"Is . . . is Dad there?" she asked.

"No," I answered, turning on the light on my bedside table.

"Do . . . do . . . don't tell him, but can you come and get me?"

"Are you injured?" I asked.

"Not really," she whispered brokenly, and I didn't know if that really meant no or it was code for yes.

"Tab, baby, are you injured?" I pressed gently.

"I'm okay," she whispered, again brokenly.

Right, I had no choice but to accept that.

"Where are you?" I asked.

"I'm outside his place. He . . . he . . . kicked me out. It's an apartment off Lincoln and I don't have my car because he picked me up at Natalie's."

Oh boy. Tab spent a lot of time at Natalie's, including a lot of *nights*.

This wasn't good.

"Your boyfriend has an apartment?" I asked softly.

"He's . . . yeah, he . . . he's," another sob. "Oh, Tyra!" she cried. "Don't tell Dad, really, really don't tell Dad! Promise!"

I was rushing to the closet to grab clothes and I answered, "Promise, baby, now talk to me. Who is this guy?"

"He's . . . he's . . . twenty-three."

Twenty-three!

She was sixteen!

"I met him . . . oh, it doesn't matter. I just need a ride."

"I'll be there as fast as I can, Tabby, honey, promise. But I need a number on Lincoln so I can get there."

She gave me the street number, shared she was sitting outside his door and I shared again I'd be there as fast as I could, she should stay where she was and if he came out, do not go back in no matter what he says, get away from him and call me.

Then, without thinking, my heart hammering, the pressure in my head increasing, my vision beginning to cover in red, I engaged my phone, scrolled down and hit go.

It rang three times before I got a sleepy, "Yo."

"Roscoe?"

"You got me."

"It's Tyra," I told him, pulling up my jeans.

"What?" he asked, sounding shocked, as he would. I had his number because I had all the guys' numbers, but I wasn't someone he would expect to get a call from unless I needed a ride or someone to mow my lawn. Mowing my lawn was, Tack had decided—and it was one of what I was currently considering the few bonuses of being attached to Chaos—part of the recruits' new duties. Seeing as a woman usually didn't need her lawn mowed at one in the morning, a call from me at that time would be a surprise.

"I take it you aren't on this mission with Tack and the boys?" I asked, now snatching a bra from my drawer.

"No."

"Who else isn't?" I asked, struggling with the phone between shoulder and ear to put my bra on.

"Recruits. Tug and Shy," he answered.

"Right. Call them. Get on your bikes and get to . . ." I gave him the address and finished with, "Now."

"Is Tack cool?"

"I don't know. This isn't about Tack. This is about something else. I need you and the boys at that address as soon as you can get there." Then I added, "Come in the mood to be menacing and look badass."

"What?"

"Just do it!" I shrieked, disconnected the call and snatched a tee out of my drawer.

I slid my phone in my pocket, found some flip-flops on the floor, slid my feet into them and tugged my tee on as I ran to the kitchen. Once there, I flipped on the light and went to my junk drawer. I rooted through it until I found what I was looking for. A can of pepper spray I bought last summer when there was a rash of break-ins in my neighborhood. They caught the guy and I forgot about it.

Until now.

I checked it and the expiration date was the month before. Damn.

Well, whatever. It was all I had, I needed it, I was going to use it and I'd have Roscoe, Tug and Shy as badass-in-training backup if it backfired on me.

I grabbed my keys, exited my house, locked up and ran to my car.

I forced myself to concentrate while driving but I was shaking. All I could hear was Tabby's sobbing in my head, her telling me her boyfriend hit her, and the knowledge she had a boyfriend at all much less the fact that he was way too old for her. None of this was good news. All of it meant she'd lied to her father (and me), and that was just plain not good. I needed to keep it together, get her sorted and do what I had to do.

I made it to the complex, a double-decker, doors to the outside walkways, the complex facing the street. I saw Tabby immediately, sitting on her ass on the bottom-floor walkway, knees up, nose bleeding, eye swelling, tears visible.

And that was when I lost what was left of my cool. That said, I may have lost it but that didn't mean ice water didn't start running through my veins. It did and instead of losing my mind, I went glacial.

I parked a spot down from where she was and got out as she got off her behind and hurried to me. I moved swiftly, rounding the hood of my car, and that was when I got a closer look.

So that was when I hit arctic.

I lifted my hands and settled them on her shoulders, whispering, "In the car, honey, lock it. Napkins in my glove box to wipe up. You stay in there, no matter what. I'll be back in a second to take care of you."

I heard the pipes of a Harley and I knew Roscoe had taken direction. I didn't look but Tabby did so I gently cupped her cheeks in my hands and forced her to facing me.

"Car, Tabby, now. Yeah?"

She was staring at me closely, scared, cheeks wet and that blood.

Damn it all to hell.

That blood.

"Did you call Dad?" she whispered.

"I did not. Tab, get in the car."

"What . . . what are you gonna do?"

"Get in the car."

"Tyra—"

"Car, baby, *now*," I ordered as I heard another Harley approach the complex and felt a presence. I looked up and saw it was Shy.

Shy was christened Shy because Shy was not shy by any stretch of the imagination. Gregarious, flirtatious and friendly, he was too young for me, I had a hot guy (maybe) but that didn't mean I didn't appreciate the fact that he was mammoth, off-the-scales hot as in *hot*. Tall, dark, lanky, messy haired, beardless, long-legged, broad-shouldered, great ass, beautiful. He, like Roscoe, was not a new recruit. In fact, he'd been around longer than Roscoe, and Tack had told me they were shortly going to take him fully into the fold and do whatever they did before they gave a boy his cut.

"What the fuck?" his low, deep voice sounded and his startling green eyes narrowed on Tabby's face.

I let Tabby go and informed him, "We've got a situation."

His angry eyes cut to me and he asked, "No shit?"

Hmm.

Maybe not a badass in training. Maybe just a badass.

Seriously, he was even more hot pissed.

"Did you call Tack?" he asked.

"No!" Tabby cried as Roscoe came jogging up to us and Shy's eyes sliced back to her.

"Fuck me," Roscoe muttered, getting a look at Tabby.

"We're handling this ourselves," I told Shy, and he looked back at me.

"You're handling what?" Tabby asked.

"This," I answered, looking back at her.

"What?" she asked louder. She was losing it and probably part of her losing it was the sound of another Harley approaching.

So I dipped my face to hers and said softly but firmly, "A man does not take a hand to a woman. A man does not get involved with a girl. And a man *definitely* does not take a hand to a girl he should never have been involved with. *That* is what we're handling."

"Tyra—" she started.

I cut her off. "Get in the car."

"Tyra!" she cried.

"Honey, please, get...in...*the car*."

She held my eyes and I held hers right back.

"I didn't want a big deal made of this," she whispered.

"Too late and, incidentally, it wasn't *you* making this a big deal."

"No." She was still whispering, looking like she'd been betrayed by her best friend. "It was you."

Shot straight to the heart.

"Tab, honey, it was him," I informed her.

"It was you," she whispered then dropped her head, looked at her feet and walked to the car.

Okay, well, that didn't go great.

Whatever.

I'd deal with Tabby later. Time to get this done.

I looked at the boys, which now included Tug.

"We knock on the door, you take my back, I'm lead," I gave them the plan.

"You are fuckin' not," Shy replied, immediately screwing with my plan.

"I am," I returned.

"You aren't, Tyra," Roscoe put in. "Take Tabby home. Get her cleaned up."

"I am," I repeated to Roscoe this time.

"That's whacked," Tug interjected.

"It isn't," I snapped, my eyes going to him. "You boys need to keep your noses clean. Two of you are about to get your cuts, and a stay in lockup for assault and battery might delay that."

"Babe, that doesn't make your plan any less whacked. The motherfucker hit a sixteen-year-old," Shy reminded me.

"He's not gonna hit you. You're Tack's woman. We stood back and allowed that, he'd lose his fuckin' mind."

I wasn't so sure about that at that present juncture but I didn't share.

Shy wasn't done.

"Not to mention, you're just a woman. This is man's work."

Wrong, wrong, *wrong* thing to say.

I therefore leaned into him but jerked my arm straight back behind me, pointing to my car. "Yes," I hissed, "and that's my girl. So, lesson, boys, he hit my girl and he took advantage of her when she was too young to get it. So this is *woman's work* and I'm fucking *lead*. This goes south, you step in. But it won't go south, trust me."

"You got a black belt or somethin'?" Tug asked curiously.

"No," I answered then yanked the pepper spray out of my pocket and showed it to him, "I've got a surprise."

Tug grinned. Roscoe's eyebrows shot up but he still looked unimpressed. Shy looked to the ceiling created by the upper walkway.

I decided we'd delayed enough and pushed through them in order to stomp to apartment number five. I felt them close in behind me as I lifted my hand and knocked, loud.

"Fuck off!" came a shout from inside.

Rude.

Not a surprise but also fucking with my plan.

"Open this door!" I shouted back.

"Go fuck yourself," was returned.

"Open this door!" I repeated. "I'm not going to ask again."

"Kiss my ass!"

"Right, then!" I yelled then stepped back and swung my arm toward the door while ordering, "Bust it in."

"Babe, a charge of breaking and entering will also get us a stay in lockup," Shy rationally pointed out.

I'd had a bad evening, a worse night and not much sleep. Tabby was pissed at me, bleeding and she'd just found out her boyfriend was a jerk. It was the wee hours of morning.

I was in no mood for rational.

I was in the mood to kick some ass.

So I shrieked, *"Bust it in!"*

"Jesus, fuckin' hell, all right, all right," Roscoe muttered, positioned, lifted a motorcycle-boot-clad foot and slammed it into the door.

It popped right open.

I shoved through the boys again and stormed right in.

I saw my mistake immediately when I saw the baseball bat swinging in the direction of my head. Luckily, I was presently Arctic Tyra and I had a mission I was not going to allow to be foiled so I had the presence of mind to duck. The bat whiffed over me, I heard Shy's growled, angry *"Fuck,"* but ignored it and I came up, armed with pepper spray.

I aimed, I shot.

My luck in life was up for debate.

My luck in that moment wasn't because the spray worked.

He howled, dropped the bat, his hands went to his face and he tripped over his feet in retreat.

"What the fuck! What the fuck! *What the fuck is that?*" he shouted.

I noted vaguely he was kind of cute so I understood his allure to Tabby. I also vaguely noted his momma needed to make a visit to do some cleaning. At the same time I stayed on target, dropped my spray and advanced.

I got my opportunity and hit him, palm open, slapping him hard right across the face.

He was in such a state, he couldn't correct himself and fell to his hands and knees.

I bent over him and asked sweetly, "Feel good?"

"Fuck!" he shouted, then started crawling and ran into a coffee table.

I grabbed his shirt, yanked him back and twisted him. When I got my shot, I slapped him again with such force, his head snapped around.

"How about that?" I asked. "Feel good?"

He swung blindly out with his arms so it was easy to avoid them.

"Fuck off! Get out! I'm callin' the cops!" he yelled.

"Yeah? You are?" I asked, leaning in. "If you were going to do that, you would have done it. But you're not. Because you don't want to answer uncomfortable questions about why your girlfriend is *sixteen*."

Then I slapped him again and he fell to his side.

"Get off me!" he shouted, getting his knees under him and starting awkwardly to crawl on them and one hand because he was using his other hand to swipe at his eyes.

I did the yanking-at-the-tee thing again and when I'd jerked him back to his ass, I grabbed onto it at the front and got in his face.

"Why she's not only sixteen, but you *hit her*," I went on. "And bloodied her *goddamn nose*!" I hissed then held him still while I slapped him then I did it again. Then I went in for a third go while his hands pulled at my forearm attached to the hand fisted in his tee and his head and body jerked to get away from me.

"Red, you're done."

My body went still at the sound of Tack's low, gravelly voice. Then I let go, straightened and turned to see Tack,

Brick, Dog and Boz standing with Shy, Roscoe and Tug inside the door.

This meant Roscoe, Tug or Shy had called the boys, and I made a note to self that the next time I enlisted Chaos recruits to dish out retribution, I made clear that our operation was flying under radar.

"What are you doing here?" I asked.

I asked Tack but it was Boz who answered.

"Enjoying the fuck outta the show. Shit, Cherry, you're cute, all badass and pissed off and kickin' squirrel-ball ass."

It wasn't a compliment I thought I'd ever get. Still, it wasn't half bad.

"Go see to Tab," Tack ordered, and I looked from an amused Boz to a very, very unamused Tack as I vaguely heard Squirrel-Balls scrambling, sniffing and breathing heavily behind me.

It was then I felt the scary, badass biker vibe in the room. It was blazing. It was serious. It was terrifying. It was all-encompassing. So much, it was suffocating. And it was not coming from the bikers collectively.

No, it was coming from Tack and Tack alone.

I bit my lip.

I'd never seen it, Tack breathing fire. I thought I had. He had a temper, no doubt about it, and that temper was scary. I might have got a hint of it after the Russians abducted me, but by the time he got to me, he'd had time to cool down.

But this.

This was something else.

"Go," he growled. "See," he kept growling, *"to Tab!"* he barked, leaning toward me.

I moved toward the door muttering, "I'll just go see to Tabby."

No one spoke.

Unfortunately, my path to escape was covered in bikers with Tack being right inside the door. When I made it to him, I turned to the side, sucked in my gut and tried to squeeze by him but failed.

He caught my upper arm and my eyes flew to his.

"My house. She needs to be home. And when I get there, babe, you better be there."

Oh boy.

I held his eyes.

Then I nodded.

He let me go.

I went to see to Tab.

CHAPTER TWENTY-FOUR

Laid Out

"TABBY, HONEY, PLEASE," I whispered to the girl lying on her side in her bed, her back to me, ignoring me as I sat on the side of her bed, pleading with her.

Suffice it to say, things were not going well.

On the way up to Tack's we stopped at a fast food drive-thru and I got her a drink, a water and a shed load of napkins. I instructed Tabby to hold the drink on her face and use the water and napkins to clean up as best she could until we got home. She did as instructed but she did it silently and she didn't once look at me.

I'd not even come to a complete halt outside Tack's house when her door was open and she was out. By the time I got fully parked, the car turned off and hustled in, she was behind closed doors in the bathroom.

I decided to wait it out because she couldn't stay in there forever, and it was the right decision. She'd come out, blood free but nose swollen with the fast food cup still pressed to her eye.

"I'll get you some ice," I offered.

She looked through me and walked to her room.

I went to get her ice.

Her door was closed and locked when I got back. I called, I knocked and doing so woke up Rush.

This was not good but it was unavoidable. Tabby would have a shiner the next morning. He'd eventually find out.

Trying to take the drama out of it, and failing seeing as it was dramatic, I shared what was happening and then watched Rush morph into a mini-me Tack Dragon.

Then he kicked his sister's door in. ·

The good news was, Tabby was no longer barricaded away from those who cared about her who could take care of her after the events of that night.

The bad news was, the door would need to be repaired.

The further bad news was, Rush was weeks away from eighteen and already kind of scary.

I decided to file that away to worry about at a later date (if I was around to worry about it) and instead prioritize.

This led us to now. Tabby took the ice and set aside the fast food cup but she also instantly curled with her back facing me, her face resting on the ice, me sitting on the side of her bed begging her to talk to me. Through this, her brother was standing across the room, arms crossed on his chest, looking like he wanted to murder someone.

I decided pleading wasn't working so I tried another tactic.

"Okay, I'll admit, maybe I lost my cool and didn't handle that too well," I told her.

Finally, a response.

"You think?" she muttered to her pillow.

"Tab, my beautiful girl, he hurt you," I whispered.

No response.

"I'm worried about you, baby, and not just because you're going to have a black eye tomorrow," I said softly.

Still no response.

I kept at it.

"I'm worried because you have a boyfriend. I'm worried because of his age. I'm worried because you didn't tell me or your dad about it."

Her eyes slid to me and she hissed, "You're not my *mom*."

"No, but I'm your friend."

Her eyes slid away while she stated, "You're not that either."

Ouch.

That hurt but I kept trying.

Putting my hand on her, I whispered, "Honey—"

Her shoulder twitched to shake my hand off but I felt something new in the room, it wasn't a good new and I turned to the door just as Tack ordered, "Sit your ass up . . . now."

Oh boy.

Seeing as his eyes were on his daughter, I knew he wasn't talking to me but I still got to my feet beside the bed.

"Can everyone just *go away*?" Tabby asked in a teenage whine.

"Ass. Up. Now," Tack demanded, coming to stand at the foot of the bed where he crossed his arms on his chest just like his son was still doing.

I assessed him.

Nope.

The dragon had awoken and he wasn't feeling tired just yet.

This wasn't good.

"Tack—" I started, and his eyes cut to me.

"Shut your mouth."

Ouch.

I shut my mouth and took a step away from the bed.

Tack's eyes sliced back to his daughter and he growled, "Tabby, won't tell you again."

I prayed she'd sit up and my prayer was answered. She did and leveled one narrowed eye on her father. The other one was covered up by ice. This was not a good stance to take for a variety of reasons.

"What'd we talk about?" Tack barked at her the instant she got in position.

"Dad—"

"What. Did we..." he leaned in and clipped harshly, *"talk about?"*

"No lies," she whispered.

"Yeah. No lies. I trusted you. And you lied."

Instantly, her bravado melted, her face collapsed and I started to go to her as tears filled her eyes.

"Do not fuckin' move, Red," Tack bit at me, and I stilled. Then, carefully, I said, "Kane, maybe now's not—"

"You got a voice in this?" Tack asked, cutting me off, and before I could answer he did. "No. You fuckin' do not. So keep your mouth shut."

I shut my mouth as I felt pressure build in my head again.

Tack looked back at Tabby.

"Got yourself hurt," he pointed out the obvious.

"Dad—" she whispered.

"Coulda got Tyra hurt," he went on.

"She—" Tab started but got no further.

"She went chargin' in there, he had a bat," Tack informed her, her one visible eye shot to me and got wide. "Eyes to me," Tack growled, and she quickly looked back at her father. "Your ass does not leave this house for the rest of the summer," he declared.

"Dad!" she cried, straightening up further and taking the ice away.

This was a bad idea. The swelling was up and the bruising had started to come out.

"Ice on your eye," Tack clipped. "Keep it on. We'll finish this tomorrow when I'm not in the mood to rip you a new asshole."

I pulled in breath.

Uncle Marsh was right. Definitely not father of the year.

But it was none of my business. Tack made that perfectly clear.

"You, bed," he grunted at Rush, and then he looked at me. "You, my room."

I pressed my lips together to stop from telling him to go fuck himself. Tab and Rush didn't need to hear that. No, when I said that, it would be for him and him alone.

Then I pulled in a calming breath that didn't calm me in the slightest, looked at Tabby and said softly, "Try to sleep, honey."

She was chewing on her lips and just nodded.

I left the room without looking at Rush or Tack.

I didn't know what he was doing to delay him getting to the room. I just knew when he finally got there I had commandeered my bag from the corner and put it on the bed. My toiletries from the bathroom were already in it and I was pawing through the mess on the floor to locate my stuff.

I heard the door close.

Then I heard, "What the fuck are you doing?"

"I would like," I began, not looking up and continuing to paw through the clothes on the floor, "when this blows over, for you to allow me some time to visit with Rush and Tabby so I can say good-bye."

This was met with silence.

I located a pair of shorts, grabbed them, moved to my bag and shoved them in.

As I was doing this, the bag was swept clean out from

under my hands and I watched it go sailing across the room where Tack sent it. I watched it land.

Then I looked up at him.

"And when I do that," I went on like he hadn't acted like the badass, biker jerk he was, "I'll be doing it just them and me."

Suddenly, with his hand wrapped around my throat, I was moving backward across the room. My breath had stopped because my lungs had seized but my heart knew what it was doing, it liked it, so it went into overdrive.

I hit wall, not gently, not hard and Tack didn't take his hand from my throat so I lifted mine and wrapped them around his wrist just as he dipped his head and got nose to nose with me.

Then he shocked the shit out of me.

"Took care 'a my girl, way you did, I don't know whether to kiss you or smack your ass."

I blinked.

That wasn't what I expected to hear.

"Jesus, fuck me, Tyra. What the fuck were you fucking *thinking*?"

"Let me go," I whispered.

"Shy told me, way he went at you, he coulda caved your fuckin' head in."

"Let me go," I repeated on a whisper.

"What were you thinking?" Tack kind of repeated.

I yanked at his hand at my throat, which, from the minute he placed it there to now, was holding me but it was just like how I hit the wall. Not gentle. Not hard.

What it was, was immovable.

"Let me go," I said yet again.

The dragon breathed fire and roared in my face, *"What were you fuckin' thinking?"*

"Quiet!" I hissed. "Tabby. Rush."

"Don't worry about Tab and Rush, babe. Advice, right now, you worry about *you*. What the fuck were you thinking?"

"Let me go!" I snapped, still yanking at his hand.

"Tell me what the fuck you were thinking!" he thundered.

"Fuck you!" I screeched. "And let me *the fuck* go!"

I yanked hard at his wrist. It went down and I let it go. I quickly slid away only for his arm to hook around my waist and haul me right back where he stepped in and pressed one hand into my belly and curled the fingers of the other one around the side of my neck.

And I was immobilized. *Again.*

"Tonight you coulda died," he ground out.

"I didn't."

"Or you coulda been made not you, he did damage but didn't take your fuckin' life."

"That didn't happen either," I snapped.

"It could have."

"It didn't."

He got nose to nose with me again and clipped, "It could have."

"He hit her!" I yelled.

"She makes that your problem, you call me, I deal with him. You don't go into an uncertain situation armed with goddamned, fucking *pepper spray*. Strike that, you don't go into an uncertain situation *at all*!" he ended on a shout.

"Well, next time, I won't seeing as there won't be a next time."

"Damn straight," he bit off.

"So, if you don't mind letting me go, I'll get the rest of my shit and then *go*."

"What?"

"Let me go, Tack, so I can *go*."

"You're not going," he growled.

"I'm not?"

"Fuck no."

"Wrong!" I shouted in his face and kept shouting. "Let me go!"

"You need to get this and you need to get it right fuckin' now and you doin' what you're always fuckin' doin', runnin' away and lickin' your wounds, means you will not be gettin' this."

"Wrong again, Tack. I don't need to get anything. Not anymore. Badass biker lessons are over because *we're* over."

His head jerked back an inch and he whispered, "What?"

"We're fucking over!" I shrieked and pushed at his abs with my hands. His middle rocked back but he came right back in.

"Fuck me, not this again," he muttered.

Oh no.

Oh fucking *no*.

"Step back," I hissed.

"Red—"

"Step back!" I screeched, shoving at him. He did the rocking thing again, but I got no shot to get away so I was stuck. Therefore I did the only thing I could. I fought my corner (as it were). "In there—" I raised an arm straight out to the side, pointing in the direction of Tabby's room before I poked him in his chest with my finger as best I could in the room allowed "—*you* made it clear where I stood. *Your brunette*," I snapped, and his face got hard, "also made it clear where I stood and where *she* stood. And I don't like where I'm standing, Tack, so you need to *let me go*!"

"What'd that bitch say to you?" he growled.

"Nothing I care to repeat. Now let me go."

"What'd she say?"

"I answered that."

"Tyra, babe, what…did…she…*say*?"

"You can repeat your question over and over, Tack, but this is going to end one way. Me leaving. So give me one last thing, let's avoid the scary biker dude hassle before I go."

"I see you're pissed, Red, but we can't work this shit out unless you talk to me so I know what the fuck I'm dealin' with."

"This is not a problem seeing as we don't have anything to work out."

I watched him suck breath in through his nose at the same time watching him get control.

And I knew he had control when he whispered, "Baby," his hand slid up to wrap around my ear, "we been through this. You don't get to decide that."

"Wrong again," I whispered back, staring him straight in the eye.

Tack ignored that and went back to our earlier topic.

"What'd she say to you?"

"Step back."

"What'd she say to you?"

"Step…*back*," I hissed.

His control slipped and he bit back, "What'd that bitch fuckin' say to you?"

Right. He wanted to know? I'd tell him.

"We enjoy a tag team with you and, seeing as I'm your old lady, I get your cock or your mouth. In my oh-so-elevated position as a hanger-on of the Club, I get to choose."

"Fuck, darlin', she's fuckin' with your head," he stated dismissively.

"She says you like it like that."

His brows shot together. "Say again?"

I didn't say again. I shared further.

"And she said she should know since she gave it to you like that."

"She said she gave it to me like that?" he repeated after me.

"Yep."

"She said she gave it to me like that." This was a statement, not a question, but it was still a question, just a question that was a whole lot scarier.

Scary or not, I still answered, "Yep."

"Where?"

"I don't know where," I returned. "Where do you have your threesomes?"

"No, babe, where were you when she said this shit to you?"

"Outside the Compound."

"Standin' on Chaos?"

His words didn't entirely make sense but I still got the gist so I replied, "Yep."

"Standin' on Chaos, talkin' to an old lady, she spewed that fucked-up shit at you," he stated, and suddenly, I didn't know why, but the change in him penetrated my anger and I realized I'd been wrong.

Very wrong.

The dragon might have woken.

But he hadn't yet breathed fire.

And I was about to learn that when a dragon breathed fire, it wasn't about noise, heat and flames.

It was about quiet, control and annihilation.

"Yes," I whispered, staring into his eyes.

He stepped back, his hands moving from me but one went to his back pocket and he pulled out his phone.

Stunned, freaked and now a little more than scared,

as the heavy air in the room pressed into my skin, I stood pressed against the wall and watched him hit buttons. I then watched him put it to his ear.

I then watched him speak.

"Dog, find BeeBee. I don't know where the fuck she is but find her. When you do, tell that bitch her ass doesn't get near Ride or Chaos. Not again. Not ever. Make that clear in a way she does not mistake it. Then you share that shit wide, brother. BeeBee is *gone*. She shows her face again, you or any of the brothers, make a statement." He paused to listen to Dog as I caught my breath at his words. "She got hold of Tyra. Filled her head with shit. Lied about what she gave me. On Chaos. To Tyra's face." This was an explanation that led to another pause. "Yeah, brother, *on Chaos* direct in the face of *my old lady*." Again a pause then, "Right. Later."

He disconnected, shoved the phone back in his pocket and locked eyes with me.

"You will not see BeeBee again," he declared, and I sucked in dearly needed breath.

When I accomplished this feat, I asked, "What does 'make a statement' mean?"

"It means, that bitch is stupid enough to come back, shit will rain down on her and she will not be stupid again."

Oh boy.

"What does that mean?" I whispered.

Tack did not whisper. "Whatever it needs to mean to get that message across."

It was then I realized I was shaking.

But Tack wasn't done. Far from it.

I knew this when he kept talking.

"Earlier, you pissed me off because you made assumptions and you hung up on me. I don't like to get hung up on. Don't do it again."

I didn't move except to keep shaking.

Tack didn't care. He kept speaking.

"I already told you once, no good woman deserves that shit. I've fucked BeeBee, you know it, we do not need to go back there and you sure as fuck are not gonna drag me back there every time something crawls up your ass. Now, with the shit she did, that will not be a problem. She didn't corner you on Chaos without someone at your back, which, if you had someone taking your back she would not have said dick or even fuckin' looked at you, you'd see her again. Now you won't. And I'll be havin' words with Hop about takin' off and leavin' you behind, knowin' he left you open for that bitch to get at you."

I was glad I wouldn't be present at that conversation.

"But, bottom line," Tack continued, "I don't do that shit. I told you that about me right off the fuckin' bat. You got stung when that shit went down when we started, you didn't get over it and you took that shit out on me. Now this is twice you've taken that shit out on me. Don't take that shit out on me again, Tyra. Face it, process it, deal with it, set it aside."

He was wrong, in a way.

I didn't inform him of that.

I just swallowed but said not a word.

Tack kept going.

"As for Hop, he don't tell me where to put my dick, I return the favor. Mitzi can be a pain in the ass. She can also be a ball-buster. Hop does not like gettin' his balls busted. They got problems at home. How he deals with that is not my business. It's not yours. It's theirs. They deal with it, we roll with it. That said, he is not the only member of Chaos who gets his rocks off when he wants with who he wants, and that might not be his old lady. You workin' at the garage, bein' with me, you might see shit like you did today. You ignore it. You don't share it. You can tell me. Anyone else, no. That's an absolute, babe. Never. Every woman connected to the Club knows it. This is a brotherhood and we have each other's backs in everything. *Everything.* But there are boys in that Club who don't mind bein' claimed. Brick, when he's got a woman, is one. Dog is another. I'm another. By that I mean, we got a woman, we don't stray. Get that now so we don't have to talk about this shit again."

I held his eyes and remained silent.

"Now's the time where you assure me you get me," Tack prompted.

"I get you, Tack," I whispered.

"Good," he returned instantly. "As for tonight, because Naomi's a bitch, rides Tabby's ass and always has, we've had problems. Tabby acts out. Her and me, we had a deal. I get her clear of her mom, she gets her shit together. She did not do that, she bore the consequences of it, you *nearly* bore unacceptable consequences of it, and I had to clean up both of your messes. That did not make me happy. My daughter gettin' hit by some motherfucker way too fuckin' old for her did not make me happy. Bein' called away from what I was doin', which was important, to deal with your and her shit also did not make me happy. In there," he pointed toward Tabby's room then his arm fell, "I was pissed. Serious as shit. When that happens, you gotta roll with that shit too."

I again didn't move or speak.

Tack again didn't care and kept going.

"As for the shit you pulled tonight, you didn't duck, I'd be in an ER right now hopin' to fuckin' Christ that you made it out at all much less you makin' it out as you. I think you get you mean somethin' to me so the threat of that is not somethin' I like either. Do not let that shit happen again, Tyra.

You got a situation, you call your man. You do not call in the boys and use your position to pull the shit you pulled tonight."

"My position?" I asked quietly.

"I've got my cut, I've got the gavel and you're my woman. Those were recruits. You call and they don't haul their asses outta bed in the middle of the fuckin' night to do your bidding, they might answer to me. They know they don't wanna answer to me. You gave them zero choice and swung their shit out there a lotta ways. Silver linin' for you, the boys, even the recruits, save Shy who's sharper than the rest of them, think that stunt you pulled is the shit. But those brothers do not have the cloud of the possibility of you permanently suckin' your food through a straw still hangin' over them. They can think it's the shit. I do not."

At that, I strongly suspected it was Shy who called in the boys.

I didn't ask for confirmation though.

I didn't say anything.

When I didn't, Tack asked, "Now, are we clear?"

"We're clear," I answered softly.

He held my eyes and he did this a while.

Then the dragon went to sleep and I knew this because the hard went out of his face, it softened, the air lightened all around us and the edge was gone from his voice when he said gently, "All right, baby, now come here."

"No," I whispered.

"What?" he whispered back.

"We're clear," I repeated then continued. "Very clear, Kane. So right now I'm going to bed and I'm doing it on the couch. Tomorrow, I want to be here in case Tabby's not still pissed at me so I can look after her. And tomorrow, after I sleep on it, I'll decide what I'm going to do about you."

He lifted a hand toward my neck but I jerked my head away and stepped swiftly to the side and out from the wall.

He pivoted with me, his hand dropping.

"Red, baby, what the—?"

"I told you, I needed time," I whispered. "You're going to give it to me."

"I just laid that shit out," he reminded me.

"Some of it, yes," I agreed and his head jerked slightly but I kept talking. "And I need to process that. I'll tell you my decision tomorrow."

"Babe—"

"Tomorrow, Tack."

The softness shifted out of his face right before he declared, "You are not sleepin' under my roof on the fuckin' couch."

"Okay, then, I'll go home."

"You are also not goin' home."

I held his eyes.

Then I whispered, "Fine," tore my gaze from his and walked to the unmade bed. I flipped off my flip-flops, pulled down my jeans, stepped out of them and shoved my hands under my shirt to yank my bra off with my tee still on.

Then I climbed into his bed, pulled the covers up and settled on my side, my back to him.

I heard nothing for a while then I heard movement. I saw him round the bed and rolled to my other side, away from him. The bed shifted when he sat on it and I heard boots dropping. The bed shifted again when he got up and I heard the whisper of clothes and a belt buckle hit the floor. And last, the bed shifted again when he got in it.

Then the room was plunged into darkness.

About a second after that, just as I expected he'd do, he rolled right into me and pulled me snug and tight to his front, his body curving into mine, forcing mine to curve with his.

I let him do what I expected he'd do anyway and stared through the dark at nothing.

"What else you need laid out, Red?" he asked the back of my hair quietly.

I didn't reply.

"It is not cool BeeBee got to—"

I cut him off, begging, "Please don't say her name in this bed."

"Fuck," he muttered. "She say somethin' else to you?"

I again didn't reply.

"It's clear she marked you, babe, what else did she say to you?"

"She was bleeding," I whispered.

"That bitch was bleeding?" Tack asked.

"Tabby," I pushed out then my breath hitched.

"Fuck," Tack repeated, and his arm got tight as his body pressed closer.

I felt the tears fill my eyes but I took deep breaths through my nose to fight them back and while I did this, Tack's hand searched and found mine. When it did, he forced his fingers through mine, lacing them, and he pressed our hands close to my chest.

"Took care of my girl," he murmured.

I deep-breathed.

"She's safe, you're safe, he's taken care of, baby. It's all good now."

I kept deep breathing.

I felt his face in the back of my hair where he whispered, "Tyra, it's all good now."

I wasn't so sure about that.

Still, I whispered back, "It's all good now."

"Sleep, we'll talk more tomorrow."

Goodie. Something *not* to look forward to.

Tack's fingers tensed in mine as his arm gave me a squeeze.

He relaxed both and urged, "Sleep, baby."

I sighed.

And, surprisingly, I fell asleep before Tack.

But I didn't have good dreams.

CHAPTER TWENTY-FIVE

Absolution

I woke draped on Tack, smelling his musk.

I opened my eyes and saw Tabby's tat under where my cheek was resting on Tack's shoulder. Somehow in the night we'd repositioned to our usual sleeping arrangement.

And as usual, it felt good.

A sharp stab pierced my heart as the day before washed through my brain.

Damn.

Right. One step at a time and my first step was, bathroom. Second, as ever, coffee. And then check on Tabby. And then...

I didn't know.

But when that step came, I'd figure it out.

Super carefully because I *really* didn't want to wake Tack, I lifted my arm that was lying across his flat belly and started to roll.

The problem with that was that Tack started to roll with me. He was bigger, more powerful and his roll took me to my back with him mostly on top of me.

Great. Awake half a minute and already my day wasn't going according to plan.

His head came up and my eyes caught his alert, totally not sleepy ones.

"Where you goin'?" he asked softly, his gravelly, early morning, warm-in-bed rumble drifting over my skin.

"Bathroom," I answered, ignoring my body and heart's response to his rumble.

His eyes drifted over my face as if he was trying to ascertain if I was lying about heading to the bathroom and instead intended to make haste to my secret chamber that would beam me to Fort Lauderdale.

Then his eyes came back to mine. "After, come back to bed."

I shook my head. "After, I'm starting coffee."

He gave into that but ordered, "After that, come back to me."

"No," I denied. "After that, I want to check on Tabby."

"She's good," he muttered, his forearm that was in the bed beside me sliding up so his fingers could glide in my hair at the side of my head. "Got up after you drifted off last night, checked on her. Sat with her a while 'cause she wasn't findin' sleep. Got her a couple Tylenol PMs. She went out, checked about half an hour ago, she's still out."

There it was. He might not win father of the year but he'd had his blowout then it was all about looking after his little girl.

Not a surprise. A relief, but not a surprise. Also sweet but I ignored that too.

Tack finished, "So after coffee, you're back here."

Whatever. I'd agree and do what I wanted.

So I lied, "Okay."

"Okay," he whispered then dipped his head and touched his lips to mine where he then touched the tip of his tongue to my lips. His goatee tickled my skin and for some reason

I felt his mouth, tongue and goatee more than I usually felt it and usually I didn't miss it. But it was like I was trying to memorize it. As if somewhere in the back of my mind I knew, soon, it would be gone and I'd never have it again.

He lifted his head and said quietly, "Hurry back to me, baby."

And usually him saying something like that quietly or even not quietly and just plain bossy would make me hurry back to him.

This time I just nodded, and that was a lie too.

He rolled off but did it with his hand sliding to my jaw, taking my hair with it and then I was free.

I rolled the other way and since I'd packed most of my stuff the night before, I went to my bag and dragged it into the bathroom. I did my thing, found a pair of loose-fitting, soft, elastic-waist pajama shorts with a cute little frilly edge on the hem and tugged them on. They didn't exactly go with my tee but, whatever. An outfit that matched was not, at that time (like it normally was), a priority.

I washed my face, brushed, flossed then packed my things back in the bag, ready for anything.

I walked out and I wanted to avoid looking at the bed but I couldn't. Even undone by the events of the day before and uncertain of my future with my man, such was the power of his charisma, I couldn't help but look.

Sheet to the waist, chest, tats, six-pack on display, up on an elbow with his head in his hand, probing sapphire blue eyes on me...all man, all beautiful, all hot.

Damn.

I moved quickly to the kitchen, started coffee then went to Tabby's room. The door was closed, though not latched seeing as it was broken. I hoped Tack was as good with a screwdriver as he was with whatever tools they used in a garage (okay, so I wasn't fucking up at work so much, still, I had no clue what they did—FYI, you could order parts without knowing how they were installed). Slowly, I pushed her door open and on quiet feet I walked to the bed.

Tack was right, Tabby was out. I was also right, she was sleeping on her right side so her left was visible in the morning light and she had a shiner. It wasn't angry but it was swollen and it wasn't a good look.

A seriously unfun lesson to learn at sixteen that guys could be dicks and some of them supreme assholes.

I pulled in a silent breath and leaned over her, cautiously shifting her long, thick hair away from her temple, cheek and neck. Then, it wasn't my place, we had been building it (until last night) but it wasn't where we were, still, I leaned down and kissed her soft hair at the side of her head.

Then I straightened, turned to the door and stopped dead.

Tack was leaning in it, arms crossed on his chest, leg crossed at the ankle, no shirt, no shoes, messy hair, faded jeans.

I swallowed.

"Couldn't help yourself," he whispered.

"No," I whispered back.

He made no reply except for his lips twitching and his warm, beautiful eyes getting warmer and more beautiful.

Since I couldn't stay in Tabby's room forever, I walked toward him then went sideways to squeeze by him.

This effort failed when Tack's fingers curled around my upper arm and he halted me right after I made it into the hall.

I watched as he leaned in and pulled Tabby's door to. Then he came to me, rounding and shifting me so he was in front of me and I had my back to the back hall. His arms slid around me and he started walking forward, thus I had no choice but to walk backward.

This seemed a theme in our relationship, Kane "Tack" Allen backing me into something.

I lifted my hands to place them on his chest and said quietly, "I'm going to get a cup of coffee."

"Later," he muttered, still moving.

Not a good choice of word.

I went silent.

Tack switched directions at his door, backed me in, stopped us to close the door with his foot, it latched then he started moving us again. Another switch in directions and I was down on his bed with Tack on top of me and my hands on his chest captive between us.

I stared in his eyes as they moved over my face and I steeled myself against how nice it felt when his hand framed one side and his thumb came out to sweep across the apple of my cheek.

"Quiet again this mornin'," he muttered after he studied me for a while.

"Mm hmm," I agreed but shared no further.

His eyes caught mine.

"She's sleepin'," he told me something I knew. "This mornin', she and me'll talk. I'll see where her head is at, why she keeps doin' fucked-up shit and then we'll see if we can get her over this crap."

"That'd be good," I replied.

"Right now, I wanna know where your head is at."

"My head is thinking of coffee," I lied.

"Bullshit," he called me on it, speaking gently.

I pulled in breath.

"Talk to me, babe," Tack urged.

"You back me up a lot," I observed, and his brows drew together.

"Say again?"

"You back me up a lot."

His head tilted slightly to the side but he didn't reply.

I gave examples. "In my office, last night in this room, just now down the hall and, um... also in this room."

"Yeah?"

"Yeah."

"So?"

I fell silent.

Tack rode my silence for half a minute then he ended it.

"Red, I know you don't want me to bring her up at all, 'specially not in this bed, but BeeBee's—"

At his words I decided it was time.

So it was me who started laying it out.

"You mistook me yesterday," I stated, interrupting him. "That wasn't about me thinking you'd do what Hop did. That was about me confronting something that was shocking and difficult to process. It was unfortunate you called seconds after it happened when I'd had no time to think about it. But then you pushed me on it when I tried not to talk about it and I had no choice but to process it on the spot, not on my time. So I did what I do. I got pissed about it." I took in a breath and finished quietly, "You shouldn't have pushed me, Tack."

His hand moved to my cheek so his thumb could glide along my lips the entire time his eyes didn't leave mine but he didn't say a word.

That, I supposed, was an apology but it also wasn't.

So be it.

I kept talking.

"I grew up in Ozzie and Harriet's house. My mom's a homemaker and bakes pies. We went to church every Sunday. My dad believes in God, the sanctity of marriage, football and shoot-'em-ups, in that order. I might have broken free from something that wasn't entirely me to live my own life but I have never, nor did I ever expect, to see two people having sex right before my eyes. That was shocking. I didn't know what to do with it."

"From here on in, darlin', you go to my room in the Compound only with me."

"It's too late, Tack. What was seen cannot be unseen."

"Red—"

"And it was *her*." I felt his body still as I felt the sting of tears in my nose and I took in a deep breath to control them before I went on, "You don't get how big that was, that it was her, because I didn't tell you."

"Tell me what?"

"That I fell in love with you during tequila and roast pork sandwiches."

His big frame gave a small jerk, his eyes flashed and his fingers tensed on my face but I kept going.

"It's stupid, ridiculous actually, I know it. And I don't care since I also know deep in my heart that it happened. Black and white, my whole life it seems I lived in black and white. I met you, suddenly all around me there was color." I sucked in breath and whispered, "Then you kicked me out of bed."

His face went soft, his eyes went warm and his head dipped closer to me as he growled a low, rough, quiet, "Baby."

I shook my head. "I fell in love with you and you didn't let me spend the night. You didn't even kiss me good-bye. And a day later, I saw you with her and you'd spent the night with her and you were kissing her good-bye."

"Fuckin' Christ, baby," he whispered, his hand flattening against the side of my head.

"That didn't sting, Tack, it *hurt*."

"Tyra, darlin', I had no clue."

"I know you didn't. That doesn't mean that wasn't what I was feeling. And seeing her yesterday at all, much less what I saw, was going to be unpleasant. Circumstances and her being her just made it worse."

"She's gone."

I nodded my head. "Yeah. But what's done can't be undone either."

"Tyra—"

"I've had five lovers."

Tack blinked and his head went back slightly.

Then he asked, "What?"

"Five. Carefully chosen. Men I could work with. Men I thought, since I knew they weren't perfect, they would become that."

"No one's perfect, baby," he interjected.

"Please listen to me," I whispered, and he slightly lifted his chin to communicate he acquiesced to my request so I continued. "I promised myself, as a little girl, that I would settle for nothing less than my dream man. Nothing less. It was crazy. I've thought on it and I don't even know why I vowed that to myself. I just did. Girls do that, sure. Then the reality of life seeps in and they get over it. I never did. My dream man or nothing. So I looked for him my whole life. I was going to live that dream, I would settle for nothing less. So I had nothing until that night at Ride when I met you."

I felt more of his heavy weight settle into me and his thumb swept my jaw as he whispered, "Red—"

"And I know you think I'm vulnerable, Tack. And I know you understand you have to teach me how to live in your world. But I'm not so stupid as to be partying with a bunch of rough-and-tumble bikers in the forecourt of a garage, drinking tequila and getting laid and through that convince myself the man I'm with is perfect, the man I'd been looking for, my dream man because I'm desperate to find him or the sex was great or I was drunk. The perfect I was looking for wasn't *perfection*. The perfect I was looking for was *the one*. And he was you."

His hand pressed in as he murmured, "Jesus fuckin' Christ, baby."

"Then you kicked me out of your bed without even a kiss good-bye."

"Christ, baby," he growled.

"And then you were a jerk. And I couldn't believe I was so wrong about you. Then you weren't a jerk. Then you were again. And, looking back, I didn't know I was doing it but I'll admit right now that you're right. I was playing games. I was doing it because I was testing you because if I was going to settle on *the one* I had to be sure he was . . . *the one*."

"Tyra—"

"You passed," I whispered, and his eyes heated as his face got closer, his hand shifting to cup my jaw and I finished, "Then last night, you failed."

His head jerked back.

"What?"

"You put your hand to my throat and shoved me against the wall."

"Tyra—"

"I'll accept beer and tequila and eating chips out of a bag and dip out of jars and ten pounds of extra weight," I told him. "I'll accept people smoking pot and making out hot and heavy all around me. I'll even do it, if I'm in the mood. Though maybe not the pot," I carried on. "I'll accept your brothers getting their rocks off whenever they want with whoever they want because that's the way of your world and also, because you're right, it's none of my business. And lastly, having had time to think about it, it's the way of *any* world. Men cheat, women do too. It happens everywhere, not just with bikers. Though, I must say, I don't ever want to see it again in the flesh," I shared, and kept going. "And I'll accept essentially being a second-class citizen in your biker world but only if I'm treated with respect to my face and that shit does not come home. I'll even accept rivers of blood because a man like you has to do what you have to do and part of the reason why you were the one is because you're a man like you."

I pulled in breath, held his eyes and finished. "What I will not accept is being shoved against the wall, a car or even a pillow with your hand at my throat."

To this, he replied immediately, "But your pulse is there, baby."

My head jerked and I felt my brows shoot together because his soft response was not anywhere near what I expected.

"Pardon?" I whispered.

"Did I hurt you?" he asked.

"That isn't the point."

"Yeah, darlin', it is. Now answer, did I hurt you?"

"No," I whispered.

"And I won't," he replied. "Ever," he went on firmly. "Not like that," he concluded.

"Tack—"

"Found my sister dead. OD."

I blinked in shock at his words, the change in subject and, well, his freaking words!

Then I whispered, "What?"

"Dead. It was me who was with her, me who found her. Felt her throat, no pulse. I gotta tell you, Red, there is nothin', not one thing in the world worse than puttin' your hand to the throat of someone you love and . . . feelin' . . . *nothin'*."

Oh my God.

"Tack—" I breathed.

"Rush was already born before she died but first thing I did when Tab was born was wrap my fingers around her throat to feel her pulse."

Oh God.

"Handsome—" I whispered.

But my time to talk was done.

I knew this when Tack kept talking.

"I grew up in the life. My dad was in a Club. His was different than Chaos. Started by veterans. Pissed. Jacked up. They had their reasons and I don't got their experiences so I don't judge. But his Club was about brotherhood, the end. Not country, not blood, but loyalty to your brothers. They thought country fucked them over so that no longer factored. Blood came second place but only if the biker was the kind of man where his old lady or kid meant somethin' to him. And they weren't about freedom to live your life the way you want even if that way is raisin' hell. They were radicals. They were into anything and everything, serious, whacked-out shit, all of it. And everything they did was to fuck The Man." His eyes held mine, they were intense, drilling into mine and his lips kept speaking. "And, 'cause 'a that shit, my dad's doin' a long fuckin' stretch, life for double homicide."

Ohmigod!

"Yeah," he muttered, watching me closely. "That a good thing to share when you're gettin' to know a sweet, feisty woman who you know's gonna mean something to you?"

Oh *God*!

"Honey—"

"My dad," he cut me off, "was about the brotherhood, not blood. Spent my life watchin' him knock my mother around. Spent my life knowin' he fucked around on her whenever he wanted, wherever he wanted and he did not give one shit that she or his kids knew. Spent that time vowin', I got a good woman, which my mom was in the beginning, that I would never, not ever, do that shit."

His eyes were hard, resolute and I kept silent because I figured it was now "later" so I had to take what was coming to me.

And I wanted it.

So I kept quiet and took it.

"Got an older brother," he kept going. "He hit eighteen, he joined the Air Force. Got the fuck out. Dad was in prison by then and Mom had convinced herself she wasn't worth shit so she just kept hookin' up with shit-heel biker after shit-heel biker that treated her like Dad or worse. Don't blame my brother for gettin' the fuck out. Do blame him for never turnin' back. Didn't hear from him then, don't now, don't even know where the fuck he is. He left me and Kimmy to that. By the time I was free, I just wanted out so bad, I couldn't see anything else. So I got on my dad's old Harley, took off and left her to that too."

He was still struggling with that decision, it was clear on his face. He wasn't hiding it from me. And it hurt to witness.

So I slid my hands up, wrapped my fingers around his neck and whispered, "Baby."

Tack was in the zone because he showed no response that I'd even spoken and kept talking.

"Searchin', that was what I was doin'. Pissed off at the world 'cause 'a my shitty life, scared as shit I had my dad in me, searchin' for somethin' that would prove that wrong, lead me to a better life. Somethin' to do to get that poison out of my system. Somewhere where I belonged. Found Chaos. Back then, they were a good Club, about livin' life, havin' a good time doin' it and raisin' hell, all of which I wanted, the last I needed. They sold pot. They had the garage as a front. And they were about the brotherhood but also blood and country. Not a lot of places in this world you can ride free and do the shit we liked to do. America is one of them. They appreciated that. That isn't to say that they abided by all her laws but that was their choice and it was a choice they could take because we live in America."

He pulled in breath and was talking quieter when he spoke again.

"But the first Chaos party I went to, old ladies were there, kids. Later ones, yeah, they got rowdy and shit went down but that first one was about family. I liked that. I liked the way the brothers were with their women, their kids. I liked the shit they had to say about what the Club was about, what the brotherhood meant. So I found where I belonged and became a recruit."

"I'm glad you found that, handsome," I said softly.

"Me too," he agreed. "But then I got my cut and was let into the way the Club was goin' and I was in, no goin' back even if I really didn't fuckin' agree with the path they'd turned down. They kept goin', meant I was followin' in my father's footsteps. But these were my brothers. So I kept my mouth shut, did my bit but planned for the future, talked the Club into explorin' different avenues while they made their way down that path, just in case they got their shit together and veered off. Didn't work but I kept at it, met Naomi, got her knocked up with Rush, married her ass and she got what she wanted. She was born an old lady. She loved the life. She bullshitted me—a miracle how she could do that while suckin' my cock—as I told her where I felt the Club should be and she said she was with me all the way. She knew before she got deep into it with me where my mind was at and she threw her hat in my ring. And when Kimmy died, she knew I'd come back full of fire to make that change and she acted like I never fuckin' told her when practically every night I'd talk about it, in our bed before we went to sleep. She liked drippin' in the rose gold I could give her 'cause 'a what the Club was into. She liked havin' a decent house because she didn't grow up in one. She liked quiet, she liked the flow, she did not have what it takes to stand by her man. A follower needs one kind of woman in his bed, a leader another. She's the woman of a follower. She mighta thought she had what it took or even hoped she did but she didn't. She only had what it takes to hold him down. And that has not changed. Her old man, Pipe, used to be a decent guy. He's just weaker than me. She didn't delay in draggin' his ass down. He didn't fight it, that's where he is and, unless he gets shot of her ass, that's where he'll always be."

Well, that fully explained Naomi and made me think even less of her, which was quite a feat.

"What path was the Club on?" I asked quietly, and Tack focused on me.

Then he rolled to my side and put his hands to my pits, pulling me up further in the bed before he shifted up beside me, rolled again, to his back so I was on top, chest to chest.

He lifted a hand, pulled the side of my hair back and continued talking.

"The Club ran drugs, babe," he said quietly, my body locked and I stared at him. "Not sales. Safe transport. And doin' that, they did all that went with it. The path got darker and darker, the Club got deeper and deeper and I didn't like it even before my mom called and told me Kimmy was fucked up."

Right, okay, first things first.

"Tell me about Kimmy," I urged.

Tack pulled in breath through his nostrils and I already knew the end was not a happy one. I still braced when he prepared by sifting his fingers through my hair and then pulling it away from my face again and burying his hand in it before he continued.

"You live our life, unless you develop a tough skin, that shit'll eat you alive. I thought Kimmy had a tough skin. She was hard, seen it all, done it all by the age of twelve. Least that was the way she acted. I was wrong. She had a soft spot. I just didn't see it so I sure as fuck didn't protect it."

Oh God.

I closed my eyes, Tack's hand slid to my jaw and I opened them.

"Yeah," he whispered, "you're gettin' it, babe."

"That's why you like mine," I deduced in a return whisper.

"And that's why I'll bust my balls to protect it."

Oh *God*.

"Go on," I kept whispering.

He drew in another breath and then did as I asked.

"I left her behind but unlike my brother, I didn't leave her. She mighta seemed hard but we were tight. She could be funny and we held together in a house that felt like a boat tossed in a storm all the fuckin' time. She got it when I took off, she even told me to get the fuck out. But, soon's I could, I reconnected with both of them but mostly Kimmy. And soon after that, I started to send her money in hopes she'd find her own way out. Brought her out to Colorado when I married Naomi. Brought them both out when Rush was born. Naomi was pregnant with Tabby, nearly to term when Mom called. Told me Kimmy was hooked on shit, totally fucked up, stealin', lyin', turnin' tricks."

I held my breath at this news trying not to look like I was holding my breath but Tack was back in his zone, a seriously bad zone, and thus didn't notice it.

"So I went back to California to sort her shit out. What I found, babe, was pissed at my mom for not tellin' me sooner. She wasn't a mess, she fuckin' defined it. So we talked, or I talked and she shouted. Saw no way to clear her of that shit unless I intervened and took matters into my own hands. Should not have done that. Should never have done that. Should have put her in a hospital. Too late now, I did it. I locked her in a room with me while she detoxed. It was not pretty. Screamin', fightin', scratchin', pukin', gettin' the shakes, Christ, those fuckin' shakes. Like seizures. Whacked. And it did not work. Up for seventy-two hours, dealin' with her shit, I passed out. She had a stash, junkies are fuckin' geniuses when it comes to hidin' their stash, took it, I woke up, she wasn't movin' and that was that. She did it with me right in the room. Me right there. My little sister killed herself and I was five feet away, fuckin' *sleeping*."

I closed my eyes but slid my hand up his chest so I could again curl my fingers around his neck and this time I did it tight.

I opened them when Tack stated, "Put Kimmy into the ground on a Friday. Hightailed my ass back to Colorado because Tabby came into the world that Sunday."

That would mark a man.

That would definitely mark a man.

And that marked my man.

His eyes focused on mine and his hand slid back into my hair, his fingers twisting in it and his words were soft when he said, "The Russians got you, didn't even think, I got to you, put my hand to your throat. I needed that pulse, babe, so I went for it. Shy shared what went down last night with that asshole and his bat, also didn't think, put my hand to your throat. It was not meant to hurt you or alarm you. It was done so I could assure myself you were alive."

This made sense. So much of it, it was sad at the same time it was beautiful.

"Okay," I whispered.

"My sister's addiction, I steer clear of any 'a that shit so I do not smoke pot, my choice, personal. Others do, I don't judge. You wanna try that shit, that's your choice too and I won't judge that either. But you wanna try it, you do it *only* with me around so I can look after you."

"I don't want to try it," I assured him, and he nodded.

Then he declared, "Outside pot, drugs do not touch Chaos."

I licked my lips before I asked hesitantly, "So I take it they veered off that dark path?"

"No, they did not. I came back with a fire in my belly to get my Club clear of that shit, stop makin' it easy for people to take the escape my sister took and make certain I did not become the man my father was. But I was smart enough to bank it. I bided my time. I built up the garage and the stores. I recruited brothers who saw things my way and we planned. The monetary success of the stores and garage had to cover the Club so their lifestyles didn't change too much when we pulled our shit off that dark path. I got enough support, I took over. It was hostile. We lost some brothers, they renounced the Club, took off, started to do their own thing. And it was unpopular in factions outside the Club. We were good at what we did and the people we worked with weren't real happy we were no longer going to provide that service. Shit got ugly, lost a brother to it, but we got clear. And one of the suppliers we worked for was the Russian mob."

I gasped. "You lost a brother?"

"Yeah."

"As in, he died?" I whispered.

"Bowin' out of safe transport of narcotics is not the same as handin' in your resignation."

Too true.

"The Russians?"

"Yeah. I still am not popular with them. And there's another reason why Arlo and High are about showin' you respect. They like the money but they also like the rush. Danger is a drug and they're hooked. They are the last of the brothers who are still tryin' to get us back in. They got ties to the Russians to keep that avenue open for us should they get me out. What they didn't expect was that the Russians would pick up someone connected to Chaos. You and me were new, the Russians didn't want you and had no clue who you were. Even so, that shit doesn't fly with Chaos. Collateral damage, no matter how that comes about, is unacceptable. Kids, women, not just old ladies but you just bein' the garage's office manager, was steppin' over a line and that line is not drawn in the sand, babe. Not for Chaos. That line is fixed in cement."

This was good to know.

"Right," I said softly.

"So Arlo and High are on board and after this is done, where it takes us, I have no clue. Maybe the Russians takin' you and Lanie, not backin' down after that shit, not givin' us our due by admittin' their mistake, sending lieutenants to offer apologies, might have been a wake-up call to just how cold those motherfuckers are. You're ours and you weren't safe. Lanie has nothin' to do with Belova's shit and she wasn't either. This means no one is. That's a serious wake-up call 'cause both Arlo and High got old ladies and High's got kids. After we sweep up that mess, I don't know how they'll go. What I know is, drugs took my sister, I worked my ass off to get my brothers where they are, livin' free and *stayin'* free by not doin' stupid, dangerous, fucked-up shit that could get our asses in the joint or worse, dead, and my Club will not be involved in that shit in any way or I won't be involved in the Club."

"So you, um...don't do anything illegal?"

He held my eyes.

Then he said quietly, "I didn't say that."

Oh boy.

Tack rolled again so I was on the bottom and he was looming over me.

Then he explained and he did gentle-like so I knew I was in for even more.

"We do what we gotta do to protect what's ours and what we do might be frowned on in the eyes of the law. Case in point, there's a twenty-three-year-old motherfucker who'll think twice before he moves on another sixteen-year-old girl and definitely he won't raise a hand to a woman. And he ain't breathin' easy and without pain learning that lesson because of you slappin' him and unmannin' him. He's doin' it 'cause once you were gone, me and the boys finished the job."

I figured they'd kept up with my lessons after I left so I nodded.

Tack went on.

"We also do what we wanna do to enjoy our lives and, you seen it, that includes shit like smokin' pot. We got beefs with other Clubs or out in the world, we deal, and that shit can turn bad. And a five-mile perimeter around any Ride store is free of drugs and hookers. We patrol it and if there's a dealer or bitch on our turf, we don't call the cops but we do take measures to remove them."

Oh boy.

Tack kept going.

"But Ride's books are clean and that means squeaky. We don't transport drugs. We don't offer enforcement. We don't sell tail. We don't sell guns. We build cars and sell auto supplies."

"Sell tail?" I squeaked and Tack kept holding my eyes when he replied, "I told you that path was dark."

Holy crap!

"So, uh...now you aren't drug transporters, pimps and gun runners, you're mechanics, hell-raisers and kind of vigilantes?"

"Yeah."

"But you were all that," I whispered, and Tack kept right on holding my eyes.

"Yeah."

"You," I pressed.

"Me," he answered immediately.

Oh boy.

"Babe, my scope was Ride and the garage. This does not mean I didn't get pulled into that shit. I did. And as a brother, I did my bit. And it took a long fuckin' time but I did more than my bit to pull all of us out."

"Okay," I said softly. "So this was why I got all those 'laters'? Because you weren't fired up to share all of this?"

"This was why," he confirmed.

I pulled in breath through my nose.

Before I could process any of what he said much less come to terms with it, Tack stated, "Love and redemption."

My head tipped on the pillow. "What?"

"That movie you made me watch, first time at your house. Love and redemption. You said, 'The most beautiful stories ever told are the most difficult to take.' You said that, Red. Right out. And I knew if you got that, when it was later and I shared my shit with you, you'd get me. I never thought my story was beautiful. I thought it was shit. But you said that and when you did, I saw it. The ride is not over but if I can keep my Club together and find a sweet, feisty woman who's got my back and enough to her that she'll stay there, holding me up not dragging me down, I figure I'd find my way to beauty eventually. And I'd find absolution because I'd know, I earned the love of that woman, a woman who's got so much to her it'll take years to dig down and find the heart of her, that would be my reward."

Ohmigod.

Ohmigod!

Ohmigod!

Did he just say that?

Did. He. Just. *Say that?*

"And you told me," Tack continued, his face coming closer, "I had that when I first met you."

"I—"

"So I was hooked to that shit, I did it, I participated in it, I was loyal to my brothers as I'd vowed I'd be and I pulled me and my Club out of it. I did that but that didn't erase what we did. *You* are my absolution."

Oh.

My.

God.

Now did he just say *that*?

"Tack—"

"And no way in fuck I'm gonna get in a stupid-ass fight with my woman, find out hours later some asshole took his hand to my daughter, justifiably lose it and then watch the woman I been waitin' for walk out my door."

Oh God.

He said that. All of it.

"Tack, honey, I—"

"I get pissed, babe, wait it out or give it as good as you get," he declared.

"But—"

"I say somethin' stupid when I'm pissed, like you don't have a say with my kids when you're practically livin' with them and *definitely* you're a fixture in my life, you tell me to go fuck myself."

"Well, I—"

"You got somethin' to say, say it. You're pissed, let it all hang out. You got an opinion, share it. What you don't do is get scared of me and what you don't do, *ever*, is walk out on *us*."

I shut my mouth.

Tack waited.

I kept my mouth shut.

Tack didn't.

"Am I clear?"

"Mostly," I answered.

His eyes narrowed. "What's not clear?"

"Rivers of blood."

His head twitched and he asked, "Say again?"

"The Russian mob."

He shook his head instantly. "No."

What did he mean, no?

"No?" I asked.

"No," he answered.

I verbalized my question. "What do you mean, no?"

"What I mean is, that is not done. But it's gettin' done. Careful, quiet. And how it gets done, you don't know. You don't know shit. So when it's done, any shit blows back, you're clear. The Club is dealin' with this. You're workin' in the office and sharin' my bed."

"I—"

His fingers came up and pressed to my lips as his eyes locked with mine.

"Trust me."

"What if you get hurt?" I said behind his fingers, and he moved his hand.

"I won't."

"But what if you do? Or Dog? Brick? Hound? Or—"

"I won't. They won't."

My voice was rising when I asked, "How can you be sure?"

"The whole point of doin' it careful and quiet is so they don't. I went with my base instinct, babe, blood would have been shed about fifteen minutes after we surrounded Hawk's truck. But doin' that shit serves no lasting purpose except the pain it might cause if someone gets hurt or dead. No, you *plan* that shit so the vengeance you seek sticks and lasts a fuckin' lifetime."

I was seeing benefits of Tack being sharp as a tack.

He kept talking.

"The mob bought that shit when they took Mara and Lawson's kids. We been workin' that now for fuckin' ever. They took you, the time had come to speed that up and be done with it. But you are not involved or in the know. You trust your man. Then, when it's done, we live easy until the next fuckin' drama. And, Tabby doesn't pull her head outta her ass, seein' as we got two years of her at least in this house, that could happen tomorrow since it happened yesterday. And by the way," he added, "I know I made my point last night but it's worth repeating. It didn't help you goin' commando on that motherfucker's ass."

"I'd had a bad day," I muttered and his mouth curved.

"Yeah."

"I didn't think," I went on.

"Got that, babe."

"Actually, to be honest, I'm not entirely certain what came over me," I admitted.

"Don't care, long's it doesn't come over you again."

I took in a breath.

Then I shared, "Well, considering I didn't exactly have control over it the last time, I can't make that promise."

"Fuck me," he muttered to the headboard.

"But I'll try," I offered. He looked at me and when he did, his eyes had changed in a way that made me catch my breath.

"You bein' cute mean we're over this current shit?"

I let out my breath and asked back, "If I say yes, will you let me up for coffee?"

His face dipped close. "Babe, I like your cute but this is kinda important."

I pulled in yet another breath and held his gaze as I whispered, "Do I really have a choice *not* to be over this current shit?"

"No," he replied instantly.

"I didn't think so," I muttered.

"Red, you're still bein' cute."

I sighed.

Then my voice softened and my arms tightened around him as I whispered, "I'm sorry that happened with your sister."

Tack closed his eyes and dropped his forehead to mine.

There it was.

Damn, there it was. He gave it right to me, but I should have known the instant I looked in his awake, alert eyes after I woke.

He'd worried about my state of mind, about the state of us, he didn't sleep and me moving through the drama, taking in all he was, all he used to be and accepting it meant everything.

And like the everything I gave him, everything Kane "Tack" Allen gave me meant the exact same.

Everything.

I kept talking.

"And that your story is difficult to take."

He opened his eyes, stared into mine and whispered, "Baby."

"But I'm not your absolution, honey. You earned it before you met me."

"You're my reward."

Oh God.

I liked that he thought that. Like, a lot.

So I agreed, "Okay."

"You're in love with me," he stated, and my breath left me.

So I had to force out my, "I—"

His head came up half an inch and he repeated, "You're in love with me."

I closed my eyes.

"Eyes, babe."

I opened my eyes.

"You're in love with me," he said yet again.

"Yes," I whispered.

"Since we met."

"I know it sounds crazy, Tack, but—"

"Since we met."

I fell silent for a moment then said softly, "Yes."

"Thank fuck you needed that fuckin' job enough to go head-to-head with me," he muttered.

"Um . . ." I started to correct, "I think I went head-to-head with you mostly because you were a jerk. It was only partly because of the job."

"Then thank fuck I was a jerk."

Who would have ever thought I'd agree with that?

Still, I did.

"Can I have coffee now?" I requested.

"No."

"Tack!" I snapped.

"I love you too, babe."

My mouth dropped open and I stared.

But although my body was still and my mind was blank, my belly got warm and my heart tripped before it got light.

Tack wasn't done.

"Watchin' that fuckin' movie, minute my fingers curled around your chin, turned your face to mine and I saw you were cryin', that's when it happened."

Oh hell.

I started crying right then.

"Or, coulda been when I saw you in your yoga shit," he muttered, watching the tears fill my eyes.

"Shut up," I whispered.

He dropped his head and touched his lips to mine.

Then he lifted it and didn't shut up.

He kept muttering.

"Another layer, I lay my shit out, all of it, it's ugly and she ends that by bein' cute."

"Shut up."

"And bossy."

"Shut *up*."

"Bossy and a crybaby."

"Shut up!" I snapped then finished, "And kiss me, for goodness sakes."

His lips dropped to mine where he said, "That, baby, you be bossy and *that* I'll do."

Then Tack slanted his head and did it.

Hard, wet, wild and thorough.

When he lifted his head, I was dazed, I was happy, later was over, my man loved me, I had it all and Tack said, "Now you can have coffee."

CHAPTER TWENTY-SIX

Toothache

TACK AND I were sitting out on his deck in the Colorado sun, feet on the railing, sipping coffee and waiting for the kids to wake up so Tack could make breakfast.

We were both silent.

I didn't know what Tack was thinking.

I was running through all the available scenarios, knowing the players involved, of how the meeting of my parents and Tack would go.

I was coming up with none that didn't involve mayhem, gunplay or me getting disowned even though I was an only child when Tack asked, "How attached are you to your house, babe?"

My head turned in his direction and I saw him calmly sipping coffee and staring at his fantastic view.

"Pardon?"

He dropped his mug and turned his head to me.

"Your house," he stated. "How attached are you to it?"

"In, uh . . . what sense?"

"In the sense that if you're attached to it in a way that convinces me to give all this shit up, we'll build a couple rooms on so Tab and Rush can have their space. If not, we'll put it on the market."

Seven hundred thousand, two hundred and ten words flew into my head but none of them came out of my mouth before Tack kept going.

"One plus, it's close to Chaos and Ride. Minus," he swung his mug out to his fantastic view but added, "and it's small."

"I … we … you," I swallowed then asked, "Are we moving in together?"

His head tipped to the side like my question was borderline insane and he answered, "Well, yeah."

"When was this decided?"

"You love me?" he asked, and my belly flipped.

"Yeah," I whispered.

"Right," he grinned. "And I love you and your biological clock is ticking so we best get started on that shit."

That … *shit?*

"Uh, you mean, the shit of having a family?" I asked, my brows rising and his grin got bigger.

"Yeah."

"I've known you six weeks," I reminded him.

"You gonna fall out of love with me tomorrow?" he shot back.

"I don't think so," I returned, and his grin turned into a smile.

"So what're we waiting for?"

"Maybe getting to know each other a little better?" I suggested.

"You got any skeletons in your closet?" he asked.

"Not that I know of," I answered.

"So we're good," he muttered, turning back to the view.

"Do you have any," I started then finished when I got his gaze back, *"more?"*

"Opened those doors wide and you saw 'em rattlin' just this mornin', Red."

That was definitely the truth.

"You've only lived through one period with me," I pointed out, and his brows drew together.

"Say again?"

"I can be hell on wheels when I'm PMS'ing," I shared.

His gaze went back to the view as he muttered, "You can be hell on wheels anytime. Like, say, how you're gearin' up to be now."

"Tack!" I snapped, and he again looked at me and he did it again grinning.

"What?"

"It goes like this," I began to explain. "We get to know each other. We have a huge-ass wedding. We spend time just us and, um…Tab and Rush, of course. Then we start on a family."

"Got it all scheduled," he noted.

"Yes," I returned.

"What's a huge-ass wedding?"

"Don't ask that," I advised. "Just show up."

His grin turned wicked and I liked it

That was, I liked it until he inquired, "You askin' me to marry you, Red?"

I wasn't even sipping coffee and, still, I choked.

Then I pushed out, "What?"

"I accept."

I shook my head and kept shaking it when I requested clarification. "Let me get this straight. Did you just accept my non-marriage offer?"

"Non-marriage?"

"I didn't ask!" My voice was rising.

"So you just wanna shack up?" he asked but didn't wait on my answer. "I'm good with that too."

Gah!

"I'm getting my huge-ass wedding," I declared.

"So you *are* askin' me to marry you," he noted.

Gah! Gah! Gah!

Sharp as a tack.

Someone kill me.

"When did you show last night?" I asked.

"Say again?"

"Last night, when I was going off on that kid, when did you show?"

"You'd just slapped him and asked, 'How about that? Feel good?'"

Wonderful. He caught nearly the entire performance.

"So you saw most of the show," I surmised.

"Reckon. Yeah."

"Do you want some of that?" I asked sweetly, and Tack grinned huge, wicked *and* sexy, leaned into me fast, hooking his hand behind my head and pulling me to him.

"You think you could take me?" he asked softly.

"Only if I get to wield pepper spray," I returned.

"No fuckin' way," he replied.

"Then no. But I'd give it a shot," I retorted, and he pulled me closer.

My breath started to escalate as his face, but mostly his mouth, got closer. It escalated further as his eyes moved over my face and it did this mainly because of the sweet, soft look in them.

Then they caught mine.

"Huge-ass wedding," he whispered.

"Yeah," I whispered back.

"That how you like it?"

"That's always been my dream."

"You didn't settle for a man until you found the one you wanted, you keep settlin' for nothin' less, baby."

My heart flipped.

I was going to get my huge-ass wedding.

To a biker.

Yay.

"Okay," I breathed.

"Seein' as you're breathin' and not through a tube, it's all out there, you love me, lookin' back on you kickin' that motherfucker's ass, gotta say, it was pretty hot."

My belly fluttered.

"Yeah?" I asked softly.

"Yeah. You bein' all riled up like that for my girl was hotter."

"It was for Tabby as well as all womankind," I corrected.

"So noted," Tack muttered, lips twitching.

"But mostly, it was for Tabby."

Tack's eyes got sweeter and softer and his hand fisted in my hair.

Then he asked quietly, "You wanna move in with me?"

"Yeah," I answered immediately.

"You attached to your house?"

"No."

"Good, we'll get you a car that does good in snow and move you up here."

"Okay."

"Start plannin' that huge-ass wedding, baby. We need to get hitched. Rush is gonna be gone in a year. We need a baby in the house."

At that, my belly melted.

"Okay," I breathed.

"I hit the heart of you yet?" Tack asked.

"Close," I whispered.

"Tastes sweet," he whispered back, and I felt my eyes get wet.

"Yeah," I agreed quietly, "it does."

I watched up close as Tack's eyes heated then his hand at my head pulled me even closer and then we were making out.

This was what we were doing when we heard Rush say loudly, "Cool. You're goin' at it. After that fight last night, didn't know what I'd come up to."

Tack's hand released my head and both of us looked over the backs of our chairs to see Rush, in cutoff sweats exposing a teenage boy-man body which laid testimony to part of the reason why he was a successful serial dater, and his coffee mug joining us. I pulled in a calming breath and tamped down my mortification of getting caught making out as Rush pulled up a chair on the other side of his dad and collapsed into it.

"I'm sorry you heard that, Rush," I told him, he turned to me and grinned.

"You say fuck when you're pissed nearly as much as Mom does," he informed me.

Great.

"Though, you don't throw shit or grab knives," he muttered then his eyes slid to his dad. "Bet that's a relief."

Tack chuckled.

Chuckled!

"Knives?" I breathed.

"Long story," Tack replied.

"Or, stor*ies*," Rush clarified.

"Naomi wielded a knife on you?" I asked Tack.

"Knive*zzzz*, plural," Rush answered.

"Holy crap," I whispered.

"Right, quit freakin' out Tyra," Tack muttered. "Your sister up?"

"She will be, she smells bacon fryin' and knows pancakes

are comin'." Rush threw out his thinly veiled request for his father to start cracking on breakfast.

"I'm not sure, honey," I put in. "She had a rough night."

"Uh, Tyra, you've eaten Dad's pancakes. Rough night, wild night, hell night, you get up for Dad's pancakes."

I suspected this was true.

"Go check on her," Tack ordered.

"A man takes a load off and right away, he's ordered to put one back on," Rush groused as he got to his feet.

"Boy, you just been sleepin'," Tack returned.

"Whatever," Rush murmured, humor in his voice as he slid inside.

If Tabby was up, I had little time.

Even if she wasn't, Rush would be back soon so I still had little time.

So I didn't delay in throwing it out there.

"Can I talk to her first?"

Tack looked hard at me. "You want to?"

"I think . . ." I hesitated then answered, "Yes, I want to."

"You think what?"

I took in breath.

Then I told him, "I think, if I'm going to be around, that I broke her trust last night. And I think, since I *am* going to be around, I shouldn't delay in getting it back."

"How'd you break her trust?"

"She didn't want to make it a big deal. I went off half cocked and made it a big deal."

"You're a big girl, babe, and you get to make those decisions. She's sixteen. She don't get that yet nor does she get to be pissed at the decisions you make."

"She gets whatever she wants, Tack. It's *her* emotions and unless they're handled with care, since she's feeling a lot of them, it's clear most of them are no good, she's acting on them and not in good ways, that cycle won't be broken unless they are. Her emotions handled with care, I mean. Not to mention, I don't think she has a woman she trusts, she was giving that to me, I took it away and I have to give it back."

"You got a plan of attack?" he asked.

"No, I'm going to wing it," I answered.

"Then yeah, you talk but I'm here. So's Rush. Sortin' Tab's shit is a family thing," he declared, and I sucked in a sharp breath.

A family thing.

"Red?"

"I waited a long time," I whispered.

"For what?" he asked.

"For you."

I watched a shadow darken his face.

"You do not get to do that shit," he growled, and I blinked.

"What?"

"Make me wanna pick you up, carry you to my bed and fuck you hard to show my appreciation for bein' so damn sweet I got a toothache, a fuckin' toothache I fuckin' like when I got pancakes to make and a daughter's shit to sort."

"Oh," I whispered.

"Fuck, I'm not even close."

"To what?"

"The heart of you. You run so fuckin' deep, I'll never get there."

God.

"Lookin' forward to a lifetime of diggin', babe."

God!

"Now you're being sweet," I accused, my voice wobbly.

"Used to it yet?"

"No."

"You got a lifetime to get there too."

Seriously.

I could take no more.

"Shut up."

"I will, you kiss me."

"Rush and/or Tabby might be here any minute."

"I didn't tell you to go down on me."

My eyes narrowed and I couldn't see it but even I knew it was ominously.

"Tack!"

"Kiss me, Red."

"Tack!"

"Fuck it," he muttered, shifted, leaned into me, hooked me at the back of my head and then *he* kissed *me*.

I was sitting in my chair, tingling from top to toe and Tack was moving into the house with both of our mugs to refill as Rush slid by him to come out, muttering, "She's gettin' up."

So Tack got his kiss before Rush came back.

And I got to sit in the Colorado sunshine knowing without a doubt I had my hands straight up in the air, tucked so secure, I was safe to enjoy the ride.

CHAPTER TWENTY-SEVEN

One of Us

IT WAS SUNDAY afternoon and I was pressed close to Tack on his bike because we were heading down into Denver. Sheila had got a wild hair and decided to throw a barbeque so she made enough potato salad for the entirety of Chaos and bossed Dog into manning the huge barrel grill outside the Compound.

So we were heading down to get our bratwurst and commune with the brethren on a sunny Sunday afternoon.

The sun was shining, the wind was in my hair, I was pressed close to my man heading toward a grilled brat and life was sweet.

And as we rode, my mind was running over the day before and my lips were smiling.

Not long after Tack left the deck, Rush returned to it, I came to terms with the fact that I was a roller-coaster type of girl and was reflecting on the fact that not only was Tack's house awesome, there was no lawn to mow, when it occurred to me that Tack was taking a long time refilling my coffee.

So I'd turned my head, looked over the back of my chair and into the kitchen.

And what I saw cemented in my mind that I'd made the right choice over tequila six weeks before.

Because I saw Tack and Tabby in the kitchen. Tack had his ass against the kitchen counter, his body facing the deck and his girl in his arm. She had both arms around her dad, leaning in, her cheek to his chest. His arm was high, his strong hand curled around one of her shoulders and his lips were to the top of her hair. He kept them there as I watched and I knew he was talking to her. I couldn't see all of his face but I guessed he was doing it gentle-like. And I figured it was a good guess because Tabby's eyes were closed and her face was soft.

I turned away, giving them their moment.

"Jealous," Rush muttered, and I looked from the view to him.

"Pardon, honey?" I muttered back and he looked at me.

"Mom. Jealous of Tabby."

I said nothing but held his eyes, a nonverbal cue that if he wanted to talk, I was listening.

He wanted to talk.

"Don't know, but it's never been good. Thought on it, it's been so bad. I always thought it was because she don't get along with her mom because Gram is awesome with us but she's even now a bitch to Mom so Mom don't know any better. But I don't think that's it. I think she made bad decisions in her life and Tabby's got her whole one ahead of her. Mom can't go back. Tabby's got time and that's what Mom wants."

I nodded because this made sense.

Rush kept talking.

"She's my sister but it ain't lost on me she's also hot so good-lookin' and young, double threat for Mom."

"You don't have to tell me," I began, "but if you want

to, I'd like to know what 'never been good' means when it comes to Tab and your mom."

He shook his head, looked at the view but shared, "Just always on her ass. My room's a mess, Mom never says a word. She's always up in Tabby's face to clean hers. When we lived there, Mom washed my clothes. Told Tabby years ago it was her responsibility to do hers. I play music loud, Mom don't say shit. Tabby does or she's on the phone or somethin', Mom shouts at her. Never leadin' into it, she just loses it right off the bat. And, when she hit high school, it got worse." Rush looked at me. "Tab's popular. Gets a lot of attention. Drives Mom crazy. Mom's convinced she's a slut."

His eyes grew contemplative and his gaze slid to the view.

"She's not a slut, honey," I said gently.

"Seein' an older guy," Rush muttered.

"Sometimes, you get told enough you are what you aren't, it gets in your head and you make it a self-fulfilling prophesy even if you really aren't that." Rush looked back at me. "She isn't that," I whispered. "She's just in trouble enough for not being it, she probably thinks she might as well do it since she's in trouble for it anyway."

Rush took a moment to consider this and I let him.

Then he murmured, "Makes sense."

"Stick by her," I urged, and his back slightly straightened.

"I will, Tyra."

And he would.

"Good, honey."

He grinned at me, his eyes moved to the view and he took a sip of coffee before he announced, "I need more coffee. You think we gave them enough time?"

He was giving them time, like me.

Really a good kid.

But I needed more coffee too. I'd only had one cup and already a full morning. I was hitting emergency status on the caffeine level.

"You've been a member of this family all your life, only you can make that call," I told him.

I got another grin and he decided, "We've given them enough time."

Oh hell.

That meant it *was* time.

I nodded, we both stood and Rush did the gentleman thing again, letting me precede him to the door and I wished he didn't. I was happy to drag my feet.

But we'd given them enough time. I knew this because Tack had his back to the door and it looked like he was preparing food. Tabby was close to her dad, hip to the counter, talking to him.

I sucked in breath for courage, opened the door and walked through it.

Tack's torso twisted and his eyes came to me. Tabby's neck twisted and she did the same.

I opened my mouth to speak. I didn't know what I was going to say but I did it anyway.

I didn't get a word out.

Tabby came flying at me and this so surprised me, at first I just stood there. Then I braced because she threw herself at me full body. I went back on a foot, my arms closing around her but her arms were already around me. Tight.

"Honey—"

"I almost got you hurt!" she wailed then shoved her face in my neck and burst out crying.

I looked at Tack. Tack tipped his head to the side.

"Jesus, bitches," Rush muttered as he closed the door and squeezed around us.

I grinned at Tack then dropped my head so my lips were at Tabby's ear.

"I'm fine," I whispered.

"I'm stupid," she sobbed into my neck.

"You aren't. He was cute," I told her, her body went still then her head jerked back and her watery eyes found mine. "He's a complete and total jerk, but he was cute."

"What?" she whispered.

"And too old for you," I went on.

"I—"

"And he let me best him in, like, a second. So he's also a loser."

Tabby blinked.

"And, I'll repeat, he's a complete and total jerk."

Tabby said nothing.

I placed one hand on the injured side of her head and slid my thumb close to her bruise.

Then I started talking and I did it quietly.

"I know we're still getting to know each other. But I also know you're a smart girl. I hate that you learned this lesson at all, much less that you did it at your age. But please, Tab, learn it. You can have family that makes you safe. You can have friends who'll take your back. But the most important person and the one who'll have the best shot at keeping you safe is *you*."

She pulled her lips through her teeth and held my eyes but said nothing.

So I carried on.

"And the best way to do that is be smart."

She let her lips go and whispered, "I was just havin' fun."

"You can have fun *and* be smart," I replied.

She looked over her shoulder quickly then back at me but I thought it was a good sign she didn't let me go.

"Can we not talk about this?" she requested softly.

"Darlin'," Tack cut in, and she looked back over her shoulder at her father as my eyes lifted to him, "if you think what happened last night could happen and you'd get off talkin' about it, you best think again."

"You and me are good," she said to him. "You told me so last night and again not ten minutes ago."

"That don't mean we're not talkin' about it," Tack returned, I felt her pull in a deep breath then she sighed.

I gave her a reassuring squeeze and let her go.

Her eyes came to me, they were timid before she let me go and stepped away.

"Sit your ass on a stool," Tack ordered. "Tyra wants a word."

I watched Tabby's tongue run over her upper lip then she dropped her head and went to a stool.

There it was. She might be messed up but she was a good kid too.

Tack went back to whatever he was doing at the counter. Rush moved to slide my mug of coffee on the counter at the stool next to Tab's then he moved to the opposite counter and leaned his back against it.

I took a stool.

"Okay," Tabby rushed out, trying to head off the attack, "I know he was older but I liked him, like, a lot. And he was nice. And he was into me and not in a gross way. I didn't think he'd ever do anything like that. You have to believe that. I wouldn't have started seein' him if I thought that."

"He get you booze?" Tack asked the counter, which I thought was a good play. An important question with an uncertain response from him at whatever Tabby's response would be but not in your face.

"Yeah," she answered quietly, and I sucked in breath.

"Kids drink, Dad," Rush said carefully, trying to soften the blow for his sister.

God, seriously. I liked that kid.

"Not born yesterday, Rush," Tack muttered, still talking to the counter before he looked over his shoulder and leveled his eyes on his daughter. "He get in your pants?"

"Dad!" Tabby exclaimed.

"Tack," I said softly.

"Jesus," Rush murmured.

"Okay, can we not talk about *this*?" Tabby asked, sounding mortified.

"Asked you a question, darlin'," Tack reminded her.

"God," she muttered, putting an elbow on the counter and her head in her hand. "This is humiliating."

"Tab," Tack prompted.

"Handsome, how about you let me talk to her about that later?" I suggested.

"Nope," Tack replied to me then to Tabby he prompted again, "Tabitha."

Oh boy.

Tabitha.

She knew what that meant because her head came up.

"No!" she declared vehemently. "Why do you think he hit me?"

Oh boy!

Dragons were awaking, two of them, father and son, so I decided to head this off at the pass.

"Right," I stated, and Tabby's eyes came to me. "It happened, it was a drama that included bloodshed and baseball bats, and we're all lucky it's over even though we're not lucky the consequences are bruises, swelling and a hard-earned lesson. But it's over." I lifted my hand, wrapped it around Tabby's neck and leaned into her. "Though, your lessons aren't," I whispered.

Tabby sucked breath in through her nose.

I kept going and did it gentle-like.

"Honey, I know you think I broke your trust last night but I didn't call your dad. One of the boys did. I also know I lost it and could have handled it better so that's my lesson to learn. What you need to learn is, I'm with your dad and it isn't really cool to ask me to keep anything from him. Not anything. But especially not something to do with you. And especially, *especially* not when you're in trouble."

"I know, Tyra," she whispered brokenly, "I heard you guys fightin'. That's on me too."

I shook my head. "You have a lot on your plate, Tabby, don't take that too. Your dad was angry at me for what *I* did, not you. Yeah?"

She took in another breath then she nodded.

I gave her neck a squeeze. "But, the bottom line is, in this room there are a lot of people who love you. And you have to be you, you should have fun, live your life, but you have to learn to do it smart and *not* put yourself in a position where people will worry about you or hurt because you're hurt."

She bit her lip.

I leaned closer. "Honey, you're you and the people in this room love you because of who you are. You aren't who your mom says you are."

She sucked in a sharp breath.

"She has her issues," I went on quickly. "I know at your age it's hard not to take them in. But they're hers. Let her have them. Don't take them on."

"Tyra—"

"That," I cut her off, "now *that* you can talk to me about. I'm here and we can talk about anything you want to talk about. I cannot guarantee I'll keep it from your dad. What I can guarantee is, whatever I do, it'll be in your best interests. It's up to you if you want to trust me again. All I can say is, you can. I'll have your back. It'll just be my decision how I have your back."

Her lips twitched before she replied, "Yeah, you kinda proved that last night."

"Kinda," I agreed, grinning.

Then her pretty face lost all its humor and she whispered, "I can't go back to her."

Tack joined the conversation at this juncture.

"You're not."

I dropped my hand from Tabby's neck and we both looked at Tack.

"But, it's not official, like, court official and if she gets wound up and—" Tabby started.

Tack turned fully to his daughter. "Darlin', you're not goin' back to your mom."

"But it's not official, Dad," she returned.

Oh boy. There it was.

She'd been worried about this just like me.

Tack studied her.

Then he declared, "Right. So I'll make it official."

I blinked.

"You will?" Rush asked.

Tack shrugged and turned back to the bowl he was whipping pancake batter in as he muttered, "Yeah."

"Court official?" Tabby asked, and Tack looked over his shoulder at his daughter.

"Legal, babe, yeah."

Tabby's shoulders slumped with relief.

Yep. She'd been worried about this.

As for me, this was another thing Tack had to worry about which I didn't think was great.

Tack turned away from the bowl, moved to the counter opposite Tabby and me and put his hands on it.

"No more twenty-three-year-olds," he ordered.

"Okay, Dad," Tabby replied quietly.

"Eighteen, no older," Tack declared.

"Okay," she whispered.

"No more booze."

She pulled in breath.

Then she breathed it out on another, "Okay."

"And definitely no more lyin', to me, Tyra, Rush, anyone."

She nodded.

"That last, darlin', take it in," Tack urged. "You earn our trust again and break it, you might find it hard to get back."

Tabby bit her lip while she nodded again.

"You're still grounded," Tack continued. "No car. You go nowhere unless I take you, Tyra takes you or Rush takes you or Tyra and me send you to the grocery store or on errands. You also got chores."

"Right," she muttered.

"But you're still goin' shoppin' today with Tyra."

Tabby perked up.

So did I.

"Right," she said softly.

I grinned at my man.

"After pancakes," he stated.

"Okay," Tabby replied.

Tack held his daughter's eyes.

Then he said gently, "Got all the love in the world for you, darlin', always. No matter what shit you pull. Never forget that."

My lips quivered.

So did Tabby's.

Then she whispered, "Me too, Dad."

Tack kept looking at her. Then his gaze moved to me.

Then he moved back to the bowl.

We ate pancakes. I took Tabby shopping. I got some Brandi clothes. Tabby got some school clothes. We came back and Rush and Tack had fixed Tabby's door. Tabby made dinner that didn't go too well but we all ate it anyway while watching back-to-back episodes of *Dog the Bounty Hunter* that Rush had taped. And, incidentally, it was another new favorite of mine, I decided this halfway through my first episode. This was partly because Duane Lee was badass and hot. This was partly because Leland was also badass and hot. But it was mostly because Dog and Beth were badass, sweet and freaking awesome. We went to bed. Tack woke me up in the middle of the night to make love to me. I made breakfast the next morning. Rush took off to hang with buds while Tabby got down to the chores her father gave her.

And now it was now, all was well and I was on the back of Tack's bike.

All too soon, we swung off Broadway into the forecourt of Ride. When we rounded Ride, I was surprised to see the grill was smoking but the outside of the Compound was deserted.

Tack parked. I hopped off and he swung off behind me.

I got close.

"After you deal with the Russians," I started, "can we take off on your bike?"

"Where?" Tack asked.

"Anywhere just as long as the ride's long and we end it alone together."

I watched his face get soft as his hand came up and cupped my jaw, his thumb sliding along the apple of my cheek.

"That's a plan, Red," he whispered.

"Awesome," I replied.

He dipped his head to touch his mouth to mine, he gave

my lips the tip of his tongue then he lifted his head, dropped his hand from my jaw but grabbed mine. We headed inside and I was touching my own tongue to where Tack had touched his, tasting him when we made it inside and were instantly assaulted by a wave of sound.

And the sound was cheering.

Tack stopped dead and I did with him as I was confronted by every member of Chaos and, if they had an old lady or a woman, those too shouted at us.

"What on—?" I muttered but shut up when Brick stomped to me and ripped me away from Tack by wrapping his beefy arms around me. He lifted me in the air and shook me so hard my head snapped around.

Then he dropped me on my flip-flopped feet with a bone-jarring thud.

"Wasn't sure, Cherry, what with those fancy-ass shoes and skirts 'a yours. But, babe, you kickin' ass for Tabby, that sealed it," he declared.

"Sealed what?" I asked dazedly, staring up at him.

"You're one of us," he answered and at his words, warmth flooded through me.

"Really?" I breathed like that was my dearest wish in the world and, at that precise moment, it was.

"The pepper spray was sissy," Boz stated, joining our group. "But no arguin' with the results."

"Feel good?" Dog asked, and I turned to him to see him grinning at Tack. "Never forget that. Open-hand slappin' him like he was a girl and askin' him if it felt good. Fuck me, that was the fuckin' *shit*."

"I wish I'd have seen it," Sheila, standing close to Dog and smiling at me put in. "Dog won't quit yappin' about it."

Dog scowled down at his woman. "I don't yap."

She gave him a look then looked at me and mouthed, "He yaps."

I stifled a giggle.

"Wouldn't think you had it in you," I heard, and my eyes went to Mitzi who had joined our group with Hop, his arm around her shoulders, and I felt my body still at seeing them. "Glad to know you do," she went on and hard-as-nails, tough-broad Mitzi gave me a genuine smile.

Mitzi smiling at me. Hop was smiling at me too.

Seemed me kicking some squirrel-ball ass was a cause for celebration and Mitzi and Hop were on a good patch.

Their business, not mine.

"Thanks," I whispered.

"Red needs a beer, so do I," Tack announced loudly, claiming my hand thus me again and dragging me into the common area of the Compound.

"Got it," Tug called from behind the bar.

I saw on the bar that someone, most likely one or several of the women, had unearthed bowls and in them they'd dumped chips, dip, potato salad and macaroni salad. There were paper plates, red Solo cups, plastic silverware and even napkins.

Clearly a special occasion seeing as there were bowls.

I grabbed a chip.

Tug offered me a beer.

I ate my chip, grabbed my beer and took a sip.

Tack tugged on my hand, I fell into him and tipped my head back to look at him.

He was smiling.

I smiled back.

Then, still smiling, he kissed me.

When he lifted his head he didn't go far so I heard it when he whispered, "My reward."

My eyes narrowed and I snapped, "You're not allowed to do that shit."

His head jerked slightly and he asked, "Say again?"

"Be sweet and make me all melty and want to jump you when I'm celebrating my heretofore unknown badassness with a bunch of bikers and their bitches. Not to mention, I'm hungry."

Tack grinned as his arm snaked around me and he yanked me close.

"You wanna jump me?" he asked.

"I always want to jump you," I answered.

"Good to know," he muttered.

"But now your badass brethren needs to feed me," I declared.

"I'll see they get down to that."

"Since you're the head honcho, you do that."

Tack's grin became a smile.

I smiled right back.

Then I took a huge gulp of beer, put it down on the bar and grabbed a handful of potato chips.

*   *   *

"Come here," Tack growled.

We were in bed in Tack's room at the Compound. I was between Tack's legs, his cock in my mouth and I'd just slid down.

I slid up, sucking deep as I did. Tack's fingers drove into my hair and fisted. I released him, my eyes going to his, my fingers wrapping around his cock and my tongue swirled the tip.

"Here," Tack mostly repeated, his rough rumble low.

I let him go and kept eye contact as I crawled up his body. I barely got face-to-face with him before his arms closed around me and he rolled me to my back. Once there, he gave me all of his weight as his hands slid over my ass and down the backs of my legs. He swung one of my calves around his ass. The other one he swung around his back.

Then one of his forearms went into the bed and the other one went between us. I felt him guide himself to me then slowly, God, so slowly, he slid inside.

He did all of this with his eyes never leaving mine.

But once I had his cock, my eyes closed and my neck arched.

"Jesus, baby, every time I give you my cock it's like you haven't had it in years."

My arms circled him, my neck righted and my eyes found his.

"I like it."

"No shit?"

"You gonna use it?" I prompted.

He grinned and pulled out an inch, slowly. Then he slid back in to the root, again slowly.

"Honey," I breathed and felt his hand on my belly.

It went up, up, up until it was wrapped around my throat.

"Started here," he whispered.

"What?" I asked.

"In this bed," he went on.

"What?" I repeated.

"You and me."

My arms and legs tightened around him.

His hand slid up to my jaw and his thumb slid over my lips.

"Love you, Red."

Yes.

"Love you too, Kane."

His thumb went away but his head dropped and his lips touched mine.

Against them, I asked, "Now, are you going to fuck me or what?"

I watched his eyes smile. Then his head slanted and his hand moved around to drive into my hair as his mouth took mine, his tongue thrusting inside and his hips jerked back then slammed in.

Finally.

One of my hands moved up into his hair and we kissed deep while we fucked hard and I came the usual twice to Tack's once.

When we were done, Tack kept us connected while his hand moved soothingly along the skin of my side and his mouth moved along the skin of my neck, his goatee tickling my skin. I kept my body curled around him, the fingers of one hand drifting through his too-long hair, the others drifting over his back and ass.

I turned my head so my lips were at his ear and I whispered, "Thank you."

"For what, baby?" he asked against my neck.

"For taking care of this." His head came up and his eyes caught mine. When they did, I admitted quietly, "I'm not sure I've done my part in helping."

"You're still here," he pointed out.

"Yes but every time we hit a rough patch, I give up and declare we're over." I lifted my head and touched my mouth to his before dropping it back to the pillow and promising, "I'll do my best to break that habit."

"Don't matter if you do."

My head tipped on the pillow. "Pardon?"

"Babe, you can declare all you want. That don't mean I'll let you walk out on me."

My lungs quit working.

"Never let you go," Tack went on.

My limbs around him tightened and my hand in his hair clenched.

"Not ever," he finished.

Not ever.

He'd never let me go.

"I love you, honey," I whispered.

"I know, baby," he whispered back.

I looked into his sapphire eyes, smelled his musk, felt the weight of his warm, hard, heavy body and the ghost of his pounding between my legs, his cock still inside me and suddenly, I squirmed.

"Fuck, that greedy pussy," Tack muttered.

"Um...I'm kinda ready to keep playing." I shared something I knew he already knew.

"Babe, I'm still hard and inside you after comin'."

"And?"

He stared at me.

Then he murmured, "Christ. She wears me out."

"Liar," I snapped. "I do not."

And I didn't. He might be forty-one but he had stamina and staying power.

I tried a different tactic, lifted my head and put my mouth to his neck as my hands moved on his back.

I trailed my tongue behind his ear then whispered my suggestion there. "Maybe I'll get some toys so I can take care of business while you're recuperating."

His head jerked back and mine fell to the pillow.

"Fuck that," he stated.

I suppressed a grin.

Tack pulled out and my lips parted at the loss of him.

"Get cleaned up," he ordered.

"For what?" I asked. "I like you inside me."

"Babe, you know I don't go down on you after I've come inside you. Get cleaned up."

Excellent.

I grinned at him.

He scowled at my grin.

Then he muttered, "Wears me out."

He was so full of it.

I took a leg from around him, planted my foot in the bed, rolled him to his back and I did all this while kissing him hard, wet and long.

When I was done, I lifted my head and whispered, "I'll go get cleaned up."

"Hurry, babe," he ordered.

The kiss worked. Then again, I knew it worked because I ended it when his fingers dug in my ass, which I'd learned was a sign Tack liked what he was getting.

Then again, my man always liked what I gave him.

So I gave him another grin.

Then I hurried.

CHAPTER TWENTY-EIGHT

Battle Scars

"Red."

The door to the garage just opened and I hadn't even got my head up to look that direction before I heard Tack's gravelly voice say my name.

"Yeah, handsome?" I asked his head, which was the only thing shoved through the door.

"Come into the garage," he ordered and disappeared.

I got up, smoothed my tight skirt down my thighs and walked on my spike-heeled pumps around my desk to the door to the garage.

I did this happily, deciding not to get uppity about his order. And I did this mostly because we'd had a *great* night the night before and I was still riding that high.

It was Wednesday, two and a half weeks after the drama with Tabby and, fortunately, not much had happened. Or it had, just that all of it was good.

The hog roast had been a blast.

The trip-down-memory-lane, tequila-infused sex-a-thon in Tack's room at the Compound during/after was even better.

And last Saturday, Tack had driven his big Ford Expedition down the mountain to my house, Rush and Tabby trailing in Rush's car. Once there, we'd loaded up a bunch of my stuff so I could move in with them.

Earlier in the week, while eating a dinner Tack wisely cooked (buttering them up, not, in the end, that they needed to be buttered) but before my introduction to the TV show *Justified* (and the dude who played the lead reminded me a lot of Shy, or at least his body did, and, incidentally the show was also good), Tack had shared the news I was moving in. Rush and Tabby, to my relief but not surprise, declared this "the shit." Thus the five-minute family meeting was over and the TV watching commenced.

Tack had ordered the recruits to move my furniture and anything else I didn't take up the mountain to a storage unit. I was going to sift through it. Tack and I would decide what to switch out, what to add and what to get rid of. In the meantime, we were renting out my house and Tack declared we'd put it on the market, "When you're ready, darlin'."

I thought it was cool he didn't rush me into this. Not that I needed an out. Just that things were happening fast. It felt less fast and more in my control knowing my house was still there. I was never going to move back, I loved my house but I loved Tack more and his house in the mountains was awesome. But at least the hold on my past was still in my grip and it was up to me when I was ready to let go.

I talked regularly to Lanie and she reported she and Elliott were doing "just fine." She didn't give a lot of detail on *what* they were doing but I guessed this was a Tack edict and this lack of information would keep me safe. I guessed this, I didn't like this but I also didn't question it. I had niggles of worry about it but my friend sounded happy. On my part, I shared with Lanie that I'd successfully helped her mom with canceling all their wedding plans, which was some serious work but it was also all done.

"And, maybe, soon, we'll be home," Lanie had said the last time I talked to her.

I figured this was an unintentional share of intel on the state of Operation Rivers of Blood but I didn't ask, not her or Tack. I just hoped she was right.

Aunt Bette, on the other hand, hoped I knew what I was doing. This she shared in her last e-mail which was in response to the one where I told her I was moving in with Tack.

Since I suspected Aunt Bette shared, this also got me a phone call from my mother who told me, "We're coming out soon, your dad and I, to meet your new young man."

For a variety of reasons, it was pretty hilarious she referred to Tack as my "young man," but I didn't tell her this. I just told her flat out what she'd find when she and Dad got to Denver.

"He's one of those Harley-Davidson people?" she asked in a horrified voice.

I visualized her clutching her dress, her mind filled with thoughts of Tack wearing leathers and eating with a huge-ass hunting knife at the same time it was panicking about how she'd break the dire news to my dad.

Though, one thing Tack had going for him, he worked with his hands.

"He's that," I confirmed to my mother and kept going. "He's also handsome. He's responsible. He's devoted. He's a good dad. He's unbelievably smart. And he loves me." I paused. "A lot."

"And you?" Mom asked softly.

"He's everything I ever wanted," I answered not softly.

"On a Harley-Davidson?" Mom asked, and I smiled.

"On a Harley," I replied, and it was then my voice got soft. "Give him a chance, Mom. I warn you, he won't care what you think of him. He is who he is and that's it. But he loves me, he takes care of me, he's a good man and I love him. And if you give him a chance and don't give in to preconceived notions, you'll like him too."

Mom hesitated then asked, "He has kids?"

I told her all about Rush and Tabby, which got me talking more about Tack, and when I was done she was silent.

"Mom?" I called.

"You *do* love him," she whispered.

One could say my apple fell far from their tree. Even so, they loved me, I loved them and my mom knew me.

"Yeah," I whispered back.

"We'll come with open minds," she declared.

That would be a first.

I didn't say that.

I said, "Thanks, Mom."

Monday night, I'd gone shopping and had dinner with Elvira and Gwen.

Last night in bed, I'd given Tack what I'd bought. A long dog tag chain with two stamped dog tags at the end. One was stamped with an American flag. The other one was stamped with the words "Ride free." We'd just happened onto it, and it couldn't be denied it was made for my man. So I bought it.

Some of the brothers wore jewelry, some of them lots including rings, necklaces and bracelets. They were all exclusively silver or leather or studs. But Tack didn't wear any at all. He didn't even use one of those wallets with the long chains on them that attached to his belt like the other boys did. So I didn't know how he'd take this.

I still thought it was made for him.

So I gave it to him while we sat in bed. Tack with his back to the headboard, legs stretched out in front of him under the covers that were pulled up to his hips. Me sitting nervously on the other side of the bed from him.

Tack had the chain dangling over his hand, the tags in his palm, he was looking down at it, his thumb moving it around, face expressionless and he asked, "You had these made for me?"

"No, I just happened onto them and thought of you."

"Thought of me," he muttered to his palm.

"You don't have to wear them," I offered, slightly disappointed but not surprised by his reaction. "You can hang them from the rearview mirror of your truck or something."

His eyes lifted to me but they gave nothing away.

What gave it away was when his hands lifted, he opened the chain and dropped it over his head to settle the chain around his neck.

"You don't have to wear them, honey," I repeated softly though I kind of wished he would since they looked freaking great on him.

"We're in bed," was his strange reply.

"Uh...yeah."

"Don't like bringin' her here."

Uh-oh.

I braced and asked, "Who?"

"Naomi."

Oh boy.

"Kane—"

"She never gave me anything."

I blinked.

Then I whispered, "She never gave you anything?"

"Birthdays, yeah. Christmases, yeah. For the fuck of it, 'cause she was out somewhere and thinkin' of me," he held my eyes, his getting heated then he finished with his voice a low rumble, "no."

"Handsome," I breathed.

"You gave me this," he wrapped a fist around the dog tags and gave them a yank, "so I should express my gratitude but I'm in a certain mood which means you're also now gonna give me head."

My nipples started tingling.

"Don't worry, darlin', after, or maybe during, I'll return the favor," he went on, and someplace else started tingling too. When I didn't move he asked, "You gonna sit on your ass starin' at me or wrap your mouth around my cock?"

"Do you like them?" I asked quietly.

"I'm never taking them off," he declared.

Wow.

"Never?" I whispered.

"Not ever," he returned.

God, I loved him.

"Babe, want your mouth," he prompted and I didn't move. "About *now*," he growled.

His intensity wasn't about getting head.

It was about the dog tags.

Yeah, my man liked them.

I grinned. Then I crawled to him and gave him my mouth but I started doing it by kissing his.

Though it ended up somewhere else.

Then that led to something else and that something else was what made Tack able to get away with ordering me around at work.

I went through the door to the garage and searched the huge space with my eyes as I walked down the stairs. I spied Tack standing beside the cherry red car.

My eyes ran over it. It was gleaming. It was old but in a way where it got more badass and awesome as time went by. The color was righteous. The shape sleek and kickass.

Bottom line, it was cool as all hell.

Tack watched me walk to him and after I rounded the hood to get to the side he was on, his arm moved and he underarm threw a set of keys to me. My hand shot up automatically to catch them and I stopped moving.

"Mustang," he stated loudly to be heard over the noise in the garage. "1967 Eleanor Fastback," he continued, like that meant something to me which it didn't until I stood standing beside what I was guessing was one.

"It's cool, Kane," I told him the truth and also did it loudly.

"It's yours, Red."

I blinked, blood seemed to rush quickly through my entire system but mostly through my head and my legs started shaking.

"What?" I breathed.

He read my lips and I knew he did because he responded.

"Your car is solid, decent, you got a lot more miles before it'll start givin' you headaches," he declared. "But it isn't you."

"Me?"

"Wild and sweet, can both snarl like a bitch or purr like a kitten."

My hand flew out, I leaned down and pressed my fingertips into the hood of the kickass Mustang my man just gave to me and I did this to hold myself up.

"You can't give me a car," I informed him.

"No? Weird. Just did."

I stared at him then asked, "Is this because of the dog tags?"

His head jerked to the side. "Babe, seriously?"

Truth be told, that was a stupid question. He'd been working on that car for ages. When he decided to give it to me, I didn't know. I just knew it wasn't this morning.

I looked down at the car.

Seriously, it was *kickass*.

So who cared when he decided to give it to me?

"Just gave you a car, Red, you got nothin' for me?" Tack asked, and my eyes went back to all that was him. Kane "Tack" Allen standing in faded jeans, a tight white tee, tats visible, hair messy, goatee overlong, stubble on his cheeks he didn't bother shaving that morning, lines radiating out the sides of his eyes, eyes that were so blue they could be used on a color wheel.

God, he was beautiful.

Every way he could be.

"Yes," I replied. "I have something for you."

Then I turned and in my tight skirt, on my high-heeled pumps, I walked back to my office. Once there, I dropped the keys to my new car on my desk, closed the blinds and locked the front door. As I was locking the front door, Tack came through the door to the garage. Once he was through, he put his hands to his hips. I moved to him, my eyes never leaving his, his chin dipping down so his wouldn't leave mine. I got close, reached beyond him and locked that too. Then I snapped the blinds on that door closed.

Then I turned and walked to my desk. I stopped there, turned toward him and, lifting my gaze to his, I shimmied my skirt up my hips.

I watched Tack's eyes drop to my hips and flare.

Then I shoved my thumbs into the sides of my panties and shimmied them down until gravity took over and they fell to my ankles.

I had just stepped out of them when my back was to the desk, Tack's hips were between my legs, his torso was pressed to mine and his tongue was in my mouth.

Halfway through, Tack grunted against my lips, "Told you you were wild."

To which I gasped against his, "Shut up, handsome, and fuck me."

"Thought that was what I was doin'," he remarked, and he was not wrong.

My fingers slid up in his hair and I breathed, "Harder."

"Wild," he muttered.

Whatever.

He gave it to me harder that was all I cared about.

I didn't know if the noise in the garage drowned us out.

I did know it got heated and the phone crashed to the floor and broke.

And I also knew I didn't care about either.

*　　*　　*

After Tack fucked me on my desk, I took my new baby out for a test drive.

When I drove back into Ride, I saw Tack walking out of one of the bays.

After I parked and walked to him, I put my hands to his chest, leaned into him and got up on my toes.

In position, I smiled huge and whispered, "You're right, honey, wild and sweet, she purrs like a kitten and snarls like a bitch."

"I take it you like her."

One of my hands slid up into the back of his hair and I didn't answer with words.

But I did use my mouth when I answered.

*　　*　　*

Two hours later, Dog pushed out of the chair opposite my desk and headed to the door, saying, "Catch ya, later."

"Later, Dog," I called.

"Later, brother," Hop, lounging on my couch, said.

Dog walked out.

Dog and Hop had been in my office the last half hour, shooting the shit.

Now only Hop was in my office and I wasn't sure how I felt about this. It had been a while since all that happened went down but I'd never been alone with him so I could deal when I was around him. Now I was alone with him.

"Cherry," he called.

"Unh-hunh?" I asked my computer screen, my back to him.

"Babe, can you look at me?"

This was voiced soft and it was a little surprising. Hop wasn't a soft kind of guy. He could have a laugh, he could tease but there was an edge to him the other guys didn't have. Or, I should say, they all had edges. It was just that Hop's was edgier.

And, on a biker, that was saying something.

Him voicing this request softly was also a little worrying.

Still, I did as he asked and when I swiveled my chair his way, I found he was no longer lounging, back to my couch. He was sitting, elbows to his knees, leaned toward me.

Oh boy.

Hop had black hair and a black mustache that ran along his upper lip, thick down the sides of his mouth and grew thicker and a bit long at the sides of his chin. He worked what would likely look ridiculous on anyone else because he had full lips, a strong jaw, fantastic cheekbones and great gray eyes that had lines radiating out of the sides of them like Tack's.

Oh, and he was a biker and that was the biker mustache to end all biker mustaches.

"What's up?" I asked.

"Shoulda never left you at the mercy of BeeBee."

I knew this was what this was about.

"Hop—"

"My defense, gorgeous, didn't think the bitch was that stupid. Maybe dumb enough to mouth off to one of the other old ladies. Tack's woman? That's a whole new brand of stupid."

I couldn't argue that.

"We don't have to talk about this," I told him.

"I left you out there, pissed Tack off and he got in my face about it."

"I'm sorry about that," I said quickly, he lifted a hand and shook his head.

"I deserved it, Cherry."

"I—"

"I did," he stressed, dropping his hand. "Most 'a the other women could hold their own against that bitch. You, I saw you come out while I was takin' off, knew she was in there, shoulda known better."

I smiled at him. "I think I proved that very night that I can take care of myself."

Hop didn't smile. "Women got different weapons and they're sharper and more lethal."

I couldn't argue that either.

Hop continued, "She's gone, won't happen again but still, what I wanna say is, it won't happen again. Way you are with Tack, way you took care 'a Tabby's business, the brothers got your back."

I felt goose bumps rise on my skin. The good kind.

I'd earned their respect.

I knew this after brats and potato salad.

It was just good to have it confirmed.

"Does Tack talk about me?" I asked.

"No, though he's my brother so even if he did I wouldn't

tell you," Hop answered, taking the sting out of his words by grinning at me.

"Then I'll tell you, I can't do sweet."

"Come again, gorgeous?"

"I can't do sweet," I informed him. "So don't be sweet unless you want me to burst into tears or something."

"Wouldn't want that," he said, still grinning.

"Treat me like the badass I am," I ordered, and his grin became a smile.

"That, I know."

My head tipped to the side at his words. "Pardon?"

"That, I know. Won't say how I know but let's just say I know you're bossy."

I knew how he knew. He was full of shit. Tack talked.

I rolled my eyes.

Then I rolled them back and bossed, "So are you going to treat me like the badass I am?"

"You got it, Cherry," he said through his still-smiling lips, but he barely got it said when his smile cleared, his brows shot together, his head whipped around, his torso jerked up and he leaned into the window to peer out the blinds.

Suddenly he was on his feet, his hand to his back pocket pulling out his phone.

"What—?" I started but he stretched his other hand out to me.

"Stay there."

Oh hell.

Hop strode to the door but it flew open before he could get there and Naomi stormed through.

Oh hell!

"Where is that motherfucker?" she shrieked.

Hop had his phone to his ear and his body between me and Naomi.

"Calm down, woman, and step outside," he growled at Naomi.

"Fuck you!" she screeched.

"Tack," Hop said into his phone. "Please, God, brother, be close. I'm in the office at the garage. Your old bitch is here and your old lady is also here."

Naomi leaned to the side and pointed at me around Hop's long, lean jeans and tee-clad body, shouting, "He gets his ass here, I'll deal with him. *Then* I'll deal with you, you cunt!"

My body jerked back in my chair at that surprising, harsh and totally uncalled for insult but Naomi was gone. This was because Hop had his hand in her chest. He reached around her and opened the door then he shoved her through and closed it.

I stared at the closed door.

"Oh no," I whispered to it as I slowly stood, vaguely hearing Naomi's shrieking outside. *"Hell* no."

I stomped to the door, threw it open, stomped to the top landing and stared down where Hop and Naomi were at the bottom of the steps.

"What did you just call me?" I asked.

"Oh fuck," Hop muttered.

"Cunt!" Naomi screeched, eyes slicing up to me.

The pressure in my head exploded and I stomped down the steps.

"Oh fuck," Hop said, louder this time.

"That's it, bitch, in your fancy-ass skirt with your fancy-ass shoes, you think you can take me?" Naomi asked.

She was rolling from foot to foot, hands up, fingers wiggling at me in a bring-it-on gesture even though Hop still had his hand in her chest and kept pushing off on it, shoving her back step by step as I advanced, my high heels clicking loud.

"You just called me the c-word," I stated.

I heard the quick beat of running motorcycle boots and vaguely sensed mechanics and body shop guys coming out of the garage but I had my target in my sights.

"Yeah, I did. I called you a cunt, you cunt," Naomi leered. "Tryin' to take my kids from me. I got the papers," she snapped.

"I got her, one 'a you get Cherry," Hop ordered, and I felt a strong arm wrap around my chest from behind.

"Stand down, sweetheart," I heard Brick say in my ear.

I stood still in his arm but didn't take my eyes off Naomi. "You have a situation with Tack, you talk to Tack about it. You do not come to my office, shrieking, making a scene and calling me filthy names."

She stopped and was leaning into Hop's hand at her chest. "Oh yeah? I do, what're you gonna do about it?"

What were we? In third grade?

Okay, I'd play.

"You don't want to find out," I warned.

"You can't take me," she declared derisively.

"You're probably right," I agreed. "But I'd sure as hell have fun with the licks I got in."

She lifted her hands. "Yeah? Bring it on . . . *cunt*."

"Stop calling me that!" I snapped.

"Cunt!" she screeched, and that was it.

And what it was it wasn't Arctic Tyra.

No.

Lady Dragon got poked with a stick and she . . . was . . . *pissed*.

Therefore I tore free from Brick's arm and ran the five feet to Naomi. Launching myself by Hop and clearly surprising all holy hell out of Naomi, I took a flying leap and tackled her to the tarmac. We landed with a bone-jarring thud, hers worse because she was under me and the breath went out of her, which was good for me. I was able to semi-straddle her (my skirt impeded a full straddle) and get in a good solid smack right across her face before Hop yanked me off and pulled me, kicking and hissing, away. Lenny, the body shop guy, got in between a scrambling-to-her-feet Naomi and me, as did Brick and Boz.

"You *bitch*!" she shrieked, barreling toward me, but the boys closed ranks and she ran into them.

"I have more where that came from, Naomi!" I shouted my taunt, struggling against Hop's hold.

"Bitch!" I heard.

"Fuckin' stop, both 'a you."

This came from our sides. I stopped struggling against Hop's hold and my head turned to see Dog standing there, his arms crossed on his chest but his eyes were aimed in Naomi's direction.

"Take a second, woman, look around you. What do you see?" He waited a second, apparently letting her do that and apparently she did it because no sound came from her though I couldn't see so I didn't know. Then Dog went on, "You fucked Tack over means you fucked us all over. You do not get to come here and do this shit. Clue the fuck in, Naomi. You're out. This can only go one way and you were around long enough to know which way it's gonna go. Advice. Be smart, settle your ass down and wait to talk to Tack when he gets here. You don't, it's gonna go the way you know it's gonna go."

"This is none of your business," I heard her hiss.

"You're on Chaos, bitch." I heard, and my neck twisted to see Arlo standing a few feet behind Dog. "You know that shit ain't right."

Something must have given because Lenny, Brick and Boz stood down by moving away and I saw Naomi glaring at

Arlo but although it seemed the situation had defused, Arlo wasn't done.

"Tack's call, 'cause you're the mother of his kids, he decides not to ban you, we'll honor that. But you ever come on Chaos again and talk with that mouth to Cherry, you pushed out Rush and Tab or not, you'll never come back. You get me?"

I was feeling love for Arlo and Naomi was saved from having to answer when the roar of Harleys could be heard. Three, to be exact (yes, that was how good I was getting at deciphering the noise of the pipes). And moments later we saw Tack, Hound and High roll in.

I relaxed against Hop but he didn't let me go.

Tack and the boys stopped their bikes about ten feet away from Naomi and got off. Tack's shades hit me and I saw them do a sweep as he walked wide to Naomi's side.

Then he asked what appeared to be no one in particular, "There a reason why my woman's knees are bleedin'?"

My knees were bleeding?

I looked down over Hop's arm, stuck a foot out and put it back.

Yep, my knees were bleeding.

"That'd be because she tackled Naomi," Dog offered then finished, "justified."

"Yeah," Tack replied, his shades moving to Naomi, "heard that shit over the phone."

I watched Naomi's back go straight then I watched her spit at Tack, "Got the papers."

"You don't say?" Tack asked, and I bit back my giggle but Hop didn't. His chuckle wasn't audible but I felt his body move with it.

"I say, asshole!" she snapped.

To this, Tack strangely responded, "Fifty thousand."

Naomi's body went still and, incidentally, so did mine.

"For each," Tack finished.

What?

"A hundred," she shot back, and my body went solid as a rock.

Was she...?

Was *she*...?

Was she selling the custody of her children?

"Fifty, be happy for it. You know I'll win in court," Tack told her.

"I don't know it," she fired back.

"You know it," he stated firmly. "Even if you don't, you and that sorry man 'a yours can't afford to fight it."

"Maybe I feel like puttin' you through the hassle anyway," she suggested nastily.

"Your call," Tack said on a shrug then continued, "but that offer has an expiration. Five seconds."

Her face paled, she looked quickly toward the office then back at Tack. "Can we talk alonc?"

Oh. My. God.

She'd come here for this.

"Four seconds," Tack said.

Her body jerked.

"Seventy-five," she haggled.

Ohmigod!

She'd come here to haggle for her kids!

"Three seconds."

"Sixty!" she snapped.

"Two seconds, Naomi."

"Fuck you, Tack!"

"Right, one second."

"Fine!" she clipped.

Tack crossed his arms on his chest. "Good. That's outta

the way, these are the terms. I have the papers drawn up. They're delivered to you. You got twenty-four hours to sign them. That's delayed even a minute, deal's dead. You think of getting any bright ideas or that moron of a man you got does and you think to reopen negotiations, deal's dead. Tab, Rush, Tyra, me or anyone connected with Chaos sees you or hears from you, deal's dead. Once signed, the kids see you when and if they want to. They don't, they don't see you. You don't call them or me or Tyra or anyone that has anything to do with Chaos or Ride. You do not show your face here, at my house, at Tyra's, at the kids' school, ever. Unless the kids instigate contact, you're gone. Agreed?"

"When do I get the money?" she asked instantly and Tack stared at her, his face twisted in a way I'd never seen.

Revulsion.

"Jesus," he muttered, "I had your gold on my finger for years."

"When do I get my money?" Naomi repeated, her tone sharper.

"Not even Rush?" Tack asked what I thought was strangely before I got it.

She wasn't even going to fight for her son and she supposedly loved him.

That got to her and I could tell because her face was now twisted too. But it was not revulsion. It was hurt and bitterness.

Apparently she needed the money more than her son. Her next words laid testimony to it.

"When do I get my money, asshole?" Naomi shot back.

"When I get the signed papers," Tack finally answered.

"Works for me," she muttered, swung her glare to me then around the group at large before she stomped to her car.

Tack prowled to me.

Oh boy.

Hop let me go, Tack tagged my hand and then I was clicking across the tarmac to the Compound. Once there, Tack pulled me inside and around the bar where he stopped me, tore off his sunglasses, threw them on the bar and put his hands to my waist. Up I went and my ass was on the bar.

"Don't move," he growled and stalked off.

I didn't move.

He came back with a huge-ass first aid kit the size of which I blocked out instantly because of what its existence said about its owners. He set it on the bar beside me, dug through it, found what he was looking for and ripped open the foil pack to an alcohol wipe. I then performed a miracle when, as gentle as he was, I didn't gasp when the sting hit me when he started swiping one of my two scraped and bleeding knees.

Looking, I also had scraped and bleeding elbows.

Damn.

Well, that slap was worth it even if I hoped none of this left scars.

After Tack finished cleaning my first knee, he'd opened another alcohol wipe and started on the other one, I thought it safe to offer quietly, "We'll sell my car and I'll put my house on the market right away. Maybe we'll get a quick sale. And I still have a little money set aside."

He was bent to the side to see what he was doing.

At my words, his body didn't move. Only his eyes shifted to lock on mine.

"Say again?"

"To get the one hundred K for the kids," I explained.

He went back to my knee, stating, "Don't need to do that shit. I got it."

My head jerked. "You have a hundred K?"

He tossed the bloody wipe down on the bar and went back to the kit to get another one, saying, "Yep."

"Really?"

"Elbow up," he ordered, ripping open another wipe then after he started working on my elbow, he answered my question, "Yep. Really."

"So my old man's loaded," I whispered, and his eyes came to me.

"Yep."

I felt my eyes get wide.

"I was joking," I informed him.

"I'm not."

Holy crap!

He tossed the alcohol wipe to the side then placed a hand in the bar on either side of me and leaned in.

"Chaos has a lot of members. All money earned is doled out equal. But, babe, you've accepted payments for our cars and bikes. Those fuckers cost a fuckin' mint. The stores are all *way* in the black. The point of decades of buildin' that shit was so my brothers wouldn't take a hit when we pulled outta the other shit. They did but that don't mean that hit was big. We all live easy."

If he had a hundred grand to toss around, he must live easy.

"I think I need a raise," I declared.

He blinked.

Then he smiled slowly and I enjoyed the show.

After it was done, he said quietly, "But thanks for the offer, darlin'."

"You're welcome, Kane."

His brows went up. "You really tackle that bitch?"

"I have the battle scars to prove it," I said by way of answer.

"Babe," he muttered.

"She called me the c-word," I offered in my defense.

That got me another smile.

It faded and he whispered, "She signs those papers, we're done with her."

Better news, Tabby was.

"Yeah," I whispered back, lifting my hands to curl them around his neck.

"All is in motion with the Russians. That plan goes down good, we're breathin' easy."

He said no more. I correctly took it that was all he was going to say and even if that niggle came back, I didn't push it. I just nodded.

But I asked, "You okay? About Naomi, I mean."

"Gives me the shudders, thinkin' a woman who'd essentially sell her kids was in my bed and worse, as long as she was. But if this means the back of her, yeah. I'm okay."

"Good," I replied on a squeeze of my fingers.

"You need antibiotic ointment on your elbows and knees."

"That might stain my blouse and skirt."

"Babe, I'm loaded. Dry clean."

"Right," I whispered.

"Though, bad news for you, your skirt and blouse are already stained with blood."

Such was the life of an old lady.

"Well, whatever, it was worth it."

Tack gave me another smile but through it ordered, "Kiss me then I'll sort you out."

I held his eyes looking deep to be sure he was okay. When I was sure, I did as he asked.

Then my old man sorted me out so I was okay.

CHAPTER TWENTY-NINE

Mr. Allen Needs a Lesson

"Shame," Grigori Lescheva muttered, lounging in a chair opposite where I was tied to mine, duct tape over my mouth, his eyes on me. "You're very attractive."

I was breathing heavily through my nose. I had no idea how easy it was to breathe, having two choices to use to take in air. Now, only having one, it wasn't so easy.

Not to mention, I was terrified out of my mind. It was hard to breathe when you were scared shitless.

"Such extraordinary hair," he continued. "And so much of it."

I didn't say anything because I couldn't. Even if I could, I wouldn't.

"Auburn," he whispered.

God, he was *creeping me out*.

"We could work something out, you and I," he went on as I sucked in breath through my nose and my pulse spiked. "However, I think Mr. Allen needs a lesson."

Oh *God*.

He tipped his eyes to the side then he tipped his chin up.

The man came toward me. My eyes darted his way and stayed glued to him as I panted through my nose, struggled against my bonds, but it was no use.

He didn't hesitate before he sank the blade in my flesh.

CHAPTER THIRTY

Targets

Seven and a half hours earlier in a house in the foothills outside Morrison, Colorado…

"STOP SCRATCHIN'."

"I can't, it itches."

"It itches because it's healin'."

"I know that, Kane."

I found myself plucked out of bed then I found my scabby knees difficult to get to since they were planted in the bed on either side of Tack, seeing as I was straddling him.

"You'll scar, you keep scratchin'," he informed me, fingers tight to my hips, head on the pillow, eyes aimed up to mine.

"It's not a big deal," I returned. "They're almost gone."

And they were. It'd been four days since I tackled Naomi and the scrapes weren't that bad in the first place.

"Leave 'em be," Tack ordered on a finger squeeze.

My eyes drifted to the headboard and I muttered, "Oh, all right."

My eyes rolled back when Tack ordered, "Grab the envelope on the nightstand."

I looked to the nightstand to see an envelope there. I

leaned into him, reaching out a hand and I nabbed it. I sat back as best I could because when I leaned, Tack's hands slid up my sides and he was holding me closer.

"Open it," he kept bossing. "Tell me what you think. You like it, I'll get it started."

My head tipped to the side with curiosity but I opened the envelope, pulled out a piece of paper that at first glance looked like it had kickass doodles on it then my body went still when those doodles penetrated my brain.

"You see you?" Tack asked and I stared at the doodles harder.

Curlicues and spikes, lots of them, familiar.

I looked harder.

There it was.

My name hidden in the design. Tyra.

I held in my hand what would be me, inked permanently into Tack.

My breath left me and my eyes lifted to his.

"Had my guy draw it out," Tack informed me then asked, "You like it?"

I didn't have it in me even to be a little bit of a smartass.

I just answered, "Yes."

"Right. I'll give him a call. Get it set up."

I clutched the sketch to my chest and fell forward, back curved, doing a face plant right under his throat.

One of his hands drifted up my spine and into my hair as he muttered, "Darlin'."

I deep breathed.

"She really likes it," he murmured.

"Yes," I whispered.

"Babe, you gotta get used to my sweet," he declared.

"Never," I kept whispering, "because you just keep getting sweeter."

His other arm curved around me and held tight.

I let him hold me for a while, taking him in with as many senses as I could before one of my hands drifted out and my fingers skimmed the tattoo on his left shoulder.

"You never told me about this," I said softly.

"Balance," he stated immediately, and I lifted my head to look at him.

"Balance?"

He nodded, his hand in my hair drifting to the side of my neck, taking my hair with it and his thumb moved out to stroke my jaw.

"Balance, baby," he said softly. "Wind. Fire. Live free. Be wild. Raise hell. But stay safe. You don't, the reaper'll get you, one way or another." He paused then finished, "That tat's a reminder. Balance. Raise hell but stay safe."

I nodded.

Then I lifted up a bit and put my sketch on the nightstand before turning back to Tack and sharing, "Honey, you know I'm going out with Elvira today. You don't have a lot of time. You need to get down to business."

Tack grinned. Then both his arms closed around me, he rolled me to my back, his mouth taking mine and he got down to business.

*   *   *

Gwen

Two hours later, Hawk and Gwen Delgado's farmhouse, South Denver...

Standing at the sink in my countrified yet whimsical kitchen, I jumped as arms closed around me from behind and I felt lips on the skin behind my ear.

"You need to quit doing that," I stated, even though I hoped he wouldn't, not ever.

I lost those lips, kind of. They moved to my ear.

"Doing what?"

I turned in Hawk's arms and looked up at him. "Dematerializing and rematerializing without making a sound. I know you're a superhero out there, honey, but in this house you're just Cabe."

"Babe, I walked through the door."

"Right," I muttered and he grinned, giving me the dimples.

Jeez. I freaking *loved* those dimples.

My thoughts left his dimples when he asked, "Wanna tell me what those four suitcases are in your office?"

"We're going on vacation," I told him something he already knew since he bought the first-class tickets. Or Elvira did, but he told her to do it.

"Uh, yeah," he replied. "To a beach for two weeks. Two weeks on a beach does not equal four suitcases."

"Yes it does," I contradicted.

"Sweet Pea, you need bikinis and..." he paused then went on, "bikinis. That's it. Bikinis don't take up four suitcases."

"You're right, Hawk, I need bikinis and I have bikinis. Five of them. And each of them has its own matching pair of flip-flops and sarong and/or cover up as the case may be. And then we *will* eat, and not just room service. And who knows where we'll go? Casual. Fancy. Island chic. Plus—"

"Stop right there," he cut me off. "I've lost interest in this conversation."

"Fine. I'll stop. Now, are you going to quit giving me lip about suitcases?"

"Absolutely, if you promise you'll never say the words 'island chic' to me again."

I also loved it when he was funny in his commando way.

"Cross my heart," I replied, sliding my arms around him.

"Excellent," he muttered, dropped his head and touched his mouth to mine.

I further loved it when he touched his mouth to mine.

He was lifting his head when his phone rang. He let me go with one arm to pull out his phone. He looked at the display, took the call and put it to his ear.

"Talk to me," he commanded.

Bossy and hot but more the latter than the former.

Something I also loved.

All thoughts of Hawk's hotness flew from my brain when I felt his body go still and watched his face wipe clean.

"When?" he barked into the phone and my body went more still than his. "Chaos aware of this?" he asked sharply and my arms tightened around him. "Find out. And dig local. They moved in Kansas City, means they could be plannin' a move in Denver." He was silent a moment then, "Frequent updates, Jorge, yeah?"

Then he disconnected.

"What?" I whispered and his eyes came to me.

"I gotta get to the office, babe."

My arms held tight and I repeated, "What?"

"Gwen," one of his hands slid up my back into my hair, "baby, I need to get into the office."

"Is Tack all right?" I pushed.

Hawk studied me briefly then did what he had to do because he knew I wouldn't give up and if he made me the consequences would not be pretty.

"Tack and his boys offered protection to a local guy who got his shit mixed with some local *bad* guys. Made a deal with an MC in Kansas City to get this guy and his woman out of harm's way while Chaos dealt with the local problem."

"Tyra's friend?" I guessed.

Hawk's mouth got tight.

"Tyra's friend," I whispered then louder, "And?"

"The bad guys found them. Early this morning, Elliott Belova got dead and his woman is in surgery, not lookin' good."

My body locked.

Oh my God.

Oh my God!

"Hawk," I breathed.

"Keep that shit to yourself for now, Sweet Pea. Serious. Do not call Tyra. Let me find out what the fuck's goin' on."

I nodded.

"Now I gotta go."

I kept nodding.

"Kiss me, babe."

I rolled up on my toes and kissed him.

Hawk kissed me back, hard but brief.

When he lifted his head, he whispered, "Love you, babe."

"Love you too, Hawk," I whispered back.

Then he let me go and *poof!* Vanished.

I stood frozen at the sink.

Then I whispered, "Oh my God," my breath hitched as a very bad feeling stole through me, "Tack."

*   *   *

Tess

Fifteen minutes later, Brock and Tessa Lucas's house,
Washington Park, Denver...

"Martha," I said into my cell phone, standing in my kitchen, "I advise against a sit-down dinner."

"Why?" she asked.

"Because you have five hundred guests coming to your wedding. First, that's going to cost a fortune. Second, it'll cost a fortune."

As Martha replied, "Tess, I've waited over four decades for this shindig. And I want it to be the...frigging...*best*... of *everything*," I watched as Joel wandered in and stole a cupcake from the array of them on the island.

"Hang on a second," I said to Martha then I said to Joel, "Honey, those are for the party."

"There're, like, a hundred of them," Joel replied, eyeing the island covered in cupcakes.

This was true with a slight exaggeration and only half of them were for the party since, when I made them, I doubled the number because I knew this exact thing would happen.

"Right, then, it's still morning," I told him.

"Barely," he replied.

He had me there so I didn't respond and Joel knew what this meant. I wasn't going to make a big deal of it because, really, there was nothing to make a big deal of.

And anyway, my boys had my baked goods for breakfast on a regular basis.

He grinned, ripped the paper off and shoved half the cupcake with its mountainous swirl of frosting in his mouth as he wandered out.

"Hello? I'm still on the phone," I heard Martha call, and I went back to her at the same time I saw Rex wander in and grab his own cupcake.

I let Rex's pilfering go without a word. Martha and a sit-down dinner at her wedding to DEA Agent Calhoun took precedence. I had a slim chance I could talk Martha out of a sit-down dinner. I had no chance I'd talk my boys out of eating my cupcakes.

Martha was wavering when Brock walked in, leaned a faded jeans-clad hip against the counter and grabbed his own cupcake.

I watched him eating it and I felt his silver eyes on me but I didn't lift my eyes to his because I was fascinated by the movements of his mouth. Therefore, during the show I lost all focus on Martha.

"Hello? Tess? It's only my wedding we're talking about," she said in my ear. "Nothing important, like, your guys eating your cupcakes which they do every...freaking...*day*."

"Sorry," I said into the phone as I watched Brock grin, swallow his last bite and toss the used cupcake paper on the counter, which made me roll my eyes. But I wouldn't make a big deal out of that either. All my boys did this all the time too. I found them everywhere, the living room, TV room, bedrooms, even the bathroom. Living with three men, I picked my battles.

After he tossed his cupcake paper, I watched him head to the fridge where I knew he'd drink milk straight out of the carton. Luckily, he had his very own carton so when I needed a splash for my coffee, I didn't have cupcake back-wash in it.

"Okay, a buffet," Martha said in my ear, and I heard the fridge open at the same time I heard Brock's cell ring.

"I think that's a good call, honey," I replied as I heard Brock answer his phone. "But with that amount of guests, we'll need to make certain there are two, with two sides for the lines to go down or it'll take a year for everyone to walk through the buffet."

"Agreed but we'll still need to do the taste testing," she told me.

"Absolutely," I replied, my lips curving.

Something to look forward to.

The fridge closed.

"I'll schedule it. Let you know at the shop when we're doing it," she told me.

"Great."

"Fuck, you shittin' me?"

That was Brock and it was said in a tone that made my head whip toward him.

And he had a look on his face that made mine go pale. So pale, I felt it.

"Martha, I have to go," I whispered into my phone as Brock's eyes lifted from the floor and locked to mine.

I did not like what I saw.

Oh God.

"What?" Martha asked.

"I have to go, honey, now. I'll call you later."

"Is everything—?" Martha started but I cut her off by disconnecting.

Then I stared at Brock as he talked into his phone.

"Has the call gone to Lawson?" Brock asked, his eyes not leaving mine. "Kane Allen and the boys?" he went on. "What about Allen's woman, Tyra?"

My body locked.

"Fuck, I'll call Lawson and I'm comin' in," Brock kept talking. "Right, be there in ten."

He disconnected.

"What?" I asked.

"Gotta go to the station."

"Is everything with Tyra okay?"

Brock held my eyes.

Then no games, no bullshit, straight out, he said softly, "No. Shit's goin' down, baby, it's not good and she may be a target from two angles."

"Those would be?"

"Connection to Chaos, who the Russian mob thinks fucked them over, connection to some guy who just plain fucked over the Russian mob."

I closed my eyes but opened them when I felt his hand wrap around the back of my neck and his mouth touch mine.

He tasted of frosting.

This normally would make me feel better.

Right then it didn't make me feel better.

His head lifted. "Gotta go."

I nodded.

"Love you, darlin'," he whispered.

"I love you too, Brock," I whispered back.

Brock went.

I lifted my phone and called Tyra.

There was no answer.

I disconnected and called her again.

*   *   *

Mara

At the same time, Mitch Lawson and Mara Hanover's house, East Denver...

"Do I have to go?"

This was Bud, sitting on a stool outside the bar that

fenced one side of the kitchen that was smack in the middle of our house and opened off into a huge, cathedral-ceiling living room.

"Yes," I replied.

"But I don't wanna shop for school clothes," he told me, and I felt the side of Mitch's front move in close to the side of the back of mine. So close, we brushed.

This, he did a lot.

This, I liked a lot.

"Don't blame you," Mitch muttered, and my eyes jerked to him then narrowed.

Mitch grinned at me.

I glared.

"Seriously, sweetheart, you know his sizes. Can't you and Billie just pick up some shit for him?" he asked.

"I can pick out clothes for Bud," Billie, sitting beside Bud at the bar chimed in then finished, "Easy."

"See, Billie can pick them out for me," Bud unsurprisingly instantly agreed with Billie's plan.

"Are you sure you want that?" I asked Bud and he shrugged.

I was visualizing Bud in t-shirts with butterflies on them when I heard Mitch mutter, "Decided," and my eyes went back to him.

"It's a family outing," I announced and watched Mitch's head jerk.

Then he declared, "I'm not going."

"You are."

"I am not."

"If Mitch isn't going, I'm not going either," Bud stated.

"I'm going!" Billie cried excitedly.

That was my girl, *all* girl, therefore always up for shopping.

"Bud and I'll go out, hit a few balls," Mitch said, "That cool with you, Bud?"

Like Bud would say no.

"Totally!" Bud cried.

See?

It was then I knew I'd lost both of them from the family outing I had planned but I hadn't exactly communicated mostly because I knew this would be the outcome.

Mitch and Bud taking off with their baseball equipment wasn't unusual. They went out nearly daily to hit a few balls and catch a few balls either at a park or a vacant diamond, and Mitch also took him to batting cages. Bud had played Little League that year and you would never have guessed a little over a year ago he'd never thrown a ball in his life. Mitch said he was a natural. It seemed Mitch was right. Bud was the best kid on his team.

Then again, it helped that those two were always carting their mitts and bat bags around everywhere they went. Heck, just the other day when we'd swung into King Soopers to grab some things we needed, Billie and I went in and came out to Mitch and Bud playing catch in the parking lot.

"We were going to have a nice lunch," I dangled my carrot.

"Good, have one with Billie," Mitch replied, not seeing my carrot as tasty. "Bud and I'll grab some hot dogs," and he said this last as his cell on the counter rang.

I looked at Bud. "What if you don't like the clothes we get?"

"Auntie Mara, they're *clothes*. What do I care?"

That was my boy, *all* boy, therefore he didn't care what clothes he wore.

Though he'd probably care if butterflies were on them.

Before I could threaten him with this eventuality, Mitch spoke.

"What?" he said in a low tone that made the hairs on my neck stand up, and I wasn't the only one who felt it. The kids did too for all our eyes went to Mitch. "Right. I'll be there as soon as I can. Leaving now."

Oh no.

Mitch disconnected and looked at me. I didn't like what I saw but I didn't have a chance to fully process it before he looked to Bud.

"Sorry, buddy, gotta take a rain check. Work. Soon's I can, I'll make it up to you."

"Okay, Mitch," Bud agreed, his voice soft.

"You okay, Mitch?" Billie asked, her eyes still on Mitch's face.

"I will be, gorgeous, once I get this work done. Won't take long," he answered Billie and looked at me. "Walk me to the door, baby."

My eyes slid through the kids while my lips smiled a fake smile I knew they wouldn't buy and I followed Mitch to the door.

He walked out of it, I followed him out and he closed the door.

Then he turned to me, lifted both hands and put them to the sides of my neck, leaning in so our faces were close.

"Your new girl Tyra?"

Oh no!

"Yes?" I whispered.

"She might be in some trouble."

Oh no. On no. Oh no!

"Mitch," I breathed.

"Don't go shoppin'. Put Billie off for a bit. Stay at the house."

"Why?"

"I just wanna know where you are all day, okay?"

I nodded. I could do that for him.

"I gotta go."

I nodded again.

"Love you, sweetheart."

"I love you too, honey."

He bent his head further, touching his mouth to mine.

Then he jogged to his SUV in our drive.

Jogged.

That was not good.

I watched him swing in. Then I sucked in breath and went inside to break the news to Billie we weren't going shopping.

And after that, call the girls.

Elvira

At the same time, outside seating, Starbuck's in Cherry Creek North, Denver...

The bitch was late.

This did not make Elvira happy.

Tapping an impatient toe, she sucked back a sip of latte, put it down, lifted her phone and jabbed at it with her finger before putting it to her ear.

The call rang through to Tyra's phone.

No answer.

When she got voicemail, Elvira disconnected without leaving a message and her hand was falling when her phone rang in it.

The display said "Hawk Calling."

Elvira took the call and put the phone to her ear.

"Which part of the words 'day off' do you not understand?" she asked in greeting.

"Tyra with you?" Hawk asked back.

"No. The girl is late."

"Russians are on the move. Tack and Tyra are both targets. Get your ass to the office now and call Lee Nightingale on your way."

Disconnect.

Elvira shot out of her chair and raced on her high heels to her burgundy Eclipse.

In most instances, except this one, it was a sacrilege, but she left her latte on the table not even half drunk.

CHAPTER THIRTY-ONE

Rivers of Blood

Tack

Two minutes before Hawk's call to Elvira, Kane Allen and Tyra Masters's house...

TACK'S CELL RANG as he was walking down the hall toward the sound of the TV in the living room where his kids were. He dug it out, looked at the display and put it to his ear.

"Yo," he answered.

"You good?" Cabe "Hawk" Delgado asked in a voice that made Tack stop dead outside his kitchen.

"Yeah. Why you askin'?"

"Tyra with you?"

Ice immediately suffused his veins.

"No, she left half an hour ago to drive down the mountain to go shoppin' with Elvira."

"I'll call Elvira, you call Tyra. Get her ass back there or to Chaos. Guard."

Shit. Fucking *shit*.

"Hawk, tell me what the fuck and do it now," Tack growled.

"Elliott Belova was whacked early this morning. Elaine Heron is in critical condition, ICU in a hospital in Kansas City. The Russians are making moves."

That ice started biting and Tack's legs started moving back where he came. "Jesus fuckin' Christ. Call your girl, I'll call my woman."

He disconnected then found Tyra and hit go.

He was at his safe in his closet, opening it with his fingers at the same time getting voicemail in his ear.

The freeze crusted over his skin.

He stopped what he was doing and hit go on Tyra again.

He had the safe open when he got voicemail again.

"Jesus fuckin' Christ," he bit off, grabbed a gun and shoved it in his belt before grabbing another one. He closed the safe and, one handed, he called Dog.

"Yo," Dog answered.

"Russians got to Belova and Lanie. Belova's dead. Lanie's critical. You hear any 'a that shit?"

"Fuck no, Jesus, brother—"

"Tyra left half an hour ago. She's not pickin' up her phone."

"I'm on my bike."

"Everyone is. Make the rounds, brother."

"Done. Later."

Disconnect.

Fuck. How in *the fuck* did shit this big happen under radar?

Tack prowled down the hall seeing both his kids standing at the end of it, faces pale, eyes on him, feeling the vibe. He stopped outside the kitchen again, held their eyes, put the extra gun on the bar and made his call to Hawk.

"Talk to me," Hawk answered.

"No Tyra."

Tack watched his daughter's lips tremble.

That was when the burn hit his chest and the ice started cracking.

"She's not with Elvira," Hawk informed him.

"Fuck!" Tack snarled so viciously both his kids jumped.

"She's mobilizing Nightingale."

"I'm down the mountain."

"Meet you at the Compound."

"Right."

He disconnected and looked to his kids.

"Rush, gun. You know how to use it, but don't touch it unless you think you need it. You and Tab lock up after me, lock up tight. Everything. Doors, windows. You keep your phones on you. You do not make any calls. You do not leave. I'll have a brother up here as soon as I can."

"What's happening?" Rush asked quietly.

"I don't know. I gotta go down the mountain to find out," Tack answered.

"Is Tyra okay?" Tabby asked, her voice shaking.

"She will be," Tack answered.

That said nothing but said it all. He knew it when Tabby blanched and Rush flinched.

And he hated it.

Tack walked to his kids, grabbing Tabby behind her head first. He pulled her in and kissed the top. He repeated this with his son.

Then he walked through them to the door.

He turned at it and announced, "I'll bring her home."

Rush had his arm around Tab and he'd pulled her close.

He nodded.

His son was a good kid.

Tabby whimpered.

His daughter felt deep.

"Love you both," he told them, his voice rougher than normal.

"Love you too, Dad," Tabby whispered.

"Love you, Dad." Rush's voice was gruff.

Tack took off.

*   *   *

Forty-five minutes later, Chaos Compound, Denver…

Tack stood by the bar in the Compound, watched Hound hit a button on the phone and his brother's eyes come to him.

"Pope in Boulder and his boys are on their bikes."

Tack nodded.

That was the last one. He'd called in all his markers. Every single one.

The door opened and Tack's eyes cut to it to see Brock "Slim" Lucas and Mitch Lawson coming through the door.

He felt Hound get close to his back but he didn't move and he didn't much like the looks both men were wearing.

"My guess, you know shit's gone down," Tack stated as they stopped in front of him.

He got chin lifts then Lucas's gaze shot to Hound and back to Tack. "Your boys out?"

Tack nodded.

"Just you two?" Lucas pushed.

"Reason why you wanna know who's here?" Tack pushed back.

Lawson said quietly, "We've got news."

"Spill," Tack ordered, and Lawson looked to Hound. "Now, Lawson," he growled.

Tack watched both Lawson's and Lucas's bodies go alert as if waiting for or preparing to attack.

"A red 1967 Mustang with tags registered to Ride Custom Cars and Bikes was found abandoned on the side of 6th Avenue. Tyra drive that ride?" Lawson asked.

Tack closed his eyes and looked to his boots, that burn in his chest searing deep. He knew then why they wanted to know how many brothers were there. If they felt they had to lock him down, they wanted to know what kind of fight they had on their hands.

"That's Cherry's ride," Hound confirmed.

"Cherry?" Tack heard Lucas ask, and he opened his eyes and looked up.

"Tyra," Hound grunted, his hand landing on Tack's shoulder.

"That all you got?" Tack asked, and two sets of surprised eyes hit him. They thought he'd lose his shit.

And he would, she didn't come out of this breathing.

Now, him losing his shit would in no way help his woman.

"That's all we got," Lucas stated.

"No blood?" Tack asked.

"No blood," Lawson affirmed.

This was not good news, it was not bad. Lescheva wasn't messy when he did his wet work, and it depended on his mood when he'd stop playing and get down to business.

"Are you confirming Tyra Masters is missing?" Lucas asked, and Tack felt Hound's hand leave his shoulder.

"If she's good when we find her, DPD could fuck this," Hound growled from behind Tack, knowing Lucas's question meant he wanted authorization to get the Denver Police Department involved in an official capacity.

"DPD won't fuck this," Lawson returned.

"DPD don't know what they're dealin' with," Hound shot back.

"DPD knows what they're dealing with and they know there's a possible hostage involved and *they* have experience extricating hostages while they're still breathing so DPD won't fuck this," Lawson retorted then his eyes went to Tack. "And I know you know, man, and I sure as fuck haven't forgot. I owe you. DPD won't fuck this because I won't *let* them fuck this."

"We'll discuss who owes who after she's home safe," Tack replied, then he looked to Lucas. "Make your call."

Lucas stepped off to the side, pulling out his phone.

"Tack, brother," Hound clipped, and Tack turned to him. "We do not need cops involved in this."

"The Russians got my woman. She needs every man on the hunt she can get."

"Tack, this could get messy." Hound reminded him of something he already knew.

"Objective, she ends this day home and breathing."

"Tack—"

"Done talkin'," Tack ground out as the front door opened.

All eyes went there to see Hawk Delgado and Lee Nightingale, another local badass, a private investigator, walking in. Hawk was carrying a manila folder.

Both men's eyes scanned the space then came back to Tack.

But it was Hawk who spoke.

"Boys out?"

"What do you think?" Tack asked back, not about to have this conversation again, then he dipped his head to the folder. "What's that?"

"You need to look at some pictures," Hawk told him, stopping and tossing the file on the bar.

"Got other things to do, Hawk," Tack said low. Hawk's head turned to Tack and they locked eyes.

"In about thirty seconds, I'm gonna tell you somethin' that is gonna seriously piss you off. But you got other things on your mind so I know you'll get over it. We'll deal with your beef later."

Fuck.

"Give it to me," Tack growled.

Hawk didn't delay.

"Ride has been under my surveillance for three years," he announced, and Tack felt Hound's fury explode behind him but he lifted a hand and kept his eyes locked with Hawk's.

"The Russians, Arlo and High," Tack guessed accurately, dropping his hand.

Hawk nodded. "We've been workin' with the Feds."

"What else?"

Hawk tore his gaze from Tack's, looked down at the folder and threw it open. He shifted an eight-by-ten black-and-white to facing them and pointed to it. It was a still shot taken in the interior of Ride's auto supply store of a man alone in an aisle.

Hawk twisted his neck and his eyes went back to Tack. "You know that man?"

Tack stared at the photo and the burn in his chest singed even deeper.

"Fuck me, that's Naomi's man, Pipe," Hound muttered then louder, "What the fuck's that fucker got to do with this?"

"Your ex's man," Hawk said, ignoring Hound and straightening away from the photo.

"Yeah," Tack forced out on a grunt. "You wanna tell me why you're takin' photos of that asshole shoppin'?"

"This guy is a fuckup," Hawk stated.

"Got a woman with the Russians," Tack warned. "Don't waste my time tellin' me shit I know."

"No, Tack," Lee Nightingale entered the conversation, "This guy is a *fuckup*. He's in deep with about every player in town."

"In deep how?" Tack bit out.

"Drugs."

Jesus. Fuck. Shit. God fucking damn it.

That motherfucker was using with his kids around. And his ex-bitch knew, let him, hid it and played Tack.

Jesus. Fuck. Shit. *God fucking damn it!*

That was why he threatened to sell Tab's car, punishing her for no reason, and why Naomi was so quick to sell their kids.

His eyes burned into Hawk. "You think to tell me some strung-out asshole with a slew of debt was in a house with my kids?"

"I did, it would compromise the investigation," Hawk returned then said quietly, "Tack, we'll deal with your beef later."

It took effort but Tack locked down the burn and prompted, "And you're sharin' this with me now because . . . ?"

"Because one of the players he's in deep with most is the Russians," Nightingale replied. "Desperate, he wiggled in, started to do favors. Got tight. Or as tight as the Russians would get with an outsider. He spends a lot of time in your shop, Tack. He spends a lot of time in his car outside your shop, eyes on Ride. He takes a lot of notes on the comings and goings of Chaos. He lives with your ex who knows you well. And he spends a lot of time behind closed doors with the Russians."

Tack immediately turned to Hound. "Call a brother to take your back. On your bike. Pick him up. You know where to take him." Hound moved and Tack called to his back, "Get that bitch too."

Hound turned. "Naomi?"

Tack didn't trust himself to speak. He just jerked up his chin. Hound took off.

Tack looked to Lawson and Lucas, the last had made his phone call and rejoined the huddle. "In about two seconds, you are not here and you keep DPD away from all known Chaos locations."

"Tack—" Lawson started.

Tack cut him off. "He's gonna talk. He's gonna do it fast. And if he's gonna do it fast, he ain't gonna be doin' it in an interrogation room."

A muscle jerked in Lawson's cheek. He was struggling; he felt he owed a marker but he was shackled by the man he was.

"Chestnut," Tack whispered, referring to Lawson's woman. "Your kids. Keep clean."

"You go gonzo, Slim and me might not be able to cover your shit," Lawson returned.

"Let me worry about that. You keep clean."

Lawson held his gaze. Then he jerked up his chin. And, with looks through Tack, Delgado and Nightingale, Lucas and Lawson walked out.

"It'd help, my boys could coordinate search efforts with yours," Nightingale stated, and Tack looked at him.

"You got a line to Dog?"

"Yep."

"Have your boy call him."

Nightingale nodded, pulled out his phone and stepped away.

"Kane," Hawk said low, and a knife pierced Tack's gut at his tone and the name Hawk used before he looked at him. "Lescheva fucked up with Winchell, Pierson and the mattresses. They lost two million in product in that mattress warehouse. Shit happens, like you lose safe transport and warehousing, you deal and you don't lose two million when you do. The higher-ups do not blame you. They blame Lescheva. Then he fucked up again when he kidnapped the wards of a police officer, took a meeting with every badass in Denver and pissed every one of us off, buying himself unwanted attention. Then he fucked up again with Belova goin' rogue and disappearing. All that guy knows? You did the best you could but he was dead even before your boys took him and his woman over the Denver city limits. His higher-ups have been all over his shit. Nightingale and his boys have been all over his shit. The Feds are all over his shit. And Chaos has been all over his shit."

"You are again not tellin' me somethin' I don't know," Tack pointed out.

"Prepare, man," Hawk replied quietly.

He knew that too.

He knew. Tack knew.

Lescheva was stone cold. But even the coldest motherfucker burned bright before he flamed out.

Lescheva's days were numbered. Tack had been working for a whole fucking year with the man's higher-ups to see that come about at the same time extricate Chaos from that bullshit forever.

And Lescheva knew it.

But that didn't mean he didn't intend to take down everyone around him when he flamed out.

And Tyra was around him.

"Got shit to do," Tack muttered.

"My boys and I are all over this."

Tack caught his eyes. "Owe you."

"No marker."

"Don't play it that way, Hawk."

"You had my woman's back and in doin' it, mine. I got yours. We're even."

He could live with that.

Tack jerked up his chin.

Then he stalked out of the Compound to his bike.

*   *   *

Two hours later, Chaos cabin outside Golden, Colorado…

Wearing brass knuckles, Hop clocked Gerald "Pipe" Dahl in the jaw with a closed fist, and the fat man as well as the chair he was tied to went down.

Naomi, tied across the room in her own chair, shrieked, *"Stop!"*

Pipe spit out a mess of blood and a tooth, grunting, "I'm tellin' you! I don't know *shit!*"

Tack, standing three feet away, arms crossed on his chest, ordered in a voice cold as ice, "Get him up."

Boz and High moved forward, grabbed the chair and hauled it up, Boz bitching, "Jesus, man, how'd you get so fat bein' a cokehead? You're breathin' after we're done with you, lay off the Doritos."

They got him up, Boz and High stepped back, Hop looked to Tack but Tack shook his head once.

Then he looked at Pipe and demanded, "Talk to me."

Battered, bloody, his head hanging down because he didn't have the strength to pull it up, he pushed out a labored breath on his, "I don't know shit."

"He doesn't know anything! Leave him be!" Naomi screeched.

Only Tack's head turned and his eyes skewered his ex-bitch.

"You are in a precarious position," he told her, his voice low, chill, his words coming slow but his eyes were flaring. "Advice, Naomi, keep your mouth shut."

Naomi looked into her ex-husband's eyes and shut her mouth.

Tack's gaze went back to Pipe. "Talk," he growled.

With effort, Pipe lifted his head and, expending more effort, he focused as best he could on Tack. "Seriously, dude. I'm tellin' you. I don't know shit. I'm into them two hundred K for blow. They're not gonna trust a cokehead."

"You do that blow in front of my kids?" Tack's words lashed out and hit true, stinging both targets.

Naomi peeped but went silent. Pipe winced as if he'd been struck.

Then he grunted, "No."

"How you get two hundred K in with the Russians for blow and not do that shit in front of my kids?" Tack asked. "You do that much, you'd have to have that rolled bill permanently fixed to your nose."

"I hid it, they never saw."

"How you get two hundred K in with the Russians for blow and not do that shit in front of my kids?" Tack repeated when he got a bullshit response.

Pipe blew out another jagged breath and his head dropped. "To relieve a debt, told 'em I'd hold onto some of it for them. Keep it safe before they moved it. Had a party. Someone found it. Stole it."

Jesus, this was one stupid-ass motherfucker.

"Where would they take Tyra?" Tack asked, and Pipe forced his head up again.

"I'm tellin' you, I *don't know*."

Tack looked to Hop and gave him a nod.

Hop moved in but this time he pulled the knife from his belt.

"Fuck me! I don't know! I don't know!" Pipe screamed. *"But I know who'll know!"*

Hop looked over his shoulder. Tack jerked up his chin. Hop moved aside.

"Oleg," Pipe stated immediately. "Dude's name is Oleg."

Tack felt eyes on him, and this was because every brother knew everything about the Russians and none of them had heard of Oleg.

"Do not bullshit me, Pipe," Tack warned.

"I'm not. I wouldn't. He's not tight with the Russians. He's only tight with Lescheva."

"Then how do you know this guy?"

"I ain't stupid, man. My neck's on the line with these fuckers. I been watchin' and not just Ride."

"What's his connection with Lescheva?"

"No clue but my guess is, he's his out."

"His out?"

"Lescheva's time is up, man. He ain't stupid. He knows that. Only one reason a man gets tight with a man outside his operation but in the family and that's because he's makin' plans. I didn't get close. I just watched but, lately, they been meetin' a lot."

"You know where we can find him?"

"A bar on Evans. Called The Drainpipe."

Tack jerked his chin up to Boz and Shy and they moved out.

Then he looked to Naomi. "You'll get the papers Monday."

She pulled in a visible breath then nodded.

"You'll sign 'em."

She nodded again.

"You'll get the hundred K never." Her face lost all its color and she opened her mouth to speak, but Tack shook his head and whispered, "You are not smart. You've never been smart. Be smart now. You know I am not payin' for blow."

Proving his immense stupidity, Pipe jumped in. "We're fucked, we don't get that money."

"That is not my problem," Tack replied then he turned and headed to the door.

"What do you want done with them?" Hop asked his back and Tack turned at the door.

"I don't give a fuck," he answered and walked out.

*   *   *

Two and a half hours later, Chaos Compound…

There was a sick, liquid noise to it but there was no denying it.

The man was chuckling.

Fuck, they'd been at him for-fucking-ever. The man was made of ice.

They needed to break him.

Now.

"Move away," Tack growled, yanking the gun out of his belt. Dog moved away from the mangled, bloodied man tied to the chair and Tack put the gun to Oleg's head. "Where would he take her?"

Oleg's eyes slid to the side to catch Tack's and he said with a heavy Russian accent, "Go fuck yourself."

Tack moved the gun and drilled a round in Oleg's thigh, the man's body jerked, he stifled a groan then Tack immediately put the gun back to his head.

"Where would he take her?" he repeated.

"Suck my cock," Oleg spit out.

Tack moved the gun and drilled another round in Oleg's

other thigh then he moved the gun, shoving it in the soft flesh under Oleg's chin.

He got nose to nose with him and bit out, "Where would he take her?"

"Eat me," Oleg grunted.

Tack shoved the gun higher and Oleg's head jerked back as a cell rang in the room.

Tack ignored it and clipped, "Where the fuck would he take her?"

"Kill me, I die knowing where she is and I die knowing you *don't* know."

"Tack," Dog called, and Tack pushed away from the Russian and cut his eyes to his brother. "Hawk. Says police band says that Lucas and Lawson got a lock on a safe house where they think Russians are holding a hostage. They've called for backup and put SWAT on alert."

"Hawk say where this is?" Tack asked.

Dog nodded.

"Let's go," Tack grunted, leading the way.

"Clean him up. Clean this shit up. Ask around. Man's gotta have enemies. Find out who they are. Then put the word out we got him available for trade. We'll make the deal after we get Cherry." Tack heard Dog order, probably Arlo and Tug.

But he didn't turn.

He walked out the door.

* * *

Half an hour later, Littleton, Colorado…

The black van driven by Brick, Tack in the passenger seat, Dog, Hound, High, Boz, Shy and Hop in back rolled up and parked behind the SUV.

Tack got out instantly and walked to the front of the van,

rounded it, moved to the curb and saw Lawson standing shielded from the house by the SUV.

"Jesus, are you insane?" Lawson clipped.

"They in there?" Tack asked.

"Broad daylight, Tack, they might have seen you."

"They. In. *There*?" Tack bit off, leaning in.

Lawson sucked in breath then ran it down. "Backup's here. Far's we know, they don't know we're here. Or they didn't until you showed. We've called SWAT. They're ten minutes out."

"Then they're in there," Tack stated, that burn he'd locked down beginning to rage out of control.

His Red was close. A street and a yard away.

"Slim has gone in for a closer look."

"Not waitin' for SWAT," Tack declared, turned and jerked up his chin at his men who were huddling at the side of the van opposite the house where Tyra was.

He stopped when Lawson clamped a hand on his shoulder and forcibly jerked him around.

Tack locked eyes with Lawson and warned, "Not a good time to touch me, man."

"Be smart, Tack," Lawson said quietly. "Tactical gets here, I promise, we'll get her out."

"They've had her six hours. I'm not makin' her wait longer," Tack fired back.

"Shit goes down, Tyra could get hit in the crossfire."

"My boys know to aim only at the shooters."

Lawson gave him a glare and muttered, "Fuck, Kane Allen, expect the unexpected."

"I'm with you."

This came from beyond Lawson and Tack looked to see Lucas there.

"Fuck, Brock Lucas, wild man," Lawson muttered.

"I'm in too."

Tack looked over his shoulder to see Hawk had appeared out of thin air.

"Terrific. Now we can add the commando." Lawson kept muttering.

"Let's go," Tack stated, pulling out his gun.

"Fuck!" Lawson clipped, but Tack, Hawk and Lucas were on the move.

Tack saw his brothers were gone. They'd already scattered to take their positions.

Tack felt Lawson move out with them.

Tack, Hawk, Lucas and Lawson strode out from the cars and moved directly to the house.

Not surprisingly, gunfire came out of the house instantly.

All four men ducked low and started running toward the house as cover fire came from every direction. There was so much gunfire it had to be more than his boys. This meant Hawk's boys were out there too. And, possibly, Nightingale's.

This served its purpose and drew the fire from the house, giving Tack, Hawk, Lucas and Lawson a clean shot to the front door.

In the din, Tack did his best to count gunshots coming from the house.

Two.

At least two men inside to take down.

Once they made it to the door, Tack immediately lifted a boot and kicked it in.

The men surged inside.

The first Russian was down before they even got into the house.

The bullet that went through the other Russian's gut came from Lucas's gun.

The bullet that went through Grigori Lescheva's brain came from Lawson's.

The men down, Tack saw her in the middle of the room.

Tyra, tied to the chair and even during the gunplay, she didn't move. Head drooping, her thick, long, wavy dark red hair hanging lank, back bowed, body limp.

Blood was seeping out of her, oozing across the wood floor.

Too much.

Little rivers of it.

Rivers of blood.

*　　*　　*

Fifteen minutes later…

The ambulance had its lights and sirens on.

There was a black van following it.

An SUV was following the van.

A Camaro was following the SUV.

Beyond that were three Harley-Davidsons.

Beyond that were two squad cars, lights on, no sirens.

The convoy drove up to the Emergency Bay at Swedish Medical Center.

Brick didn't come to a full stop before Tack was out, running to the back of the ambulance where the paramedics were running.

"You can't park here!" he heard shouted but his eyes were glued to the doors that were opening then the gurney that was being tugged out.

The instant its wheels hit the ground, Tack moved in, wrapping his hand around her throat.

He felt the pulse.

"Sir, step back."

Tack ignored that too.

Her green eyes came to him and he sensed her hand come up.

He tagged it and squeezed tight as the paramedics gave up on him and started running the gurney into the ER.

Tack ran with it, hand at her throat, other hand in hers, eyes locked.

"Don't let me go," she whispered.

"I won't let you go, Red."

"Don't let me go."

"I won't let you go, baby."

"Don't let me go."

This last wasn't verbalized. Just her mouth moved with the words.

Tack didn't answer because her hand went limp in his as the light flashed out of her eyes.

Fuck him. Fuck him. *Fuck him.*

She let him go.

Everything he had focused on his hand at her throat.

No pulse.

"Sir! Step back!"

Kane Allen stepped aside and watched them race the gurney through swinging doors that closed behind it, hiding her from sight.

* * *

"It was too easy," Tack muttered.

"What, brother?" Dog asked from close.

"Redemption," Tack answered.

"Brother," Dog murmured then clapped a hand on Tack's shoulder.

They stood together for a while before he felt Dog move away to give him space.

When he was alone, he lifted his hand to his chest and

pressed in. The metal dog tags she gave him were cold against his skin, but that cold felt like a burn.

Then her words came to him.

Truth, honesty, perseverance, strength, love of all kinds and forgiveness are all beautiful, Tack. The most beautiful stories ever told are the most difficult to take.

"You were right, Red," he whispered to the doors. "You were right, darlin'."

*   *   *

Gwen

I moved away from the girls in the waiting room and wandered to the hall.

Bikers everywhere. Some had their arms draped around women. Some were alone, standing back to the wall, motorcycle-boot-clad feet in front of them, heads bent, eyes to their boots.

Two teenaged kids were close to the end of the hall, both on their behinds on the floor, backs to the wall. They both had their knees up. The boy had his arm around the girl's shoulders. She was leaned into him, her face in his chest. He had his eyes glued to Tack.

My eyes moved to him too.

Amid the bevy of bikers, Tack stood alone, one hand to his waist, one hand wrapped around the back of his bent neck, eyes to the floor, standing in the middle of the hall just outside the double doors, close to the kids that, at a glance, I knew were his.

Out of nowhere, I felt a pair of lips at my ear as a hand slid from my waist to my belly.

"Go to him, Sweet Pea," Hawk whispered in my ear.

I nodded and moved.

I walked through bikers and when I arrived at Tack, I moved

right in, sliding my arms around him, pressing my front close to his, my cheek to his chest, closing my eyes, holding tight.

His arms moved around me and held tighter.

"She'll be okay," I whispered.

"Okay, Peaches."

"She'll be all right," I kept whispering.

"Okay, babe."

I opened my eyes and looked down the hall through the bikers.

Standing at the end, Hawk had his arms crossed on his chest, his face blank, his eyes locked to me. Brock had his arm around Tess's shoulders, tucking his wife tight to his side, her head resting on his shoulder. Their eyes were on Tack and me. Mitch had both arms around Mara, hers were returning the favor and her cheek was resting on his chest. Their eyes were also on Tack and me. Elvira stood beside Hawk. The fingers of both her hands were pressed to her mouth. Her outfit was killer. And her eyes were on Tack and me.

As I watched, Hawk moved to slide an arm around Elvira's shoulders and when he did, she leaned full body into his tall frame, giving him most of her weight and, as usual with my man, he stood strong and took it.

"Everything will be all right," I whispered and gave Tack a squeeze.

I knew he'd already lost hope when Tack didn't squeeze back.

*   *   *

Tyra

I felt a hand at my throat.

I opened my eyes.

Tack's handsome face was all I could see.

Weirdly, except his hand wrapped light at my throat, I felt nothing. Not a thing.

Until his rough, gravelly voice came at me.

"Welcome back, Red."

Then I felt my lips smile.

EPILOGUE

Dreams Come True

I STOOD AT the basin in our bathroom wearing my bra and panties, my eyes moving over my body.

Nothing there.

This was because, when I got out of the hospital, approximately half a second after Tack carried me into the house (even though I could walk, just not very fast) and he lay me in bed, he'd started researching. He found the best plastic surgeon in the country, and since then I'd taken two trips out to Los Angeles to have procedures to erase the scars from the five stab wounds Grigori Lescheva's henchman had given me.

"Got that day burned in my brain," Tack had growled after he'd handed me the plane tickets and explained our destination. "Do not need to look at your beautiful body and have it burn deeper. But you *definitely* are not gonna live with the scars 'a that shit in your head *and* on your body. No fuckin' way."

After his explanation, I decided, who was I to argue?

So I didn't.

It was just over nine months since that day and all physical remnants of it were gone.

My man saw to that.

I shifted so my back was to the mirror and looked down. Above my hipster panties was Tack's dragon. His tattoo artist was just that, an artist. The tattoo was the...freaking... *coolest*. All in black, its wings spanning the small of my back, the tips skimming my hips, spiky head turned to the side, the dragon's body curled up as if to attack with its feet, its talons pointed to my behind.

It hurt like hell to get but Tack was right, it was worth it. I liked having his mark on me.

I liked how much he liked it more.

And boy did he like it.

These thoughts made me turn back around. I leaned into the counter and both my hands slid along my belly, my eyes dropping there and I caught sight of my rings.

The second day I woke up in the hospital, I did it with a huge-ass diamond ring on my left finger. It was a raised princess cut diamond, two carats with smaller round diamonds surrounding it, more diamonds set in the gold in the rise up to the bigger one.

The minute I saw it, regardless of the drugs pumping numbness through my system, I smiled.

Pure Tack.

The biker boss to end all biker bosses, his woman was unconscious when we officially became engaged. He did what he did and got what he wanted however that had to come about.

I didn't argue about that either. When Tack walked into my room five minutes later, I just lifted my hand (albeit weakly), wiggled my fingers and whispered, "I accept."

Tack had just smiled back, came right to me, bent in and kissed me.

It kind of sucked that our engagement kiss was soft,

gentle and brief seeing as I was highly drugged, had five stitched holes in my body, IVs and was recovering from an alarming loss of blood.

But none of that made that kiss any less sweet.

We didn't have a huge-ass wedding and we didn't delay in that either.

Lying in a hospital bed, my dream changed. After what I endured, what Tack endured trying to find me and the fact that my heart had stopped beating for one minute and forty-six seconds, my priorities changed.

Live life. Do not delay. Ever.

That didn't mean our wedding didn't kick ass.

It *so* did.

The minute I was up to it, Tack put me on the back of his bike and we lucked out that the weather was good the whole way as we rode over the Rockies and into the Napa Valley.

It was a long ride.

I loved every fucking minute of it.

Everyone met us there, Chaos, Mom and Dad, Aunt Bette and Uncle Marsh, Tabby and Rush, Hawk and Gwen, Brock and Tess, Mitch and Mara, Elvira and even Tack's mom.

I discovered that Tack's mom was, not surprisingly, beaten looking. But she was also friendly and loved her son if in an unusual distant, hesitant way I didn't exactly get and I didn't like all that much. But that distance meant she went right back to San Diego and kept distant. We rarely ever heard from her. Tack was used to this and it didn't bother him so I decided not to let it bother me.

As for my mom and dad, they had met Tack when they came to Denver after my incident. While I was drugged up, Tack left Mom with me and took Dad for a cup of coffee. There he laid it out, all of it about Chaos, the Russians and how that made me a target. There he also laid it out about the fact we loved each other and he intended to spend the rest of his life with me and make a family.

This was also very Tack, up front and honest, and apparently my father appreciated it.

I knew this when I was less whacked out and more lucid and I approached my father about his talk with Tack hoping to head him off the path to judgment.

I shouldn't have worried (though I didn't know that).

"Honey, God makes those decisions, I don't," Dad shocked the shit out of me by saying. "I just know it wasn't him who stabbed you with a knife. I also know it was him who nearly got riddled with bullets to get you out. And I know he got you out alive. And last, I figure the path to redemption is thorny but I'm guessing that man will make it through mostly because he's got a strong woman at his side. And I know *that* because I raised that woman."

Seriously, it sucked I was laid up in a hospital bed because that meant I couldn't give my dad a big hug.

And, for your information, bawling while recovering from stab wounds hurts like a bitch.

I didn't know if Mom and Dad came to Denver with open minds. I just knew they respected Tack's honesty and they saw how Tack, Tabby, Rush and Chaos treated me so if their minds didn't start out open, they ended up that way.

Tack and I got married in a vineyard.

I was wearing a simple but kickass ivory dress and not simple and more kickass ivory spiked heels. At my side was an immensely sad but faking it for me Lanie. Tack wore jeans and an unbelievably cool ivory shirt with subtle western-style stitching and not subtle totally kickass rocker-biker black embroidery across the upper chest and his shoulders at the back. Through the nuptials, Dog stood by his side. And when we were pronounced man and wife, a collective biker howl split the air that made me laugh and cry at the same time.

After I slid my wide gold band on his finger, he slid the thin, diamond-embedded gold one on mine, we partied hard and long and, as it raged on, rowdy. The owners of the vineyard luckily were game and joined in rather than taking the alternative of calling the cops.

Everyone left but Tack and I stayed a week for our honeymoon. Then we extended our honeymoon and rode the coastal road of California.

Only after we'd done that did we go home.

It wasn't near enough time riding the roads with my man with the wind in my hair. But it still was time I savored.

Every second.

Both Lanie and I missed Elliott's funeral because we were both still in the hospital. But she waited for me and my moral support, and I took her to his grave when Tack and I got home from our honeymoon. I also held her while we stood at his grave and she sobbed in my arms. Not long after, she moved back to Connecticut to be close to her mom, dad and sister. I missed her every day but I understood her play.

Too much Elliott in Denver.

He was a fuckup, got himself dead and Lanie in the ICU. But even so, she loved him and still wasn't over him.

She hadn't dated since. Not once.

I was worried about her and planning a trip to go out and shake her shit up.

Life was too short and too precious to lay it down to grief.

My friend was beautiful, she was funny, she was loving and she needed to wake the fuck up.

She was breathing.

She needed to start living.

And she was going to do it even if I had to kick her ass.

Yes, I was a badass biker babe, and if my friend didn't sort her shit, she'd answer to me.

On this thought, the bathroom door opened and my eyes went to it in the mirror to see Tack walking in wearing nothing but faded jeans and my dog tags hanging around his neck.

Mm. Nice.

My eyes dropped to his chest to see my ink on his upper ribs, under Tabby, close to his heart. The dog tags rested right next to it.

He had my tattoo done before I got out of the hospital.

On the inside of his right forearm was another new tattoo. A set of scales, unbalanced. The top scale had the word "Red" inked in killer lettering sitting on it, and dripping over the sides were rivers of blood. The bottom scale had the word "Black" and drifting up was a ghostly, hooded, skull-faced reaper with eerie blue eyes and a scythe in his skeletal hand. The support holding the scales was made of the words, "Never Forget."

Every member of Chaos had this tattoo. The "Red" was me and a reminder that I got out alive, but barely. The "Black" represented their fallen brother (whose last name, incidentally, was Black) who went down when they'd first instigated plans to pull themselves off the path of evil to strike out toward redemption. The message of the tattoo was a reminder that if they weren't smart, the scales could unbalance and it wasn't worth the loss of what was at stake.

Brothers and blood.

Nothing more important in life.

Not one thing.

Even Arlo and High got that tattoo. One could say what happened that day was a wake-up call. No money or adrenaline rush was worth what happened to their brother or Tack and me.

So all was good in the Club.

No, actually, all was good with everything.

Absolutely everything.

And it was about to get better.

My eyes lifted from my ink on my old man to catch his as he made his way to me. He held my gaze as he fitted his front to my back, one of his hands gliding along my arm to rest on mine at my belly. His other hand came up and wrapped around my throat.

He did this often. In fact, all the time. I knew what it meant and as the weeks wore into months and he kept doing it, it troubled me so I'd gently approached him about it.

"Don't question it," he'd replied just as gently. "Just give it to me when I think I need it."

What could I say? They were his demons and he had to create his methods of coping. And this was one.

So I agreed and let it go.

As for me, the first thing I saw after waking up in the hospital which was also the last thing I saw every night before going to bed and the first thing I saw in the morning was my coping mechanism.

It was a hellish six hours and I couldn't say I didn't have dark moments when those hours drifted into my brain and haunted me.

What I could say was, once I made my way to Tack, he let in the light.

I watched him tip his head and felt the tickle of his goatee whisper against the skin of my shoulder before I felt his lips touch there and I melted back into him.

He lifted his head and again caught my eyes in the mirror.

"You're quiet this mornin'," he said softly.

"I'm pregnant," I replied, and felt his body go still behind mine but his fingers at my throat flexed and his hand over mine at my belly pressed deep.

We held each other's gazes in the mirror for long moments before he whispered, "Say again?"

"I'm pregnant, handsome."

His hand again pressed against mine at my belly as I watched his eyes flare.

Then both of his hands moved so his thumbs could hook into the sides of my panties and he yanked them down.

A tremor ran through me at this maneuver and the area between my legs instantly got wet.

Then Tack put his fingers to my hips and turned me to him, his mouth slammed down on mine and I got wetter. His tongue thrust into my mouth as my arms slid around his shoulders, his fingers clenched into my hips, jerking me up and I got even wetter.

My ass landed on the basin and my legs wrapped around his hips.

One arm tight around my back, his other hand roamed as he kissed me and I kissed him back. His hand slid over my side, my ribs, up and in, he found my nipple, caught it between thumb and finger and rolled.

I gasped into his mouth, my hips shifting on the counter to gain better access to his.

His hand instantly left my nipple and went between us.

"Fuck, please be ready," he growled against my lips as his hand worked his jeans.

"I'm ready, honey," I breathed against his.

He kissed me again then he was inside me. I gasped in his mouth and my legs tightened around his hips. He leaned in, I went back and he braced one hand against the basin, the other arm still wrapped around me and he pounded in deeper and, better still, harder.

"Yes," I whispered.

His arm around me jerked me slightly out from the basin so he had better access and I moaned as fire shot through me because this meant he could go even deeper and drive in way, way *harder*. I knew because he did just that.

He fucked me and kissed me as my hands moved on him, all over him, every inch I could get, fast, feverish but when I was close, one hand sifted in his hair and clenched as my other arm went around his back and squeezed.

"I'm there," I gasped.

"No shit," he muttered. I vaguely felt his mouth smile against mine but I was paying a lot more attention to the fact that I was coming.

He lasted a long time, I held him tight and he built it again so I climaxed again before he finally groaned in my mouth.

Except during my recuperation and after the cosmetic procedures, this hadn't changed. Tack was always hungry for me. I was always greedy for him.

No. It *had* changed. It kept getting better and better.

His lips were working my neck and my hands were sliding over his skin when I turned my head and asked, "So, I'm taking it that was Kane 'Tack' Allen's way of communicating he's happy he knocked me up."

Tack's head came up and his lips surrounded by his badass biker goatee were smiling.

"Yeah, babe. That's my way of communicatin' I'm glad I got you knocked up."

"Good," I said softly.

His smile faded as his hand came up to my neck, palm

under my ear, fingers in my hair behind it, thumb moving out to sweep the apple of my cheek.

God, I loved it when he did that.

His eyes watched his thumb move then they came to mine and I held my breath at what I saw.

"I got there," he whispered.

"Where, baby?" I whispered back.

"God wouldn't 'a given me you and all you could give me growin' inside you if I was not redeemed."

My heart tripped and my belly flipped as I breathed, "Handsome," lifting a hand to curl around the side of his neck and moving my head so my forehead was resting against his.

His soft words brushed against my lips and it was the sweetest touch he'd ever given me when he said, "I love you, Red."

"I love you too, Tack."

We held each other close, connected and savored the moment before he lifted his head and announced, "We got a party to get to, darlin'."

He was not wrong.

He touched his lips to mine, pulled out gently and, still gentle, slid me off the counter and onto my feet. He held me close until my legs felt firm under me. Then he dropped his head and kissed my throat.

I closed my eyes.

Second sweetest touch he'd given me. Definitely.

I opened my eyes when Tack stepped away and adjusted his jeans. I turned to the basin and twisted on the taps to clean up.

All was right in the world and I knew this when Tack wandered out of the bathroom bossing, "Hurry up, babe. Takin' the time to fuck you means we're runnin' late."

My eyes to the reflection in the mirror of the door he disappeared through, I rolled them.

Then I cleaned up.

Back in my panties, I reached to my moisturizer but stopped.

We had pale yellow tile in our bathroom rimmed with thin tiles of white. I'd dumped Tack's old, mismatched towels and added new, thick emerald green ones. They were hanging on the towel rack.

My eyes moved.

My moisturizer and toner bottles were the deep-hued color of moss. My toothbrush was bright pink, Tack's was electric blue. There was a little bowl by the tap where I tossed my jewelry when I was washing my hands or preparing for bed. It was ceramic painted in glossy sunshine yellow and grass green. My eyes went to the mirror. My undies were cherry red lace.

I grinned at myself in the mirror.

I lived in color, every day, and my life was vibrant.

I rubbed in moisturizer hoping our baby got his or her dad's sapphire blue eyes.

But I'd settle if they were my green.

*   *   *

Sitting on top of a picnic table outside the Compound in the warm, late June Colorado sun having a moment of alone time, I heard the clickety-clack of high-heeled shoes and my eyes turned to see Elvira bearing down on me.

And when they did, my lips curved into a smile.

Only Elvira would wear to a barbeque at a biker stronghold a tight, butter yellow, cleavage-baring, halter-top dress with a pair of bronze sandals that were so fuck-me, even as a girl I would describe them as that.

She looked like she was about to step out to a trendy eatery, not about to bite into a grilled brat.

With a grace borne of practice, she climbed up and sat her ass down beside me at the picnic table whereupon she announced, "Trouble's a-brewin'."

I felt my eyebrows draw together at this very strange yet totally Elvira opening. "Pardon?"

Her head tipped in the direction of something and my eyes moved there.

I saw Shy, now a full member of the Club, being Shy. That was to say he had on a pair of faded jeans that fit him all too well, a tight black t-shirt that also fit him all too well, his dark hair was a sexy mess, his mirrored shades were shoved on the top of his head and he was openly flirting with a young, attractive biker babe.

He was smiling at her and his smile was wicked.

She was also smiling at him and her smile was come-hither.

Shy was clearly going to get him some. And from copious experience witnessing Shy in action my guess was, he was going to get that some and soon. Hell, just that week I'd seen him charm a woman who was buying wiper fluid in Ride into his bed in the Compound and he'd done it in ten point seven five minutes. I knew this because Hop and I had timed it.

Not a surprise and also not a rarity, not by a long shot. Thus I didn't know what trouble was "a-brewin'" until I started to look away and my eyes caught on Tabby.

Oh boy.

She was standing about ten feet away. She was also looking at Shy, and the way she was looking was like her entire world just came to an end.

This was not good.

Tabby had pulled her shit together. This didn't mean she didn't come home drunk once, as in drunk and puking all over the entryway. And this didn't mean Tack didn't lose his mind when she did and she didn't get a lecture. But she was a teenager. That shit happened. Tack knew it and busted her chops but he didn't go overboard.

Mostly, she was Tabby, sweet, cute, smart, charming. She and her dad were tight. She and her brother were tight. And she and I were tight. She got good grades. She came home (mostly) by curfew. She dated boys of an appropriate age who only slightly scared the crap out of me seeing as they were all good-looking and players-in-training but were also totally into her. And it helped Tab's dad was a badass and he more than slightly scared the crap out of Tabby's boyfriends.

But this wasn't good. Not only because Tabby was seventeen and Shy, at twenty-two, was out of her league for at least another year but also because Shy was Shy. He was a dawg. He racked 'em up and nailed them down so fast, if it could be recorded as a world record, it would.

And he was a brother. It was not as if Tack wasn't aware of all this.

On this thought my eyes slid to my old man to see he was, indeed, aware of all this. All of it. I knew this because his face didn't look happy and it didn't look that way even though his eyes were covered by his own mirrored shades and those shades were pointed in the direction of Tabby and Shy. Tack had Mitch, Dog and Gwen's father, Bax, standing close to him talking but I knew he wasn't involved in the conversation.

His mind was on his girl. And his brother, the dawg.

Crap.

"'Cause 'a Gwen then 'cause 'a you, I been to my fair share of these boys' jamborees and it hasn't escaped my notice that boy is *fine*," Elvira stated at my side. "He's rough, he's young, he makes me feel like a cougar, but that don't mean that boy ain't *fine*. So fine, a girl could convince herself she don't mind he's a player. 'Love 'em, leave 'em' could be tattooed across his chest and a girl could convince herself she don't care just so she could see the weapon he's packin' in those faded jeans. May have been some time since you bitch-slapped your way to kicking that motherfucker's ass, girlfriend, but I think your girl there has tastes that run toward heartbreak. And it looks like this is not lost on your man and he's not takin' to it too good."

Tack must have felt my eyes because his shades came to me. They locked with my eyes and then he slowly shook his head. We weren't close but I still knew he blew out a sigh.

No, this was not lost on Tack.

"Makes matters worse," Elvira kept talking and I tore my eyes from Tack's shades and looked at her, "that boy won't go down to no bitch slappin', sister. He gets a whiff he's got a go and she comes of age, you better arm yourself with more than pepper spray. I'm thinkin' ... machete."

"No way Shy would go there," I informed her, and her eyebrows went up.

"Girl, you crazy? She's gorgeous and he's on a mission to have a bedpost that's made up 'a nothin' but notches."

"She's also his brother's daughter. He won't go there," I told her authoritatively because I knew, Shy might be a dawg, but he was also smart, a good guy and loyal and he'd rather cut off his own arm than disrespect Tack like that.

"Then your problem is her, 'cause a girl don't look that forlorn unless she's in deep," Elvira returned. "That ain't no crush. She likes him, straight up."

She was not wrong about that.

My eyes drifted to Tabby who had, fortunately, been

engaged in conversation with Meredith, Gwen's mom, Roberta, a friend of Mara's, Tracy and Camille.

"Oowee!" Elvira suddenly screeched. I jumped, twisted and saw Gwen approaching, her tiny, new baby Asher bundled in her arms. Elvira had both her arms extended, fingers wriggling. "Give me that little cuddly baby commando." Gwen arrived, transferred Asher to Elvira who immediately cuddled him close to her chest, dipped her face to his and cooed, "Who's gonna grow up, kick ass and take names? Who's gonna be my little badass?"

"Elvira, stop putting ideas in his head," Gwen ordered, and Elvira kept Asher snuggled close to her substantial cleavage but her head snapped up.

"Girl, he can't even cogitate. Calm down."

"He's Hawk's. He has superhero powers. They're latent, you can't sense them, but they're there. Trust me. Stop giving him ideas. He's not going to grow up to be a commando. He's going to grow up to be anything *but* a commando." She looked to me. "I don't know what that is. I also don't care. Hawk being Hawk, I'm pretty certain every bullet in his arsenal is stamped with a male chromosome that will not be denied. I'm screwed. I already envision decades of living through fights, blood, drunkenness, puke and pregnancy scares. I don't need to be finding assault rifles under beds and sitting on ninja stars that have fallen into my couch."

Elvira lifted a hand to the side of baby Asher's head, covering the whole of it, but her target was his ear and I knew this when she snapped, "Gwen, shut yo' mouth. If he don't grow up commando, how's he gonna make his fortune, make men quake in their boots and nail down his own fine piece of ass?"

Gwen's eyes on Elvira bugged out then they went to the

heavens. "Someone, deliver me. Or better yet, deliver Elvira. Maybe to China."

"I don't mind China," Elvira told Asher in a baby-talk voice. "They got good food there and they created Jet Li. Now that's a boy who knows his shit, Asher, *and* he's got a kickass name. His momma couldn't 'a made up a better name for a badass. With a name like that, only one route that boy could go down in life, the route straight to badass." Her head came up and her eyes locked on Gwen before she finished, "Kinda like the name Asher Delgado."

"My next boy I'm naming Nigel," Gwen shot back.

"Ha!" Elvira hooted. "Like Hawk would allow that."

"They're boys, I get to name them. We have a pact," Gwen retorted.

"Yeah, you make sure I'm around when you tell Hawk you're gonna name his kid Nigel. We'll see about that pact," Elvira returned.

Gwen looked at me. "Are there weapons in the Compound?"

"Uh . . ." I mumbled, thinking there undoubtedly were.

"Never mind. Bullets mean questions. Poison, now, poison can go undetected," Gwen muttered, and I grinned.

Elvira dipped her head to whisper to Asher, "Mommy's silly."

Tess joined our party at this juncture, sitting at my feet on the bench seat of the picnic table.

"Hey, girls," she greeted.

She got greetings back from Gwen and Elvira with Elvira waving Asher's little baby hand at her for good measure.

"Thanks for bringing that cake. It was awesome," I told her.

"No problem," she murmured, smiling at me.

"Yeah, well, you would know," Elvira muttered. "Others of us not fast enough or experienced enough with the brethren didn't get our asses in there to get our piece before the bikers fell on that shit like vultures. You would think those scary biker dudes never had a slice of cake *in their lives.* By the time I got there, not a crumb left. Not even a swipe of frosting on the plate." She looked at Tess. "Means you owe me, girl."

"Honey, I own two bakeries. You can walk in any time and get your fix," Tess replied.

"Freebie?" Elvira asked.

"You're the one who always insists on paying," Tess said by way of answer.

"Well, you got mini-hot guys to raise. I don't want to be the one who keeps you from keepin' them clothed. 'Specially now, seein' as they're of the datin' age."

Tess closed her eyes in despair at this thought and I knew why. Joel was already dating, and Tess was already living her version of the threat of fights, blood, drunkenness, puke and pregnancy scares.

Elvira's eyes drifted to the congregation in the direction of Joel and Rex who were both standing with Hawk, my Uncle Marsh and Aunt Bette, the visit of the latter two being why we were throwing this barbeque. "Shee-it, they're growin' like weeds. I reckon both 'a them are gonna be taller than their daddy. And it's stamped all over them they're gonna be just as hot."

"Tell me about it," Tess murmured, her eyes also on her boys.

I watched Brock walk to that particular huddle and when he got there, he lifted both hands, wrapped them around the backs of both his boys' necks and, I suspected, he gave them a squeeze before he dropped his hands. After this move, both boys shifted slightly closer to their dad, not close-close, but the invisible bond had tightened.

Then I watched Brock's eyes scan the crowd and find

Tess. He gave her a sexy smile before he turned away and gave his full attention to the huddle.

Watching this, my belly warmed.

Tack was a good dad, a good man and a great husband.

I had that, what Tess had. And my kid would have that, what Brock gave his boys.

And I liked that.

Then it penetrated that something was happening. Bikers were moving, a word was drifting through then all the males were shifting toward the open tarmac. I spied Mitch carrying one of those big, long baseball bags, Bud striding beside him, Leo, Camille's husband, next to Bud, Derek, LaTanya's boyfriend, next to Mitch.

Holy crap.

Were bikers going to play a game of baseball?

Mara came in from the opposite side to where I was looking, sat on the bench seat by Elvira's fuck-me shoes as her girl Billie climbed up behind her, got on her knees on the table and peered over Elvira's shoulder to coo at Asher. At the same Tess's best friend, Martha, came to stand beside Gwen.

"Mitch and Bud have struck up a game of baseball," Mara announced, and she smiled up at Gwen. "Not a surprise."

Holy crap!

I stared as the men congregated.

Bikers were going to play a game of baseball.

"Does Bud sleep with a mitt on his hand?" Tess asked Mara.

"Close enough," Mara answered.

I watched Mitch turn his head from the huddle and look toward Mara. Then I watched as he gave her a sexy grin too.

Well, I supposed if commandos and police detectives

could show at a biker barbeque then bikers could play baseball.

My eyes drifted from Mitch to Brock to Hawk to Tack.

In the beginning, the woman posse took me under their wing.

But now, we were all family. And this wasn't because Elvira was rabidly friendly.

No, it was because Hawk, Brock and Mitch stormed that house at Tack's side. This meant, to Tack, they were different kinds of brothers. Not of blood. Not of the cut. But that bond was unshakable all the same.

It was on the more than occasional basis that I was out shopping, having coffee, drinks or dinner with one, several or all of the girls.

It was only occasional but not unheard of that Hawk, Brock and/or Mitch was sitting in the Compound having a beer.

Tack had made his statement. There was no going back now.

Not that I would want to.

Aunt Bette, Meredith, Roberta, Tabby, LaTanya, Tracy and Camille joined our klatch as did Sheila, Mitzi and the other old ladies.

"I take it this is the cheering section," Aunt Bette noted.

"Seems to be," Martha murmured.

"Right, before we gotta figure out who we're cheering for, how 'bout we get the important stuff outta the way?" Elvira suggested, I looked to her to see her eyes on me and she asked, "When you due?"

My body locked.

"Pardon?"

"Girl," she said softly, "you're surrounded by your girls. Do not think that contentment in your eyes is lost on us. The sun is shining. The food is good. The vibe is happy. But that look on your face don't say sun, food and good company. It also don't say you got yourself some. It says something a whole lot bigger. Make that vibe happier. When you due?"

I felt eyes hitting me from all around, primarily Aunt Bette's and Tabby's.

But Elvira was wrong. I had gotten myself some. I didn't share that primarily because of Aunt Bette and Tabby.

Not surprisingly, Aunt Bette and Uncle Marsh had outwardly accepted Tack, his kids and my biker-babe lifestyle. Though, considering shortly after I entered that world I'd been kidnapped and, later, stabbed five times, I didn't know what they thought of it.

Nor did I know what they'd think of this added evidence that I was happily mired deep in it.

Still, because Elvira was nosy but she also was right, my girls were around me and outside of Tack (and his badass brothers) there was no safer place to be, I answered, "January."

"Yee ha!" Elvira hooted, Asher jumping in her arms then his rosy baby lips gave a baby smile as all the women surrounding me cheered, whooped and I got hug after hug.

Tabby's included her body giving a slight jerk as her breath gave a slight hitch and my arms giving her a not-so-slight squeeze.

My girl was happy she was getting a baby brother or sister. Or, maybe, it was just that my girl was happy for her dad and me. Or, maybe, both.

My last hug was from Aunt Bette. It lasted the longest and it was the tightest.

"Sometimes it happens in weird ways," she whispered before she let me go, "but dreams come true."

Boy, Aunt Bette paid attention to e-mails.

I felt the sting of tears in my eyes and she let me go, looking away quickly and I gave her that play.

Okay, so, I guess Aunt Bette inwardly accepted Tack, his kids and my biker-babe lifestyle too.

Good to know.

My dampening eyes found my old man's.

He was standing, one arm thrown around Rush's shoulders, but his attention was all on me and he was grinning his sexy grin at me.

Yes, I thought, sitting in the sun, my girls around me, holding his gaze, taking in his smile and carrying his child, Aunt Bette was absolutely right.

Sometimes it happens in weird ways that included fights, blood, drunkenness, kidnappings and pregnancies.

But dreams came true.

*   *   *

"It was good form, your brothers not pulling knives or shooting anyone when Mitch, Brock and Hawk's team beat your team in baseball," I noted, lying cuddled naked in bed with a naked Tack in his room in the Compound.

It was late. The barbeque was over. Aunt Bette and Uncle Marsh were at their hotel. Tab and Rush were at home. And Tack and I decided to keep partying in private.

"Lawson didn't tell me he had a secret weapon," Tack mumbled. "Fuck, you see that kid hit?"

"Yep."

"Jesus," Tack muttered. "Got an arm on him too. He's only eleven."

"I noticed that too."

"And Lucas's boys weren't far behind him. Older, fuckin' powerhouses."

"Yep."

"We didn't stand a chance."

"Nope."

Tack fell silent.

I did too.

Then I broke it with, "Rush make his decision?"

Rush had graduated high school and told his father he was thinking of joining Chaos. I was surprised this wasn't a given but, for some reason, it wasn't.

"Not yet."

"What's holding him back?"

"I don't know, maybe our shit gettin' a woman he cares about stabbed five times?"

My head popped up from his shoulder and I looked through the dark at his shadowed face.

"Me?"

"Only some shit you can shield your kids from, darlin', my kids ain't dumb and their mother had a big mouth that also was loud, both of those making it harder to shield them at all. They heard me and Naomi fightin'. They heard what it was about. Hard as I tried, bitch wouldn't shut up. This only led to what happened to you. And, babe, you know Pipe went down."

Only weeks after my drama, Naomi's old man had gotten into his car, started it and got blown to smithereens. Lescheva might have been out but the Russians kept good books. They knew who owed them a debt, and those kinds of debts got paid.

Elliott paid it.

Pipe Dahl paid it too.

Naomi didn't waste time moving on to her next victim. She shacked up three months later with a biker in Boulder.

Rush saw her occasionally.

Tabby, never.

As for me, even though I never saw her, Boulder wasn't far enough away. But it was something.

"Rush isn't all fired up about Chaos," Tack finished.

"But you're not on that path anymore," I pointed out.

"Darlin', you got stabbed five times and his stepdad got dead."

"Pipe dying had nothing to do with Chaos."

"Not sure Rush sees it that way."

"He couldn't do better than the Club," I announced heatedly, and the air in the room went still but I ignored it and kept talking, "What's he going to do? He loves cars. He's great with them. You got him that bike for Christmas and every good day with clear roads we've had since then, he's been on it. He knows everything about cars and bikes. And—"

"He couldn't do better than the Club?" Tack cut me off to ask.

"Well, yeah. Brothers and blood. What's more important than a lifetime of loyalty to both?"

"Jesus," Tack murmured.

"What?" I asked.

"Jesus," Tack repeated.

"What?" I repeated too and his hand came up and cupped my jaw.

"Your what is that those layers keep strippin' off, baby. And sometimes, when they do, what's uncovered shines out so bright, it takes the wind out of me."

His words took the wind out of me.

Tack went on, "This mornin', you gave me one of the most precious gifts a woman can give her man. And now, you just gave me another one."

What did I do?

"I..." I faltered then asked, "How did I do that?"

"I claimed you into my world and then you gave me you. But, Red, me claimin' you and you existing in my world is one thing. You accepting it is another."

Oh, that's what I did.

My body relaxed into his and his hand slid from my jaw into my hair as I pointed out, "I took my place in it a long time ago, honey."

"You love me, you love my kids, you feel deep for my brothers but until now, I didn't know you also loved the life." His hand in my hair pulled me close so he could touch my mouth to his before he let me back an inch and finished, "And that's a gift, baby. One that means the world to me. Thank you."

Ohmigod!

I was thinking I just heard Tack say, "Thank you."

"Did you just say 'thank you'?" I asked in order to confirm.

"Spoke English, babe."

"You just said 'thank you.'"

A pause before he muttered, "Now she's bustin' my balls."

"I am not!" I snapped.

"Now she's servin' up attitude."

Well, I *was* doing that.

"Give me a break, handsome, I've been with you just shy of a year and in that time I've been kidnapped, I kicked ass *twice*, I was stabbed, got married and you got me pregnant. Through all that, you've not once said 'thank you' to me. Even when I got that mammoth parts order right without having to ask you a single question. Let me savor the moment."

"Yeah, I was savoring that moment too and that moment was tender until you got feisty."

"Uh...you pledged your troth to me, Tack. It's not like you don't know I get feisty."

"I pledged my troth," Tack repeated.

"Yeah."

"You just said I pledged my troth."

"Yes, that's what I just said."

"What's a troth?"

"I don't know, I just know you pledged it."

I heard and saw Tack shake his head on his pillow then he stated, "Babe, advice. A man expresses his gratitude, you do not throw attitude. You kiss him and, maybe, suck his dick to show your appreciation."

Okay, now we were back to the Tack I knew.

"I think I've already cemented my biker bitch status, Tack, this very conversation being evidence of that. Lessons are no longer necessary."

"Right, then, how about you get busy suckin' my dick 'cause I want you to?"

That went through me like a hot knife through butter and my legs shifted.

"Always greedy," he muttered.

"Like you don't like it," I muttered back.

"Hard to talk, you got a mouth full of my cock," Tack remarked.

That went through me too.

"Quit turning me on when I'm feeling feisty," I snapped.

"Red, best time to turn you on is when you're feeling feisty."

This was true.

"Babe," he prompted when I made no move then, "Tyra," he prompted again when I still made no move.

"Oh, all right. I'll get busy."

"Obliged," he muttered, a smile in his voice but his hand

didn't leave my hair to let me get down to business. It pulled me close so my mouth was touching his. "Think about this, darlin', before you go down on me and brace, baby, 'cause I'm about to get sweet and you need to process it fast so you can move on to suckin' me off, *not* fast."

As requested, I braced but I also held my breath.

Tack didn't delay in trumping the best sweet he'd ever given me. Something he did often. Something his words proved I'd never get used to.

"I thank you for helpin' me make that baby inside you. I thank you for takin' your place in my world and likin' it. I thank you for bein' a good stepmom to my kids and givin' Tab what she needed and never had. And I thank you most of all for bein' you, givin' as good as you get in all the ways you can, makin' sure my life is never boring and makin' sure I go to bed content and wake up happy to face the coming day."

My throat closed because my heart swelled so big it took up my entire chest but I didn't get a chance to start crying because Tack kissed me. I did give a little sob into his mouth before I got over it and decided to concentrate on kissing him back.

After that, I got down to business.

*   *   *

Tack

Tyra was out, her body heavy against his when Tack gently rolled her to her back.

He rolled into her and, as he'd done countless times since that day, his hand moved over her skin.

The scars were gone but their memory remained. He

knew each location where the knife plunged into her flesh, and he ran his fingers across the skin he'd paid a fucking mint to make smooth again.

And, as always, he ended the journey of his hand at her throat.

Resting lightly there so as not to wake her, he let her pulse beat into his fingers and he did it until it washed the memories away.

But this night and the ones to follow for the next seven months, the path of his hand didn't end there as it usually did.

It moved down to her belly.

And into the darkness, to his sleeping woman, he whispered, "You don't know this, baby, but some men have dream women too."

Since she was asleep, for once, Tyra Allen had no reply.

Palm flat against his woman's warm, soft skin, Kane Allen settled into his wife in the bed in the room where they started and he fell asleep.

*   *   *

Seven months later, Rider Allen was born.

And the first thing Tack did was wrap two fingers around his throat.

Gwendolyn Kidd has met the man
of her dreams.
Night after night he comes to her bed,
but she doesn't even know his name...

Please turn this page for
an excerpt from

MYSTERY MAN.

CHAPTER ONE

D-e-a-d, Dead

THE NEXT MORNING I was sitting at my computer in my home office.

I should have been working. I had three deadlines over the next two weeks and I'd barely begun the work. I was a freelance editor. I got paid by the hour and if I didn't work that hour, I didn't get paid. I had a mouth to feed, my own. I had a body to clothe, a body that liked all sorts of clothes, it craved them, so I had to feed the habit or things could get nasty. I had a cosmopolitan addiction, and cosmos didn't come cheap. And I had a house I was fixing up. Therefore, I needed to get paid.

Okay, that wasn't strictly true. I wasn't fixing up my house. My dad did some of the work. My friend Troy did the rest. So I should say that I had a house I was guilting, begging and emotionally blackmailing others into fixing up.

But still, it needed fixing up, and cabinets and tile didn't march from Cabinet and Tile Land into my house and say "We want to live with you, Gwendolyn Kidd, affix us to your walls!"

That only happened in my dreams, of which I had many, most of them daydreams.

Like right then, sitting at my computer, one heel on the seat, my chin to my knee, my eyes staring out the window, I was thinking about my Mystery Man, the Great MM. I was day-dreaming about changing our first meeting. Being smarter, funnier and more mysterious. Being more alluring and interesting.

I'd hook him instantly with my rapier wit, my flair for conversation, my ability to discuss politics and world events intelligently. I'd tell my humble stories of expansive charity work all wrapped up with enticing looks that promised a lifetime of mind-blowing orgasms, making him declare his undying love for me.

Or at least tell me his name.

Instead, I was drunk when we met, and definitely not any of that.

I heard my doorbell go, a chime then a clunk and I started out of my elaborate daydream, which was beginning to get good.

I got up and walked through my office into the upstairs hall making a mental note, again, to call Troy and see if he'd fix my doorbell for a six-pack and a homemade pizza. This might mean he'd bring his annoying, whiny, constantly bitching new girlfriend though, so I changed my mind and decided to call my dad.

I got to the bottom of my stairs and walked through my living room, ignoring the state of it, which was decorated in Fix-Up Chic. In other words dust rags, paintbrushes, power tools, not-so-power tools, cans and tubes of practically everything, all of it jumbled and covered in a layer of dust. I made it through the area without my hands going to my head, fingers clenching my hair and mouth screaming, which I counted as progress.

I got to the entryway, which was delineated by two narrow walls both fit with gorgeous stained glass.

Two years ago, that stained glass was my undoing.

Two years ago, approximately six months and two weeks prior to meeting my Mystery Man, I'd walked one single step into this ramble and wreck of a house, saw that stained glass, turned to the Realtor and announced, "I'll take it."

The Realtor's face had lit up.

My father, who hadn't even made it into the house yet, turned his eyes to the heavens. His prayer lasted a long time. His lecture longer.

I still bought the house.

As usual, I should have listened to my dad.

I looked out the narrow side window at the door and saw Darla, my sister's friend, standing out there.

Shit.

Shit, shit, *shit*.

I hated Darla and Darla hated me. What the hell was she doing there?

I searched behind her to see if my sister was lurking or perhaps hiding in the shrubbery. I wouldn't put it past Ginger and Darla to jump me, tie me to the staircase and loot my house. In my darker daydreams, this was how Ginger and Darla spent their days. I was convinced this was not far from the truth. No joke.

Darla's eyes came to me at the window. Her face scrunched up, making what could be pretty, if she used a less heavy hand with the black eyeliner and her blush, and if her lip liner wasn't an entirely different shade as her lip gloss, not so pretty.

"I see you!" she shouted.

I sighed.

Then I went to the door because Darla would shout the house down and I liked my neighbors. They didn't need a biker bitch from hell standing on my doorstep and shouting the house down at ten thirty in the morning.

I opened it but not far and moved to stand between it and the jamb, keeping my hand on the handle.

"Hey, Darla," I greeted, trying to sound friendly and pretty pleased with my effort.

"Fuck 'hey,' is Ginger here?" Darla replied.

See!

Totally spent her days looting.

It took effort but I stopped my eyes from rolling.

"No," I answered.

"She's here, you better tell me," she warned then she looked beyond me and shouted, "Ginger! Bitch, if you're in there you better come out here, right fuckin' now!"

"Darla!" I snapped. "Keep your voice down!"

She craned her neck and bounced on her toes, yelling, "Ginger! Ginger, you crazy, stupid bitch! Get your ass out here!"

I shoved out the door, forcing her back and closed it behind me, hissing, "Seriously, Darla, shut up! Ginger isn't here. Ginger is *never* here. You know that. So shut up and *go*."

"*You* shut up," she shot back. "And *you* get smart. You're helpin' her..." She lifted her hand, pointed her finger at me, thumb extended upward and then she crooked her thumb and made a gunshot noise that puffed out her cheeks and made her lips vibrate. I would have taken a moment to reflect on how good she was with verbal sound effects if the serious as shit look in her eye wasn't scaring the crap out of me.

So, instead of congratulating her on the only real talent I suspected she had, I whispered, "What?"

She dropped her hand, got up on her motorcycle-booted toes so we were eye to eye, and said in a soft, scary voice,

"D-e-a-d, *dead*. You and her, you don't get smart. You get me?"

Then I asked a stupid question because the question was asked often and there was always only one answer. The answer being yes.

"Is Ginger in some kind of trouble?"

Darla stared at me like I had a screw loose. She lifted her hand, did the gun thing with the sound effect, finger pointed at my head. Then she turned around and walked swiftly down my front steps.

I stood on my front porch staring at her. My mind absently noted that she was wearing a tight tank top, an unzipped, black leather motorcycle jacket, a short, frayed jean skirt, the wearing of which was a crime in several states for a variety of reasons—both fashion and decency—black fishnet stockings and motorcycle boots. It was around forty degrees outside. She didn't even have on a scarf.

The rest of my head was caught up with my sister and Darla's sound effect.

Shit. Shit. *Shit.*

*   *   *

As I drove, I kept trying to tell myself this was a good plan. Knowing that my first plan, the one where, after Darla left and I went back into my house, I walked directly to the phone and called my father, was the right plan and this plan was garbage.

But my father and his wife, Meredith, had disowned Ginger a while ago. It was approximately ten seconds after they came home from a vacation to Jamaica and lost their happy, island holiday mojo when they saw their daughter. She was on her knees in the living room, her head between the legs of a bare-chested man, his jeans opened, his head lolled on the back of the couch because he was passed out. Ginger was so whacked on whatever she was taking she had no idea her activities were getting her nowhere.

And, incidentally, the living room was a disaster, as was the rest of the house.

As you can probably see from this story, I was loath to bring my father into another situation involving Ginger. Especially since this wasn't the worst story I had, it was just, for Dad and Meredith, the last. They were currently living a carefree, Ginger-free existence and I didn't want to rock that boat.

Therefore, I didn't call Dad.

Instead I thought of Ginger's boyfriend, Dog. Dog was a member of a biker gang and Dog was as rough as they come. But I'd met Dog. I liked Dog. Dog was funny and he liked my sister. She was different around him. Not a lot, but at least she was palatable.

Okay, so Dog was likely a felon. As ironic as it was, he was a good influence on Ginger and those didn't come around very often. As in *never*. Not in twenty-five years. So, since I was getting the hint from Darla, Ginger's one and only friend, that Ginger's trouble was a little worse than normal, I needed firstly to do something about it. Secondly, since this was Ginger, call in reinforcements or better yet, lay the problem on their door.

Enter Dog.

I drove to the auto supply store on Broadway and found a spot on the street. Even before I knew Dog, and thus figured out this was probably a front for a biker gang's nefarious dealings, I knew about this store.

It was called Ride, and I'd shopped there mainly because I could find an excuse for shopping anywhere. But Ride was awesome. It had cool stuff in there. I bought my windshield wiper fluid there. I bought new car mats there last year and they were the bomb, supreme car mats, the best I'd ever had. And when I was in my twenties and going through one of my many phases, in an effort to pimp my ride, I went there and bought a fluffy, pink steering wheel cover and a glittery, pink Playboy Bunny thingie to hang from my rearview mirror.

Everyone knew Ride had a triple-bayed garage in the back but it wasn't for normal cars and motorcycles. It was for custom-built cars and motorcycles, and it was world famous. They built cars and bikes and they were extremely cool. I'd read an article in *5280* magazine about the place. Movie stars and celebrities bought cars and bikes from there and, from the pictures, I could see why. I wanted one but I didn't have hundreds of thousands of dollars so that was a bit down on my List of Things I Want, right under a Tiffany's diamond bracelet, which was directly under a pair of Jimmy Choo shoes.

I got out of my car and walked down the sidewalk to Ride hoping my outfit was okay. I'd put my hair in a girlie ponytail at the top back of my head, I was wearing low-rider jeans, low-heeled boots and my biker jacket. Mine wasn't like Darla's. It was a distressed tan leather, had a bit of quilting around the high waist, was lined with short, warm fur and had a six-inch tuft of fluffy fur at the sleeves. I thought it was *hot* and the deal I got on it was hotter. However, I wasn't sure about the fluffy fur. I didn't think bikers were concerned with animal rights. I thought they'd think it was an affront to their brotherhood and they might garrote me.

Welp! Nothing ventured, nothing gained.

I straightened my shoulders, walked into the cavernous store and turned direct to the long counter at the front. It held one cash register even though sometimes the place could get packed. Since I didn't have his cell, my intention was to ask if someone there knew how I could get hold of Dog. I didn't expect to see tall, broad, inked-to-the-max, long-blond-haired Dog standing at the other side of the counter. There was one big, rough biker guy on his side of the counter, three on the outside, and all of them turned to me the minute I walked in.

"Hey, Dog," I called on a smile, walking toward him but stopping dead when his eyes sliced to me.

Uh-oh.

His eyes narrowed and his face didn't get near to hiding the fact that one look at me made him extremely pissed off.

"Do not shit me," he growled. I took the nanosecond before I peed my pants to try to remember the moves I'd learned in the one half-hour self-defense class I took.

When I made no response and didn't move, Dog repeated, "Do not come in here and fuckin' shit me."

"I'm not shitting you," I told him because, well, I wasn't.

His brows flew up. "That cunt sent *you*?"

Uh-oh again. Dog was using the c-word. I suspected that the c-word wasn't worda non grata in Biker Club Land like it was in the rest of the English-speaking world but still, it said a lot.

Before I could speak, Dog did. "She sent *you*. Jesus, Gwen. You got one warning, woman. Get your head outta your ass, turn that sweet tail a' yours and *get…outta… here*."

Wow. Dog thought I had a sweet tail. He was scaring me but he wasn't entirely unattractive so I thought that was kind of nice.

I focused on the matter at hand, took a deep breath and walked forward. All of the bikers went on alert or, more accurately, scary biker guy alert, so I stopped moving.

Then I said to Dog, "Ginger didn't send me."

"I'm bein' cool with you, babe, go," Dog replied.

"No, really, she didn't. Darla came around this morning and she freaked me out. She did this." I lifted my hand up and did the gun thing with the sound effect thing and my gun blast was nowhere near as good as hers but I forged ahead. "She seemed serious so I thought I'd check in with you, make sure Ginger is all right."

"Ginger is not all right," Dog returned instantly. "Ginger is *far* from all right."

I closed my eyes. Then I sighed. I did the sigh thing loudly. I was good at that since my sister made me sigh a lot and I had practice. Then I opened my eyes.

"I take it you two aren't together anymore," I surmised.

"No, babe, we are *not*," Dog confirmed.

Damn.

"What'd she do now?" I asked.

"You don't wanna know," Dog answered.

"Are the police after her?"

"Probably."

I studied him. Then I asked, "But that's not why she's in trouble?"

"Ginger's got all kinds 'a trouble, babe. But if the cops are after her, that's the least of her worries."

"Oh boy," I whispered.

"That's about right," Dog remarked then his eyes shifted over my shoulder.

I was turning to see what he was looking at when I heard a deep, gravelly voice ask, "Who's this?"

Then I saw him.

I wasn't into biker dudes but I could seriously make a turn to the Harley side for *this* guy.

He was tallish. He was broad and ripped and there was

no "ish" about either of those. He had a lot of tattoos up his arms and neck that I instantly wanted to examine, up close, to the point of cataloguing them and maybe writing books about them. He had salt-and-pepper hair, mainly pepper, *black* pepper, and it was long with a bit of wave but not too long or too wavy. Ditto with the pepper in his salt-and-pepper goatee that hung a bit long at his chin in a biker way that was mammoth cool. His cheeks were a couple days' past needing a shave, which looked good on him too. He had spikes of pale radiating in the tan skin around his blue eyes.

There were only two words to describe all that was him: *Biker Yummy.*

"Hey," I whispered, and his eyes went from over my shoulder, looking at Dog, to me and my whole body did a shiver.

Then his blue eyes did a body scan and it shivered again.

They locked on mine and his gravelly voice growled, "Hey."

Another shiver.

Yowza!

"Tack, she's cool. She's with me," Dog stated. My body did a lurch and I turned to see he was around the counter and heading my way.

"I am?" I asked, and Dog's gaze pinned me to the spot and said without words, "Shut the fuck up!"

I shut the fuck up and turned back to Biker Hottie.

"Sheila know about her?" Biker Hottie asked.

I turned to look at Dog who was standing next to me. "Sheila?"

"How many bitches you need?" Biker Hottie went on.

"She's not my woman, brother, she's a friend. She's cool," Dog answered.

"All right. So who is she?" Biker Hottie, otherwise known as Tack, pushed.

"Her name's Gwen," Dog answered. Tack looked at me and I froze.

Then I watched his lips move to form my name softly.

"Gwen."

Another shiver.

I'd always kind of liked my name. I always thought it was pretty. Tack saying it made me freaking *love* it.

"So who are you, Gwen?" he asked me directly.

"I'm, um . . . a friend of Dog's," I told him.

"We established that, darlin'," he informed me. "How do you know my boy here?"

"She's Ginger's sister," Dog said quickly. Tack's entire, powerfully built frame went wired instantly and it was so damned scary, I forgot how to breathe.

"Tell me she's here to drop the money, brother," Tack whispered in a voice that was as scary as the way he was holding his body, if not more.

"She and Ginger aren't tight," Dog explained. "Like I said, she's cool. She's good people."

"She's blood of the enemy, Dog," Tack whispered.

Uh-oh-uh-oh-uh-oh.

I didn't want to be blood of the enemy, not anyone's enemy, but especially not *this guy's* enemy. He was hot but he was also freaking *scary*.

Time to sort things out pronto.

I pulled my purse off my shoulder and tugged it open, muttering, "Ginger. A pain in my ass. A pain in my ass since the day she cut off all the hair on my Barbies. She was three. I was too old for Barbies but they were *mine*. She couldn't leave them alone? What's with cutting their hair?" I looked up at Dog and said, "I think that's what psychos do. We should have known then. She's three, wielding scissors and causing mayhem and heartbreak." I kept blabbing as I dug in my purse, found my checkbook and then kept scrounging for a pen declaring, "She was always, *always* a bad seed."

I yanked out my checkbook, flipped it open, clicked my pen smartly, put the point to the check and looked at Tack.

"All right, how much does she owe you?" I asked irately, not happy to be bailing Ginger out *again*, especially when money and angry bikers were involved.

It was at this point I noted that Tack was staring down at me and he wasn't being scary anymore. He was looking like he wanted to laugh. It was a good look.

I didn't want to see his good looks, not his expressions or the rest of it all over his face (and hair and tats and body). I wanted to go home, whip up a batch of cookie dough, and eat it. All.

"Well?" I snapped.

"Two million, three hundred and fifty-seven thousand, one hundred and seven dollars," Tack answered. I felt my jaw go slack and his white flash of a smile surrounded by his dark goatee dazedly hit some recess of my brain. He finished with, "And twelve cents."

"Oh my God," I whispered.

Tack was still smiling when he dipped his head to my checkbook. "Think you can get that on one line, Peaches?"

"Oh my God," I repeated.

"You need mouth-to-mouth?" Tack asked, leaning in. I took a step back, clamped my mouth shut and shook my head. "Shame," he muttered, leaning back.

"My sister owes you over two million dollars?" I whispered.

"Yep," Tack replied.

"Over two million dollars?" I repeated, just to confirm.

"Yep," Tack confirmed.

"You haven't made an accountancy error?" I asked hopefully.

Tack's smile got wider and whiter. Then he crossed his big, tattooed arms on his wide, ripped chest and shook his head.

"Perhaps this is foreign currency and you forgot. Pesos, maybe?" I suggested.

"Nope," Tack returned.

"I don't have that kind of money." I told him something I was guessing he already knew.

"Sweet jacket, Peaches, but I was guessin' that," he replied.

Well, the good news was, the tufts of fur didn't turn him off. The bad news was, my sister owed him over two million dollars.

"I think it'll take me a while to raise that kind of cash," I explained then finished, "maybe eternity."

"Don't got eternity to wait, darlin'," he responded, still grinning so huge, if he burst out laughing it would not surprise me.

"I figured," I muttered, clicked my pen, snapped shut my checkbook, shoved both in my purse and lost my mind.

I mean, I had reason to lose my mind and that reason had a name.

Ginger Penelope Kidd.

I looked up at Dog and demanded to know, "Why me? Why? Just innocently being born and seven years later, *zap!* God curses me with the sister from hell. Is it too much to ask for a sister who giggles with you and trades makeup secrets? Is it too much to ask for a sister who finds a great sale, calls you immediately but peruses the racks to stash great deals she knows would look *hot* on you, so you'll get a shot at them before anyone nabs them? Is it too much to ask for a sister who'll come over and watch the new *Hawaii Five-0* with you so you can both perv on Steve McGarrett and wish you had a Camaro? Is it? *Is it?*" I ended on a shout.

"Gwen, babe, think you should calm down," Dog muttered, and I could swear I could read on his face that he was wondering if he should knock me out for my own good.

"Calm?" I yelled. "Calm?" I yelled again. "She owes you guys over two million dollars. She cut the hair off my Barbies. She stole the lavalier my grandmother gave me on her deathbed and pawned it to buy pot. She got drunk and stuck her hand down my boyfriend's pants at Thanksgiving dinner. He was straightlaced, went to church and, after Ginger's antics...the hand down the pants was only the culmination, he caught her snorting coke in the bathroom too...he thought my family was insane, possibly *criminally* insane, and he broke up with me a week later. He might have been straightlaced and, looking back, probably boring but at the time *I liked him!*" Now I was shrieking. *"He was my boyfriend!"*

"Peaches," Tack called, and my body swung to him to see he'd moved into my space.

I tipped my head back and snapped, "What?"

His hand came up, fingers curling around my neck, then he dipped his face into mine and whispered, "Baby, calm down."

I stared close up into his blue eyes and instantly calmed down.

"Okey dokey," I whispered back.

His eyes smiled.

My body shivered.

With his hand at my neck, I knew he felt it and I knew it more when his fingers curled deeper into my flesh.

Something flashed in his eyes that made me shiver someplace he couldn't see but I could feel. A lot.

Time to go.

"I could probably sell plasma and a kidney but I don't even think that will get me enough money, so, um, can I just leave my sister to deal with this?" I asked politely, wanting to move from the strength of his hand but scared to do it.

"No one takes a blade to you for Ginger," he said quietly.

"Okay," I replied.

"Or at all," he kept going.

"Um…" I mumbled. "Okay." I said this because I didn't want anyone to take a blade to me for Ginger or at all and I didn't want that in a big way.

His fingers curved deeper into my neck and he pulled me up a bit so I was almost on my toes and his face was closer. Way closer. Too close. *Shiver* close.

"I don't think you get what I'm sayin' to you." He was still talking quietly. "This Ginger shit heats up, you get on radar, you mention my name, yeah?"

Oh no. This didn't sound good. This sounded worse than owing a biker gang two million dollars. And I suspected there weren't a lot of things worse than that but, if there were, Ginger would find them.

"Um…if you're asking 'yeah?' as in 'Yeah, I get you,' then no, I don't get you," I told him honestly because I was thinking with Tack honesty was the best policy.

"All right, Peaches, what I'm sayin' is, you get in a situation, you mention my name. That means protection. *Now* do you get me?"

"Um…kind of," I answered. "But why would I get in a situation?"

"Your sister has shit where she lived, she's shit where she didn't live, she's shit everywhere. You walked in here and had no clue. Don't bumble into another situation because others…" he paused, "…they might not find you cute like I do."

"Okay," I whispered, liking that he found me cute at the same time regretting my decision not to call my father or, say, get on a plane and fly to France. "If I um…have to use your name…um, what does that mean?"

"It means you owe me."

Oh boy.

"Owe you what?"

He grinned but didn't answer.

Oh boy!

"Owe you what?" I repeated.

"I gotta get on my bike and get you out of a situation, we'll talk about it then."

"I'm sure I'll be fine," I assured him and said a short prayer in hopes of making that true.

His grin got bigger.

Then he let me go but slid my purse off my arm and before I could make a peep, he dug into it. I decided to let him have at it. He'd already touched me and I wasn't certain I wanted that to happen again. I wasn't certain what my response would be but I *was* certain that jumping his bones was high up on the list of possibles. I also figured he could best me in a fight for my purse so I was going to let him take what he wanted. My best lip gloss was in that purse but at that point, if he wanted it to give to one of his bitches, I was willing to let it go.

He came out with my cell, flipped it open, his thumb hit buttons, he flipped it closed, dropped it into my purse, then slid it back on my arm.

"You got my number, darlin'. You need it, use it. You don't need it, you still wanna use it, don't hesitate. Now, do you get that?"

I hitched my purse further up on my shoulder and nodded. I got that. He thought I was cute.

I fought back another shiver.

"Nice t'meet ya, Gwen," he said softly.

"Yeah," I whispered, "later." Then I turned to see Dog grinning down at me and I said, "Later."

"Later, babe," Dog replied in a way that made it sound like he'd actually see me later, which made me have to fight back another shiver.

I turned to the silent biker boys behind me, saw them all smiling, found this scarier than them being scary, lifted a hand and called, "Later."

I got a bunch of chin lifts and one "Later, darlin'."

Then I got the hell out of there.

THE DISH

Where Authors Give You the Inside Scoop

♥ ♥ ♥ ♥ ♥ ♥ ♥ ♥ ♥ ♥ ♥ ♥ ♥ ♥ ♥ ♥

From the desk of Jaime Rush

Dear Reader,

Enemies to lovers is a concept I've always loved. Yes, it's a challenge, and maybe that's what I like most. It's a given that the couple is going to have instant chemistry—it is a romance, after all! But they're going to fight it harder because they have history and a good reason. Each person believes they're in the right.

That's how Kade Kavanaugh feels. Being a member of the Guard, my supernatural world's police force, he has had plenty of run-ins with Violet Castanega's family. They live in the Fringe, a wild and uncivilized community of Dragon shifters who think they are on the fringe of the law as well. And mostly they are, except when their illegal activities threaten to catch the attention of the Muds, the Mundane human police. Because Rule Number One is simple: Never reveal the existence of the Hidden community that has existed amid the glitter and glamour of Miami for over three hundred years. Mundanes would panic if they knew that Crescents—humans who hold the essence of Dragons, sorcerers (like Kade), and fallen angels—lived among them.

Violet is fiercely loyal to her Dragon clan, even if it does sometimes flout the law. But when one of her brothers is murdered by a Dragon bent on firing up the clan wars, she has no choice but to go to the Guard for help. There she encounters Kade, whom she attacked the last time he tried to arrest her brother.

My job as a writer is to throw these two unsuspecting people together in ways that will test their loyalties and their integrity. And definitely test their resolve to resist getting involved with not only a member of another class of Crescent, but a sworn enemy to boot. Juicy conflict, hot passion, and supernatural action—a combination that truly tested my hero and heroine. But their biggest lesson is never to judge someone by their name, their heritage, or their actions. I think that's a good lesson for all of us.

We all have magic in our imaginations. Mine has always contained murder, mayhem, and romance. Feel free to wander through the madness of my mind any time. A good place to start is my website www.jaimerush.com, or that of my romantic suspense alter-ego, www.tinawainscott.com.

Jaime Rush

From the desk of Kristen Ashley

Dear Reader,

While writing MOTORCYCLE MAN I was in a very dark time of my life. An *extended* dark time, which is very rare. Indeed, it's only ever happened that once.

In fact, I wrote nearly an entirely different book for my hero, Tack. He had a different heroine. And it had a different plot. Completely. But it didn't work for me and it has never seen the light of day. I abandoned it totally (something I've never done), gave it time, and started anew.

I had thought it was rubbish. Of course, on going back and reading it later, I realize it wasn't. I actually think it's great. It just wasn't Tack. And the heroine was not right for him. But never fear, I like it enough; when I have time (whenever that is in this decade), I intend to rework it and release it, because that hero and heroine's story really should be told.

Nevertheless, when I finally found the dream woman who would belong to Kane "Tack" Allen in MOTOR-CYCLE MAN, I was still questioning my work because things in life weren't going so great.

You see, sometimes I battle my characters. Sometimes they urge me to take risks I feel I'm not ready to take. Sometimes they encourage me to glide along an edge that's a little scary even as it is thrilling. And when life is also scary, your confidence gets shaken in a way it's tough to bounce back from.

But Kane "Tack" Allen is an edgy, risky guy, so he was pretty adamant (as he can be) that he wanted me to just let go and ride it with him. Not only that, but lift up my hands and enjoy the hell out of that ride.

But as I was writing it, I still fought him. Particularly the scene in Tyra's office early on in the book, where they have a misunderstanding and Tack decides to make his feelings perfectly clear and in order to do that, he gets Tyra's attention in a way that's utterly unacceptable.

I fretted about this scene, but Tack refused to let me soften it. I even sent it to my girl, a girl who knows me and my writing inside and out. If I remember correctly, her response was that it was indeed shocking, but I should go with it.

Ride it out.

In releasing MOTORCYCLE MAN, I was very afraid that my life had negatively affected my writing and the risks Tack urged me to take would not be well received.

As you can imagine, I was absolutely *elated* when I found I'd done the right thing. When Tack and Tyra swiftly became one of my most popular couples. That Tack had rightly encouraged me to trust in myself, my instincts, my writing, and give myself to my characters to let them be precisely what they were, let them shine, not water them down, and last, give my readers the honesty. They could take it. Because it was genuine. It came from the soul.

It was real.

And because of all this, MOTORCYCLE MAN will always hold a firm place in my heart. Because that novel and Kane "Tack" Allen gave me the freedom I was searching for. The freedom to ride this wave. Ride it wild. Ride it free.

Lift up my hands and ride it being nothing but me.

♥ ♥ ♥ ♥ ♥ ♥ ♥ ♥ ♥ ♥ ♥ ♥ ♥ ♥ ♥

From the desk of Christie Craig

Dear Reader,

Here are two things about love I took from my own life and used in TEXAS HOLD 'EM:

1. Love can make us stupid.

Sexy PI Austin Brook is a smooth-talking good ol' boy Texan. Where women are concerned, he wings it. Why not? He's got charm to spare. But one glance at Leah Reece and he's a stumbling, bumbling idiot. First he accidentally blows his horn as she's passing in front of his truck, causing her to toss up her arms and drop her groceries. Wanting to help, he snatches up a plastic bag containing a broken bottle of wine and manages to douse Leah with Cabernet from the waist up. And since he likes wine and wet T-shirt contests, it only makes her more appealing and him more nervous.

For myself? On a first date with a good ol' Texan, we were both jittery. I'd dressed up in a short skirt. The guy, thinking he should be a gentleman, pulled my chair out in the crowded restaurant. I had my bottom almost in the seat when he moved it out. *Way* out. *He* might've looked like a gentleman, but there was nothing ladylike about how I went down. All the way to the floor, legs sprawled out, skirt up to my yin-yang. Laughter filled the room. Snickering in spite of his apologetic look, he added, "Nice legs."

Later when he dropped me off at my apartment, I struggled to get the door of his sports car open. Forever the gentlemen—hey, that's Texans for you—he rushed to open my door, and then shut it. Standing close, he heard my moan, and completely misunderstood. He dipped in for a kiss.

I stopped him. "Can you open the car door?"

"Why?" he asked.

I moaned again. "Because my hand's still in the door."

With a bruised butt, and three busted fingernails, I eventually did let him score a kiss. It's amazing I married that man.

2. Love is scary.

Divorced, and a single mother, I wasn't looking for love when I met Mr. Craig. Life had taught me that love can hurt. And I'm not talking about a sore backside or fingernails. I'm talking about the heart.

Neither Austin nor Leah is open to love. Isn't that what makes it so perfect and yet still so dad-blasted frightening? We don't find love; love finds us. And like me, Leah's and Austin's pasts have left them leery.

At age six, Leah realized her daddy had another family, one he obviously loved better because they had his name and he called that home. Oh, when older, she still gave love a shot, got married, expected the happily-ever-after, and instead got a divorce and a credit card bill for all his phone sex. It's not that Leah doesn't believe in love; she just doesn't trust herself to know the real thing.

Austin, abandoned by his mother at age three, passed from one foster home to another, and learned caring about people gave them power to hurt you. His last and final (he swears) heartache happened when his fiancé dumped him after he got convicted of a murder he didn't commit.

As scary as love is, Leah and Austin give it another shot. Not to give away any spoilers, but I think it'll work out fine for them. I know it has for me. I'll soon be celebrating my thirtieth wedding anniversary. So here's to laughter, good books, and getting knocked on your butt by love.

Happy reading!

Christie Craig

♥ ♥ ♥ ♥ ♥ ♥ ♥ ♥ ♥ ♥ ♥ ♥ ♥ ♥ ♥ ♥

From the desk of Laura Drake

Dear Reader,

There's just something about the soft side of a hard man that I've never been able to resist—how about you?

Max Jameson looks like a modern-day Marlboro Man. He's a western cattleman, meaning he's stubborn, hard-working, and an eternal optimist. But given his current problems, there's not enough duct tape in all of Colorado to fix them.

To introduce you to the heroine of NOTHING

SWEETER, Aubrey Madison (aka Bree Tanner), I thought I'd share with you her list of life lessons:

1. Nothing is sweeter than freedom.
2. It is impossible to outrun your own conscience.
3. "When you're going through hell, keep going."
   —Winston Churchill
4. There are more kinds of family than blood kin.
5. A stuck-up socialite can make a pretty good friend when the chips are on the table.
6. Real men (and bulls) wear pink.
7. "To forgive is to set a prisoner free, and discover that the prisoner is you." —Louis B. Smede

I hope you'll enjoy NOTHING SWEETER. Keep your eyes open for a cameo of JB and Charla from *The Sweet Spot*, and watch for them all to turn up in *Sweet on You*, the last book in the series!

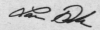

From the desk of Rebecca Zanetti

Dear Reader,

I met my husband camping when we were about eight years old, and he taught me how to play Red Rover so he could hold my hand. He was a sweet, chubby, brown-eyed boy. We lost touch, and years later, I walked into a bar (yeah, a bar), and there he was. Except this time, he was six-foot-five, muscled, with dark hair, a tattoo, a leather jacket, and held a motorcycle helmet under one hand. To put it simply, I was intrigued. He's still the sweet guy but has a bit of an edge. Now we're married and have two kids, two dogs, and a crazy cat.

People change…and often we don't know them as well as we think we do. In fact, I've always been fascinated by the idea that we never truly know what's in the minds or even the pasts of the people around us. What if your best friend worked for the CIA years ago? Or the mild-mannered janitor at your child's elementary school is a retired Marine sniper who didn't like retirement and has found a good way to fill his life with joy? What if your baby sister was a criminal informant in college?

What if the calm and always-in-control man you married is one of the deadliest men alive?

And what if you're now being threatened by an outside source? What happens to that calm control now? That was the main premise for FORGOTTEN SINS. Josie Dean, a woman with a lonely past, married Shane Dean in a whirlwind of passion and energy. Then he disappeared two years ago. The story starts with him back in her life, with danger surrounding him, and with the edge he'd always partially hidden finally exposed.

Of course, Shane has amnesia, and in his discovery of finding himself, he reveals himself to the one woman he ever truly loved. He'd always held back, always treated her with kid gloves.

Now, not knowing his deadly training, there's no holding back. The primal, arousing man she'd believed existed has to take the forefront as he protects them from the danger stalking him from his past. Yeah, he'd always been fun and sexy…with hints of dominance in the bedroom. Now the hints disappear to unveil the true Shane Dean—the man Josie hoped she'd married.

I hope you truly enjoy Shane and Josie's story.

Best,

Rebecca Zanetti

RebeccaZanetti.com
Twitter, @RebeccaZanetti
Facebook.com/RebeccaZanetti.Author.FanPage

♥ ♥ ♥ ♥ ♥ ♥ ♥ ♥ ♥ ♥ ♥ ♥ ♥ ♥

From the desk of Kate Meader

Dear Reader,

FEEL THE HEAT is the first in my smokin' Hot in the Kitchen series, about an Italian restaurant–owning family and the sexy, sizzling chefs who love them. And don't we all want a hotter-than-Hades, caring, alpha chef like Jack Kilroy in our lives? A man who cooks, defends his lady, and knows how to treat her right both in the kitchen *and* in the bedroom is worth his weight in focaccia (and the British accent doesn't hurt). But sometimes we've got to work with what the gods have given us. So if you have a husband/boyfriend/sex slave who believes guy cooking = grilling, but outside of the summer months, you won't catch him dead in an apron, read on.

"But he just makes a mess" or "I'm a better cook," I

hear you whine. Who cares? The benefits to encouraging your man to cook are multifold.

1. Guys who cook know how to multitask. If he can watch a couple of bubbling pots, chop those herbs, and pour you a glass of wine, all while *you* put your feet up, it'll eventually translate to other areas. Childcare, taking out the trash, maybe even doing the dishes as he whips up that *coq au vin*.

   Guys who cook know how to get creative. You might ask your man: "Is this made with sour cream, babe?"

   Cue worry crease on guy's brow that looks so adorable. "No, I didn't have any so I used Greek yogurt instead. Does it taste okay?"

   Hold praise for a beat "That's so creative, babe, and less fattening."

   (Positive reinforcement is key during the early training phase.)

2. Guys who cook have a direct correlation to a woman's TBR list. He's brought you that glass of Pinot and he's back in the kitchen where he belongs. Now you can get down to the important stuff—making a dent in your stories about fictional boyfriends who probably cook better than your guy. (In the case of Jack Kilroy, Shane Doyle, and Tad DeLuca, the sexy heroes of the Hot in the Kitchen series, this conclusion is a given.)

3. Guys who cook will evolve into guys who shop for groceries. Nuff said.

4. Guys who cook make better lovers. Chefs have very skillful hands, often callused and scarred from years

of kitchen abuse. Those fast-moving, rough hands are going to take your sexytimes to the next level! As long as your guy is burning himself while he learns, it can only be beneficial to you further down the road.

So get your guy in an apron and let the good times roll. Remember, chefs do it better...

Happy cooking, eating, and reading!

Kate Meader

www.katemeader.com